THE TRUE LOVE AFFAIR

Book Four of The Chandler Affairs

by

G. W. Renshaw

The True Love Affair

Javari Press,
Calgary, Alberta, Canada.
http://www.javaripress.ca/

ISBN: 978-1-895487-12-1 (pbk)

First paperback edition, April 2017.

Set in Gentium Book Basic
Printed in the United States of America

There was almost no light in my room, but by the red glow of the numbers on my alarm clock I could see vague shadows in front of me at the foot of my bed. They looked suspiciously like a pair of feet that were blocking my way to the door. My eyes followed the shadows up the dark mass to a quiet blue flame hovering in midair. It moved, becoming brighter for a moment. There was a sound of someone exhaling, and the pungent burning smell became more intense and caught in my throat. The smell wasn't tobacco.

It was brimstone.

I scurried backward, crab-walking with my butt almost on the floor, until my head hit the night table. The lamp on top teetered and fell to the carpet. I felt the lamp shade brush by my hair as it went past, narrowly missing my head. The crunch of a breaking light bulb was close and immediate.

Adrenaline poured through my system again. I chose to interpret it as anger rather than fear. A male voice with a distinctive lisp familiar to a previous generation of movie-goers spoke in the darkness.

"Nice reflexes, doll, but you should put something on. You look cold."

I knew that voice. There were no unnatural urges, and I fought down my instinctive panic. It was far too late for modesty, so I stood up, pushed past the figure, and put on the robe that was hanging on the door. I tied the belt by touch, viciously yanking the ends as I did so. I would have a hell of a time getting it undone later, but that was the least of my worries.

I found the wall switch without much trouble and flicked it upward with a satisfying snap. The result was painfully bright, and I couldn't help blinking several times. It didn't make any difference to what I saw, which was exactly what I was hoping I wouldn't.

Humphrey Bogart, circa 1941, stood in my bedroom, dressed in a well-tailored, three-piece, pin-stripe suit. He'd tossed his fedora over the post at the bottom of my bed.

I really liked normal cases. None of them involved Sam Spade showing up in my bedroom at oh dark seventeen. Especially considering what the bastard had done to me the last time we'd met.

He waved the sulphurous cigarette at me in greeting, and took another puff. How do you even smoke sulphur? The stench tickled my throat, and I made a great effort not to cough. I'd be damned before I'd let him make me cough.

"Put that out. You'll stink up the whole apartment."

"Whatever you say, toots." The cigarette vanished as if it had never existed. The smell did not go with it.

CONTENTS

DEDICATION

To Heinrich Cornelius Agrippa (1486–1535): polymath, physician, legal scholar, soldier, theologian, and occult writer who understood that women are no less intelligent, talented, courageous, or skilled than the men who think them inferior. In 1529, he published a book that brilliantly argued that doctrine long before its merits became obvious to all but the foolish.

"...the true distinction of which Sexes, consists meerly in the different site of those parts of the body, wherein Generation necessarily requires a Diversity: for both Male and Female he impartially endued with the same, and altogether indifferent form of Soul, the Woman being possess'd of no less excellent Faculties of Mind, Reason, and Speech, than the Man, and equally with him aspiring to those Regions of Bliss and Glory, where there shall be no exception of Sex."

– Declamation on the Nobility and Preeminence of the Female Sex by Heinrich Cornelius Agrippa (1529)

ACKNOWLEDGEMENTS

Thank you. Yes, you. I hope you enjoy reading this book as much as I enjoyed writing it. Please, let others know what you think of it by leaving an online review and raving to your friends about how good it is.

This novel was written with the generous help of experts who gave up their valuable time to answer just one more question from a sincere, but sometimes clueless, author.

In alphabetical order:

Nikki Berube, editor and friend, who found annoying little details that needed fixing.

Lexi Larissa Bonette, the unicorn riding pirate-ninja, for her help with translation.

Sandra Fitzpatrick, my lovely wife, and financial, tax, and biochemistry consultant, without whose love, cleverness, and encouragement I might have been another wannabe.

Thomas Gabriel Frensson, internationally renowned musician and Nightwish fan, for his help with translation.

Tereasa Maillie, who tried her best to get me an interview and instead ended up being kidnapped by aliens. Such is the life of a Librarian.

Mickey Mikkelson, Creative Edge publicist and friend, who has helped Veronica to reach more people who need her.

Jenna Miles, who continues to educate me in the finer points of being a young woman, as well as beating me up in aikido, Krav Maga, and baton class. The cake is a lie; the popcorn is true; the porchetta is delicious.

* * *

Any variances between the information given to me and what appears in my writing, are mine. All mine. I refuse to share the credit with anybody else.

If they want credit, let 'em make their own mistakes.

CHAPTER 1

La Rana Dorada

I tried my best to ignore Bruce's knee, but it kept going up and down like a pump that was sucking the life out of him.

The coffee table in front of him was covered with paper towels where he'd spilled the water I'd given him. He leaned back on the sofa before he did more damage. The way his hands were shaking, it was a good thing I hadn't offered him anything hot.

Bruce Froberg was in his late forties and good-looking. The problem that had brought him to consult a private investigator was his 27-year old wife, Cindy, who had disappeared from their home sometime during the morning of March third. It was now the sixth.

"What makes you think your wife has been kidnapped?"

"All the money was withdrawn from our joint account the morning she disappeared. That was the day after my pay cheque had been deposited. It can't be a coincidence."

I decided that honesty was the best policy. "I'm sorry, but that doesn't sound like a kidnapping to me."

"No! You don't understand. I found a note, and she would never have taken the money unless she was coerced. Kidnapping is the only thing that makes sense."

He handed me a folded, letter-sized piece of paper. He hadn't thought to wear gloves, of course.

We have kidnapped Cindy. We will not harm her as long as you do not contact the police and you pay our ransom. We will contact you with the details.

The note was printed. I looked at it carefully and saw tiny, almost-invisible yellow dots on the paper.

"Do you have a colour printer at home?"

He looked puzzled by my question. "Yes." Most people don't know that their printer's serial number is encoded on the document as faint dots. I had a bad feeling that the code would match his printer. I've never heard of a kidnapper relying on the victim to create their ransom note for them.

"Doesn't it seem strange you haven't heard from them yet? Especially after she withdrew all the money from your bank account."

"She was forced! She must have been! Please, isn't there something you can do?"

He seemed legitimate. I wasn't getting any creepy stalker vibes from him.

"The first thing we should do is call the police."

"No! They said they'd kill her if I do. I want you to act as my agent when they call."

"Try to stay calm. The note doesn't say anything about killing her."

In fact, the note's language seemed off to me. Most people would have said *kidnapped your wife*, not *kidnapped Cindy*. Using her name indicated familiarity, or possibly a desire to avoid the phrase *your wife*. Neither option was good for Bruce.

There was always a possibility that he'd gotten rid of her and was using me as an alibi by making it look like she'd been abducted. My gut, however, said he was one of those men who dearly loved his wife. Either that or he was a great actor.

"All right, I'll need a letter of authorization so I can talk to your bank." He didn't hesitate to write one for me by hand.

We finished up the details of our contract, and I showed him out. Then I headed for his bank.

* * *

Bruce had been a customer for a long time, and the manager was anxious to cooperate. At first, Bruce had offered to come with me, but I didn't want him getting freaked out by whatever I discovered. I suspected that this affair was not going to turn out the way he thought.

As a courtesy, the bank manager let me see the surveillance videos of Cindy's visit. To me she certainly looked nervous, which was to be expected, but she never looked anywhere other than at the floor or the teller. A person under duress would also be under surveillance by her abductors, and someone who knows that they are being watched almost always glances toward their watcher at least once. My feeling that something was hinky about Cindy Froberg was growing. That was too bad. Bruce seemed like a great guy.

She left the bank with three thousand dollars in cash and a bank draft for another sixty-two and change.

My next step was to phone every airline that flew out of Calgary International. I was hampered by having no idea whether she was travelling alone, or where she might have gone. It required cunning.

"Hi. My mother left a few days ago on holiday, and I need to know where she went."

"Do you know the flight number?"

"No, she didn't tell *anybody* in case her office tried to get hold of her. It's been, like, three years since she had a vacation. I'm not even sure she took this airline."

"I'm sorry, but..."

"*Please.* She left her heart medication on her night table. I have to send it to her or she'll *die*." I was proud of the quiver in my voice.

"Don't worry. A local pharmacy can phone her doctor to confirm her prescription and get it filled where ever she is."

"But she *can't*," I said, projecting as much desperation as possible. "She's in this research study, and the pills aren't available yet. *Please*."

"All right. Just one moment." This was the fifth airline I'd called, and I was getting thoroughly sick of listening to elevator music while on hold. I expected another "I'm sorry, I don't have a passenger by that name listed."

"I found her. Her destination is listed as Puerto Vallarta, Mexico. Did you say she's on vacation?"

"Yes. Why?"

"Her ticket is one-way. Are you sure..."

I interrupted the man with profuse thanks as befit a worried daughter and hung up.

As far as I was concerned the case was solved. I called my client and asked if Cindy had a passport. She did, but when he looked it was missing. Despite the obvious evidence he still thought she'd been coerced into taking it. His faith in his wife was touching, and I was not going to enjoy watching his bubble burst.

More phone calls and e-mails failed to turn up a Cindy Froberg at any of the hotels or resorts in the area. Bruce refused to allow me to contact the Mexican police unless I was sure that I knew exactly where she was. If we wanted to learn more I would have to go to Mexico.

He didn't even blink at paying the expenses. He *actually* loved his wife.

Poor me. I was going on a field trip.

* * *

Mi hermanita Kali had driven me to the airport when I left and she picked me up when I got back.

The end-of-case celebration included thick steaks, my travel stories, chocolate mousse, and a bottle of aged *ron* from the duty-free shop.

"How did you like Mexico?" she asked as I grilled the steaks. Kali was handling the salad, dressing, and potatoes. The latter were in the oven, gently baking to perfection. She'd picked up plenty of sour cream, and our bacon bits were so real they were probably still rooting for truffles. The chives came fresh from my herb garden in the living room.

"It was interesting. My client is satisfied if not happy."

"Interesting as in quaint and pleasant, or as in bone-freezing terror?"

"A bit of both, with sex, an international bank swindle, and Colombian cartels thrown in."

She stopped shaking the jar containing the dressing, and waited for me to tell my story.

* * *

Puerto Vallarta is lovely in the spring. The bougainvilleas are in bloom and their fragrance drifting on the vagrant breezes tends to catch visitors unaware. The weather is not yet hot enough to scorch bare feet on the beach sand. The winter tourists are fleeing back to their more temperate abodes leaving plenty of vacancies for those of hardier dispositions.

It's the perfect place to stay if you have been kidnapped.

With my backpack slung over one shoulder, I found the airport's security office. I was in luck. There was a gorgeous young man behind the counter. When he looked up his eyes widened as if he recognized me. It was my first time in Mexico, so that was unusual to say the least.

* * *

"He was probably just flirting," Kali said.

"Who's telling this story? You'll spoil the foreshadowing."

* * *

"Hello," I said in Spanish, "I'm investigating the disappearance of this woman." I showed him a picture of Cindy, as well as my private investigator credentials. Although I wasn't licensed in Mexico, I hoped they would at least buy me a little professional courtesy. "She flew in on the third of March."

He treated me with the utmost respect and didn't even glance at my credentials.

"Of course, *señorita*," he said. "Would you like to see our surveillance videos?"

I thought he wanted to feel important and *macho by* helping a female investigator from a foreign country. He immediately led me to their surveillance office.

* * *

"That's more than a little weird," Kali said. "I thought you would need a warrant or something to see that kind of thing?"

"Normally, yes. At the time I thought he was just being nice."

"At the time?"

"Shush, you'll spoil the story."

* * *

He took great pride in showing me his skill in handling the computer system. It only took him a few moments to find her coming out of the arrival gate, collecting her luggage, and buying a taxi ticket. The camera outside caught the license number of the cab. He printed the image for me, as well as a blow-up of the frame best showing the driver who got out to help her with her bags.

At no time did I see anybody with her. Nor was she paying much attention to her surroundings. She definitely didn't look frightened. If anything, she looked relaxed and eager.

In short, there was still no evidence of a kidnapping, and mounting evidence against it. Things were not looking good for my client's marriage.

My new friend, Ramón, was so helpful that he insisted on escorting me to the taxi booth. That turned out to be more useful than you'd think. On the way, he chased away several men who offered me a ride, but who were only trying to sell condo time-shares to tourists. Just in case I needed any further help he also gave me the contact information for his cousin who was a municipal police *comandante*.

Another odd thing was he seemed nervous, even as he offered to show me the sights in their lovely city when I had time. Ramón was entirely yummy looking, and I accepted. My only regret was that I couldn't drag him off to a hotel room right away. He smelled good.

* * *

"You *didn't*," Kali said. "You slept with *literally* the first man you spoke to in Mexico? Damn, *hermanita*."

"I've given up feeling guilty about what my libido wants. Apart from not doing anything excessively dangerous, that is."

"If you say so."

* * *

The man at the taxi booth remembered *la señorita hermosa* from several days before, mostly because her destination was Boca de Tomatlan which is the furthest south you can go by road along the coast. It's a small village whose big claim to fame is that you can get a water taxi to the other coastal villages further south. It wasn't a tourist destination.

He identified the driver in the photo. When I offered him a small "service fee" to have dispatch call the taxi for a pick up, Ramón grabbed his hand before he could take my money and shook his head at the man. I had the distinct feeling that I was missing something. No knight's armour was *that* shiny and I didn't think I was being subtle about wanting to end up in bed with him later. It wasn't like he had to try to impress me further.

Dispatch said the driver would be there within half an hour. While I waited, I got a recommendation for a good, relatively cheap hotel where, of course, the taxi guy's nephew worked. It was already after noon so I doubted I'd be lucky enough to locate Cindy that day.

Now that I knew where I'd be staying, I also confirmed a date with Ramón for that evening. Apart from dinner, I wondered how many sights we'd see outside my hotel room.

I'd leave that entirely to him.

* * *

"Good afternoon, *señorita*," the driver said as he got out of the taxi to help me with my minimal luggage.

I handed him my prepaid ticket. "*Buenos días. Llévame al Holiday Inn Express.*"

He finally looked at me, and when he got to my face he stared. I thought maybe my Spanish was rusty and he hadn't understood, but instead of being puzzled he only became more respectful. Fawning would be a better term.

What the heck, I decided to go with it. If he thought I was a VIP it might help my investigation. He gallantly helped me into the back seat of the taxi, and we headed for the hotel.

"I'm looking for a woman you picked up a few days ago," I said, still in Spanish. "She was headed for Boca de Tomatlan." I passed him the picture I had of Cindy. That was a mistake. There was a blaring horn as we almost side-swiped another car while his attention was distracted.

"I remember," he said. "She gave me extra to stop at a bank on the way and to wait while she did some business." I saw him sneak one hand from the wheel and wipe it on his trouser leg. His eyes kept shifting from the road to the rear view mirror. He'd see me looking at him and immediately shift his attention back to the road.

"Which bank?"

"*Banco de Finanzas*, near Boulevard Francisco Medina Ascencio."

"And then?"

"I drove her to Boca where she took a water taxi."

"Did she ask you to do anything else for her?"

"No, *señorita*."

"Good. You have done well." I relaxed in the back seat, and watched the scenery as we drove the rest of the way to the hotel in silence.

When we arrived he insisted on carrying my backpack to the front desk for me. I tried to look like I expected it. He had a quick, whispered conference with the desk clerk who was also nervous afterwards. I couldn't hear most of what he said, but I thought I heard "*ella es la rana dorada.*" That made no sense. I'm a golden frog?

* * *

Kali stiffened. "Holy shit, he thought you were *La Rana Dorada?*"

"What, you've heard of her?"

"Hell, yes! No wonder they were terrified of you! Do you have any idea who she is?"

"Patience."

* * *

I thanked my driver and slipped him a twenty-dollar bill as a tip. That was probably about four times what he usually got, but I wanted him to remember that helping me had its rewards in case I needed him later. Besides, it all went on my expense account.

When I asked for an economy room the clerk profusely apologized. Mysteriously, all the economy rooms were booked, but he would be happy to upgrade me to a luxury room for no additional charge. The constant VIP treatment was making me nervous.

I had no idea who they thought I was, and I couldn't ask anybody without blowing my cover, so I went with the flow and ignored the whole thing.

The room was indeed luxurious, and my first act was to explore the bath tub. At six Ramón arrived to take me to dinner. *Bravos* was a nice restaurant in the south end of the city where I had the braised lamb shank on gnocchi, which was excellent.

He was quiet as he drove me back to the hotel. Again he seemed nervous, like he was about to put the moves on the president's daughter.

I succeeded in getting him over his shyness. As predicted, we spent the entire night sightseeing in my room. Ramón was a good testimonial for why Latin lovers are in high demand.

* * *

Kali snorted. "From what I've heard of them, you got lucky."

I smiled in remembrance. "Oh, you'd better believe it."

She put her forefinger in her mouth and made gagging sounds.

* * *

The next morning a minor earthquake woke me at an annoyingly early hour. Ramón was trying to put his trousers on while sitting on the edge of the bed. I rolled over and grunted into my pillow.

"I apologize, *chiquita*," he said as he leaned over to kiss me. "It is time for me to go to work. Perhaps you will be free this evening?"

I forced myself to wake up enough to consider his offer.

"I'd like that, but don't know if I'll be here. It depends on how my investigation goes. I'll call you if I'm available."

I was aware of how trite that sounded, but we'd talked about this last night. To be even more trite, we were ships passing in the night. He was fun and charming, but we either hooked up again or we didn't.

"I look forward to it," he said. I never saw him again.

Now that I was awake there was no point in putting off getting out of bed. I had breakfast in the hotel restaurant, then went to find a taxi.

It took a while to dicker with the driver. In Mexico the taxi fares aren't metered. Instead, they are set by convention and most are negotiable. The fare to Boca de Tomatlan wasn't small.

Boca was pretty much what you'd expect from a coastal Mexican village. It was situated where the highway turned inland, so the main business was serving the people along the coast who didn't connect with a road.

Captain Garcia was taking a well-deserved break when I found him. His water taxi ran on a schedule rather than continuously, so he had a fair amount of the day off unless there was maintenance to be done. For once, I was being treated like a normal person.

I bought him a drink and showed him the photo of Cindy. He recognized her immediately. Not from her initial arrival, but because he saw her almost every day on his runs.

"I took her to a villa about 15 minutes down the coast from Cabo Corrientes. Almost every time I pass by she is either swimming naked in the ocean with her boyfriend, or they are making love on the beach. Their displays offend some of my passengers." From his grin, I suspected that the captain did not share their sense of moral outrage.

"Can you take me there? I don't doubt your word, but my employer will want photographic proof of her presence."

The captain made a big production of miming how big an imposition that would be, then got to the heart of the matter.

"It costs a lot to run my boat, and it would be difficult to do for just one passenger."

"What if we took a smaller boat? I'm sure there must be some for rent, and of course I would pay you for your time and trouble."

Again I was treated to bad acting. I put a hundred-dollar bill on the table between us which instantly vapourized his anguish.

"I have a nephew who owns a boat. Maybe he will let us use it."

The nephew was willing, for a cut of his uncle's payment, to let us use his boat. For some reason I expected something like a three-metre boat with an outboard motor. Instead, it was 12 metres long with *three* huge outboard motors. On the side it said Cigarette. It didn't plough the seas; it skipped over them with the bow pointed upward while I hung on, and tried not to imagine what would happen if we hit a wave and flipped. The engines roared and we would have needed bullhorns to talk to each other.

Half an hour later Captain Garcia slowed the boat, and we puttered quietly past a twenty-metre long beach at the base of a low cliff. We were far enough out from shore that we wouldn't disturb the inhabitants unless they actually looked up and saw us.

The boat's binoculars made the on-shore activities clear. A naked, bronzed man with a thoroughly impressive body and no tan lines was languidly wading ashore as Cindy came down the stone steps from the house. She was carrying two drinks and wore nothing but sunglasses and a pair of flip-flops. Her long blonde hair fluttered behind her as she handed her boy toy one of the glasses.

My phone has a good camera, but I'd recently bought something better for surveillance work. The 40X zoom was worth every penny as I recorded about ten minutes of video. Cindy, her long blonde hair fluttering behind her as she handed him a glass, as they sat on a beach towel and sipped, as they put down their glasses and started kissing, and as they got serious. I recorded several good shots of the man's face as he turned around over her stretched out body. She looked like she was having a lot of fun. I'd have been envious if it wasn't for my recent adventure with Ramón.

I didn't bother to record the whole performance. Bruce didn't need, and probably didn't want, that much detail.

"I've seen enough," I said, and the captain started the engines to take us back. He gave the couple a final glance and opened up the throttle. This time I scrunched down in my seat to avoid whiplash.

* * *

It was well after dark by the time I got back to my hotel room. I ordered room service to make up for my missed dinner, then composed a tactful text message to Bruce asking him what he wanted me to do now that this wasn't a kidnapping case.

Captain Garcia and his nephew had identified the boy toy as Carlos Rodriguez. He was a well-known beach bum who cultivated an air of romance to catch the attention of women like Cindy. I included a single photo from that day's shoot: one that tried to straddle the fine line between obvious proof of her infidelity and not tearing his heart out.

It wouldn't have surprised me if I didn't hear back for a day or two. I could imagine the shock it would be to him, and if it was me I'd have taken a while to start thinking rationally again. Instead, he texted me back within the hour. He'd found his own evidence after I'd left for Mexico.

"*C stole 300K from invest acct meant for kids uni. Recover if possible. Leave her there.*"

The poor guy was thinking of his children while his wife lived it up on the beach with 370,000 dollars of his money. As far as I knew, Bruce's only crime was being over 25 and marrying a bitch.

The situation offended my sense of fairness, and I intended to do something about it. The question was what I *could* do, given that I had no legal standing in Mexico, almost no contacts, and had no real idea how their banking system worked.

Maybe I could run some kind of scam and get her to take the money out of the bank, but no obvious plans for that presented themselves to me. Besides, it would probably leave me with an outstanding international arrest warrant. That would be awkward. I'd been in a similar position before and preferred not to do it again. I'd have to sleep on it.

I was tempted to call Ramón, but I'd need more sleep than I'd gotten last time we'd had a pyjamaless party.

The next morning I called my one remaining contact to see what he could offer.

"*Comandante* Vasquez," said a deep, important-sounding voice.

"Good day, *Comandante*," I said in Spanish, "your cousin Ramón gave me your number, and said I should call if I needed any help. My name is Veronica Chandler."

"Of course *Señorita*—Chandler." Again, he sounded a lot more respectful than I'd expect of a busy police commander getting a call from some random *chica* his cousin had hooked up with. The pause before my name sounded like he didn't believe that my name was real either. *Here we go again.*

"There is a woman living in a house about four kilometres south of Cabo Corrientes. She stole a considerable amount of money from my client, and he would like it back. Do you have any suggestions as to how we might do that?"

"Do you know where the money is now?"

"In the *Banco de Finanzas.*"

"What is her name?"

"Cindy Froberg."

"Do you wish the woman—detained?" he said very softly. His tone of voice suggested he wasn't talking about a legal arrest.

I had to tread carefully. "No, that won't be necessary. As long as the money is returned she can live her life as she pleases."

"You are most generous, *Señorita*. I shall make inquiries. Do you have a number where you can be reached?"

I gave him the number of the hotel and my room number. I wasn't going to sit and wait, so I changed and told the desk clerk that I'd be in the swimming pool in case I got a call.

Two hours later one of the staff approached me with a telephone on a silver tray. I didn't think they actually did that except in movies.

"This is *Comandante* Vasquez. I have made arrangements for you to receive your money. Would a bank draft be acceptable? If not, the manager can have it in cash, but not before tomorrow. He apologizes for the delay."

I was stunned. Getting the money out of Cindy's hands wasn't anything I would have bet on five minutes ago. I wondered how many corners he'd cut to do it, but I wasn't going to look a gift horse in the mouth.

"Certainly, *Comandante*. A draft would be perfect. Thank you."

"I can pick you up at your hotel and take you to the bank if you wish. Let's say twenty minutes, if that is convenient."

"I'll be ready."

It was almost exactly twenty minutes later that there was a knock on my hotel room door. I'd just gotten out of the shower and managed to dress in the other set of clothes I'd brought with me. When I answered the door, he slipped in as if he didn't want to be seen.

"I hope that I am not early," he said.

"Not at all. You didn't have to pick me up. I could have called a taxi."

He drew a folded piece of paper from his pocket.

"That wouldn't be wise. I am only the *comandante* of one *delegación*, you understand. I might not have been able to protect you if you had been seen by others."

I was about to ask him what the hell he was talking about when he opened the paper. It was a wanted poster much like ones you see on TV.

The woman looking back at me from the picture almost looked like she could be my twin, although her hair was considerably different. Her name was Teresa Maria Gacha Ochoa. She was 23, just two years older than me, and she was wanted for multiple counts of murder, extortion, and assault. All of her alleged crimes involved elaborate and creative forms of torture. She was closely affiliated with a major Colombian drug cartel, and her sweet young face, combined with the pleasure she took in her job, had earned her the nickname *La Rana Dorada*—The Golden Frog.

Oh, crap. It was pure luck that I hadn't been picked up by immigration or the *Federales* when I entered the country.

* * *

"I told you so," Kali said as she took the potatoes out of the oven. "From what I've heard, that woman started killing professionally when she was fourteen. She even scares the other cartel enforcers."

* * *

I'd learned Spanish from Kali and her parents. It hadn't seemed significant until now, but I it meant I spoke with a Colombian accent. No wonder these people thought I was a cartel assassin and were giving me tons of respect. If I didn't play this right I would be in big trouble. I'd allowed them to believe I was someone else without understanding the consequences, so I wasn't going to be able to explain this as mistaken identity now.

From what Kali had told me of life in Colombia, the cartels had an exceedingly short fuse for any act that even faintly hinted at disrespect. A *gringa* taking advantage of their reputation would land me in a big, deep pit of pain that I would never get out of.

The only way to survive this was to keep playing the part, and to get the hell out of the country as soon as possible.

It was almost noon. The timing would be tight.

"I'll need to check out before we go."

It took all of five minutes for me to pack, and another five minutes to check out. Vasquez drove to the bank with lights and siren, which wasn't exactly inconspicuous. At least it made us immune to traffic stops.

While he drove I checked my phone. There were some flights out at 3:00 and miracle of miracles, there was an available seat. I booked it and hoped nothing would hold me up.

Out of curiosity I also looked up Golden Frogs. They live in the rainforest of Western Colombia. The females are larger than the males, and have enough poison on their skin to kill twenty adult humans.

Oh, goody.

* * *

The bank manager was terrified of us and handled the details himself. I didn't want to know what he thought I'd do to him if he didn't cooperate. Cindy's account was closed, and the full amount issued to me as a bank draft. He made it clear that there were no service charges.

"Do you want to leave a message for the account holder?"

There was no way that my client's name was Colombian, and giving it would blow my cover. My real name wouldn't mean anything to her either.

"Just tell her who I am," I said, trying to sound like a psychopathic cartel assassin. Whatever they sound like. "She should understand."

"*Comandante*," I said as we left the bank, "there is one more favour you could do for me. I need a ride to the airport. My flight to Bogotá leaves at three."

"Of course, *señorita*. It would be my pleasure."

Again, I let him drive with lights and siren. After a while he spoke diffidently.

"*Señorita*, I was wondering if I could ask you for a small favour?"

"Go on," I said. "I'm feeling generous."

"I am, as you know, the *comandante* of a *delegación*. As such, I could be useful to your friends, as I have been useful to you. I would be grateful if you would mention me to them when you get home."

And so the other shoe dropped. He wanted a position in "my" cartel. At least he had guts, given the reputation of *La Rana Dorada*. I hoped that the smile I gave him was as cruel and evil as it should be.

"You have been most useful. I see no reason why we should not work together in the future."

Out of the corner of my eye, I could see him smiling to himself.

* * *

I had him drop me off outside the main terminal, but I insisted he not accompany me. After all, it wouldn't be good for our future business dealings to draw attention to himself in my company. Besides, the airport was *Federales* territory where he would have no jurisdiction. He agreed with my logic and left me at the entrance.

Puerto Vallarta airport is perfect for the con I was pulling on him. International flights depart from a separate building with access by a long, curved walkway. He couldn't see which flight I was taking without actually being with me.

I went to the WestJet check-in for my flight to Calgary. My first thought was to send a message to the *Federales*, telling them to keep an eye on Vasquez. Unfortunately, I would likely have to explain my involvement to them, and that would probably cause them to view me unfavourably as well as drawing attention to our bank scam.

I briefly wondered if I could have done this legally, but even if Mexico had an extradition arrangement with Canada it would take time and paperwork to charge Cindy with theft. If she had caught any hint of it she'd have been in the wind. It was best to let sleeping dogs lie.

After check-in, I bought a bottle of 12-year old Jav's *ron* at the duty-free shop. I felt like I deserved it.

* * *

"The rest you know, since you picked me up," I said as Kali finished her steak. As the story-teller, I had fallen behind.

The Mexican affair had been a nice, normal case. I didn't have to deal with any literally inhuman monsters, or any uncanny events. I like nice, normal cases. They're normal. Normal is good.

Between us, we finished off the bottle of *ron*. Or rather, it finished us off. By then, Kali found it hilarious that I'd been mistaken for a cartel as-sassin. Both of us were acting silly but not stupid, so we might have been under the legal limit for driving. Theoretically, Kali could have driven home.

Under no circumstances was that going to happen. Kali's parents had died in a car crash, and although alcohol hadn't been involved, we had a zero-tolerance pact between us for driving after drinking. Around one a.m. I crawled into bed, and Kali crashed on my sofa.

My cat, Yoko Geri, showed what he thought of me going away without him by abandoning our bed to curl up with Kali. Damn it, I'd been look-ing forward all week to him purring me to sleep. Just because she'd fed him while I was gone didn't mean that he had the right to be fickle.

Tomorrow I would give the bank draft to my client and get paid. Maybe I'd be up in time for lunch.

* * *

It was wonderful while it lasted. There was an endless, deserted expanse of white, Mexican sand, warm sun, and a soft blanket on the beach. The air smelled of the sea and tropical flowers. Ramón was glorious and there was a complete lack of any clothing. The waves were warm, Ramón's beautiful, brown eyes gazed longingly into my own sort of hazel ones. He tasted of salt.

The forest fire kept distracting us from more important things.

I opened my eyes. The glowing numbers on my alarm clock said 5:17, a number I prefer to associate with thoughts of supper. The rum had par-tially worn off, but I was still groggy from lack of sleep. It took a few seconds for my brain to fully acknowledge that there was a burning stench in the air.

The blankets went one way, and I went the other. As soon as my bare feet hit the carpet I crouched down to get below the smoke layer, just as we were taught in school. How the hell could a brick and concrete build-ing be on fire? Why weren't the fancy new smoke detectors that had been installed only a month ago making a frantic racket?

I crawled toward my bedroom door where my bath robe was hanging. I hadn't bothered with my pyjamas when I went to bed, and if we ended up outside I wanted to be wearing something more than a deeply con-cerned expression. The weather wasn't *that* warm.

An angry and muffled meow came from my bed. Yoko must have seen

the error of his ways sometime during the night, and left his other woman. I'd grab him once I was robed and had assessed the situation.

There was almost no light in my room, but by the red glow of the
numbers on my alarm clock I could see vague shadows in front of me at
the foot of my bed. They looked suspiciously like a pair of feet that were
blocking my way to the door. My eyes followed the shadows up the dark
mass to a quiet blue flame hovering in midair. It moved, becoming
brighter for a moment. There was a sound of someone exhaling, and the
pungent burning smell became more intense and caught in my throat.
The smell wasn't tobacco.

It was brimstone.

I scurried backward, crab-walking with my butt almost on the floor,
until my head hit the night table. The lamp on top teetered and fell to
the carpet. I felt the lamp shade brush by my hair as it went past, narrowly missing my head. The crunch of a breaking light bulb was close
and immediate.

Adrenaline poured through my system again. I chose to interpret it as
anger rather than fear. A male voice with a distinctive lisp familiar to a
previous generation of movie-goers spoke in the darkness.

"Nice reflexes, doll, but you should put something on. You look cold."

I knew that voice. There were no unnatural urges, and I fought down
my instinctive panic. It was far too late for modesty, so I stood up,
pushed past the figure, and put on the robe that was hanging on the
door. I tied the belt by touch, viciously yanking the ends as I did so. I
would have a hell of a time getting it undone later, but that was the least
of my worries.

I found the wall switch without much trouble and flicked it upward
with a satisfying snap. The result was painfully bright, and I couldn't
help blinking several times. It didn't make any difference to what I saw,
which was exactly what I was hoping I wouldn't.

Humphrey Bogart, circa 1941, stood in my bedroom, dressed in a well-
tailored, three-piece, pin-stripe suit. He'd tossed his fedora over the post
at the bottom of my bed.

I really liked normal cases. None of them involved Sam Spade showing up in my bedroom at oh dark seventeen. Especially considering what
the bastard had done to me the last time we'd met.

He waved the sulphurous cigarette at me in greeting, and took another puff. How do you even smoke sulphur? The stench tickled my
throat, and I made a great effort not to cough. I'd be damned before I'd
let him make me cough.

"Put that out. You'll stink up the whole apartment."

"Whatever you say, toots." The cigarette vanished as if it had never
existed. The smell did not go with it.

On the bed I saw movement where Yoko Geri was trying to escape from the blankets. He'd be safer where he was.

Bogart only had about nine centimetres on me. He was from an earlier era when leading men didn't have to be tall. I reared up to my full height of 163 centimetres and folded my arms across my marginally adequate chest. I was hoping to convey angry authority rather than fear.

"What are you doing here? We had a deal that you wouldn't answer a summons in North America for the next hundred years." To my irritation, he sat on the end of my bed. At least he missed sitting on Yoko.

"We do, babe," he said, waving his hand as if he still held the cigarette. "Nobody summoned me. I came to see you on my own nickel."

"I don't care why you're here. Get out of my apartment right now."

He leaned back like he was posing for a cheesecake photograph. Even Bogart's quirky smile was ruggedly handsome. That didn't help my state of mind at all.

Would it be better for me to stay in the bedroom, and hope that he ignored Kali? Or should I wake her up, and hope that two slightly drunk brains were better than one in figuring out what to do about this?

"Sorry, doll. No can do. I need your help."

I gave up. Ignoring his statement, I went out into the living room. Bogart got up, grabbed his fedora, and sauntered after me.

Kali was fast asleep on the sofa in a borrowed pair of my pyjamas. My spare blankets were tucked around her. Her long, black hair was tied back in a pony tail, and it curled across her breast like a sleeping kitten. I sat beside her and shook her gently. She made sleepy noises.

"Time to get up?"

"No, but we have a visitor."

"That's nice," she said, rolling over.

"Kali, wake up! There's a problem!"

She groaned and opened her eyes. It took her a while to focus on the scene illuminated by the light coming from the bedroom. I watched her eyes track from me to our visitor. She sniffed, and I could see her try to process.

"Is that...?"

"Brimstone? Yeah."

Her brain engaged. She bolted upright, the blanket clutched to her chin.

"Is that...?"

"Prince Sitri of Hell? Yeah."

I turned to the demon, who was studying my original Maltese Falcon poster on the wall.

"Would you please stop looking like Bogart, and doing the 1940s dialogue? It's creepy."

He actually looked crestfallen. "I'm sorry, I thought it would make you feel more comfortable."

Sitri turned to mist and solidified again. He was now a normal human. He looked a bit like he could be David Tennant's hotter brother and...

"Put some clothes on!" I yelled. As befit a lust demon, he had a body that just wouldn't quit. That was another complication I didn't need right now. He did his dissolve-and-solidify trick again, this time appearing in form-fitting jeans, and a tight military-green t-shirt emblazoned with a picture of a Scottish long sword above the stencilled words "front toward enemy." That was marginally better. I tried not to look at him.

My psychologist, Trinity MacMillan, had been working with me for the past several months to help me get over my last meeting with Sitri. I strongly suspected she didn't actually believe what I'd told her, but at least she believed that I experienced it as real and was willing to go with that.

I checked in with my brain, and it seemed to be working more or less normally. I didn't feel any weird sexual urges. Weird for me, anyway.

There was no reason to sit in the shadows, so I turned on the living room light. When I turned around, Sitri was holding out his hand to Kali.

"Hi, I don't think we've met," he said. "I'm Sitri." She stared up at him like a caged squirrel looks at a starving wolverine. He slowly withdrew his hand.

"How are you feeling?" I asked her.

"Okay," she said, never taking her eyes off him.

"Look at me."

She turned to face me without hesitation. If she was feeling anything abnormal toward him it didn't show on her face. For now, it looked like he wasn't doing anything perverted to either of our brains.

Enough of the small talk.

"What do you want?" I was tired, mildly drunk and had a demon in my living room. It's possible that I may have sounded somewhat cranky.

He was looking at me with a boyish grin. It slowly faded as I failed to be either charmed or impressed, and he became serious.

"I want to hire you."

"In the middle of the night? You must be joking."

"Not at all. Somebody is getting in my way. I need you to find out who."

"You want to hire a private investigator? Seriously?"

"Yes, I do. Seriously."

"This isn't some revenge thing for the Blakeway affair is it?"

"Why would I want revenge? We both got what we wanted last time we met."

"So this doesn't involve souls and Faustian bargains?"

He looked like I was correcting him on the use of the proper fork at his first formal dinner.

"Why, do you think it should?"

"Don't give me that crap. You have a lot of gall showing up here after what you did to me." I let my anger build to counteract my fear.

He didn't try to deny it. Instead, he looked—ashamed?

"I'm sorry. I know you've been having a difficult time dealing with the effect I had on you. It—I didn't realize what I was doing until later."

"You are telling me that you can control it?"

He looked unhappy, which had to be an act. "Yes. I'm sorry. I forgot it was on. Normally, I'm nothing like that. I'm so sorry."

Being anywhere near him still scared me, but I wasn't going to let him intimidate me no matter who he was. I got up in his face.

"If you even *think* of pulling that shit again, on either of us, we're done. Do you understand?"

"Yes. I'm sorry."

He looked like a little boy whose puppy I'd run over. I wasn't about to buy it as sincere, but I accepted his apology for now.

"Fine." I let some of my anger seep away. It didn't cost me anything to be more polite while we found out what he actually wanted. As long as he didn't want us to become best friends. *That* wasn't going to happen.

"What do you mean 'getting in your way'?" Kali said. That was my girl. It meant she'd gotten over the worst of her panic and was thinking more-or-less clearly. Now it was two against one.

He tried to sit on the sofa by Kali, but I beat him to it. Instead, he had to sit by himself across the coffee table from us in my comfy chair.

"Okay, so this is the thing," he said, leaning forward. Both of us instinctively leaned back. "Six weeks ago a magician in Oslo summoned me. I thought, hey, I'm not busy. I'll go play. I was delayed, and when I arrived he was dead. The same thing happened again a few days later in Tokyo, then again three weeks ago in Tbilisi."

"Where?" The name didn't sound familiar.

"It's the capital of Georgia," Kali said.

"Isn't that Atlanta?" I said before thinking. "Or is it Augusta?" Kali gave me a *get with it* look. "Oh, the *country* Georgia. Right." I turned back to Sitri.

"You actually get summoned every week or so? I didn't know there were so many magicians in the world who were that desperate to get laid."

"It's been getting busier lately, now that Midland has synchronized with Downland."

I sighed. One of the many problems I'd discovered in dealing with demons is that, even when you understand all the words, you feel like a six-year old at an astrophysics conference. They seem to assume that you know a lot of things that you don't.

"What are you talking about?"

He paused and got a look on his face I recognized from my conversation with the demon Beleth over a year ago.

"Let me guess," I said. "It's complicated."

He shrugged and leaned back in the chair.

"Yeah, it is. The short answer is that the time rate has been slowing in your universe for a long time, and now it's synchronized with ours."

"Why would our..." Kali said. "Never mind. Go on."

"Anyway, nobody's ever killed a summoner like this before, and I knew I'd need somebody I could trust in this world to figure this out. There was only one name on the list—you. I killed three weeks being a tourist in your world and then came to see you."

Heaven save me from incompetent amateurs during an investigation.

"Why didn't you come as soon as it happened? The first 24 hours after a homicide are critical."

Again with the look.

"It's a bit embarrassing. You could say that I needed to become sober first."

"You were drinking?"

"No."

"Drugs?"

"No. Nothing like that."

"Then why would you have to...? Never mind. We'll add that to the list of questions for later. What exactly do you want me to do? Not that I'm going to agree to anything without a lot more explanation."

"I need you to find out what's happening to my summoners, and who's doing it."

"Is that all? You don't want me to stop the killer too?"

"If they were able to delay me from appearing in your world, I doubt that you would be *able* to stop them. I'll take care of that when the time comes. I hope."

I considered my options. Of course, I could refuse but I had no idea what the consequences would be. Going to the police was pointless. Not only were the three victims in widely separated jurisdictions, but explaining how they were related would be a problem. The various national police services wouldn't listen to an outsider. It would be worse if I told them that a demon was the common denominator among the cases.

For better or worse, my involvement in three other affairs involving demons meant I was likely the only demon-savvy investigator on Earth. Lana Reviere in England was another possibility, but she didn't have as much experience as I did. As he said, there was one name on the list.

Oh, happiness and joy. I'd better add that to my resume so I can get more cases involving the paranormal. Just what I need. It's not as if I enjoy normal cases or anything.

"Fine. I'll take the case on one condition. If the killer is a human, then I get full jurisdiction over his or her punishment."

"That's unlikely, but okay. If the killer isn't human then they're mine."

I had a nasty feeling that I'd regret this. I looked at Kali. She looked thoughtful, then nodded slightly. So be it.

"Fair enough. Now, about my fee..."

"One thousand dollars an hour plus expenses," Kali interrupted. "Thirty-thousand dollars in advance as a retainer." What she'd just asked for was ten times my normal rate.

He didn't even blink. "No problem. When do you want it?"

I yawned as I looked at the kitchen clock. It wasn't yet six a.m.

"No earlier than this afternoon. You're leaving now, and we're going back to sleep."

"I was hoping..."

"This isn't open to negotiation."

He looked slightly disappointed. Too bad.

"Okay, I'll see you in about six hours. Will Canadian dollars be acceptable?"

"Perfectly," I said, and he was gone. We watched the seat of my comfy chair as it slowly adjusted to having no weight on it. Kali and I looked at each other.

"Is he gone?"

"Probably. It's not like we can do anything about it if he isn't."

"I hope that neither of us regrets this," she said, then yawned. It was contagious.

"The only thing I regret right now is being awake."

I got up and went back to my bedroom. Yoko Geri had given up trying to get out of the blankets by the time I untangled him. He gave me an annoyed chirp when his head appeared, but he decided to stay in bed with me anyway. I hoped we'd get to sleep in.

I already regretted accepting the case. Regardless of what happened this afternoon, this was probably going to be an extremely long day.

CHAPTER 2

Laundry Day

Morning had broken, and I really wished I could put it back together again.

My clock read 11:38, so I had to get up soon. I could hear Kali moving around in the kitchen, which meant that breakfast would soon be ready. She had always been an early riser, and I had no doubt that she'd been up for at least an hour, even after last night's festivities.

"Good morning," she said, as I shuffled from bedroom to bathroom in my robe. My response might not have actually been either audible or intelligible.

A hot shower revived me somewhat. By the time I got dressed, and stumbled into the kitchen for breakfast, I was more or less functional.

"How are you feeling?"

"Just dandy," I said, as I poured the elixir of life from the coffee machine.

"I made breakfast for you."

The first sip of caffeine hit my system. "Remind me to tell you how wonderful you are."

I sat down at the counter, and a plate of bacon, scrambled eggs, and fried potatoes *aux herbes de Provence* appeared in front of me.

We devoted ourselves to breakfast for several minutes.

I decided to go first. "What do you think of this deal with Sitri?"

"I think he was too willing to pay an insanely high price for your services."

"You mean I'm not worth it?"

"Don't fish for compliments. I'm just saying that when somebody is willing to pay ten times your normal fee he's either desperate, or he's playing you for a sucker."

"Did you actually say 'playing me for a sucker'?"

"You aren't the only one who can read old detective novels."

She poured herself a second cup of tea and sipped it.

"I don't trust him, and I'm going to be watching him like a hawk. Ever since you nearly got eaten I've been feeling protective."

"Have I told you lately that I love you?"

"I love you too, and if he tries to hurt you again, he's going to wish he hadn't. All our attempts to stop him before were defensive. I'd like to see how well he reacts to offensive magic."

"Or a tactical baton, for that matter."

"That too."

I finished my second cup of coffee just as the clock reached noon. I had time for one deep breath and exhalation and as expected, Sitri appeared in the living room. I'd said "after noon" and being a demon, he'd taken me literally. He had a thick envelope in his hand.

I just hoped that his story was true, and that he genuinely did need me. It could give me some much-needed leverage to get through this case in one piece. The thought also helped to nudge me farther away from fear and closer to indignation.

"Hi." He sounded chipper, the fiend.

"The next time you come to see me you will use the front door. I don't appreciate having people randomly appear out of thin air in my home."

He looked genuinely surprised, as if this had never occurred to him.

"Oh, okay. Sorry. Here's your retainer." He handed me the envelope.

Inside was a stack of brand new, crisp $100 bills. From the thickness of the packet, I could easily believe that there were 300 of them.

I read a lot, and big chunk of it is science fiction and fantasy. There are stories where supernatural riches evaporate the next morning, or diamonds turned out to be common rocks. Call me crazy, but when a demon offers me a stack of cash I wonder about the tiny details, such as where he got it, and whether it's real.

Sitri sat on the sofa while Kali and I elected to stand. I examined several of the bills at random. They felt right. All of them had the correct security features, and all of them had different, non-sequential serial numbers. I even got out a flashlight and checked the hidden numbers in the maple leaf. The bills were either real or were amazingly good forgeries.

"Where did you get these?"

"From a bank in Toronto."

"You stole them?"

He looked indignant. "Of course not. I traded them for US dollars."

The longer I was around demons the clearer it was becoming that historical demonic cunning had little to do with diabolical intelligence. It had much more to do with them being bloody-mindedly literal, and completely lacking any sense of subtext. He'd sit there and answer my questions all day without telling me what I actually wanted to know.

"All right, where did you get the US dollars?"

"From a bank in New York, in exchange for a cashier's cheque. It's all legal."

"And the cashier's cheque came from...?"

"A bank in Lagos."

Patience, Veronica. Assaulting your client won't do you any good, even if you can. I'm not particularly good at patience.

"Which you got in exchange for...?"

"Nairas, of course. That's what the gold merchant gave me. Well, a cheque for them. He didn't have 8.6 million on hand."

"And you gave the gold merchant...?"

"One hundred seventy Canadian coins. Like this."

A coin appeared in his hand and he put it on the coffee table in front of me. It was about the size of a quarter, and the Queen's portrait was showing.

"You just happen to have a collection of Canadian gold coins?"

"Well, duh. Of course not. That would be cray-cray. I made them."

He seemed to love slang. First the 1940s Bogart stuff, and now this. I managed to keep myself from sighing deeply.

Kali came out of the kitchen where she'd been brewing herself another pot of tea, and picked up the coin. She turned it over.

"First Special Service Force," she read. I took the coin from her and looked at the emblem. I should have known.

"You made $30,000 worth of Devil's Brigade commemorative coins?"

"Sure, why not? Actually, it was more like fifty thousand so I could cover any immediate expenses you might have."

"What happens when the counterfeits are detected?"

"They aren't counterfeits. They are exact duplicates of the coins put out by your mint."

"You are saying that the gold is real?" He looked offended.

"Well, duh..."

"You can stop saying that now."

"Of course the gold is real. They wouldn't be exact duplicates if it wasn't. I even made sure that it was isotopically pure, just your minted ones."

My first cases involved the demon Beleth who had created some silver medallions with isotope ratios that were impossible in this universe. Sitri must have been talking to her about me. I'd have to remember that.

"If you were just selling gold, why make gold coins? Why not a gold brick or just a lump of metal?"

"Coins don't have serial numbers. Gold bricks do. A lump would have led to questions about where it was mined. Investors buy and sell gold coins all the time, so that seemed the safest way to get the money."

This was a ridiculous ethical problem to present to me after a disturbed night. Technically, Sitri was a counterfeiter and had committed a federal offence. He'd also gotten money for counterfeit merchandise, so from that point of view the money in the envelope should almost certainly be considered stolen.

Counterfeiting was illegal because it produced things that looked like money, but which weren't worth as much as their face value. A criminal had to make a dollar coin for less than a dollar each, or there was no point in doing it. That's why they prefer to make hundred-dollar bills.

Counterfeit money also wasn't backed by the country's economy. A dollar originally represented a certain amount of metal that was stockpiled so that in principle you could trade a dollar bill at the bank for a dollar's worth of gold. That's why old bills say, "pay to bearer on demand." Things were more complex now, but the principle was the same.

I had no doubt that Sitri could produce coins that were indistinguishable in any way from the real thing. Unlike paper money, or Canada's one- and two-dollar coins, the value of gold coins is in the metal, not in the ridiculously low face value assigned by the mint. With these coins, you could either buy coffee at Tim Horton's for the five dollar value embossed on the front, or trade in the ounce of metal for at least several hundred dollars. Was it counterfeiting if the fakes were worth exactly as much as you said they were? It was difficult to see how that could be considered fraud.

The gold dealer had probably already melted them down for the metal, so the fact that they were recently in the form of Canadian currency was moot. Another consideration was that only the original gold dealer had been "swindled." The cheque was presumably issued in good faith and the cashier's cheque likewise. The U.S. currency he got in exchange for that was real, as was the amount of Canadian currency. By the time it got to me, the money was probably as clean as any money could ever be.

I could take the moral high ground and refuse the payment on a debatable principle, but he'd been completely honest about how he had gotten the money. Next time he might not be. Sitri would just come back with more money from a different source. Possibly one that was even more tainted. As far as I knew, he didn't have any legally gotten wealth with which to pay me. Not in this world, anyway. Was money from another world legal tender in this one?

At least this was a victimless crime. The Canadian government wasn't out any money. Neither were the gold buyer, or any of the banks he'd dealt with. Economically, the gold coins might as well have been nuggets from a creek bed.

I fought a mild rear-guard action with my morals.

"Don't you have to have certificates proving you've bought the coins from the mint?"

"You do? I didn't know that, and he never asked. Don't worry about anything coming back to haunt you. I even opened a chequing account in Toronto for the remainder so that the bank would be happy."

"How did you—never mind." If he could counterfeit currency, then fake identification was probably a completely trivial effort.

"Why did you go to all that trouble? Why not just create hundred-dollar bills?"

"They have serial numbers. It would have taken too long to change the mint's procedure so that the numbers on my bills would have been unique. I wanted to protect you. As I said, this will never come back to haunt you."

I had to admit that I was impressed. It was an effective and novel money laundering scheme. There was one more point that I wanted an answer for before I accepted the money and the job.

"I'm still unclear about why you need a private investigator for this. You're a Prince of Hell. According to the Key of Solomon you're supposed to have, what, sixty legions of demons at your command? Why don't you send them to figure out what's happening?"

He rolled his eyes. Seriously, he looked like a thirteen-year old being told by an adult that One Direction weren't the finest musicians in history.

"Honestly, the things you people believe. I guess that a lot of it is our fault," he said, leaning forward again in an attempt at sincerity. "The truth is that what you call Hell isn't at all like you think it is. Just because I can do things you can't, you assume that I can do anything. As much as it pains me to admit it, we all have our limitations. Yours are different from mine, and in this case you are the only person who can do the job. That whole 'prince of sixty legions' thing is mythology. I've never commanded any troops. All I have is an administrative assistant for what you'd call my day job. Besides, none of us know this world like you do and I've never done any kind of investigation."

That much was obvious. I sighed. "What will you do if I refuse?"

He shrugged. "I'd have to contact Lana. She's the only other investigator with demonic experience in your world."

Great. Either I take the job or he goes after Lana. At least I knew I'd survived such cases before. I wasn't sure about how she'd do.

No pun intended, but to hell with it. The only way I could move forward with this case was to take his story at face value, and keep my eyes open for anything that might come back to bite me. Possibly literally.

I almost asked him about the day job he'd mentioned, but I didn't want to go down another rabbit hole right now.

I sat in my comfy chair, feet on the coffee table with my legs crossed at the ankles in front of me and opened my laptop. I was about to start a new case file, but instead I created a new folder, then opened the new case file there. This would be the third affair in which demons showed up. I might as well keep those cases separate from my normal work load. I tried not to think about the implication that there might be a lot more such cases.

"All right, tell me about the first victim."

CHAPTER 3

CSI Oslo

Now that we had recovered from our drunken revels, Kali drove herself home. I wished I could go with her.

Interviewing Sitri was frustrating. He was willing to give me all kinds of information about the case, but most of it was useless. I didn't care where the victims had gone to school, or where they got their ritual robes. He had no clue how a real investigation worked.

I asked him about that, and he admitted he'd been watching cop shows and noted that a lot of the detectives told witnesses that any detail could be significant. I didn't dare to correct him in case he started filtering the details too much.

When I'd gotten as much information as I could, I stood up and stretched. I heard a couple of vertebrae popping back into place. My brain felt like I'd been watching question period on CPAC all afternoon.

"If I'm going to investigate these homicides, I'll have to have more detailed information about the scenes than what you've given me," I said. "Things like coroner's reports, crime scene photos, and reports on physical evidence."

"I can do better than that," he said. "How about if I recreate the scene for you?" He reached out to touch my arm.

I had time to say "what?" and then I was...

* * *

...standing in what appeared to be a basement. It took my eyes a while to adapt to the much lower light level. The tiny windows were covered with plywood. I wasn't completely sure by the small amount of light leakage around the edges whether I was seeing daylight or streetlights. Candles the length of my forearm and as thick as my wrist provided a flickering illumination of the room: the four large ones on the floor and several smaller ones scattered about the room on shelves and tables. The furniture looked like it might have been bought at IKEA once upon a time. Now it was threadbare, stained, and generally knocked around.

The air was musty and damp. The floor was cold on my bare feet.

"You could have let me put my slippers on first," I said to Sitri, who was standing beside me. "Where are we? Oslo?"

My fuzzy slippers appeared in his hand, and he passed them to me. I tried not to be too concerned that I was in a foreign country without anything but the clothes I was wearing, and completely dependent on the good will of a demon to get me home. There wasn't anything I could do about it now.

"Not in the sense you mean," he said. "This is just Halvorsen's basement. I recorded the scene, and you can think of this as a three-dimensional playback. The spot where you are standing is where I arrived when I was summoned."

It looked real enough, and if this was a holographic image we must still be in my apartment. That made me feel considerably better. At least I wouldn't have to explain myself to the Norwegian police. Especially since the extent of my Norwegian was the single word skål. That was sure to go over well if they offered me a drink instead of arresting me.

The previous affair with Collin Blakeway had given me an observer's knowledge of ceremonial magic. As Sitri had said, I was standing in the triangle of evocation, the area where summoned demons were supposed to appear and be contained. In front of me, painted onto the concrete floor, was the elaborate magic circle intended to protect the magician from the demons he summoned.

Lying on the circle itself was a man in his late thirties. He was bald and wore a goatee. He was wearing a well-made, floor-length black robe, embroidered with various mystical symbols. Either he was a tailor, or he spent a lot of money getting someone to do it for him. The whole evil magician effect he was trying for was somewhat spoiled by him having blond hair instead of black. He was also extremely dead, judging by the amount of blood pooling beneath him and oozing over the concrete.

The first time that Sitri and I had met he'd told me a great occult secret: All the rituals and symbols that were supposed to protect people against demons were just useless superstition. For that matter, so were the summoning rituals themselves. For thousands of our years, the demons had come and gone when they felt like it, solely for their own amusement. That the circle hadn't protected Halvorsen wasn't a surprise. The questions were who had answered the summons before Sitri could get there, and why they'd decided to break the rules of their own game by attacking the magician while he was "protected."

I walked around the room. It was difficult to see details in the dark corners, which made me wish that Sitri had used a flash or something when he made the recording. I found myself stepping around things, which was absurd. If this was just a holographic playback, then nothing was real. For that reason I didn't try to pick anything up.

Sitri knelt by the body and turned it over. One of the victim's arms flopped as he did so.

"How did you do that?"

He looked at me like I'd asked if that was a nose in the middle of his face.

"With my hands?"

"Sorry, I didn't know we could actually touch things."

If the recording could be changed, we had to be careful. I stood over him, not wanting to contaminate the crime scene any more than necessary. I needed to know what the limits of his recording technology were.

"Can you replay this scene from the beginning?"

"If you wish."

"Not yet. I just wanted to know if we were making permanent changes to the crime scene."

"We can recreate the scene from the beginning as many times as you choose. It's just a recording."

I looked closely at one of the candles standing on the floor. HDTV had nothing on this. There was no pixelation, motion blurring, or any other hints that this wasn't reality. I poked at it, and my finger stopped at the apparent surface. I rubbed it. It felt waxy. As far as I could tell, this was a real candle, with a real flame that was giving off heat and light. I knelt on my hands and knees, bringing my face as close as possible to the floor. It smelled like old concrete. I looked around again.

"I thought this was a single image, but it seems more like a movie."

"It *is* a single image. Why would you think differently?"

I waved my hand at the candle I'd poked. The flame flickered.

"Oh that," he said. "The flame is part of the recording, so of course it burns during playback."

"I don't get it." This was beginning to sound to me like the magical pictures at Hogwart's.

"Anything that is in motion when the recording is made continues to move in the playback. For example, if you were throwing something it would continue to follow the same trajectory it would in real life. If something had been tossed into midair when I recorded it, then it would fall to the floor during the playback."

"In other words, what you're saying is that the candle is burning because there was a flame there when you took the picture?"

"Exactly."

It still sounded like magic. I decided to let it go for now.

"What's the resolution of the recording?"

"I'm not sure. It must be somewhere around the size of an atom so the chemical compounds are properly recorded."

Damn. I wasn't sure off-hand how big an atom was, but the resolution must be somewhere around a billion pixels per inch. My friends in the police force would kill for whatever kind of recording device he had used. So would every scientist on Earth.

It helped me to think of it as a still camera version of a Star Trek holo-deck. At least, that analogy made me feel like I had some idea what was going on. Camera memory cards came to mind, and I wondered what the capacity of his camera was. On the high side of freaking ginormous was my best guess.

I turned my attention back to the body. It had flopped over on its back and the blood was still seeping from a wound in the chest. The blood looked, acted, and smelled fresh. It appeared he'd been dead for only a few minutes before the recording.

I reminded myself that this was a hologram and tore the robe to ex-pose the wound. I examined it with my fingers. This might look real, but as long as I kept my mind on the whole holodeck thing, it didn't bother me any more than cleaning out a chicken for dinner.

The wound was an elongated puncture that had gone through his lower sternum without leaving an exit wound on his back. To me, it looked more like a blade thrust than a bullet hole. The recording was de-tailed enough that the blood felt wet, and appeared to coat my hands. I'd have been a lot less cool with this if it was a real crime scene.

"It looks like he was stabbed." I poked one finger into the hole and felt bone fragments. Damn, Sitri's camera recorded the interior struc-tures of objects too. "Whoever it was must be pretty strong to go through bone like that."

Sitri stared at the body for a moment.

"The only contaminants I can find in the wound are cedar oil and bronze."

"Really?" I didn't ask how he was doing that. If this was their idea of a snapshot, I wondered what their idea of Photoshop was. Maybe that's how he'd made the gold coins.

The wound contaminants were unusual. I'd expect a knife or sword to be made of steel. Maybe using a bronze weapon was part of the killer's signature. Some kind of history buff? Or somebody who thought they were from another time? Maybe the killer *was* from another time.

The cedar oil was puzzling. Maybe I was reading too much into it. The killer might coat the bronze in cedar oil to keep it from corroding, or perhaps the weapon had a bronze blade on the end of a cedar handle. I suspected that the list of possible weapons that matched that description was pretty short unless it was a homemade shiv of some kind.

Of course, it might not be a weapon. Maybe it was some kind of tool or ornament.

"Who uses bronze weapons?" I said to myself. Sitri thought I was talking to him.

"Nobody. They break too easily. That's why the Iron Age supplanted the Bronze Age."

"Or it could be somebody *from* the Bronze Age. Can your people travel through time?"

"No. It's theoretically possible, but as far as I know we don't have the technology yet."

My hands were pretty messy, but from watching Star Trek I knew that nothing created on a holodeck could leave so I just wiped my hands on my clothes.

"That helps a little. We can tentatively rule out Leonidas of Sparta as our murderer." I looked at the wound. "I wish there was some way to determine the shape and composition of the blade."

"I might be able to do that for you."

I drew back as a grey substance oozed out of the bloody chest. I couldn't think of anything good that was grey and came from a wound. It puddled in a mound on the surface. Half a minute later, the oozing stopped.

"You wanted the shape of the weapon. That should be an accurate model."

"What is that stuff?"

"Just a quick-setting plastic."

I poked at the goop. It was now completely hard. I used both hands to pull on the surface knob. I wiggled it slightly, and it easily came free with a slight sucking sound. Gross. When the fat part inside got to the ribs, I had to work it from side to side, and rotate it back and forth to get it through the cracked bone.

The shaft had irregular triangular fins all the way down from the passage of the head. That was a problem with making a casting from the injury: The head of the weapon made the biggest hole so we'd never be sure what the shaft behind it looked like. The head itself was leaf-shaped, and appeared to have bulges along the flat sides.

"Have you seen anything like this before?" I asked him.

"No. If I need an ancient weapon, I'm more of a sword kind of guy. They look cool with a flaming blade." I could see that appealing to a demon.

"Not bad work for a crime scene that doesn't exist. I wish we could take the casting with us, though. I suppose we could come back with my camera and take pictures of the interesting parts."

"I don't understand. Why not just take the casting with us?"

"Um, I guess that's a good question. Maybe I should have found out more about your recording technology. I assumed that anything in the scene has to stay here, like on a Star Trek holodeck."

I'd confused him again, or maybe I'd confused myself.

"I don't know what a holodeck is, but you can take the casting anywhere you want."

Uh oh.

"You'd better tell me more about these recordings."

"I'm not sure what you want to know. In principle, it's simple. I took what you'd call a snapshot of the room when I arrived. The playback just recreates the scene."

I looked down at the bloody smears on my hands and felt queasy.

"When you say *recreates* you mean, *physically recreates*, don't you?"

"Of course. As far as I know that's the only way to do it. I'm sorry, did you think this was some kind of virtual image? For most purposes, we are in a real, exact duplicate of the room I recorded."

"So anything we take from here...?"

"Is a real, physical object, almost the same as having taken it from the original crime scene."

I tried not to think too much about sticking my fingers in the wound, and the blood stains on my clothes.

"I wish you'd told me that before. What if this guy had some kind of disease?"

"Don't worry," he said, "Even if Halvorsen had been alive when the recording was made, this copy would still be dead. The recording data is compressed and the playback has tiny errors in it. Not enough to notice, but it makes life processes impossible. You can't catch any diseases from the recording, although I suppose the bacteria we've brought with us would eventually cause the corpse to rot if we maintained the playback long enough."

"Great. That makes me feel *so* much better," I said. The sarcasm was lost on him.

I looked at the body—Halvorsen—for a moment. I had two more crime scenes to process. I'd have to be smarter next time. I knew all the procedures in real life, but I'd never worked a homicide investigation all by myself, and of course never from a physical recreation of the scene.

I was beginning to think that Kali's idea of charging ten times my normal rate might be on the low side.

* * *

As soon as we got back to my apartment from where ever we'd been, I told my client I was going to take a shower.

"Do you want supper? I could get some while you do that."

"Good. For some reason I don't feel like cooking." *Yeah, handling a raw steak is* just *what I want to do right now.*

I scrubbed myself from head to toe, paying special attention to my hands and arms up to my elbows. After I finished I also washed off the wound casting in the bathtub and scrubbed it with my back brush. I put cold water in the tub to soak my t-shirt and jeans to get most of the blood stains out. Half an hour after arriving back home I finally felt clean. Afterwards, I put on my usual business attire.

I came out of my bedroom to find a large pizza on the coffee table.

"I thought you were cooking." He looked at me blankly, and then the wonderful smell reached me. "Never mind. This isn't a recording of a pizza, is it?"

"No, I had Vincenzo make it for us."

It was almost seven o'clock. I was starving. The pizza was right-out-of-the-oven hot and incredibly delicious. The crust was light and fluffy, indicating that it had been allowed to rise for at least half a day. There was also the slight smoky flavour of a pizza that had been baked in a real, wood-fired oven. Being a true Neapolitan-style pizza, the crust was soft and we had to eat it with a knife and fork.

"This is incredible," I said between bites. "Where did you get it?"

"*Il Pizzaiolo del Presidente.*"

I paused with my fork in midair. "I thought I knew all the restaurants nearby. Where's that?"

"It's a little place on Via Tribunali in the centre of Naples."

"Naples, as in Italy? You went to *Naples* just for pizza?" Man, it must not suck to be a demon. "It has to be, what, one or two in the morning there?"

He shrugged.

"Vincenzo was only too happy to open for me."

My last bite of crust paused in midair again.

"I already had that spare coin I showed you, and he gladly accepted it. Five dollars seemed like a bargain for a pizza this big."

I finished the bite before responding.

"That's one hell of a tip you gave him."

"Don't you think it was worth it?"

"Oh yes. As long as Vincenzo is happy, who am I to complain?"

We turned our attention back to the now-clean casting. I did some research about Norway on my laptop while asking questions.

"Is there any kind of tradition that links the killing of magicians with specific materials or weapons?"

"Not that I'm aware of. If there were they'd be your traditions. As far as we're concerned, they're just people like anybody else."

"According to this, handguns are fairly common in Norway. If there's no reason to use an exotic weapon, why wouldn't the killer just shoot him? It doesn't seem to be a knife, unless it was somebody's first attempt at a shop project. It doesn't make sense."

Sitri put down the casting.

"It might make more sense if the killer wasn't human. My people tend to be traditional about some things. Any of us who are hunters would probably use a bow. There are also traditions among your people about ancient weapons being more effective against occult creatures. That's probably why your myths about vampires haven't been updated to them being shot through the heart with an assault rifle. It wouldn't feel right to you, although in reality it would probably work just as well as a wooden stake."

It's hard sometimes to tell if a demon is jerking your chain or giving you important information.

"Are you telling me that *vampires* are real?"

He looked startled. "No. Well, not as far as I know. It was just something I saw on television. The young woman on the show kind of reminded me of you."

I looked more closely at the casting and tried to picture the original shape that made the wound. It wasn't hard to convince myself that the murder weapon was either an arrow or a small spear. Either way, it was a weird choice.

Even a wooden stake would have been more sensible.

* * *

I threw Sitri out shortly after dinner, pleading that I wanted to get some sleep for the next day's investigation. He seemed to buy the excuse.

The truth was that I needed to have a stern talk with myself.

Sitri, at least in his current form, was highly attractive. We'd been alone together for about nine hours, and he'd been a perfect gentleman the whole time. A handsome, charming gentleman with a great body. He'd kept his promise not to use his lust ray, or whatever it was, on me.

Given my libido, he didn't have to. But he'd used it on me once, and even after therapy I was still terrified of it happening again. It played to my weakness entirely too well.

I didn't understand how I could be angry with him for what he'd done, afraid of him doing it again, and attracted to him all at the same time. For all I knew, this wasn't his real form either. He could be a pulsating slime monster with tentacles. That thought helped a little.

I had to keep my emotions under control. He was a client, and I had to stay professional. He also wasn't human, although my libido called that a distinction without a difference. Humans are not as discriminating as they like to believe they are, and all my senses told me that Sitri was a desirable human male regardless of where he came from.

I refuse to describe the dreams that I had that night. Kali would have thrown a pail of ice water on me just for mentioning that I'd had them.

And at this point, I would have cheerfully filled the bucket for her.

CHAPTER 4

Georgia on My Mind

Marina and the Diamonds was singing *Girls* on my bedside table. I fumbled for the phone and actually managed to find the right button to answer it. I even managed to make a sound into it that was vaguely humanoid.

"*¿Que pasa, hermana?*" Kali said in response. Perky cow.

"*¿Que hora es?*" At least, that's what I think I said. For all I know I could have been speaking Klingon. She must have understood, both the grunt and my mental state. She switched to English.

"It's about quarter past ten. Did I wake you?"

I make another proto-human sound.

"How's the case coming along?"

Normally, she would never ask about a case if she wasn't terribly worried about me. Of course, in this instance, she knew exactly who my client was, and what the case was about.

"Believe it or not, it's going well. Sitri's behaving himself and he's even making a decent attempt at giving me reasonable answers."

"Do you honestly believe that?"

"For now. The few facts I have so far seem to be fitting together."

"I'm worried," she said. "Whatever he looks like, however he acts, he's still a demon. I don't want you to get hurt."

"Funny you should mention that, because neither do I. You'll be glad to know that we may have been mistaken about him."

"What do you mean? Just hearing you say that makes me nervous."

"Apparently, Arthur C. Clarke was right. Any sufficiently advanced technology is indistinguishable from magic."

She sounded even more concerned. "I don't understand. What does advanced technology have to do with this? Are you sure he isn't doing anything weird to make you hallucinate or something?"

I remembered my dreams. They had been wildly erotic and vivid, but that wasn't demonic influence. That was just me.

I was enjoying this. She'd pegged Beleth and Sitri as demons when I was sure that they were just weirdos pulling a con of some kind. Now was my chance for petty, mean-spirited revenge on her by blowing her mind.

"Sitri isn't a demon. At least, not in the traditional, pitchforks and pointed tail sense."

"If you say so. I'm listening."

"He's an alien."

Dead silence.

"No way," she finally said. "An alien? As in...?"

"From another universe. One with some pretty awesome technology."

"Are you telling me that he has gizmos that do all his magic for him?"

"Well, not gizmos as such. At least I haven't seen any. But between what I've seen, and what he's told me, I'm pretty sure he's telling the truth."

"Veronica," she said slowly, "you have a history of not believing in magic. How do you know that he isn't passing off his demonic powers as technology to lull your suspicions? That sounds like it would be a demonic kind of thing to do."

"Honestly, I don't know. I'm not completely buying his whole story, I'm just saying that so far it makes more sense than anything else."

"Why would aliens go around pretending to be supernatural creatures?"

"Have you ever seen *Stargate?*"

"Are you seriously giving me an example where evil aliens pretend to be gods to exploit humans? Oh, that makes me feel *so* much better about you being with him. Just be careful. Don't get any forehead tattoos and keep me in the loop. If I don't hear from you by tomorrow, I'm calling the police." The implied threat was clear. She'd call our mother.

"I'll let you know as soon as anything changes."

"You'd better."

* * *

Now that I was awake, Yoko Geri was bunting my free hand with his head and demanding to be petted. I indulged him for a few minutes and then managed to slide out of bed. He immediately jumped down and headed for the kitchen. Hope springs eternal in the kitten stomach.

My cruelty knows no bounds. Instead of catering to his desperate needs, I waited until after I had a shower and put some clothes on before making breakfast for both of us. Two cups of coffee later, I was almost sure that I'd reclaimed most of my humanity.

I spent the next hour or so making lists and preparing for my next move. Around noon, I dialled the phone number that Sitri had given me.

Whether he had bought a burner phone, was intercepting the call with some alien technology, or heard me through a magical amulet was unknown. I was hoping for option number one.

He picked up on the third ring. "We're sorry, your call cannot be completed as dialled. Please deposit three souls, and use area code 666 to reach your party. Beeeep."

It took me a moment to recognize the voice as his. It took me considerably longer to form a reasonably polite reply. I was not at all in the mood for cuteness.

"Cut the crap. Do you want to catch this guy or not?"

"Wow, somebody got up on the wrong side of the crypt today." Like Kali, Sitri was a morning person. What more proof of demonic origin did one need?

I hung up on him. Yoko Geri jumped onto my lap, and I took great delight in playing with him instead of thinking about the case.

Marina sang to me again. I scratched Yoko's neck through the first verse. I ran my hand down his back, pulling gently on his tail through the second. He made a halfhearted attempt at killing my hand, and then started licking it. Sometimes, kittens are almost as strange as human men.

When the song started to repeat I answered the phone.

"Well, what's it going to be?" I said.

"I apologize. Sometimes my old habits come out. Let's get this guy."

"Apology accepted. Meet me at my place in five minutes." I hung up again. My sidekick was lying on his back waving his paws in the air. Being a sucker, I rubbed his tummy. After I had extracted my hand from the ravening nest of claws and teeth, I picked up the gym bag I'd packed just as there was a knock on the door. I let Sitri in.

"Where are we going?" He asked.

"Back to Oslo."

* * *

Of course the basement hadn't changed. The recording started at the beginning, with Halvorsen lying face down, just as he'd fallen.

I brought a couple of battery-powered lights. They did a reasonable job of illuminating the room.

I opened my equipment bag, and started laying things out. Sitri seemed confused by all my gadgets, but he kept quiet about them. He must have assumed that I knew what I was doing. It was nice to be the one dealing out confusion for once.

The fact that I kept perplexing Sitri made me more and more comfortable about working for him. Unless this was an overly elaborate scam, I'd seen no evidence of supernaturally great cunning on his part.

Like most of my clients, he was just a guy who wanted answers.

My first step was to do the obvious thing that I should have done last time: I put on nitrile exam gloves. Then I checked the room access. Unlike a previous client who had been doing rituals in her basement, Halvorsen had permanently boarded up his windows for privacy. The screws were all in place. Nobody had gotten in or out that way.

The door was locked with a sliding bolt on the inside. I unlocked it and opened the door. I was going see if it was possible for someone to have opened the bolt from outside with a shim. What I saw stopped me for a moment.

The back side of the door looked like the static pattern on an old, analogue television. So did the space outside the door.

It was utterly creepy, like the real world was a mask, and I'd seen behind it. It wasn't a comforting thought. In fact, it freaked me the hell out.

Sitri must have seen me tense. "Just ignore that. The recording only shows objects inside the room. That's just a texture to let you know you're looking at something that wasn't recorded," he said.

Tentatively, I tried putting my hand on the static. It felt like a solid glass wall and was neither hot nor cold. Despite the visual movement, there was no sensation of motion. I closed the door again. I had what I needed anyway. The jamb protected the bolt from being shimmed. The bolt itself was brass, so a magnet wouldn't work to move it. Nobody got in or out that way either.

There was no way to see into the room from outside, and all exits were sealed from the inside. It was a classic locked-room mystery.

I wasn't sure whether that made me feel better or not. The good news was that it pretty much ruled out a human killer, so I didn't have to worry about handling jurisdiction questions or punishment when we caught him. The bad news was that only a demon could have gotten in and out.

It was time for more of my own magic. With his help, I used a tape measure to get the distance from the entrance wound to the bottom of Halvorsen's heel. Then I set up a camera tripod, straddling the spot where we both agreed the guy should have been standing when he was shot. I duct-taped a laser pointer to the top of the tripod.

I'd brought the plastic adjuster rod I'd removed from the Venetian blind on my kitchen window. We rolled Halvorsen over, and I got Sitri to carefully insert the rod into the wound. I had a plastic protractor that was left over from high school, and I used it to estimate the angle of the wound. If I ever needed to do this again, I'd have to invest in one of those fancy ones that coroners use. I adjusted the tripod so that the laser pointer was aimed at the triangle of evocation at the same angle. A cheerful red dot appeared on the far wall.

In theory, laser pointers are relatively safe, but I didn't have a pair of tinted safety goggles, and I didn't want to risk staring at the beam. I used Sitri as the target on the assumption that a demon would be immune to getting his eyes seared out. The dot appeared on his throat. Good, the shooter had been shorter than him although not by much. I wiped the plastic adjuster rod on the victim's clothing and handed it to my client.

"Do you know how to shoot a bow?"

"Just the basics. I'm not by any means an expert."

"You don't need to be. Hold this in your hands as if it were an arrow you were shooting. Aim at the laser."

Sitri obligingly stood with his left arm extended, the rod resting atop his fist, while he pretended to hold an invisible bow string near his ear at full draw.

"Crouch down a little. A little more. More. Hold that."

The laser was now shining along the length of his makeshift arrow. I quickly measured from the floor to the top of his head.

"Okay, you can stand up now. Our shooter is about 178 centimetres in height. Is that a more normal height for a man, or for a woman, where you come from?"

"That's nearly my height. There are a lot of women that tall, but most of them are shorter. My height is fairly typical for a man."

"All right, for now we'll assume that we're looking for a male from your neighbourhood who is an archer." I explained my reasoning about the killer not being a human. He thought about it.

"Unless one of us brought the killer here and then took him away afterwards."

"Granted, and I'll keep that in mind, but the simpler explanation is usually the more probable."

I had him reset the scene and examined the concrete beside the body. I worked outward until I found a slight scrape on the floor. Sitri held Halvorsen's body on its side for me so that the wound was pointing at the scrape. I measured the distance, then added the length of the casting.

"What are you doing?" He finally asked.

"That scrape looks like it was made by the nock end of the arrow. When Halvorsen fell, he landed on his side, propped up by the shaft sticking out of him. The shooter pulled it out, and let him flop on his front. We should now have an approximate total arrow length."

I had him stand again, and marked the length on the plastic shaft. When he drew the fake arrow back to the mark, it was almost too short for him.

"That's good."

"What does that tell you?"

"The length is consistent with the height we got earlier. The shooter is either a man, or a tall woman slightly shorter than you."

Once more we reset the scene. I knew people in the Identification Unit who would have killed for this technology. This time I examined the triangle of evocation with a magnifying glass and a flashlight. Shining the light along the floor allowed any particles to cast long shadows so I could see them. I could even distinguish Sitri's shoe prints.

There also appeared to be smaller prints present that had no visible tread pattern. Maybe the shooter was wearing slippers. The footprints were narrower than Sitri's, but that could just be the shoe style. There were also some dust particles on the floor, but nothing that looked significant. Halvorsen hadn't been a particularly fastidious housekeeper.

From my limited experience, demons liked to appear to humans in some more-or-less nonhuman form. That the shooter had human-looking feet didn't necessarily tell us anything about what the rest of him looked like, but it might cut down the suspect pool a bit. At least the footprints weren't hooves.

The floor between the triangle and body also showed some faint disturbances. By using oblique lighting and a certain amount of squinting, I could see where the slipper-wearing killer had approached the body. There were no scuff marks apart from the arrow nock, so it didn't appear that the killer had rushed Halvorsen and attacked him. It looked to me like the killer had calmly walked over to the body and removed the arrow postmortem.

I suspected it wasn't a forensic countermeasure. It was just the behaviour of a hunter. Nor was there any sign that he was in the least concerned with having committed murder.

* * *

After packing up the equipment we jumped to Tokyo.

This crime scene was different, at least on the surface. The ritual room was smaller than the one in Oslo, and it was above ground. A single bed was standing upright in a corner. The circle was painted onto a sheet of cloth rather than the wooden floor.

I'd read that the average Japanese home was less spacious than ours. The cloth circle and triangle could be spread on the floor as needed, then taken up when the room was used as a bedroom. Kobayashi-san's wound was similar in shape and location to Halvorsen's. It appeared to have been made by a similar weapon. The measured height of the shooter was also the same, within experimental error.

Once again I went over the triangle. I was hoping that the cloth would preserve more evidence than the bare concrete had.

Jackpot.

"What are those?" Sitri said, almost in my ear, as I was hunched over the triangle. I managed to convert my instinctive defensive reaction to a push at the last moment instead of a punch. He'd been squatting and landed on his butt.

"Don't do that when I'm working!"

"Sorry." He backed up.

I used tweezers to pick up the small objects, and place them in a plastic bag.

"They look like bits of some kind of leaves," I said. Before I could stop him, he picked up the last one with his fingers. There was a flash of light and a fat spark. He shook his hand like the object had stung him. The leaf was now a small piece of ash.

"That was—strange."

"What happened?"

"I'm not sure. It was painful."

I tried not to be impatient. Rather than the usual demonic run around he honestly seemed to be trying to describe the indescribable.

"In what way?"

"Something like an electrical current. That shouldn't be possible." He stopped talking.

"Look, I'm trying to help here. Be specific. Why shouldn't an electrical shock be possible? If it has anything to do with the crimes, I need to know."

He looked down at the offending piece of ash, then at me.

"There's a property of the universe your physicists haven't observed yet because they only have one universe to study. My world has a—I'll call it a charge—of minus one. Yours has a charge of zero."

"How does this apply to leaves?"

"When I'm in my own universe everything is at the same charge, so a knife would cut me, and I'd bleed normally. When I come here, my body is—again, I'm not sure you have a term for it. I wish I could just give you the mathematics. It's like when you wet your hand, and stick it into a puddle of molten metal."

"Oh? Is that something you do for fun?"

"Not usually. I just remember the experiment from school. The water instantly evaporates and forms a boundary layer around your hand. As long as you are quick, the metal never touches your skin, and you don't get burned."

"Okay, now I remember seeing that on *MythBusters*. Your point?"

"My point is that my body is foreign to your universe and the charge is different. There's a boundary layer between the two that tries to keep them separate. There can be interaction between them if the contact is slow enough, or at a low enough energy, but it would be almost impossible for a significant electrical current to get through."

"What if somebody shot you with a gun? I'm just curious, you understand."

"The bullet would flatten or ricochet. A knife would slip off, bend, or break, unless you held it against my skin long enough for it to sink in. Oxygen diffuses into my lungs the same as it does yours, but slower. I have to watch how I exert myself while I'm here. You could easily win a foot race against me."

If true, that was an astoundingly trusting thing for him to have told me.

"All right, the leaves sound significant. Could they be from the Downland?"

"I don't think so. We'd be at the same potential. And they aren't pine needles. They're cedar. I have one in my front garden."

"Cedar again. Interesting."

I took my pocket knife and tried to cut one of the other cedar needles in half. No matter how hard I pressed it just sat there. When I looked at the blade it had a notch in it. The leaf was unharmed.

"Has anything from this world ever affected you like that?"

"No."

"And we haven't found anything else in these crime scenes that gives you a shock. It must have some significance. All we need to figure out is what it means."

"In theory there might be another explanation, but I don't believe it. It's impossible."

"If it's impossible, why mention it?"

"Perhaps I've picked up your habit of thinking out loud. Forget it. I wish I could be more help, but I'm not primarily a physicist. All I have is the basic courses that everybody takes." I looked at him.

"Yeah, right. Basic courses."

* * *

The next site was outdoors in an abandoned industrial area on the outskirts of Tbilisi. It wasn't possible for me to sight see. The static pattern started about 20 metres from the circle and included the sky. I tried very hard not to look at it.

The victim, Javakhishvili, was a clean freak and had carefully swept the concrete pad to make a canvas for his work. The meticulously drawn chalk circle must have taken him hours to complete. His attention to detail hadn't prevented the killer from putting a hole through his chest.

In all three cases the victims had been killed by what appeared to be a single arrow through the heart. The shooter had amazing skill.

Between the good weather and Javakhishvili's obsession with sweeping the area clean, we found another clue. There was a fresh piece of leaf on the ground between the triangle and the circle. It probably came from the shooter's footwear.

The leaf looked like some kind of mint. I took pictures of it, then tried to crush it to release the smell. It was like trying to crush a leaf made of glass, except that it didn't break no matter how hard I tried to bend it. Sitri watched my grunts and straining with interest.

"Catch," I said as I dropped the leaf.

He automatically held out his hand before he thought about it. There was a much bigger spark between them and the leaf disappeared.

"Ow, that hurt. Why did you do that?"

"I needed confirmation. We now have weird things present at two of the three crime scenes."

"Is that good?"

"It's data. We won't know if it's good until we fit the pieces of the puzzle together. Did it actually hurt?"

"Yes, a lot. Please don't do that again."

I considered the pain he'd put me through before. We wouldn't get anywhere if I kept trying to get revenge. It was time to call us even.

"I won't."

I examined the triangle, and again found narrow footprints. It looked like the shoes were dusty. Unless you were looking from the right angle, the prints were almost invisible. After taking pictures, I called Sitri over.

"Would you run your hand over the concrete?" I asked. "There shouldn't be enough material to cause you anything more than a tingle."

He cautiously did as I asked and pulled his hand back when he got to the place where I knew there was a footprint. There were some tiny snaps and crackles, like when I touched a door knob after walking across a carpet.

"Tingles?"

"Yes. Right here."

"Good. That confirms that the footprints belong to our shooter."

Since this scene was open, anybody could have come in normally. We tried various scenarios for a shooter outside the triangle, but none of them gave us a reasonable height for the killer.

I also spent a lot of time on my knees, looking for any other footprints. There were none. All the evidence pointed to a single shooter appearing in the triangle, taking the shot, retrieving the arrow, and then vanishing without walking back to the triangle. That scenario might also account for Sitri's delay in being able to answer the ritual call.

When we finished processing the third crime scene, I stood up and stretched. My knees were sore from kneeling on concrete, and despite the apparent time of day, my watch said it was approaching midnight. My stomach gurgled loudly, and agreed with my watch.

"Next time we do this we bring food. I'm starving."

"I know a nice little place nearby," he said, grabbing my hand.

Before I could answer, the universe jumped, turned inside out, and settled down again.

* * *

We were standing in front of a pink stucco building with a wooden door set in a white Roman arch. Above the door was a line of writing in a rounded alphabet that I didn't recognize.

About 20 metres behind us was a busy, four-lane highway. To my left was a car park filled with vehicles. A steady flow of people went in and out of another building on the far side of that. The people coming out were all either carrying wine bottles, or pushing carts loaded with cases. It came as no surprise when I looked beyond the car park to the vineyards stretching into the distance.

"Shall we?" Sitri was holding the door open for me.

The noise level dropped considerably once the door closed behind us. We were in a small restaurant with stone walls and floor. Hand-painted ceramic tiles were inlaid on both in tasteful accents. The ceiling was a beautiful, muted blue with white stencilled flowers and dancing figures along with more of the enigmatic writing. Small shelves on the walls held various antiques and wine bottles. Above the shelves were framed photographs of people in ethnic costumes. Ukrainian? I wasn't familiar enough with Eastern Europe to identify them, but didn't Ukrainian use the Russian alphabet?

"*Mogesalmebit' Kakhelebi restorani*," a smiling man in a white apron said.

Restorani sounded like a great idea, so I went along as the waiter led us to an intimate two-person table in the corner.

We were seated with a flourish that felt like genuine Old World courtesy, rather than a gimmick for the tourists. The waiter produced two menus in the unknown script and spoke to Sitri who answered at length in what seemed to be the same language. I recognized the behaviour of someone ordering from the menu. I didn't understand a single word.

The waiter gave us both a charming smile, and went off to the kitchen.

"Where the hell are we?"

"Sorry," Sitri said in English. "I should have warned you. This is the Kakhelebi Restaurant, about 15 kilometres east of Tbilisi." I looked up at the inscription on the ceiling.

He followed my gaze. "It says that the Kahkheti region had been a wine-growing area for the past 8000 years." I looked back at him.

"You're kidding. This isn't an image or playback or something?"

"No, you're actually here. South of Russia, north of Armenia and Turkey, east of the Black Sea. I've ordered brunch for us."

"Holy shit."

The first thing to arrive was a bottle of Rkatsiteli wine which was poured for us with great ceremony. The server said something in a tone I interpreted as pride, so I smelled the bouquet and took a sip. It was smooth as oiled glass. I gave the waiter a smile and a nod, which he returned before leaving.

"What did he say?" I whispered.

"It's from their own vineyard. Is it good?"

'Oh, yes."

Next was *imeruli khachapuri*, a fairly flat, round loaf of bread. I broke off a piece, and the hot cheese filling slowly oozed out. The bread was still warm from the oven. Need I say more?

"I'm almost certain that the murderer isn't human," I said. "Apart from the locked room in Oslo, I can't see how anybody from this world could have known about the summonings in enough time to get to the next destination. Even if they have their own jet and can travel internationally without worrying about visas, it isn't possible."

I picked out the clean casting from my bag.

"The bronze arrow head is another problem. I could imagine a serial killer who has a thing for arrows, but bronze? Either he's using antiques, or he'd have to make his own, and I bet they don't last long. That may be why he collects them afterwards, or it might be a forensic countermeasure. Or both. So, who has a thing for bronze-tipped arrows?"

He looked at the casting.

"Perhaps somebody who has been around since the Bronze Age?"

"You said you don't have time travel."

"We don't."

There was an uncomfortable silence, at least from where I sat. I might as well get it out in the open.

"How old are you?" He sat back in his chair.

"I'm not trying to be difficult, but the answer depends on what you mean by time."

"Of course it does."

"That's not fair. I'm trying to be as honest as I can. If you are talking about birthdays at home, I'm 176 years old. Our medical science is more advanced than yours." He kept his eyes on me while he spoke. I could feel my eyebrow rise.

"That's surprising."

"That I'm so old?"

"That you're so young. Your name is mentioned back to at least the 1500s. Is it like a hereditary title, or are you Sitri the Tenth or what?"

"I'm the original. The real difference is how old I am *here*. I told you that the time rate between our worlds recently synchronized. By your calendar, I'm over two hundred thousand years old."

I tried to wrap my mind around the concept that I was having lunch with someone who might have watched the first humans leave Africa. I gave up. It wasn't registering.

The next course came on large platters. Grilled vegetables of all kinds and skewers of lamb that had been roasted over charcoal. When the waiter put the meat platter down, he smiled at me and said *gaamot!* which I assumed was Georgian for *bon apetit*. The food was succulent and delicious in a way that spoke of fresh ingredients, simply prepared by a master chef. Thinking of the pizza from Naples, I wondered if they did take out.

"Let's get back to the case. You mentioned that something delayed you from answering a summoning. What was it?"

"I wish I knew. Normally, if I want to come to this world, I just do. On these occasions it was like the process was sluggish. Initially, I didn't think I was going anywhere, and I tried again. By that time, Halvorsen was dead. It was the same all three times. The total delay was on the order of 15 seconds."

"How do you travel? What could affect it?"

He blew out a long breath.

"As to how, the actual mechanism is *really* complicated. I mean, we're talking about moving between universes here. There aren't many things that could affect it either."

"Why not?"

"Okay, imagine digging a tunnel through a mountain range. On your side you have a sophisticated boring machine. On the other side are primitives with stone knives."

"Gee, thanks."

"It's just an analogy. People with technical knowledge from your side could disable your boring machine, but that would be obvious, and it wouldn't affect the boring process itself except to stop it. From the other end, there's nothing that the natives could do to affect the tunnelling."

"So it's impossible."

"No, just extremely difficult. If somebody from the Downland appeared in Oslo just as I was trying to jump they might be able to prevent the tunnelling for a few seconds by causing turbulence in the bulk between the two points. That would be something like creating a pocket of molten rock in the mountain so the tunnel collapses every time you try to bore through. The thing that bothers me is that I don't know how much energy they'd need to do so, but it would probably be huge. I'm not sure that it's practical."

I decided to save questions about *a bulk* until later.

Dessert was *churchkhela*: walnuts threaded on a loop of string, then repeatedly dipped like hand-made candles in thickened grape juice. We were told that they were left hanging in the sun for several days to dry before being served.

After a meal like that, my stomach was ready to believe that Sitri wasn't such a bad guy. My mind was almost ready to agree with it. Almost.

"Is there any way to be sure about the energy cost?"

"I could do the calculations, but until this case is done I don't want to go home now that I'm sober."

"You mentioned that before, and that it has nothing to do with alcohol or drugs. What do you mean, 'sober'?"

I poured him another glass of wine.

"About 85 years ago, our time, we had a high-energy physics experiment go wrong. As a result, our universe split into two pieces. Physical conservation laws required that one section, the Downland, have what I called a negative charge. Your universe isn't part of ours, and since it never split, it has a neutral charge. It's the charge difference between the two that allows me to do all the fancy stuff you've seen, now that our time rates are the same. It's like carrying my own power supply with me."

"So your power isn't unlimited."

"No. Since my body is much smaller than your universe, eventually I'd use up my charge if I stayed long enough."

"What does this have to do with you being sober?"

"I'm getting to that. As some of your researchers suspect, the brain's functioning relies on quantum effects. The new negative state made us all a bit crazy. It's a delicate balance, so it wears off after a few weeks here, and comes back after a few weeks at home. That's why I waited before coming to you. I had to wait for my brain to stabilize."

"What exactly do you mean by crazy?"

He looked embarrassed.

"Frankly, we're all sociopaths. It's been a huge struggle for us to get anything important done in the past few decades. Nobody wants to co-operate unless there's something in it for them, and trust is in short supply."

"I assume that you have something like computers."

"Of course."

"Is there any way for you to start the calculations, and then jump back here until the answer is available?"

"Yeah, I could do that. It shouldn't take more than a few hours to set it up. I should have thought of that."

I felt charitable. "Don't sweat it. Maybe your brain is still adjusting."

The bill arrived, and the negotiations began. I didn't want Sitri giving out more gold coins. It was too obvious. That meant he had to dip into his stash of real Canadian currency. He and the owner discussed the 40 *Lari* bill over the manager's computer. Sitri handed him two Canadian twenties, and they called it even.

The website they used for deciding the exchange rate was in English, so I leaned in to read the screen over their shoulders. I'd have called it even too if a customer had given me a 60 percent tip.

According to the sun, it was just after noon when we left the restaurant. I had time to inhale the country air before the universe leaped, pirouetted, and we were standing in my living room. In Calgary, it was after two in the morning.

"I'll call you late this afternoon," he said, and before I could answer he was gone.

CHAPTER 5

Back to School

Teleporting all over the globe gave me a new appreciation for the term jet lag.

For a moment, I had an evil thought about calling Kali to let her know I was okay. Instead, I nobly sent her a text about my adventures that she could read when she got up.

Yoko sauntered out of the bedroom, and chirped at me to let me know that I should keep more regular hours. He also had to sniff all my clothes and my shoes before he would come to bed. Apparently I'd been interesting places.

I did not set my alarm clock.

When I woke up, I was lying on my back. There was pressure on my chest, and something was tickling my eye. Yoko Geri was sitting on me and sniffing my eyelids.

He'd done that before for no obvious reason. In this instance, I suspected he was delicately suggesting that his breakfast was long overdue. Turning my head, I looked at the clock. It was after noon.

It was definitely time to get up. I had to pee, and brunch in Georgia was ten hours ago.

That's when the reality hit me. I'd been in denial until then, pretending that the case was, in some sense, proceeding normally.

Holy crap, I'd had brunch in *the Republic of Georgia*, just popping over for a quick bite after working on recordings of murder scenes that made the Enterprise holodeck look like a 19th century Daguerreotype.

If just *one* of the Downland technologies was made available on Earth, it would change the world. I'm not a natural pessimist, but I doubted it would be for the better. For one thing, unless people saw you somewhere else at *exactly* the same time as a crime was committed, alibis were a thing of the past. Not to mention how drug and human trafficking cartels would enjoy the new shipping technology.

Maybe Hell on Earth wasn't just an expression.

I shuffled into the bathroom and turned on the shower. Naturally, my phone rang just as I wet my hair. I turned off the water and had to fumble before I found my phone.

"Hello?"

"I got your text. Are you serious?"

"Yes, I'm serious." I yawned. "It was a busy day yesterday."

"So what's Georgia like?"

"Same as anywhere else. Nice people. Great food. Mostly I saw the inside of a restaurant next to a wine store. Maybe I can go back and pick up a few cases. Wine cases, that is. The bottle we had with lunch was almost good enough to convert me to being a wine snob."

"I hope you are being careful."

"Yes, Mum. I put a condom on my dessert and everything." All right, maybe that was uncalled-for but if you'd seen the size and shape of *churchkhela*, it wasn't completely ridiculous.

"Don't take that tone with me. I'm worried that you are having too much fun figuring out the mystery, and forgetting about one important detail."

"That being?"

"Your client tore a man apart and ate him right in front of you. What happens to you if he gets hungry again?"

"I'm almost certain that won't happen."

"You know who else says that?"

All right, I'll be the straight woman. "Who?"

"Turkeys. Just before Thanksgiving."

I wished I could tell her that she was wrong.

* * *

I ate my late breakfast while I considered my next move. After that I called Sitri.

"Hello?"

Good. I'd scared him out of being cute on the phone.

"I've been thinking. Our evidence points to a skilled archer from the Downland shooting all three victims. Do any names come to mind?"

"Leraye is the only one I can think of. He's big into archery. He's also fascinated by death. I don't know him that well, but I do know that he's pissed that humans have gotten away from arrows lately. He doesn't like humane weapons."

"He sounds like a promising suspect. Does he have anything against you personally?"

"Nothing that I know of. We don't interact much in parliament. We don't have any areas of interest in common."

"Okay, we'll need to talk to him as soon as possible."

"That could be difficult. Even for a Downlander he isn't sociable. Of course, there's also the detail that he's in the Downland."

"Could you talk to him?"

"Sure, but if he's behind this I doubt that he'd tell me anything."

"Is he a hunter? All the shots were through the heart."

"Not as far as I know. He's more into battles and duels."

"That's troubling. Is there any way we can get any intel on him?"

"I know some people who owe me favours if I add a few threats. They can watch him for me. I can do that while I'm setting up the energy calculations."

"All right, do it. It'll be worth it, if only to eliminate a suspect."

After we hung up, I looked up the online University of Calgary telephone directory.

"Archaeology Department," the voice on the phone said.

"My name is Veronica Chandler. I'm an investigator looking for someone who is familiar with Bronze Age weapons who might be able to answer some case-related questions for me."

"Your best bet is probably Professor Schliemann. He's teaching for the rest of the afternoon, but he should be in his office tomorrow around eleven if that's convenient."

"That'll be perfect, thank you."

"I'll let him know you're coming."

* * *

The University of Calgary is a nightmare for visitor parking. Fortunately, I can walk there from my apartment in 40 minutes.

The sky was overcast with darker clouds to the west. Just in case, I wore my rain jacket.

The Archaeology Department was on the seventh floor of the Earth Sciences building, and unlike some other departments that had turned their space into a labyrinth, it was a simple rectangle. I found the right office without too much difficulty, and tapped on the open door.

"Dr. Schliemann?" He was writing something by hand and waved me in without looking up.

The professor wasn't as old as I'd expected. He looked to be in his thirties, and resembled a younger James Spader.

While he finished writing, I had time to glance around his office. That, at least, was everything I expected from an archaeology professor. Books and papers were everywhere. A couple of ancient-looking statuettes served as book ends. The one thing that seemed out of place was a line of inflated silver balloons on a top shelf. It took me a moment to recognize them as the inner bladders from boxed wine, with plastic eyes glued on either side of the valve. He looked up to find me staring at them.

"What are those?" I asked.

"Chac-pigs," he said, smiling as if he expected me to get the joke. When I didn't, the smile vanished.

"You aren't a student," he said.

"No, I'm a private investigator. Veronica Chandler. I called yesterday."

"Oh?" He shuffled some papers on his desk, finding and discarding a couple of message slips before locating the right one. His eyebrows went up as he read it.

"Ah. Of course." We shook hands. "You said you need someone to answer questions about the Bronze Age?"

"Yes. I'm assisting with a homicide investigation, and we have reason to believe that a Bronze Age weapon was involved." I pulled out the casting and handed it to him. "This is a casting taken from the wound. I was hoping that you could identify what kind of weapon made it."

"What makes you think that I can help?"

"Our technician found traces of bronze and cedar oil in the wound. We think that the killer is using either an original Bronze Age weapon or a modern replica."

"Interesting."

He looked at it, turning it over in his hands several times.

"Hmm. It's difficult to discern the exact shape of the weapon, but it appears to be consistent with arrow heads made in Greece. Probably fifth to third century B.C.E. The bronze heads were cast with a socket for the end of the shaft, which forms these bulges on either side. I have some pictures."

He dug out a book from the shelves, narrowly averting a minor avalanche, and flipped pages until he found the right ones. The pictures did indeed look like the sort of arrow that could have made the wound.

"Were you able to get a chemical analysis of the bronze?"

"I don't think that's available from the lab yet," I lied. I'd have to ask Sitri if he could do that. "Is it important?"

"It would be useful to compare it with the composition of period bronzes. That would tell us whether the killer used an original head or a modern replica. It's possible that it could also narrow the location where it was made."

"I'm amazed you think that it could be an original. I assumed they were all in museums."

"No, they're available. A lot of ancient battlefields are littered with them, and there isn't much to be learned from studying thousands of duplicates. Sometimes we can map the positions of the artifacts to give us a sense of how a battle was fought, but it is impossible to keep people from looting the sites. You can even buy original arrow heads on eBay. Because of the limited academic interest, they aren't classed as antiquities so there's little or no government regulation."

"Even to me, that doesn't seem right."

"No, but the private market for artifacts has been around for hundreds of years. We aren't going to be able to stop it now, regardless of how many guards are hired."

"Do you have that bronze chemical composition information?"

"Certainly." He rifled through pages until he found the right table.

"Would you be able to scan that, and send it to me?" I gave him my business card.

"Yes, of course. I'll send it right away. It shouldn't be a difficult comparison. Modern bronze is almost always made with aluminum, rather than tin or arsenic."

"Great. I'll let you know what the results are."

"Thank you. I must admit, this is the first time I've consulted on a homicide investigation, or any kind of criminal investigation for that matter."

"Maybe you can use this story to inspire students who wonder why archaeology is relevant."

While we were shaking hands, my eyes went back to the balloons.

"I'm curious. What is a chac-pig?"

"Are you familiar with the chacmool?"

I shook my head. He pointed out one of the statues on his shelf. It was a reclining figure with its head turned toward us.

"It's a common pre-Columbian Mesoamerican figure. It's also the name of the student association for the U of C Archaeology Department. Years ago, somebody at a social noticed that the wine bag looked like a pig when it was inflated. Eyes were added, and it became our unofficial mascot, the chac-pig."

I looked at the chac-pigs. They looked back at me. Accusingly.

"I see."

Really, what else can you say to that? That archaeologists should get out more?

* * *

When I got home, I checked my e-mail and found the analysis from Doctor Schliemann. The tables gave compositions for various locations. I called Sitri.

"Can you get a chemical analysis of the bronze from the wounds?"

"I'm not sure. All I found in Halvorsen were trace amounts. It was the copper and tin that stood out from the normal tissues. Most other elements would be lost in the background."

"Could you check the others? I got the recipe for original Greek bronze from an archaeology professor, and I want to compare them."

"I'll let you know in an hour or so."

I decided to tidy my apartment while I waited. Domestic things tend to get a bit out of control when I'm as deeply involved in a case as I was with this one. Sitri called back two hours later.

"I have the analysis. There was a small splinter of bronze in Javakhishvili." It took me a moment to remember that he was the Georgian victim. "How do you want it?"

"Can you e-mail it to me?"

"Sure, no problem."

My laptop pinged a few minutes later. The bronze sample was amazingly close to the composition used by the Greeks near Thessaloniki.

Our killer was using an authentic, Bronze Age arrow.

Excellent. That was one more detail nailed down.

Now we just had to figure out what it meant, and how to stop him.

CHAPTER 6

Life Sucks

S itri and I were sitting in my living room. I'd made a pot of coffee, but it turned out that he didn't like it. He was sipping his tea.

"I'm beginning to get a bad feeling about this," I said. "Is this a general problem, or is somebody targeting you specifically?"

"I have no idea. I assumed it was just me."

"Why?"

"I suppose because I assume that *everything* is about me. A long time ago I wasn't that way at all. It's become a habit since the Incident."

"What incident?"

"That physics accident I mentioned. It's a long story."

"We'll leave that for now. Who can travel between universes? I know that you and Beleth can. Anybody else?"

"There are 73 of us, unless somebody is crazy enough to do it without authorization."

"Why 73?"

"That's the number of ministers in our parliament, plus Belphegor, who is the prime minister. We're the only ones who are allowed to come here."

"Wait a minute, are a member of your government?"

"Is that so difficult to believe? I'm not just a pretty face you know."

"It's not that. I just never pictured a demon as having a life. In all the stories, demons just show up, do something bad, and then vanish. As far as I know, nobody's ever thought about what demons do when they aren't running around menacing people."

"I assure you we have lives like anybody else. We have families, jobs, and homes. Our children laugh, play, and scrape their knees."

"You have children?" It sounded stupid to me as soon as it passed my lips. I must have blushed or something. He snorted.

"Not personally. Before the Incident I was too caught up in my work for a long-term relationship. Afterwards, it didn't seem to matter."

"You mentioned that before. What sort of work did you do?"

"I was a relationship counsellor."

"You're kidding."

He looked insulted, and I tried to picture a prince of demons as a marriage counsellor. That wasn't working. Picturing Sitri, the client, worked a lot better.

"How did you get from there to eating people?"

He looked sick. "I've never engaged in cannibalism. How could you say such a thing?"

"Then what happened to Collin Blakeway?"

"That was theatre. I killed him, but that's all."

"And the body found in his car?"

"That was from an image I took of him earlier. It was never alive, but this world's technology isn't good enough yet to tell the difference."

That made me feel better and answered another old question: how had Sitri managed to eat an entire adult human in a minute or two? Answer: he hadn't.

This was getting too bizarre for me. It was time to get back to the case.

"All right, I'm glad you told me. How can we find out if anybody else has been targeted by our killer?"

"The only way would be for me to go home and ask. Do you want me to do that?"

I considered it. "It's not that I don't trust you, but you have no experience as a trained investigator. Is there any way we could bring the ministers here one at a time? Is there any way to guarantee my safety?"

"No, and no. You have to understand that sociopaths tend to be suspicious. If news about these attacks has gotten out, they'll be afraid that it's some kind of trap. If you insist on doing this, I'll have to take you to the Downland."

That was not something I wanted to hear. It took me a couple of throat clearings before I could speak again.

"There's no way in hell... I mean, I'm not interested in being in the middle of a group of six dozen demons who might do something unnatural to me at any moment just because they have poor impulse control."

"That wouldn't be a problem."

"If you can't guarantee my safety here, why do you think you can there?"

"It's not a matter of me guaranteeing anything. It's a matter of physics. When you are there *you'll* be the foreign matter in *our* universe. You'll have the same kind of quantum brane around you that I do now."

"Quantum brain?"

"B-R-A-N-E. The boundary layer between me and your universe. In the Downland it would be between you and our universe."

Part of the mess in my living room was my baton, which was still lying on the coffee table. Sitri picked it up and handed it to me.

"Hit me," he said.

"You're joking."

"No, I'm not. Hit me as hard as you can."

I flicked the baton to extend it, and tapped him on his temple. It wasn't enough to injure him, but if I'd done it to anybody else they'd have grabbed their head and started swearing. He just sat there as if he was still waiting for me to whack him.

"Harder."

It was his funeral. I put a bit of wrist into it this time. He should have dropped. It felt like hitting a concrete wall. He didn't even move.

This time I wound up and put my whole body into it. It was the kind of thing they tell you in baton class never to do. If I'd hit anybody else like that it would have been a killing blow. Despite the rubber grip, all I got for my trouble was a sore hand when the baton vibrated.

"The same thing will happen to you in the Downland. You could be injured under extraordinary conditions but for all normal purposes you'll be invulnerable, like I am here."

"That's—What about the Downlanders?"

"Being in their own universe, they'll be just as vulnerable as you are right now."

"Your world doesn't have a red sun, does it?"

He looked confused. "No, it's a yellow, main-sequence star like yours."

"Never mind. What do you mean by extraordinary conditions?"

"A nuclear bomb would do it. If it was big enough."

Wow. I'd better add glowing green rocks to my list of things to avoid.

"There's one other thing," he said. "Part of our technology consists of nanites that allow us to speak other languages."

"What?"

"Microscopic machines."

"I know what nanites are. I just never thought of that as part of your magic."

"I hope you don't think less of me."

"It actually makes me feel better. So, you don't speak Georgian?"

"Not without the nanites. They do all the translation for me."

"I'm guessing that Downlanders don't speak English either."

"No, we don't. The main language is Kalijiriki. It's also my native language. Our problem is that I won't be able to translate for you. Not only would it be inconvenient, but to the others it would imply that I have a special status with you. They'd refuse to cooperate."

"You *do* have a special place. You're my client." He blushed. "Oh, you mean *that* kind of special status. Couldn't we explain it to them?"

"It wouldn't help. Nobody would believe us. They would assume that you are acting on my behalf to set up some kind of trap for them because that's what they'd do. If you want to conduct your own investigation, you'll have to be able to speak Kalijiriki."

"Why can't I speak English, and everybody else translate?"

"Technically that would work, if anybody would go for it. You want something from them, so they'll insist that they speak their own language. It gives them at least a psychological advantage. You'll have to have your own nanites."

This is how it starts in all the stories about demons. First you accept one harmless bit of help. Then another. Soon you find yourself trapped. What could be wrong with accepting the gift of languages?

A picture came to mind of Sitri lurking around a school yard, wearing a trench coat and with a hat pulled low over his face. *Come on, little girl. The first language is free. What's the harm?*

I stalled. "Why do the nanites translate your own language when you already speak it?"

"They were originally developed for travellers in our own world. Kalijiriki is the main language, but not the only one. Later, Midland languages were added for the ministers."

In the past several days Sitri had been acting like a complete gentleman. As far as I could tell, everything he had told me was true. He wasn't acting like a demon but then how did demons act?

That was easy. In most of the stories they were charming and they lied. Then the slime and fangs came out.

There was a big difference between believing his story about just being a guy from another world, and letting him put something in me whose workings were completely mysterious, and over which I had no control. I wondered what else did these nanites did and...

I sucked in air as a sudden thought hit me. My heart raced.

Oh. Hell. No. Goddamn it, no.

"Do the language nanites have any medical function?"

"No. There are other nanites to handle that." *Shit.*

"Is it possible to transfer the medical nanites between people?"

"You mean between adults? Yes, but the procedure hasn't been done for centuries. We all have them so, except for newborns, it isn't necessary."

"What happens if you just injected one person's medical nanites into another?"

"Nobody would do that. The invading nanites would detect the native ones and convert. There wouldn't be any point to it."

I was getting frustrated. "I'm not making myself clear. What if the person didn't have any of their own?"

He thought for a moment, which made me want to hit him. "That would be bad. The nanites are keyed to the individual and would think that the recipient's genetic material was damaged. They would try to turn the recipient into the donor on a genetic level."

Oh shit. This could not be happening.

"How long would they take to damage a person?"

"I have no idea. As far as I know it's never happened. It would be entirely too easy to identify the culprit of such an attack because their DNA coding is stored in the nanites."

"Is there any way to find out if a person has nanites in them, and whether they were transferred properly?"

"Sure. That's easy. In the rare case that external intervention is needed to save someone's life the nanites can be remotely polled for information. In a healthy person the nanites would report that things are normal. If they don't belong to that person, they'll report that *everything* needs fixing. Why?"

This was my day for bad thoughts. Another one occurred to me.

"After Collin Blakeway whacked me on the head, the paramedics were confused that they couldn't find any evidence of brain damage. What did you do?"

He looked relieved. "Oh, I see what you're getting at. Don't worry. The medical nanites have some functions that are independent of the individual, just as your bandages can be used on anybody. I just gave you some of mine in first-aid mode to fix your immediate damage."

"Are you telling me that I have bugs crawling around inside me?" I felt a bit ill at the thought. I was not as calm as I wanted to be.

"Not anymore. In that mode they fix the immediate damage and then deactivate. They'll be gone by now."

"But you could have given me your nanites in normal, fix-everything mode?"

He looked confused again. "Sure. But I'd never do that."

I grabbed my phone. It was a good thing that I had the required number on speed dial. The way my hands were shaking, dialling ten digits in a row would have been impossible.

Sitri looked concerned. "Veronica, what's wrong?"

I heard the other phone ringing.

"Last autumn Kali was stabbed. Beleth was there, and when I asked her for help she put her hand on Kali. It didn't look like anything happened but the bleeding slowed down and Kali healed really quickly afterwards."

"She transferred her nanites," he said. It wasn't a question.

"We have to find out if she used the right procedure."

"*Hola*," came from the phone.

"Where are you?"

"And hello to you too. I'm at home..."

"Stay there. We'll be right over."

I heard her say, "we?" as I hung up.

Sitri held out his hand to me. I took it, and the universe danced.

* * *

Kali screamed when we appeared out of thin air in her living room.

"What the hell?" She was still holding her phone. She was also in her usual at-home outfit: a black baby doll, black fishnets, and combat boots, with a pink Hello Kitty bow in her hair.

"I'll explain in a minute." I pushed Sitri toward her. "Do it."

She backed up. "What are you doing?"

"It's all right. Just let him touch you."

"Like hell," she said. "Not unless you explain what's going on."

She must have thought that her BFF had gone to the dark side and was letting the demon have her.

"Please, just let me touch your arm," he said. "It's for your own good. We'll explain later, but time might be running out."

She looked at me. I nodded and tried to look reassuring.

Sitri held his hand out like he was approaching a strange dog. She looked at it like it was going to bite her. She jumped slightly when he put it on her bare forearm. The scene was held for a few seconds while both she and I breathed heavily and waited for something terrible to happen.

"Everything is fine," he said after an eon. "She used the emergency transfer protocol. They're functioning normally." I didn't know that I'd been holding my breath.

Kali pulled her arm back from his hand. Since she wasn't dead or his sex slave, she opted for being pissed.

"What the *hell* is going on?"

"It's okay, *hermanita*. I had to be sure you were all right. Maybe you'd better sit down."

"Why wouldn't I be all right? I don't want to sit down. What I want is to know what the hell is going on."

"Remember when Alyssa Blakeway cut you? You lost a lot of blood."

"Gee, thanks for the news flash. I was there. You stopped it and saved my life."

"No, I didn't."

"What?"

"I could barely slow the flow at all. I had help."

"Are you telling me that Alyssa saved my life? That would be ironic."

"No. Alyssa was out cold. The only other person there was Beleth."

I watched the emotions cross her face: *What? What! Oh my gods.* She stood there with her arms crossed protectively across her chest. Her voice was quietly furious.

"You let that demon do something to me, and you didn't tell me?"

"I'm sorry. I didn't know she had left anything in you until now."

"SHE WHAT?" Kali is not quiet when she's emotional. "What did she do?"

"Don't worry, Kali," Sitri said, "you're fine. She just transferred a portion of her nanites to you to stop the bleeding."

"What the fuck does *that* mean?"

"The nanites are molecule-sized machines. They repaired the blood vessels before you bled to death. They also take care of infections, cancer, and any metabolic problems. Oh, and you'll live longer." He was trying to sound upbeat about the whole thing. It was the wrong approach to take.

She pointedly ignored him and focused on me.

"Why didn't you tell me?"

"I told you—I didn't know," I said as calmly as I could. "Kali, you were bleeding to death in my arms. I couldn't do anything to save you. Beleth was the only one there who could help you."

"You could have asked me."

"No, I couldn't. By then, you were unconscious. I asked her for help, and all I saw was her putting her hand on your back. At the time we thought she was a demon. I assumed she just somehow magically stopped the bleeding. I didn't know that her tricks were based on technology."

She stared at me for a long, cold moment. Then her face softened a bit.

"Okay, I suppose I'm good with being alive. But you could have told me later what happened."

"I forgot. You were alive and getting better. I'm really sorry. I guess I didn't want to ask too many questions about how it happened. I only found out about the nanites a few moments ago."

Sitri was about to speak. I elbowed him in the ribs. He got the hint, even though the jab didn't hurt him. My elbow was another matter.

"What did you mean, I'll live longer?" Kali said to him. "That's just because I can't get any diseases, right?"

"I don't remember all the details, but there's more to it than that. The nanites perform a variety of functions to keep your DNA and cells healthy, including repairing any genetic damage you get in the future. Your cells will never age."

Holy mother Isis and all her children. Kali looked overwhelmed. I'd read enough to get the gist of what he was saying. I chose my words carefully so the question would be clear to him.

"Are you saying that Beleth made Kali immortal?"

I don't know who looked more shocked: Kali or Sitri.

"Of course not. There's no such thing as true immortality. There are plenty of ways she could die."

I don't know who looked more uncomfortable: Kali or me.

"Like what?" she said.

"Mostly accidents, or acts of malice. If somebody decapitated you the damage would probably be too great for the nanites to fix before your brain died. You could be blown apart by a bomb. Or you could starve to death in a locked room. Don't worry, you aren't immortal."

"If I avoid any swordsmen, terrorists or cells, how long will I live?"

"There are other things than those that could kill you..."

"Damn it! Don't be so literal. How long?"

"I don't know. Nobody in Downland has died of anything except violence since the technology was invented."

"When was that?" I asked.

"The first version nanites were invented about 400 years ago. The improved version I have in me was created about 50 years later."

Kali flumped on the couch. I didn't blame her.

"Fill in the blanks for us," I said. "How do these things work?"

"The general principle is easy. They are given to infants by their parents. New nanites reproduce in the body, and fix known genetic problems, then collect information about the body. When there are enough of them they form a consensus of what is normal for that person, and act to maintain it. If an anomaly is found, they kill the diseased tissues and stimulate new growth. That's far easier than trying to program them for all possible ills. They also have some general first-aid capabilities, which is what they used to stop Kali's hemorrhage, and to repair your brain damage. There are some other details that allow for puberty, pregnancy, intestinal flora, creating new memories—that sort of thing."

"So what happens if Kali gets a cold?"

"That's the point. She *can't* get a cold. The moment a virus enters her body it's identified as being foreign and destroyed."

"What about poisons?"

"Almost all of them cause death over a period of hours or longer. If an unfamiliar chemical is found near tissue damage, the nanites assume that it's toxic, and tear it apart. Any elements that are toxic by themselves, such as arsenic, are encapsulated in an inert shell, transported to the skin, and excreted in microscopic pellets. You'd never notice them."

Kali didn't move or speak until he mentioned my brain damage.

"Wait, he put those things in you too?"

"I got the first-aid-only version. He says they're gone now."

She started crying.

"I don't want to live forever. I want these things out of me!"

"I'm not sure that's possible," he said.

"What do you mean? Get them out! Now!"

"I don't know how. Nobody's ever wanted them removed before. They're designed to keep people alive under a variety of adverse conditions, so they have no off switch."

"What about mine? They turned off after a while."

"That only happens in first-aid mode. It can't be done in normally functioning nanites, or somebody could use it to perform an assassination. Even the first-aid functions haven't been used for centuries. When everybody has the nanites, nobody needs first aid. I only know about it because, as a minister, I might want to heal a Midlander some time."

"How did Beleth give me hers?" Kali asked.

"The nanites can execute commands received through the host's nervous system. Essentially, she told them to move into you."

"Why can't I do that? Order them to move out of me."

"The transfer protocol was designed for emergencies like yours, back in the days when not everybody had them. It's like donating blood: Only enough nanites are transferred to support the patient without endangering the donor. If you had too few nanites then none of them would migrate. I don't understand. Why do you want to get rid of them?"

"You're telling me I'll live for centuries. Maybe longer. I'll outlive everybody I love. If I have children, I'll outlive them. I don't want them!"

"There are good things about it," Sitri said. I shook my head to get him to shut up, but he didn't seem to notice. "I understand that the nanites can be commanded to turn ovulation on or off. You now have complete control over your menstruation and fertility. Isn't that something that women want?"

"Sitri," I said as reasonably as possible, "please leave now. I'll call you when I'm ready to resume work on the case."

If there were any remaining doubts about Sitri's lack of diabolical cunning they were gone now. From his expression he had no idea why Kali was crying, or why his latest revelation didn't make her feel any better. At least he had the sense to leave without shoving his foot further down his throat.

Kali cried while I held her, and I flashed back to the day that her parents had been killed. After a while she stopped sobbing but tears were still rolling down her cheeks. She was going through tissues fast enough that I doubted the box would last long.

I went to her kitchen. Normally, I'd have made her tea, but the situation was too serious for that. We were into hot chocolate territory: hot chocolate with hazelnut, nutmeg, vanilla, Cointreau, and a ball of vanilla ice cream instead of a marshmallow.

When I handed her the cup, she began crying again.

"It's going to be okay, *Kalita*. This isn't the last time I'll ever make you hot chocolate. I'm going to be around for a long time."

It was a good thing that Sitri had left. Even with his fancy language nanites there was no way he'd have figured out what she was saying. Unfortunately, over the years we'd both had practice in understanding each other while we were crying.

"Not as long as I will. You'll die, and George will die, and Mum and Dad will die. Everybody else I've loved is already dead. I'll be all alone." Her tears flowed again. My shirt was getting soaked.

I could imagine Sitri cheerfully telling her that she'd meet new people, as if loved ones were interchangeable parts. Dumb-assed man.

No, that was grossly unfair to him. He was a true stranger in a strange land. This wasn't his universe, let alone his culture, and Kali's problem wasn't one that anybody he knew had been forced to face for several hundred years, if then. He couldn't be expected to understand.

"Maybe it's not that bad. Sitri said he isn't an engineer, so he doesn't know everything about their technology. We might still find a way of removing the nanites, or turning them off or something."

She sniffed. "Do you really think so?"

"You aren't going to believe this, but he's a freaking relationship counsellor in his real life. Or at least he was until something they call the Incident occurred, whatever that was. All he's had is their version of basic science courses. Trust me, he's not an expert in this stuff. He's probably just read the quick user guide."

She'd stopped crying and was wiping her eyes with a tissue.

"I feel like a freak."

I was probably thinking slightly more clearly than she was right now. Eventually, it would occur to her that one solution would be to offer me her nanites, but that was a short-term solution at best.

She'd also want to give them to George and our parents. But what about George's family, as stupid and racist as they were? And anybody I eventually wanted to spend my life with? What about their friends? The ripples kept moving outward. It sounded like a great idea until the list of people who would be around for centuries or millennia became too large.

People would have to murder horrible in-laws to get away from them. Inheritances would vanish except in the case of an accident or murder. Ex-lovers would be around forever, and a life sentence would cost billions in taxes. People who expected an economic disaster would hasten it by hoarding, not for a few decades, but for centuries. Everybody would become a billionaire. There was no way that the economy could support that. Our whole society would collapse.

The only sensible thing was to get the nanites out of her. Either that, or accept that, at some point, she would probably take her own life in a violent and messy way.

Hell on Earth indeed. I had to help her, even if I had no idea how as yet.

"You aren't a freak. You're alive, which you wouldn't be if this hadn't happened. And as long as we're alive we can try to figure out how to fix this."

She sniffed again.

"I guess so."

"Good. Now, drink your chocolate before it gets cold. I have a busy day ahead of me."

"Why? What's happening?"

She had far too much to worry about without me adding to her load.

"I have to go out of town to interview some people about the case. I'll be back in a day or so."

CHAPTER 7
Parliament of Fouls

I did offer to stay longer, but Kali said she wanted to be alone for a while. She seemed thoughtful rather than depressed, so I respected her decision. I wished it was later in the year. George would be home from university after his final exams, and she could really use his company.

When I got home, I waited a while until I was sure that I was in control of my emotions, then called Sitri.

"I know you don't understand why Kali is upset. I'm not going to try to explain it to you right now. Just don't mention anything to do with the medical nanites in her presence unless she asks you specific questions. And for heaven's sake don't try to make her feel better. Just give her the facts."

There was silence for a moment. I imagined him trying to figure out what to say that wouldn't get him into more trouble.

"All right. I'm sorry. I promise."

"Good. Now, tell me about how the language nanites work."

"They interface with the language areas of the brain. You can still hear the person speaking their native language, but your brain interprets the words in a way you can understand. Written language is handled similarly, but of course through the visual centres of the brain, not the auditory."

"What about speaking?"

"That's more complicated. When you decide to say something, your brain assembles the words and sends commands via the motor nerves to produce the sounds corresponding to them. The nanites restructure the phrase you were going to say into the required language, then substitutes the correct muscle movements to pronounce them."

"In other words, if I'm talking to a Spanish-speaking person, I can intend to say hello and my mouth will actually say *hola*."

"Exactly. It takes some getting used to."

"How do you switch languages?"

"The nanites mostly figure it out from what the other person is speaking, just as you can tell that a person is speaking French without understanding the words. Or you can select a language intentionally. The user interface is quite intuitive."

"How many languages do they translate?"

"Just the main ones in both worlds. About a five thousand."

I had maybe expected a dozen. Holy crap.

"Now the big questions. Can I turn them off?"

"Certainly. Otherwise, they would interfere when you speak your native language causing something like a mental echo."

"And they do nothing else? No side effects? No hidden surprises?"

"No."

"Is there a procedure for you to give me some of your nanites?"

"Yes. They aren't dangerous the way already acclimatized medical nanites would be."

"Are they dangerous at all? In any way? To any degree?"

"No."

Somewhere in my brain, a distraught voice was yelling, *what do you think you're doing?*

Screw it. I could spend weeks arguing with myself for and against this. Ever since my trip to Europe I'd wanted to learn more languages.

"All right. Come on over."

* * *

How surprising. It turned out to be a strange experience.

Sitri placed his hands on my head like a priest giving me a blessing. I was tense, waiting for something to happen, but there was no sensation other than the growing warmth of his palms. After a moment he removed his hands.

"*Kukofiki ingu uli?*" I heard the unfamiliar words, but my mind immediately registered, "do you understand me?"

"*Ada,*" I heard myself say, although what I had thought was 'yes.'

Holy crap, I was fluent in a language I didn't know two minutes ago. I wondered which one it was.

"Good," he said in English. "You can understand and speak Kalijiriki. Now you just have to learn to control it."

There was a bizarre sensation in my head like I heard the words twice.

"What's wrong?" I said. My mouth didn't work properly. All my words were slurred. Was this what having a stroke felt like?

He tried to comfort me by touch. "Don't worry. You just have to turn off the translators when you are speaking a language you already understand, or your brain gets the message twice. Just think that you want them off." Again, I heard him with the echo. My head was aching.

I tried to concentrate on ordering the nanites to shut themselves off.

"How's this?" My words were still slurred.

"Try picturing the nanites waiting for orders," he said slowly. If he spoke slowly, I could understand him better despite the mental reverberation. "Then imagine a switch being turned off. Make sure that the meaning of the switch is clear in your mind."

I did my best to visualize all these little gadgets in my brain coming to attention and waiting for orders. The switch image that I used was one of the old knife switches from 1940s horror movies.

I tried several times. Each time I slurred. After a while I couldn't hold down the panic. I fought against it. Fear wouldn't do me any good.

Try telling that to my damaged brain. I was almost afraid to try speaking anymore.

"Did it work that time?" This time my speech was clear.

"*Kukofiki ingu uli?*"

"Not at all. I remember what it means from when you said it before, but there's no connection in my head."

I slumped back against the back of the sofa, beyond relieved it had worked. A rivulet of sweat tickled its way down my side from my armpit. My shirt was soaked. The whole process was unnerving, and I was glad that nobody else was there to see how much I'd been freaking out. "I suppose that to turn them on again I can just flip the switch the other way?"

"That should work. After a while it'll become the natural thing to do. Most of the time you'll want them off, unless you are visiting a foreign location like I am."

We practised for an hour. After a while, I could turn the translators on and off with only the occasional slip.

As far as I could tell my mind was the same. I was no more confused than normal. I took a deep breath and let it out slowly.

"Okay. What else does a tourist to the Downland need?"

* * *

Our plan was to stay for about twenty-four hours. Our brains should be safe for much longer than that, but I wanted a big safety margin.

My luggage was less than I'd expected. All I'd need would be my clothes, a fanny pack for toiletries, my duty belt, and some food.

Like Sitri, I could eat and drink while in another universe, but the nutrients were absorbed much slower than usual. It would be easier for me to carry my own food and water for a short trip.

There was one other thing that I had with me. It isn't every day you get to play tourist in Hell, and I wanted pictures. *Aren't the lakes of fire pretty this time of year? Especially wreathed with those clouds of brimstone smoke.* I'd already floated over a lake of fire in an erupting volcano. It would be interesting to see if there were differences.

When I told Sitri he was amused. The popular conceptions of Hell were nothing like the Downland. Where we were going the current weather was usually mild and dry. I took Sitri at his word because I didn't have much of a choice. He said I'd look like a complete idiot if I showed up wearing a fire proximity suit. Besides, that was one work cos-tume I didn't own. My friend Danielle's boyfriend was a fire fighter. I wondered if he could loan me one.

* * *

The universe jumped, although not as much as before. I didn't realize how much I'd braced myself for scorching heat, the smell of sulphur, and screaming souls until we arrived.

We were standing in a quiet pine forest. The terrain looked a lot like Banff National Park must have before white people arrived. The path un-der our feet looked more like a game trail rather than a hiking trail.

I shrieked and almost lost my balance backward when I turned to look at Sitri. The Pegasus wings and leopard head he'd had the first time I saw him were back. I think my scream scared him.

"Don't do that!"

He looked down at his nude body.

"Do what?"

"Why do you look like that?"

"Sorry, I forgot to tell you. Most people in Downland have a look they've adopted. It's a sort of fashion statement. This is mine. People we meet will expect it."

"Great. Just warn me before you do anything like that again."

I drew in a deep breath, intending to let him know that I wasn't amused by his omission. I was distracted by the air. It seemed oddly thin, or something. There was too little oxygen in it.

I took another deep breath. There was enough oxygen for standing here, but not as much as I expected.

"What's the altitude here?" I asked, breathing more quickly. That didn't help.

"About 600 metres above sea level. Why?"

"That's less than Calgary. Why am I having trouble breathing?"

"Remember the boundary layer around you? It doesn't let you absorb the oxygen as quickly here as you do at home. When you breathe in, hold the breath for a moment before letting it out. Remember, low density and low energy things can penetrate the layer, but it takes time. Breathe in, hold it to let the oxygen penetrate, and let it out."

I tried doing as he suggested, and my breathing problem eased. It took me a few minutes to get the best rhythm going. I guess that meant he was right about my personal force field as well.

"Veronica?" he said in a conversational voice.

I turned to look at him just as he slammed a rock the size of a water-melon into me. From the way his considerable muscles bulged, it looked like he was putting everything he had into it.

Despite being blind-sided, I tried to dodge. The rock still hit me squarely on the top of my head. There was a cracking sound.

I might have felt something. Maybe I was fooling myself because I ex-pected to be in pain. The rock certainly felt something. It split in two and landed at my feet.

"What the hell did you do that for?"

"I wanted you to be comfortable that you are protected here."

"I could have been killed!"

"As I told you, not unless I used a large nuclear bomb."

I touched my head carefully. It didn't hurt at all. As far as I could tell without a mirror, my hair wasn't even mussed. I couldn't think of a snappy comeback, so just to make myself feel better I punched him in the upper arm as hard as I could. I didn't expect the result.

He yelled and clutched his arm where I'd hit it.

"Why did you do that?"

"Oh my god! I didn't think that would hurt. I was just upset you hit me with a rock."

"Remember that I'm a native here. I can be injured just as easily as you can when you are at home."

"I'm sorry. I'm not used to being invulnerable. I won't do it again."

"I'm beginning to understand how we appear to act in your world. Apology accepted."

"Now that we're through hitting each other, where are we going?"

"This way."

He started walking. I followed.

We'd been travelling for a few minutes. It was beautiful country, but there was no sign of a parliament, a capital city, or even a trail marker.

"Is this like a massive city park or something?"

"We don't have cities since shortly after the Incident. Our technology allows us to have decentralized services, so there's no need for them. There are still some small towns where people with similar interests live, but even those have been going out of fashion."

That made sense. If you can teleport from one place to another by thinking about it, you don't need a transportation system. Food delivery, ditto. Probably each house had its own power system. If they had police, they could be anywhere they were needed in the blink of an eye.

"Do you have hospitals?"

"For trauma cases and occasional obstetric emergencies, yes."

We continued walking.

"By the way, did you hear anything back about Leraye?"

"I did. It doesn't look promising. As I said, we haven't crossed paths much. My sources tell me that he is a sadist. His favourite thing was inciting a battle, and then watching the people die slowly from arrow wounds. As far as he was concerned, the more pain the better."

"I notice you're using the past tense. What happened to him?"

"Your technology. Arrows have been replaced by bullets. My sources tell me that he's pissed because he thinks they're too efficient."

"That's not true. From what I've read of the U.S. Civil War, a lot of soldiers died horribly of infections after being shot."

"Hey, you're preaching to the choir. He's the sadistic sociopath, not me. I was into love and sex. I understand he's been getting into anti-personnel mines lately. He thinks they're fun."

And this Leraye was a member of their government. Sheesh.

"I admit that a sadist doesn't sound like our killer. Those shots were neatly placed to cause nearly instant death, not suffering. Damn, I was hoping we had our man."

We walked for another half hour.

"Are we there yet?" I said in a purposely whiny teenager voice.

"Almost." Of course, he didn't get the joke.

A few minutes later we came out of the forest. We were looking down onto a plain. Whatever else happened in this world, the view was worth the trip. I took some pictures.

I assumed that the temple on top of a low mound down below was the parliament building. It wasn't exactly like the Parthenon before it was blown up in the late 1600s, but it reminded me of it. I doubted that the Parthenon ever had antennas on the roof.

The mound itself was covered with grass and flowers. It was too far away to be certain what they were, but there were a lot of them and they were definitely red. I had my suspicions.

"Something with poison in it," I said to myself.

"What?"

"Never mind. Just a line from an old movie. We should switch to Kalijiriki now."

At the base of the mound was a formal garden that would not have looked out of place at Versailles. From what I could see it appeared to completely circle the temple. Several figures were walking about, sitting on stone benches, and generally enjoying the sunny day.

As we got closer, we passed one who was a zebra with a hissing snake for a tail. The zebra part ignored us. The snake malevolently watched us as we passed by. Another had a bloated, pear-shaped body on long, spindly legs. Her head was small and conical with no neck. At least I assumed it was female from the floppy breasts hanging down to her waist and a lack of obvious genitalia. This was more like the Hell I'd been expecting. If these were fashion statements, what did they say about their wearers?

"When we get inside there are a couple of rules. The first is that violence within the council chamber is forbidden, no matter what the provocation. We had to make that rule after the Incident to prevent ministers from trying to murder each other."

"Okay, don't rip any arms off. What else?"

"Jumping directly into parliament is forbidden to prevent people from sending a bomb to get rid of the competition. That's why we had to walk here."

"Wow, and we thought Elbowgate was a big deal. What if somebody doesn't follow the rules?"

"It isn't honour that enforces that one. It's technology. When we get inside the Prime Minister is the one you have to convince. With his help the others will at least talk to you."

"I thought we were just going to talk to some individuals. Can't you get him to play ball?"

"I'm only a minister. He's the one who overthrew the previous regime and established the oligarchy."

"What previous regime?"

"We had a constitutional monarchy before the Incident. The king and those loyal to him were violently deposed."

"Out of curiosity, what was the old king's name?"

"Iblis."

Oh goody. I just loved these little surprises. I got to negotiate with the guy who kicked Satan out of Hell.

"You couldn't have mentioned this before?"

"Does it make a difference?"

"I suppose not." What's a teaspoon of water when you are drowning?

"He'll may to distract you by offering you immense riches, and try to convince the others not to help you."

"Why would he do that?"

"Because he can. Remember, we—they're—all sociopaths. For them, it's all about self-interest, manipulation, domination, and control. Each believes they are the only real person. Everybody else is a meat puppet."

"Any pointers about how I might win him over?"

"He has a thing for research. Present yourself as a researcher, and he might buy it."

"So, what's the name of this charming individual?"

"Belphegor."

"Never heard of him."

"As far as I know, he's never been to Midland. He keeps saying that you are all animals."

I looked at the massive building atop its mound, and thought about manipulation, domination, and control.

"He's right. He's about to meet the Honey Badger."

* * *

The mound was only a couple of metres high, and looked artificial. A wide marble staircase led up to the parliament building itself.

The immense bronze doors swung aside for us. They had to be at least three by five metres each. I felt like an ant entering a lion's mouth.

Worse yet, I was beginning to feel less like a honey badger, and more like a small, twenty-one-year old girl from Cowtown who was about to sass the prime minister of Hell on his own turf.

Well, Veronica, you wanted to be in the big leagues some day. It looks like you're here. I kept reminding myself that a rock had shattered on my head without me feeling it. I am Honey Badger. Hear me roar.

I hoped.

The council chamber occupied the whole width of the building, although the length was truncated. Maybe the back third of the building was offices or something.

Bigger than life statues lined both sides. The last one on the left depicted an incredibly handsome man with wings. At the far end was a dais nearly the width of the hall and probably as tall as Sitri. There was something sitting on a throne-like chair in the middle. I assumed that was Belphegor.

Well-upholstered chairs were lined up in two groups before the dais with an aisle between them. Most of the chairs were occupied, and even compared with the Canadian Parliament, it was a zoo.

Literally.

Several dozen creatures were yelling and gesturing with no pretense of order. Each one's appearance was unique. Somebody must have made a point just before we arrived, and this was the resulting discussion.

The noise level slowly went down as the ministers noticed us. I hoped like hell that Sitri knew what he was doing.

The Prime Minister casually crossed his legs and looked down on us. He was about two and a half metres tall with horns like a Texas steer. His skin was blood-red. He was taking pains to appear bored.

"What is this *thing*, Minister Sitri, and why have you brought it here?"

I had to beat them at their own game. Sitri was about to answer when

I pushed him aside. For once his body didn't feel like a statue.

"I'll handle this. My name is Veronica," I said as loudly as possible while striding up the aisle. Thank heaven I'd learned how to project in high school drama class. "I have come to discover who is killing the Midland magicians who have tried to summon Prince Sitri."

There was a buzz from the ministers. I scanned their faces—those who had faces. Most of them seemed confused or surprised. A couple of them seemed to be purposely neutral in their expressions, like they were hiding something. I took note of which they were. Belphegor raised one hand. The ministers immediately quieted.

"Why do we care what happens to Midland animals?"

He was entirely too casual about it. His ministers, on the other hand, stirred and muttered. They cared, all right.

"You don't. What you do care about is that somebody is spoiling your fun."

That got a bigger stir from the audience. I saw Belphegor's mouth twitch, so I kept up the pressure. There weren't any obvious stairs leading up onto the platform, so I took two running steps, jumped, grabbed the edge and pulled myself up. I felt the lack of oxygen and hid it by breathing as deeply as possible through my nose. Gasping like a beached fish wouldn't do my image any good.

Belphegor stood and roared with outrage that someone else was on his dais. I confronted him and spoke quietly.

"You can't afford to let someone ruin your people's entertainment. Are you familiar with the Midland phrase 'bread and circuses'?"

Now he just looked confused. He might be good at manipulating his ministers, but I was an unknown, an outsider, and he was trying to figure me out. All I had to do was to be a moving target.

With his height I was looking at his stomach, so I completed the *lèse-majesté* by climbing up on the throne so we were approximately eye-to-eye and leaned in. My stabbing finger stopped just short of his chest.

"Don't be an idiot."

"Prime Minister..." Sitri started to say.

"Shut up," I bellowed at him. He shut up. The reverberation in the hall was impressive.

"Somebody is doing things that shouldn't be physically possible. Sitri was somehow detained on his way to Midland. That implies an amount of power beyond anything you have, and that, in turn, implies an unknown threat that is attacking at least one of your ministers. What is next?" I scanned my audience. "*Who* is next?"

Belphegor looked over his motley crew. I glanced around again. A lot of them were looking nervous. There's nothing like making the danger personal to get a sociopathic politician's attention.

One exception was Beleth. For some reason it hadn't occurred to me that I'd see her here, even though Sitri said that only ministers got to come to Midland. She was smiling in a way I didn't like as she wiggled her fingers at me in a saucy greeting.

"What you say may be true," Belphegor said, "but if so we will handle it ourselves."

"I doubt that you have the mental capacity. I am a researcher trained in just this sort of inquiry. I'm offering to discover the identity of your enemy. Refuse my help at your peril."

Outwardly, I remained calm, although my mouth was dry and I had to remind myself not to gasp for breath in the thin air. Intellectually, I knew I wasn't in any physical danger, but emotionally I expected them to torture and kill me if I made a mistake.

The only danger to me was that Sitri might be arrested or incapacitated. That would strand me here with no way home, unless one of the other ministers could be persuaded to take me back.

I wondered if anybody else knew about my prior relationship with Beleth. She'd been to Midland. She also seemed to have some kind of affection for me—if that was the right word. Asking her for a ride home would put me even further into her debt. At least it was a viable plan B. The others were unknown quantities and it might be a messy form of suicide to try to get their help.

On top of that, my escape from Downland had a definite expiration date. In a few weeks I'd be just like them.

The Prime Minister, in fact everyone here except Sitri and me, was suspicious and secretive. One of their biggest fears was that somebody would mount a sneak attack on them. I seemed to be doing fairly well at dominating them into helping me. Now let's see if I could demonstrate some manipulation and control.

"You have only one choice. Instruct your ministers to answer my questions fully and truthfully, or lose your all your positions to an outside force. Of course, any prime minister who would be stupid enough to deny my help wouldn't deserve such a position in the first place."

I hopped down from the throne and purposely turned my back on him as if I was about to play to the audience. I wanted him to believe I was dismissing him as unimportant and impotent. I just hoped I'd pissed him off as much as I thought I had.

Belphegor gave another angry bellow and struck me from behind. Since I didn't see it coming, I didn't instinctively flinch and spoil the effect. I felt a gentle push and braced myself by flexing my toes and ankles. There was a second bellow from him, this time one of pain. I turned slowly to see him clutching his broken hand. The idiot had punched me. I bet that it would be a while before his nanites fixed that much damage, and in the meantime he knew that I was in control of the situation.

"So much for your prohibition on violence within these walls," I sneered. "Accept my help or die. It's your choice."

If Belphegor had never been to Midland he probably wasn't as well versed in the physics as those of his ministers who made regular trips. The look in his eyes was one of fear and loathing. He had no idea how a puny little Midland girl had managed to survive his attempt to rip her in half, as well as making him look like a fool in front of his entire government.

The ministers knew. I could see worry in their eyes as well. They would wonder why a Midlander would come here to help them. Except for Beleth, they probably knew nothing about me personally. With any luck, she'd keep her knowledge secret, and by the time the rest of them came to any kind of conclusion I'd be long gone.

Belphegor made up his mind, not that he had much choice. He addressed parliament.

"This—person—has graciously offered to help us against a threat we had not previously suspected. Answer her questions fully and truthfully." He resumed his seat, trying not to show that he was nursing his hand. A drop of blood leaked from it and dripped onto the dais.

Regardless of orders or how harmless their information might be, I doubted that most of them would want to be seen talking to me, or risk others overhearing what they would see as an admission of weakness.

"If anyone is concerned about giving their testimony where it might be overheard, I'll be staying until tomorrow. Drop by and see me." I snapped my fingers at Sitri. "Come."

I jumped down from the dais and marched toward the exit as if I owned the place and expected a prince to jump when I said frog. He obediently followed me out.

We got to the bottom of the stairs when the whole thing caught up with me.

"I have to sit down," I said, a lot less firmly than I wanted. He helped me down onto the cool seat of a stone bench.

"I don't blame you. Are you sure you aren't a sociopath as well?"

"I hope not."

We sat on the bench as if we'd stopped to admire the view.

"That was an incredible performance," Sitri said. "How did you know what to do?"

"Hints that you gave me, of course. Apart from that I just played on his nature. I out-manipulated, out-dominated, and out-controlled him. By the way, will there be any problem that I didn't leave an address?"

"No. Your body has a Midland energy signature. They can track that to find you."

I took several deep breaths, holding each one before letting it out. "Good. How do you manage to breathe so naturally in my world?"

"Practice."

Sitri, alleged Prince of Sixty Legions, sat beside me in the garden under the warm sun. The breeze brought with it the scent of the surrounding flowers. I was right; they were poppies. It was a beautiful day in Hell. I took several pictures. We sat quietly for a few minutes before he spoke.

"Remind me not to get in the way of this 'honey badger' you mentioned."

I took several more deep breaths. There were traces of other perfumes coming from the gardens. I'd gambled and won. I felt like maintaining my feminine mystique.

"Honey Badger don't give no warnings."

* * *

We were back in the woods, about a kilometre from parliament hill. I was not happy.

"Are you joking?"

"Why would I do that? If you stay at my house nobody will talk to you. They'll assume that Belphegor is monitoring them even though that's illegal."

"What about a hotel?"

"There aren't any. Nobody needs them. A traveller can go back home in an instant. They don't need other places to stay."

"Can you at least get me some blankets or something?"

"Of course."

Sitri vanished to where ever it was he lived. About five minutes later he returned with a stack of blankets and two pillows.

"I checked the weather report again. The forecast still calls for it being warm and dry tonight."

"If your forecasts are like ours, there will probably be a tornado."

"The one-day forecast accuracy is at least 95%."

"That's what they all say."

This was the last time I was going to let someone else make my travel arrangements for me. It wasn't that Sitri was stupid or malicious. The problem was he had lived his entire life in a highly technological culture where every problem had a known solution that was implemented by commanding nanites. He wasn't used to thinking outside the box.

If the weather report was believable, I should be comfortable sleeping in the forest wrapped in my blankets.

The most ridiculous things kept tripping me up. A madman with a sword, or an artillery battery, wouldn't be able to scratch me, but mosquitoes were another matter. Apparently their density and energy level was low enough for them to try to suck my blood. I wondered if the mosquitoes were also sociopaths, and how one could tell.

Sitri was confused by my complaints. His medical nanites also fixed insect bites. The allergens weren't around long enough for them to itch. Bastard.

I am not much of an outdoor girl. To me, roughing it means that the restaurant only has two Michelin stars. Sitri brought me another Neapolitan pizza for supper, so I decided to forgive him for not thinking things through. I saved my sandwiches for later.

At least there was plenty of firewood. I found a nice flat rock outcrop where I could build a campfire without burning down the forest. That might have been somewhat counterproductive to my investigation. There were several flattish boulders nearby that would serve as chairs if I needed them.

A few minutes after Sitri left for the night I heard a twig snap. Something moved in the undergrowth. It seemed smaller than a person. Maybe it was a deer. Were there deer in Hell? Sociopathic deer? The bushes parted.

"Hello, Veronica," Beleth said. She was wearing the same highly professional outfit she'd been wearing in parliament: bare feet, and something like a black baby doll with pink fur trim, and without the underwear. I wondered if she'd been shopping in Midland, or if they had a Victoria's Secret in the Downland.

I waved toward one of the boulders and sat on another. "Fancy meeting you here."

"You were impressive today. I've never seen anybody twist Belphegor's tail that well before. You realize that he's had to give himself administrative leave as punishment for striking you?"

"He has a tail? I was too busy to notice."

She laughed as she sat down across the fire from me.

"Just for once I wasn't being literal."

"Oh. If he's upset about getting detention, he should have picked on someone his own size. What brings you to my neck of the woods?"

"Sitri and I have a problem in common. Shortly after our little party with Alyssa Blakeway, I noticed an unusually high rate of attrition among my summoners."

I got out my notebook and made some notes. I'd have brought my laptop, but I didn't know if it would work here, let alone if I'd be able to charge it in the Downland. A pencil seemed like a safer bet.

"What rate of attrition do you usually get?"

"Zero, I suppose. At least, before I answer the summons." She smiled to herself at fond memories of carnage. That wasn't at all creepy.

"And now?"

"One hundred percent. I find that somewhat annoying."

"I can imagine. How many summoners have died?"

"Seven."

"I'll need names, places, and dates for all of them."

She recited the information without pausing. I wondered if there were nanites for an eidetic memory. Now *that* would be worth having, as long as I could turn it off when I needed to. Like when Sitri turned up naked in my living room. A mosquito tried to fly into my eye and I swatted it.

The first one is free, little girl.

"Was your movement across universes slower than usual?"

"Why, yes. Now that you mention it. The whole process took far longer than normal. What does it mean?"

"I wish I knew. By the way, what's your area of specialization?"

"I'm not sure what you mean by that."

"When Sitri visits Midland, he causes men and women to fall in love with one another. What's your line?"

"Sitri is a prude. I like to be more diversified: men, women, pillows, furries."

"Horses."

She waved her hand dismissively.

"I'm over that. Unless I can interest you in..."

"No," I said quickly. "I'm fine. Thank you."

She got up and brushed the leaf litter from her legs, naked butt, and the baby doll.

"Wait," I said. This was the hard part. "I want to thank you for saving Kali's life."

"All right," she said. She stood there looking at me expectantly. Right, demons are literal.

"Thank you for saving Kali's life." She shrugged.

"You're welcome. I didn't do it for her. I did it for you. I've spent too much time on you to have things fall apart just because your friend dies."

That didn't sound in the least bit good.

"What do you mean by that?"

"If your friend had died, you'd have been biased against us. As it is, you feel some gratitude toward me."

"So Kali was just a pawn so that you can call in a marker?"

"Don't worry. Not for a while yet." And with that, she vanished into the darkness.

Was Beleth just yanking my chain? Either way, she continued to piss me off. If she'd asked for my help, I might have given it, but I did not appreciate being manipulated.

Have I mentioned that I deeply hate bullies?

* * *

I saw the next demon coming despite the darkness. I have no idea how the forest survived.

After a while he was close enough that I could see through the glare. He appeared to be a huge wolf with a serpent's tail. Fire kept belching from his mouth. I armed myself with my notebook and pencil.

"I need your name for the record."

He roared, and a flame engulfed me. I managed not to move, and held my breath just in case inhaling smoke and flame was as bad for me here as it would be at home. When the flame stopped, I was still sitting and looking calm. This whole superwoman thing was kind of cool.

"Don't give me that crap," I said, "or I'll become angry." I was counting on them having no idea what my capabilities were. And I couldn't help myself. "You wouldn't like me when I'm angry."

He changed into a man with the head of a raven, although the raven had wolf's teeth. That was rather unattractive. He made the mistake of trying to tackle me. Perhaps martial arts weren't big here; maybe he didn't know any better. Maybe he thought that Belphegor had been clumsy or something.

As he flew through the air, I simply put my foot up into his stomach, grabbed his arms, and rolled backward. He sailed over me and landed, head toward the ground, against the side of a tree. The stubs of numerous dead branches were sticking out of the trunk, and he appeared to be impaled on them. That was *so* going to leave a mark.

As he slid toward the ground, I could see several spots of blood on his back. I nonchalantly got to my feet and faced him.

He staggered to his feet and pulled a knife from its sheath. It wasn't a type I'd seen before. Instead of waving the point at me, he held it back against his arm like he knew what he was doing.

When the slash came I parried it, jumped in so close that I body-checked him, and grabbed him by the throat. At the same time I grabbed his wrist and brought my knee up hard and fast. With my hand squeezing his vocal cords, he was unable to scream. All he could do was gurgle as his elbow broke.

He collapsed, physically and psychologically unable to respond. He was used to Midlanders being pushovers while he was invulnerable. His eyes widened just before I kicked his head hard enough to put him out.

I went back to the fire, picked up my notebook and pencil, sat on a convenient boulder so I could just see him in my peripheral vision and ate another slice of pizza.

A minute later, slight sounds from the huddled body told me he was awake. He was protecting his right arm while struggling to sit up.

He waited while I finished the last bite and swallowed. Wanting to make a point, I made sure that I wiped my mouth delicately with a napkin before speaking. When he'd stewed long enough, I turned to face him and rested my elbows on my knees. Steepling my fingers, I gave him a Kubrick Stare and a slow smile.

"Now, what shall we talk about?"

* * *

It was a long night, and when morning came I was still sitting by the fire. Sadly, the pizza had given out hours ago. I'd been there so long that the rocks and twigs were beginning to ooze through my boundary layer and were poking me in tender places. I'd put the pillows under my butt. At least the blankets were nice and warm.

As the light grew, I let the campfire die out. By that time I had also re-arranged my notes into alphabetical order.

I'd had six visitors in the woods, excluding Sitri who'd already given me his story. The number of victims they were reporting varied:

Beleth – 7
Dantalion – 8
Furtur – 5
Gemory – 10
Sitri – 3
Vual – 2
Zepar – 3

I heard Sitri long before I saw him. He seemed to be crashing through the undergrowth in preference to using the trail.

"Were you out partying last night with your buddies?"

"No, I was on the computer all night."

"So why are you stumbling around in the bushes?"

"I heard what happened to a couple of your visitors, and thought it would be healthier for me to give you fair warning that I was coming. Have you completed your investigation?"

"In the Downland, yes. How are the calculations coming?"

"They're done. The killer needed at least 1.7 times more energy than would have been available to anybody from Downland."

Shit, that was so not good. Now I needed to ask a lot of questions about advanced physics. All of them could wait until after I'd had breakfast, a shower, and a couple of quality hours in bed with my cat and a pillow. Preferably not one that Beleth had been snuggling with. Or whatever she did with them. I didn't want to know.

I closed my notebook. "It's time to go home."

CHAPTER 8

I Don't Mind a Reasonable Amount of Trouble

Nine hours later I woke up with that jet lag hangover you get from going to bed too late. Yoko Geri had left me. If I insisted on not sticking to a reasonable schedule, he'd just make do without me.

According to the clock it was time for supper. That sounded like an excellent excuse for calling Kali. She answered on the first ring.

"Yo, how's my favourite demon hunter?"

"Yo? You've been watching too much American television. Do you have any dinner plans?"

"No, I was just going to thaw some stuff."

"Good, because we're going out, and I'm buying."

* * *

Kali deserved only the best, so I made reservations at Maison Chandler.

Apart from good food, I hadn't seen Dad in a few days and wanted to say hi. Also, family members don't have to pay for our meals there as long as we don't abuse the privilege when they are too busy.

I called his direct number, and asked if it would be convenient for us to drop by. He assured me that he would find us a table somewhere.

The dining room was bustling when we got there. I was playing dress-up in my LBD. Kali shocked me by reversing her usual colour scheme. She was wearing a red gown with black lace trim. Even her combat boots were red.

"Good evening, Elise," I said to the *maître d'hôtel*. In theory, she should be the *maîtresse d'hôtel*, except that it doesn't mean the same thing in French. Dad thought he could handle being accused of sexism by non-francophones better than he could being accused of running a bawdy house.

"Good evening, Ms. Chandler. May I show you to your table?"

She started toward the dining room, then veered toward the kitchen.

Dad had put us at the chef's table. I wondered if this was a family honour, or whether putting us amid the controlled chaos of the kitchen was a subtle hint that I should have called earlier. There was a small vase containing pink carnations as a centre piece. My father and his pink fixation. Sigh.

Chef Chandler met us at the table.

"Good evening ladies," he said graciously. He pulled out Kali's chair and seated her, then insisted on doing the same for me. "How are my two favourite daughters?"

"Fine," Kali said. It looked like she'd come to terms with her near-immortality. At least, well enough to be acting like her normal self.

Andre came over, filled our water glasses, and disappeared again.

"Me too," I said, stifling a yawn.

"Would you like to try these?" he said as Andre came over with two small plates, and placed them before us.

The plate held a fluted Portobello mushroom cap, sauteed in butter, and crowned with pieces of pickled ginger. It was sitting on a slice of jicama slightly smaller than the cap, with triangular notches cut around its circumference. It looked elegant and smelled wonderful.

The *amuse bouche* was too big to be finger food, so I went after it with a knife and fork. The mushroom turned out to be stuffed with grilled shrimp that was flavoured with lime juice and cardamom. The mushroom itself had been marinated in soy sauce. A dusting of sugar on the jicama slice offset the saltiness.

"Delicious," I said. Kali made a yummy sound in agreement. Dad just stood there and waited, smiling.

The next bite was more exciting. The inside of the mushroom cap was coated with a dab of wasabi. It caught me as I was breathing out, and for a moment it felt like someone had dragged a red-hot wire through my sinuses. From the look on her face, Kali had hit the land mine at the same time I did.

"Surprise," Dad said.

"Interesting," I managed to say. The good thing about wasabi is that, unlike hot sauce, it's a hit-and-run condiment. Not more than five seconds after my head exploded, everything was back to normal.

We finished our appetizers, being careful to always inhale while chewing.

The plates were cleared, and we got a salad of raw vegetables drizzled with Dad's version of Indonesian peanut sauce. The sauce was hot, sweet, and salty, all at the same time. There were no surprises this time, and Dad took the time to sit for a moment and chat with us.

"What have you girls been up to lately?"

Kali almost choked on a broccoli floret, so I answered for her.

"This and that. I'm working on a case. Kali's looking forward to summer and The Return of the George." I said the latter in a dramatic voice.

She was taking a sip of water to recover from the broccoli and almost choked again.

"Try not to kill your sister," Dad said. "It wouldn't be polite before the main course."

I saw the look that Kali gave me. I had to change the topic.

"Speaking of entrees, I've been thinking about those cooking classes." It had been over a year since my friend Andrea had suggested that I teach cooking classes. Somehow, it had gotten shelved with a lot of other things. Right then it was a good neutral topic. "Few people want to learn how to run a restaurant kitchen, but they want to be able to cook like a chef instead of just following recipes in a cookbook. I was thinking about teaching them technique, how to combine ingredients and give them some recipes to start them off. What do you think?"

"That sounds like a good plan. Once you have a detailed curriculum, I can tell you how much the supplies will cost per student."

"Also, I can talk to a supplier about getting a deal on knives," I said. "That way the students can try different ones and buy the ones they like."

"When did you want to start this?"

"I'm not sure. It depends on how long this case takes."

"Let me know." He turned to Kali, who had now finished her salad and was about to take a sip from her water glass. "So, when are you and George getting married?"

The spray of water was impressive.

* * *

Dad had to go back to work, and I had a lot to tell Kali. Between the salad and salmon she listened with wide eyes to my account of the Downland. I had some of my tourist pictures on my phone, and her eyes got even wider. One of them was taken in the council chamber just as we were entering. When I'd finished my story, she homed in on the point that she felt she could get a handle on.

"You can speak *five thousand* languages?"

"Apparently. So far I've only done Kalijiriki."

"I've never heard of it."

"You wouldn't have. It's the top language in the Downland."

"Say something in Kalijiriki."

I flipped my mental switch.

"*Ov alishibishie wasi ko akao.*"

"*Madre de dios.* I couldn't understand it, but it sounded good. How about German? I know you don't speak German."

"*Ich kann Deutsch sprechen als wäre es meine Muttersprache. Möchtest du, dass ich dir ein Wiener Schnitzel mache?*"

"As far as I can tell you sound like you just arrived from Berlin. Did you just ask me something about wiener schnitzel?"

"Yes, and I said I speak German like a native."

"You are a disturbed woman, *hermanita*. What's next in the case?"

Before I could answer, Andre came by with two pieces of Black Forest cake. On the top of each, in pink icing, was inscribed "KOH."

Kali looked at it, then at me.

"I don't get it."

I sighed. Dad was being that way again.

"You should have taken chemistry. It's a pun: The cake is a lye."

She sighed. We looked toward the grill where Dad grinned at us for a moment before giving instructions to one of the line chefs.

"So, what's next?"

"I need to sit down with my client, and ask a ton of questions about physics so I can understand what's happening. That should be fun. After that we'll have to see."

We caught up with Dad to say goodbye, thank him for supper and ask him to give our compliments to the kitchen staff. I suggested that he, Mum, and Kali come for dinner in a couple of days.

He made me promise not to get back at him for the wasabi.

* * *

Sitri came over late the next morning. After a good ten hours of sleep I was feeling better about things. I'd also had a chance to transcribe my notes so I could read them.

"I have some ideas," I said, "but first I wanted to go over where we are now in case there are some details I've missed."

He sat on the sofa. Yoko Geri decided that he was more fun than I was, and sat beside him. I didn't know that Sitri was a cat person. I should have guessed that Yoko was a demon cat.

"Seven ministers have lost a total of 38 summoners spread out all over the world. Most of the deaths have been in North America and Europe, which is also where you'd expect most of the summoners to be." He nodded his agreement.

"All the deaths have occurred within the past two months. In each case, the Downlander being summoned had trouble coming through into Midland, and the magicians appear to have been shot through the heart with an arrow. Unfortunately, you are the only one who thought to record the crime scenes. Most of them didn't even care enough to look at the body. The ages and sexes of the victims are all over the place, so the killer doesn't have a type, other than summoner."

"All right," he said. "What does that tell us?"

"Not much by itself, but the interesting thing is that the only ministers who have been affected deal with promoting sexual relationships. Somebody doesn't like sex. None of them have had a client live through the summoning ritual since this started, so we know that the killer is intelligent and organized. All the humans died under what appear to be identical circumstances, which suggests a single killer or a tightly co-ordinated team. Our height measurements, however, suggest one person."

"The killer is likely male, and his preferred weapon is a bow and arrow. He is an expert with his weapon, indicating a considerable period of practice. That means that he was shooting long before he started killing people."

"He also has a thing for the Bronze Age. Specifically, Thessaloniki between 500 to 300 B.C. according to Dr. Schliemann."

"That's about as far as I can go with the forensic evidence. Now we get to the difficult parts. Let's take them one at a time. Technologically, he must be able to detect when specific ministers are coming to Midland, because not everybody is affected. How would he do that?"

"I don't know. I'm pretty sure that it's not possible to be that specific. Whether I trigger the transfer or someone else does, it should look the same from here. Sort of like what I was saying about the tunnelling machine. From the destination side, all you can tell is that the earth is shaking. It's not like the device has a signature, or beacon, or something like that."

"Could he be watching magicians, and then blocking the next transfer that starts during a ritual?"

Sitri stared at nothing out my balcony window.

"Maybe. No. It's the same problem that you would have trying to dodge an energy weapon. Since the beam travels at the speed of light, by the time you see it you've already been hit. The transfer between universes is essentially instantaneous. He couldn't detect it in time to block it."

"Crap. I hate cases that are impossible."

"Sorry," he said. He seemed genuinely remorseful.

"In this case it isn't your fault. Maybe we're missing something obvious."

I looked at the clock. It was time for lunch.

I made us some sandwiches. It wasn't inspired, but it was tasty. While I was cutting the bread, I thought about impossibilities. How do you do something that looks impossible, but isn't?

The answer might be so simple that it would never occur to the literal, highly-technological Downlanders. Score one for the stone age Midlanders.

"Sitri, I know that the stuff that looks like magic from our side is just technology, but do your people ever do magic for entertainment?"

He looked blank. I tried to explain.

"In my world, we have entertainers who pretend to be doing something impossible when in fact they are just doing something that *looks* impossible."

He looked blank again.

"Here, I'll show you."

I got my roll of butcher twine from the drawer, and cut a piece about half a metre long. I held one end in each hand.

"Is there any way for me to tie an overhand knot in this string without letting go of the ends?" I demonstrated the knot I meant.

"No, of course not. Unless the string or your arms can move through each other in a higher dimension. Knots, by definition, require one end to move through a closed loop."

"Watch."

It had been a couple of years since I'd done this, and it was the only piece of magic I knew. I hoped that I remembered the effect.

Holding the ends, I looped the string over one wrist, moved my hand through the loop in a complicated looking way, and then separated my hands.

There was a neat overhand knot in the middle of the string.

"That's impossible," he said. He sounded worried. I tried not to smile.

I untied the knot and did it again. And again. Each time he was carefully watching me. Each time he declared that what I'd done was mathematically impossible.

The last time, I slowly moved my hands into an intermediate position, having him check at each point that I wasn't doing anything suspicious. Then I had him grab the two ends of the string and remove it from my hands. The knot formed without me completing my motions.

Sitri looked at me like *I* was the demon.

"How is that possible? Do you have some dimensional technology that we don't know about?"

"No, it *is* impossible. I cheated." I showed him how I actually let go of one end, and immediately grabbed it again in a different place.

"Why didn't I see that?"

"That's the point of stage magic. I did this several times right in front of you without you catching on. Maybe our killer is doing something similar. We've been concentrating on this end of things, where our killer can't possibly see you coming. What happens on your end? How do you know that someone is calling you?"

"I get a message that someone's doing my ritual, and if I'm not busy I show up and play."

"How do you get the message? Where does it come from?"

"Um, you might not like it if I tell you."

"What's not to like? I have a client who's a demon, and who has me chasing a serial killer across two universes. You also take me on fun camping trips to Hell where the crazy lady who loves horses and pillows too much told me she has diabolical plans for me. Hit me with your best shot."

"We seeded this world with nanites that let us know when somebody is invoking us."

And here people thought it was the CCTV cameras, NSA, and internet that had destroyed our privacy.

"In other words, you bugged our entire planet just so you could play with a few people's minds."

"It sounds so sordid when you put it that way, but yes."

I considered that with my newly found Downland technical expertise.

"I'd imagine that the bugs are something like simplified versions of the language nanites. They listen for key phrases and broadcast a coded message. To what? Your personal language nanites?"

"That's it exactly. That way we know what language to expect when we appear at the summoning."

"That's very interesting indeed. Is there any way to reprogram the bugs?"

He sat back and looked thoughtful. "I don't know. Nobody's even suggested such a thing. I suppose so. Yes, now that I think of it. There must be."

"Suppose he reprogrammed the nanites to send a signal to him, then wait before forwarding the signal to you."

Now it was his turn to ponder.

"You're right. That gives him time to kill the magician. I'd get the delayed message, and it would look like the magician was killed in the fraction of a second between the invocation and me arriving. He'd actually have been killed some time earlier."

"So why is he doing things the hard way, and temporarily blocking your access to Midland as well? It isn't necessary."

"Being a Downlander, he's doing it because he can. He's taunting us. Or maybe it's a safety mechanism to keep us from showing up in case the murder takes longer than he expected."

"Okay, let's move on to the blocking. How is he doing that?"

"Now we're back to impossibilities. As the calculations showed, in order to cause enough turbulence to disrupt the transfer between Downland and Midland he'd need more energy than any of us could command by ourselves."

"What if he has an accomplice?"

"Highly improbable. The co-ordination would have to be precise to within an incredibly tiny fraction of a second, and that wouldn't be at all easy. Also, you said we've seen no evidence of two people being involved."

"Okay, stop looking where he wants us to, and look where he doesn't. Could it be one of my people after all?"

"No. Think of it like this. Downland has a charge of minus one. Midland has a charge of zero. No matter who the killer is, the best he can do is to move over one world, and gain a potential difference of plus or minus one."

His eyes bugged out. It was an unnerving effect. Seriously, he looked like Marty Feldman for a moment.

"There is another."

"Don't go all Yoda on me. Spit it out."

"Upland. He could be from Upland."

"Why am I just hearing about this now? What's Upland?"

"It's the other half of Downland..."

"I never would have guessed."

"...but with a charge of plus one. The charge difference between the universes is two. In theory, somebody from there could cause a space-time disturbance near Downland, using the greater difference in charge. That's 'near' in a higher-dimensional sense, of course."

"Of course," I said. I was still young, and sarcasm is my friend. "Would this person have any trouble moving around in our world?"

"No more than I do. There would be big trouble if the two of us met, though. With a charge difference of two the charge would tunnel through our boundary layers, and there would be a discharge. Like the breakdown of an insulator under too high a voltage. That explains what happened when I touched those leaves."

"How big is the trouble we're talking about? All you got from the leaves was a painful shock."

"The leaves were very small. Again, I'd have to do the calculations, but if we casually touched—fingertips, for example—I'd expect something about the same as one of your electrical substations being shorted out. A few megawatts. It would be disastrous for any Midland people nearby. If there was intimate contact the discharge would be a lot more."

I decided not to make any obvious jokes. "Okay, I admit I'm curious. Why would sex give a bigger—discharge?"

"How much do you know about nuclear weapons?"

I was having the weirdest conversations lately. "Not a lot. Take two pieces of uranium or plutonium and smack them together to cause a chain reaction."

"That's one geometry. Another is to have one piece of fissile material in the shape of a cylinder with a plug cut out. The other piece is fired into the cylindrical hole to exceed critical mass. Having one piece surrounding the other is more efficient at capturing the neutrons."

"And having sex with an Uplander mimics that geometry?"

"Exactly. In theory."

"How Freudian. Okay, so, important safety tip: don't screw the psycho killer from another dimension when we find him."

"Not my thing anyway. I'm only interested in women."

"All right, we're making progress. In general, we have a who and a good theory as to how. Now we need a why. Are the Uplanders as crazy as the Downlanders?"

"Yes and no. Since the Incident, we don't know much about them except in a theoretical sense. From indirect evidence, it looks like their psychosis may be different from ours, and that could cause you trouble."

"I don't mind a reasonable amount of trouble. How are they different?"

"Everybody in the Downland became a sociopath. It seemed natural for us to present as demons." He paused.

"Quit stalling. What about the Uplanders?"

He sighed.

"They're gods."

CHAPTER 9

Mousetrap

There's not a lot you can say after a line like that. I looked at Sitri. He looked at me. I looked at him more. My brain helpfully informed me that it had nothing to offer other than the obvious.

"Gods? Please tell me that you are joking."

"I can't do that. We know that the Uplanders consider themselves to be gods. We think that the positive charge on the Upland made them narcissists. We haven't had enough contact with them to make a complete diagnosis. We don't dare."

"Why didn't you mention this before?"

"I didn't think of it. As I said, we never have any contact with them. It didn't occur to me that one of them would be insane enough to try something as dangerous as this."

"If the killer isn't a Downlander, most of what we thought we knew about the killer's psychology is probably wrong. He's not doing this to have fun, or because he thinks of us as non-persons. He's doing this because he believes that he's superior, and in the—damn. The killer believes he has the right to do away with people who are trying to bargain for a sexual relationship. Either he hates sex, or he hates the morality of the bargaining."

"From what we know, that sounds reasonable."

"Oh, good. I'm glad something about this is beginning to be reasonable. So far all we've done is to eliminate one suspect pool of nut cases in favour of a fresh pool of different nut cases. No offence intended."

"None taken."

"The good news is that the pool probably got smaller. From what I remember of mythology, gods who hate sex are fairly rare."

"There's more bad news. If he's from Upland, I can't help you."

"Why not? This is your case. Don't you want to catch him?"

"I didn't say *won't*. I said I *can't*. With my negative charge, If I went there, the results would be unbelievably catastrophic."

"Define catastrophic."

"I've been researching your world and its weapons. Are you familiar with the Tsar Bomba?"

"Vaguely. Big nuke built by the Soviets during the cold war to show that they could?"

"Yes. Fifty megatons. The largest nuclear device ever built by your people. Blast radius of 60 kilometres."

"Okay. So?"

"Bigger. Much, much bigger."

I let out a long breath. "Okay, no Sitri in Upland. Gotcha. What happens if I go there?"

"It would be just like you visiting Downland. You'd be nearly invulnerable. If you had the rest of our nanites you'd also be immensely powerful. Just like a Downlander coming here."

I firmly pushed that thought aside for later. Superwoman's invulnerability plus all the powers. *The first one's free...*

"I just had a thought about the bug nanites. Can you check their programming? See if there's anything like the delays we were discussing?"

"It isn't my area of expertise, but there are people I can ask."

"Do the best you can."

Three hours later Sitri appeared in my living room.

"I told you not to..."

"Come on," he said, reaching for my hand.

"Where are we going?"

"There's been another murder."

I grabbed my equipment bag, gave him my hand, and the universe cavorted.

* * *

I'd been to three crime scenes, and seen three dead bodies. Those were recordings. This one was horribly different.

We were standing in a normal, middle-class bedroom. On the floor at the foot of the bed were some sheets of cardboard that had been taped together to make a square about two metres across. A smaller-than-normal circle was drawn on them.

The magician was sitting cross-legged in the middle with a tablet on the floor in front of him. I could see the ritual on the screen. There was a wet patch on the front of his robe that was spreading downward. I was surprised that he hadn't fallen over when he was shot.

I backed up a pace, then squatted to examine the triangle of evocation. There were faint smudges of mud or soil on the cardboard.

We'd been there for about four seconds when the corpse moved.

He raised his head, and the stringy hair fell away from his face. He must have been all of fourteen-years old. The surprise and pain on his face froze me for a moment. He tried to say something, but there was a lot of blood in his mouth. Too much. As I reached toward him, the light went out in his eyes, and he toppled on his side.

I knew enough first aid to know where to feel for a pulse in his neck. There wasn't one.

Sitri put his hand on my shoulder, but before he could say anything there was a knock on the door.

"Eric? Supper is ready." The speaker was a woman. Her accent sounded like we were somewhere in the mid-western United States.

I had time to look into Sitri's eyes before he grabbed my bag and the universe sprang away.

* * *

We were kneeling on the floor of my living room, my gear bag beside us. It felt like a long time before either of us moved.

I was used to the bodies in the recordings. I could be clinical about it, knowing that the victim was days or weeks past help.

I'd never watched a person die in front of me before. Even when I shot Ronald Brandau, he'd fallen out of my sight. I'd seen him later, but by then it was over. I hadn't looked into his eyes as he went away forever.

We must have missed the killer by no more than seconds. I took a breath, then let it out.

"Veronica?"

"I'm fine." It came to me that I'd been staring at a random point on the carpet since we'd arrived. I blinked and looked at Sitri.

He was still holding my hand. I felt his other hand on my shoulder and a gentle pressure as he turned me to face him. I let him hold me.

My eyes were wet. I could tell because my vision was blurred. I was not going to cry. I wondered who the girl was that Eric wanted.

Maybe he was a bad person, a budding psychopath who wanted a sex slave he could throw away when he tired of her. Or maybe he was just a fourteen-year old boy who thought that Sitri—the old Sitri—would make the girl he liked like him back. Not understanding that *making* somebody like him was a terrible idea. Either way, I promised myself that was going to catch his killer before this happened again. I was not going to cry.

The tears came anyway. After a while I felt something weirdly solid dripping on my neck. Sitri was crying too.

We knelt like that for several minutes. He was holding me gently, like a friend. The only weird thing was that his body felt hard, not conforming to mine at all. For the first time I noticed that he smelled like dry-roasted peanuts. The new Sitri was a truly nice guy. I sniffed and pulled back slightly. He let me go without hesitation.

I looked him in the eyes and saw my sorrow mirrored in his.

"Let's get this bastard."

* * *

The first step was for Sitri to go home.

"You need to get the ministers to agree not to answer any summonings for a while."

"They won't agree unless we give them a good reason. Saving human lives isn't something they normally take into account."

"How about their own lives? If the bad guy slips up and lets them through a moment too early they could be blown to pieces. Besides, the killer is ruining their fun. If they agree to stay out of this for a few weeks we should be able to end this."

"They'll probably go for that."

"I'll see you later. In the meantime, I'm going to think about how to arrest a god." He vanished and I wiped my face.

The first step should be easy. All I had to do was to perform the summoning ritual for Sitri or one of the others, and our killer would show up.

Working on this case had brought home to me how many of our usual speech idioms are based on religion: No way in hell. I'll be damned if I will do that.

The devil is in the details.

My first concern was to do the ritual somewhere that wouldn't put innocent people at risk. Arresting a god was not going to be easy, regardless of who it was.

The second thing was to record the whole process. If something went wrong it would be useful to be able to look at it later so we could figure out what to do next time. Assuming, of course, that any of us survived the first time. That certainly wasn't a given.

Thirdly, I had to pick a team with a good chance of success. That wasn't easy considering that we had no idea which god we were dealing with, or what his powers in Midland might be.

* * *

Sitri returned from his diplomatic mission the next morning.

"The ministers have agreed to stay out of Midland for two months."

"That's better than I'd expected. That should stop further murders."

"Unless the killer decides to go after us directly," he said.

"At least it solves your problem if the killer commits suicide by invading Downland."

"He doesn't have to. He can send rocks from the Upland into our atmosphere and let them penetrate the ground when they hit."

"Shit, I hadn't thought of that." Why waste troops when you can just nuke your enemy from orbit for free?

"The good news is that I found out about the bugs. As we suspected, they've been tampered with. We did the simplest thing and added a delay to his signal that's longer than the one he added to mine. That way we'll know about a summoning before he does."

"Is there any way to trace where his signal is going?"

"No. There's an ID associated with it, of course, but it's not a name. We have no way of knowing who it belongs to without a directory of Upland call numbers."

"I guess we can't have everything. I'm stuck on how to trap the god once he shows up. Any ideas?"

"There are some Downland weapons that should be powerful enough to have a good chance of knocking him out. A directed blast should catch him without killing anybody not in line with it."

"We aren't talking about a nuke, are we?"

"No, portable versions can't be directed. I understand your concern about collateral damage."

"Good, because if we can't take out our target without leaving the rest of the area untouched, we're not doing this."

"The device I'm thinking of should do the trick."

When you are planning a battle with an unknown god, words like "good chance" and "should" are not comforting.

One thing that was on our side was that being in our universe made him nearly invulnerable, but it didn't automatically give him other super-abilities. If we could get handcuffs on him, he wouldn't be able to break them by himself.

Of course, he might have nanites that would dissolve the cuffs for him or something. Sitri cheerfully mentioned a list of the available functions that he'd heard about. It was a long list and did not make me happy. Nor did it make me happy when he mentioned that there were undoubtedly custom functions available that he didn't know about. Upland had no doubt developed fun toys of their own.

Sitri also mentioned he could get some old police equipment from Downland that would temporarily deactivate most nanites, including the ones used for universe hopping. It was designed for just this purpose before everybody became too sociopathic to care about policing. I wondered if this gave an answer to another problem.

"Will they deactivate a person's medical nanites?"

"No, that would have violated the prisoner's basic rights. It won't affect language nanites either for the same reason."

Crap. So much for a quick solution to Kali's problem.

"How about any offensive nanites he might have? Any guarantees?"

"No. We have no idea what Upland has developed since the Incident to support their self-image of being gods."

"In that case, plans involving handcuffs might be premature."

I wanted Stan Watkins and Kali on the team. With any luck, Kali's medical nanites would at least make her somewhat resistant to any whammies that the killer might throw, and her detailed knowledge of mythology would probably be handy. Stan was already read-in on the whole demon thing, and, with any luck, between the two of us we should be able to take down the suspect as long as there were no lightning bolts involved. As long as he didn't have super-strength, sitting on him should work.

The word "luck" wasn't any more comforting than the others.

Sitri would work the Downland weaponry and cop equipment. Otherwise, he would stay out of the way. We didn't need him doing a supernova impression with the killer while any of us were nearby. The good news there was that they had to touch to set off any sparks. We should be safe as long as there was an air gap between them.

I now had a plan for taking down our killer. There was just one small problem left to solve before we went after him.

What could we do with him once we had him? I had no idea, so I called a war council with Kali and Sitri. I didn't want Stan to be put in the position of conspiring to commit a potentially criminal act until we knew what crime we'd be committing.

"We could kill him," Sitri said. I wish the thought hadn't occurred to me as well.

"That's not an option," I said. "We have no way of doing that here, unless we want to set off a multi-megaton bomb, and you can't take him home with you."

"Is there any other way?" Kali asked.

"Sure there is," Sitri said. "We could tie him down and put a strong, low-density fibre across his throat with heavy weights attached. Eventually, it would get through his boundary layer and choke him."

Kali and I made similar faces.

"How long would that take?"

"To get through the boundary? I don't know for sure. My guess is a couple of days. Or we could encase him in cement and throw him in the sea. In several years he'd suffocate."

"No." Kali and I said simultaneously. I spoke for us. "Saving lives, yes. Committing slow torture, no."

"We could keep him here until the crazy wears off," Kali said. "Maybe we can get him some therapy."

"That's a great idea," Sitri said, "but we don't know how much of his insanity is due to the Upland environment, and how much is due to something specific to him. Something makes him different from the others."

"Why do you think he's crazier than the average god?"

"The others aren't going around personally killing people by the handful. How long would therapy take?"

"It depends," I said. "I could be anywhere from a few weeks to many years."

"It's the most humane plan," Kali said.

"Okay, we tie him down with a nanite neutralizer nearby until he's relatively sane, then get him therapy. What happens afterwards when he goes home?"

"He'd become a narcissist again," Sitri said. "We don't know what else would happen. After all, if his environment drove him crazy once, it probably would again."

"I could take him to Upland and shoot him," I said. "At least it would be quick."

"You can't do that while the neutralizer is functioning. You'd also have to take the neutralizer hardware with you, so he couldn't use whatever powers he has, and that wouldn't be a good idea. It's made of Downland matter, so it would become a bomb waiting to go off."

"Good. The idea sucked anyway. I don't feel like killing anyone ever again."

We sat around for several minutes. Nobody said anything. Yoko Geri wandered by, decided we were boring, and went into my bedroom.

"Any other suggestions?" I said.

There was another period during which we all examined the floor at our feet.

"I have an idea," Kali said. "We don't have to capture the killer this time. All we need to do is identify him. Right now we're planning in a vacuum. Once we know who he is, maybe we can come up with a better management plan. We could go to the Upland and reason with him or turn him over to authorities there. Maybe he's doing something wrong by their laws."

"That might work," Sitri said. "You could argue that his actions have stirred up Downland and might provoke a war. That would certainly make them worried. They aren't the only ones who can throw rocks."

"It's a plan, but I'm the only one with translators who can go."

"From what you've said, that's easy to fix," Kali said.

"I thought you wanted to get rid of your nanites, not get more."

"I still do. But you said the translators can be turned off. They don't have to affect the rest of my life, even if they can't be removed."

"Damn," I said. "Even after everything we've gone through you still manage to surprise me. Are you sure about this?"

"If we're going to convince a god to stop smiting people, somebody on the team has to have actual people skills."

"You are hilarious."

"So, how do we do this?" Kali asked Sitri.

I remembered how bizarre it had been when I got my translators. I was happy that there hadn't been witnesses. I didn't want to leave Kali, but it seemed like the best thing to do.

"I'll be back in an hour."

* * *

I walked around the neighbourhood for a while, then found a park bench across the street and enjoyed the sun.

Once again, my life as a P.I. was taking me places that I'd never considered or wanted. I thought about the unresolved questions from my first case. Why me? Why here? Why now?

The question of timing might be easy. Downland time had become synchronized with ours. Sitri hadn't explained why, but it made sense that the two events were related.

I considered my meeting with Beleth in the Downland woods. Maybe she'd arranged this somehow. Hell, maybe she'd arranged for Kali to be knifed so I'd have to ask for her help. That woman gave me the creeps, and I wouldn't put anything past her. Her motive was still a big question mark.

If Beleth had some kind of plans for me, then perhaps this *was* all about me, and all these cosmic events were happening here simply because it was where I was.

Wow, and we thought the gods were narcissists.

* * *

I took a deep breath before unlocking my apartment door. I wasn't sure what I'd find inside.

Kali and Sitri were sitting on the sofa chatting in Kalijiriki. I turned on my translators.

"I take it that there were no problems," I said in the same language.

"None at all. She's a natural," Sitri said.

Well, thank you very much.

"I suppose the next step is to do the ritual."

"We have to figure out how to protect you first," Sitri said. "This guy doesn't miss. He might be able to shoot you before we could prevent it."

I smiled. There were some pieces of superior Midland technology that he didn't know about.

* * *

It was two days before we had everything in place. The ritual would be held during daylight so we could see what we were doing, and so that nobody in the area would wonder why people with lights were sneaking around in the dark where they shouldn't be.

Kali had loaned me a ritual robe that covered me down to my ankles. It was loose and nicely hid the bulkiness of the tactical vest that Stan had borrowed from work. He'd gotten one of the fancy new models with ceramic plates protecting my vital areas. It was not as heavy as I'd expected, but it wasn't light. Regardless, I shouldn't be moving in it much. I was also hugely in favour of anything that was capable of stopping an armour-penetrating bullet—a Bronze Age arrow shouldn't be a problem for it. Hopefully, neither should shrapnel from whatever kind of weapon Sitri was bringing to the party.

Taking a page from the Georgian magician's play book, our ritual site was outdoors in an abandoned industrial site outside the city. Most of the building itself had been removed, leaving only a big concrete pad, some orphaned pillars, and two concrete rooms like bunkers on adjacent corners. Sitri set up his equipment in one of those.

Kali drew the circle to make the ritual look legitimate, while Stan and I installed six video cameras in various locations. All of them were set for maximum zoom, and were as far as possible from the circle while still getting a good view.

We'd all come in Kali's Audi, which was parked behind one of the bunkers in case we needed a fast get away. In that location, there was a good chance that it would be protected from any blast damage.

There's that word "chance" again.

Sitri's super-weapon was completely unimpressive. It looked like a large coffee can without a label.

Sitri said that the weapon was directional, so I didn't have to worry about being hit. He also said that it was a bit sensitive, and he wanted us out of the way while he installed it. The rest of us waited in the car. The thought of him making a mistake with a directed-energy weapon powerful enough to knock a god on his ass was not comforting. None of us had asked what the weapon did. I was afraid that if I knew, I'd be too nervous when the time came. Kali and Stan probably just preferred not to know.

A few minutes later Sitri came to get us.

"It's ready. I've buried it under the triangle and pointed it straight up."

Show time.

The vest was awkward, so Kali helped me with the robe. I carefully stepped into the circle. The cowl tended to droop over my face, but I left it in place to make the disguise more believable. I turned to the marked page in the Key of Solomon, and began reading aloud.

It wasn't the most fun I've ever had. The invocation was long-winded and full of run-on sentences and weird words. From experience, demons tended to show up about two hours in. I recited the half hour leading up to that rather than the whole thing..

After a while Sitri flashed a light from his bunker. The killer's signal had been sent.

I'd be lying if I said I was nervous. I was terrified, but it was too late to run now.

What I expected was that the killer would show up, maybe monologue a bit, and then shoot an arrow at me. At some point Sitri would trigger his weapon, and we'd have an unconscious god we could identify.

The best laid plans of mice and men, et cetera, et cetera.

Mist formed above the triangle of evocation, and as soon as I could see a figure materializing the Downland weapon went off. That's putting it mildly.

The shock wave blew me over. The damned cowl completely obscured my vision until I remembered I had hands. All I could hear was a loud roaring sound, and my entire body was tingling inside and out, like a full-body electric shock.

A painfully bright, vertical shaft of blue-violet light reached up into the sky, and immediately flickered out. It had ionized the air, and the glow dissipated over the next few seconds. When I looked up, there was an expanding hole punched in the cloud layer overhead that was outlined in red where the water vapour had exploded into plasma. The strange prickling sensation throughout my body remained, like the feeling of getting too much sun. The sensation probably only lasted for a few moments, but I was too stunned to be sure of anything. There was no sign of the figure in the triangle. Orange afterimages danced in front of both my eyes. Holy crap, what kind of gadget was that?

I blinked a few times and got up. Where the triangle had been, there was a shallow, cylindrical hole containing blobs of molten, spitting steel. It took me a moment to figure out it was what was left of the rebar from the concrete slab.

I looked around, trying to spot our target. A few moments later I jumped as a stiff body hit the ground several dozen metres away on the other side of the pad. He was not moving. His bow and quiver fell closer a second or two later followed by a lone sandal.

I saw Kali and Stan run over to the god, then pause for a moment in surprise. Kali took out her camera, and started taking pictures from every angle she could. Stan turned the stiff body over so Kali could take more pictures.

I removed the ear plugs I'd been wearing as a precaution.

"Out cold," Stan called, "but still breathing. And not a god."

"What do you mean, not a god?"

"See for yourself."

I staggered over, the weight of the vest doing odd things to my still-recovering balance.

The unconscious killer was tall, as I'd predicted, wearing a short Greek tunic in the male style, and with a golden sandal on one foot. There was also long black hair, now hanging loose, a pretty face, and a fine set of breasts and hips. Her chest was moving as she breathed.

Great. So much for my profiling skills. Most serial killers were male. Ours wasn't.

I went back over to her weapons. Kali joined me, still taking pictures.

This was our girl, all right. The bow was typical of the pictures of Bronze Age Greek weapons I'd looked up. The arrows were exactly what we'd expected from the casts, including the bronze heads.

"All right," Stan yelled, "time to scarper."

Sitri and Stan were already taking the equipment to the car. I staggered across the pad, and Kali put her arm around my waist to help me.

"Don't worry about me. I'm fine."

She grabbed the hem of the robe with her other hand to get it away from my feet. "No, you aren't." I must admit, it was easier to walk in a straight line with her support. I was still unsteady on my feet. I blamed the tactical vest, but I didn't want to waste the time removing it while in sight of someone who was sure to be pissed when she woke up.

By the time we got to the car everybody else was ready to go.

We had no idea if the video cameras were intact. We were leaving them behind for two good reasons. Firstly, we didn't want to spend the time gathering them up right now and secondly, we wanted a record of what the goddess did after she woke up. We'd pick them up later.

Kali drove a lot more aggressively than usual, leaving a spray of dirt and dust behind us until we got to the highway where she pushed 160. Stan didn't say a word.

I showed Sitri the pictures of the goddess on Kali's camera. It was a long-shot at best and he didn't recognize her.

By the time our expedition got back to Calgary I was beginning to think that we were terribly clever. We'd managed to trick a goddess into our trap, knocked her out, and gotten good pictures.

Now all we had to do was to identify our homicidal goddess and figure out how to make her stop killing people.

CHAPTER 10
Guess Who's Coming to Dinner?

Several hours later I was hunched over my toilet throwing up. I hadn't gotten much more than a scratch and a few bruises from our adventure, and after the fact the operation shouldn't have been that stressful. I felt a bit feverish too. Maybe I was coming down with something.

By the next afternoon I felt a lot better, although I'd gained a headache. I popped several pain killers before Sitri and I drove out to the ritual site to retrieve the cameras in my car, Binky.

We approached the area cautiously in case the goddess was still around. There was nothing moving but birds.

Amazingly, all the cameras had survived. Maybe we had luck on our side after all. We stored them in Binky before going over to the circle to see what the damage was.

There wasn't much to see. The former triangle area looked like a core about as deep as the length of my forearm had been taken out of the earth. The goddess, her sandal, and her weapons were gone. At some point she must have woken up and decided to call it a day.

"I wonder if she knew what hit her?"

"I doubt it," he said. "Even though she must have fallen about three hundred metres when the beam cut out, it was the initial blast that would have knocked her out."

"Ouch. By the way, I was wondering why you triggered the weapon as soon as she showed up."

"I didn't. I set it up with a pressure sensor to fire automatically as soon as she arrived."

"Gee, thanks for letting me know ahead of time. I could have hit the ground as soon as I saw the mist instead of being knocked flat."

"Sorry." We'd make a Canadian of this boy yet.

We were passing by one of the bunkers on our way to the car when Sitri looked puzzled, then threw himself onto me, bashing me into the concrete wall. It felt like being slammed by a truck. An instant later, something hit the wall very hard and stuck in the concrete.

It was a golden arrow. After a moment, the colour faded to that of a normal bronze-headed arrow with a cedar shaft.

At the far side of the concrete pad, a tall, black-haired woman wearing a knee-length Greek tunic was pulling another arrow from her quiver with a fluid grace that spoke of many hours of practice. She looked furious.

"Get us out of here," I whispered to Sitri. I don't know why I whispered when she could see us right in front of her.

"I can't. She must have her own neutralizer. That's how I knew she was here. Most of my nanites aren't working."

I wasn't sure, but maybe that was a good thing. If she was neutralizing all the nanites in the area then she couldn't throw a fireball at us either, or whatever it was she did when not turning people into shish kebabs.

"Maybe she's open to talking," I said.

"We only want to talk to you!" Sitri yelled in Kalijiriki.

She fitted the arrow to the string.

"Why are you doing this?" Sitri was still trying to shield me, so I couldn't get a full view. All I knew was that she was slowly stalking toward us.

"I must." She had a contralto voice that would have been sexy under completely different conditions.

He dodged again, pulling me with him. The next arrow skimmed by his arm. There was a sharp crack like a high explosive detonating, and the arrow disappeared in a blast of light. He was thrown sideways into me and we both went tumbling across the concrete. The side of his shirt was gone leaving a charred hole exposing his burned shoulder and chest.

"Shit, that hurt," he gasped, grasping his arm.

"You're bleeding," I said, more to confirm it to myself than to give him information. His body had shielded me from most of the flash, but there were still purple spots dancing before my eyes.

"Stop! He's from Downland!" I yelled. Her only answer was to ready another arrow.

I grabbed him by his good arm and pulled him into the bunker. If we tried to run, she'd just shoot us in the back. Even if we got to Binky in time, she'd just shoot out the tires. Been there, done that.

The room had an industrial steel door. It wasn't in good shape, but at least it moved when we leaned on it. There was a hole where the lock should have been. As the door squealed shut, another arrow whistled through the gap. Fortunately, neither of us were in the line of fire. The arrow ricocheted off the far wall and fell to the floor without touching either of us.

We both leaned against the door. We had to decide what to do next and we had to do it quickly.

"See if you can find something to hold it closed," Sitri said.

I quickly dug my way through the junk in the corners. There was nothing obvious to use as a brace. I grabbed some old pieces of wood that might work as wedges.

The sound was so loud that I felt it rather than hearing it. I could imagine that this was what a fly felt when hit by the snapping end of a bull whip. Sitri flew face-first across the room and smashed into the opposite wall. Concrete flakes and dust rained down from where he hit and daylight showed through the hole he made. He was trailing smoke and flame from his clothing.

Fortunately, I was well out of the line of fire, and already close to one wall. When the shock wave slammed me back I didn't go far. My ears were ringing, and the concussion switched my brain to its lowest setting. I slid to the floor, expecting a vengeful goddess to come through the door and finish us off. She must have turned off her neutralizer to throw the fire ball I'd been expecting.

Nothing else happened. She had us at her mercy. What was she waiting for?

I managed to get to my knees and crawled over to the door. Bits of debris painfully ground into my knees and hands.

The door itself was still in place, but a rough oval had been blown out of the centre of it at about the height of Sitri's back. The sharp, metallic smell of vapourized steel overlaid the smell of rot and animals that had been in the bunker air. The steel remaining at the edges was glowing and dripping.

I slowly raised my head and looked through the hole. I expected an arrow in the eye for my trouble.

Nobody was out there.

I almost touched the glowing hot door before I realized that would be a truly stupid idea. Instead, I staggered over to check on Sitri.

He was barely conscious and badly burned. He had areas of crispy skin on his back where he'd been in contact with the door, and the parts of his clothing that weren't burned off were in shreds. Some of the cloth was still on fire. I took off my t-shirt and used it to smother the flames.

From the amount of damage, whatever she'd done to him had been much worse than what we'd done to her with the land mine.

My head was slowly beginning to clear, and it dawned on me what must have happened. The goddess hadn't thrown a fire ball. She'd touched the door at the same time Sitri was leaning against it, and the metal had acted both as a conductor and a fuse. If we'd been anywhere other than Midland, this whole area would be a huge smoking crater.

I couldn't try to open the door until it cooled, so I sat beside Sitri, and watched him breathe and moan. I hoped his medical nanites were online and up to the task of healing him.

I tried my phone to call for back up, but being in my back pocket when I was slammed into the wall hadn't done it any good at all. We were on our own.

Sitri moaned louder.

If it had been anybody else, I'd have taken him directly to a hospital whether he wanted to or not. That wasn't an option. They wouldn't be able to treat him. I could imagine trying to explain to the nurses why they kept breaking needles against his skin while trying to start an IV.

My guess was that the only thing anybody in Midland could do was to try to help his nanites along by making sure that his wounds were clean and dressed.

"Don't move." I had no idea why, but it's what they say in movies when somebody's injured. I seriously needed to make time to take some kind of field medicine course. Preferably one intended for combat troops.

His voice was a hoarse whisper. I had to lean close to hear him. "What happened?"

"Either she didn't care that you are from Downland, or she didn't know what would happen if you touched. My guess is that the two of you short-circuited through the door. You're badly burned. Can you move?" I know, I just contradicted myself, but I didn't know how badly the goddess was injured, and if or when she'd be back to finish us off.

He moaned again, tried to rise, and fell back against the wall. This was not looking good at all.

"It's too bad you can't turn off pain."

He grimaced, then relaxed.

"Thank you for reminding me. I'm not thinking very well."

"You can do that? Cool."

He looked like hell. Whether his nanites were working or not, it couldn't be a good idea for him to be teleporting us around in his condition. We'd have to do things the old-fashioned way. I grabbed a piece of 2x4 to pry open the door.

"I'm going to get the car."

Our luck held. Binky hadn't been affected by the blast. I carefully drove onto the concrete pad and stopped in front of the bunker door. This was not the time to risk a flat tire.

The only thing that let me get Sitri to the car was that he was from Downland. I was able to drag him across the floor by his arms without doing him any more harm. With his minimal help I managed to get him into the front seat.

I wasn't feeling too spry myself. At some point my nose had started bleeding. The blood dripping off my breast reminded me to put on my t-shirt.

By the time we got to my place he'd recovered enough to stumble along with me holding him up. I took him in the back way. Mercifully, we didn't meet anybody in the hall or the elevator.

He was still close to unconscious when I put him on my bed. I had almost no first aid supplies in the apartment, so I used my kitchen scissors to cut off the remains of his clothes. Fortunately, they were ones that he'd bought in Calgary or the scissors would have broken. I removed everything so I could check for hidden damage.

His back and arms where he'd been in contact with the door were charred, with red, oozing burns. I cleaned those as well as I could and bandaged them using a spare bed sheet that I cut into strips. Assuming we survived, I'd put it on his bill.

The rest of the back of his body wasn't as badly damaged, just bright red and blistered. His front was untouched. Since it was all I had, I used sunburn spray on him. The label said it contained an anaesthetic as well as an antibiotic. It probably couldn't do any harm.

I had some sports drink in the refrigerator. I brought two bottles in for him to drink when he felt like it. Again, it couldn't hurt.

Despite his injuries, he had the most impressive body I had ever seen. I firmly told myself to be professional. My stomach was acting up again, which made it easier. It's hard to be lustful when you feel like you are going to throw up. Maybe I had a concussion.

Leaving him to rest, I bagged his ruined clothes and threw them out. I could always lend him my robe later. Then I had a shower and changed into something that didn't smell like sweat, smoke, and barbecued flesh. That's one thing they never mention in stories. Regardless of what species it is from, cooked meat smells delicious. My stomach heaved again.

My head was throbbing so I also took more headache pills. Once he was conscious, I'd see if he wanted anything to eat. It was about that time, although personally I didn't have much of an appetite.

There was a knock at the apartment door.

That was weird. Who could have gotten in without buzzing?

Aka wate. That's Downland for *oh crap.*

I'd completely forgotten that I'd invited Mum, Dad, and Kali over for supper.

* * *

I opened the door to tell them that something had come up just as Kali was about to use her key.

"Hi, dear," Mum said as she breezed past me. Dad was smiling. Kali was about to say something generically smart-assed.

Dad stopped to kick off his shoes. "Whatever we're having, it smells great."

They all ground to a halt before I could respond. Mum looked angry. Dad looked like he was trying not to show anything. Kali's mouth was open. I turned to face the direction they were looking.

"Hey Veronica, where are my clothes?" Sitri said from the doorway of my bedroom. He was slurring his words and steadied himself with one hand on the door frame. He was wearing nothing but my makeshift bandages on his torso, one of which he touched with his hand. "Why did you tie me up?"

Of course, with medical nanites, he'd never seen a bandage in use before.

He was swaying a bit, and he wasn't completely functional. It took him a moment to notice that we had company. I could imagine him thinking, "I'll bet this is one of those awkward Midland things" followed immediately by, "I wonder what I should say."

He opted for simplicity. "Hi."

"Excuse me," I said, gently steering him back into the bedroom, and closing the door. I pulled my bath robe off the hook. It barely came to his knees, but it would have to do.

"How do you feel?"

"Not great, but I'm getting better. Why are your parents here?"

"I forgot I'd invited them over for dinner. Are you capable of jumping elsewhere?"

"I think so. Yes. Definitely."

I was going to tell him to go home, but realized that would cause even more questions. "Go back to your place, get some clothes on and come back here." I said as forcefully as possible while whispering.

I opened the door and rejoined my guests, closing the door behind me.

All three were still standing there, staring at me. I felt like an actor who has made her dramatic entrance, and then completely forgotten her lines. I had to say something.

"Um, it's not what it looks like. Honestly. Um. We aren't even dating. No, wait, I mean, he isn't my boyfriend. He's a client."

I saw Mum's mouth harden even further.

"No Mum, I'm not sleeping with my client."

"Really?"

I looked at their unbelieving faces.

"You know what? Forget it. Look, I've had a really rough day and I forgot about dinner. I'm sorry, but we'll have to reschedule."

The bedroom door opened behind me, and Sitri came out. Instead of my robe, he was dressed in slacks and a dress shirt.

"Don't worry, I'll get supper," he said cheerfully. "Back soon." He was out the door before I could figure out what was going on.

Screw it. Just go with the flow. I put on my gracious hostess smile.

"It seems we're having dinner after all. Won't you come in?"

* * *

I was facing a literal tribunal. My parents sat on the sofa. Kali sat beside them, which told me whose side she was on. It would have helped if I could have gotten her alone to explain what had happened that after-noon.

"So, Mum, what have you been up to lately?" I said as lightly as I could while not feeling well.

"Just the usual—fighting crime." She still wasn't buying that I wasn't playing house with a client. "You?"

"I've been working on a case for the past week or so. It's proving to be tougher than I'd first thought."

"At least you're taking time out for recreation."

"Janet," Dad cautioned. He looked supremely uncomfortable. Kali still looked pissed or maybe worried. Maybe she thought that Sitri had used his lust ray on me.

"Look, I'm not..."

The door opened. I knew Sitri didn't have a key but, however he'd opened it, my guests must have assumed that he did. Wonderful. That really helped to sell the story that we weren't lovers. Sitri came in with a stack of pizza boxes and a waft of delicious smells. My stomach simultan-eously wanted food and was disgusted by the thought. I'd have to get my-self checked.

"Okay, everybody. Supper is ready."

I got plates, knives, and forks while he put the boxes on the coffee table and opened the top one. He didn't bother with cutlery. He just grabbed a slice and rolled it so it didn't droop.

"Come on, dig in," he said before taking a bite, "or Vincenzo will be deeply offended."

Maybe fortune would favour the bold.

"You heard the man," I said. "Let's eat."

The conversation was a little strained at first.

Kali kept glaring at me. My brain felt like it was wading through hip-deep water. I was definitely coming down with something.

Dad looked—formal. Like he was trying desperately not to notice that his recently teenage daughter had a well-built, naked man of undeter-mined age in her bedroom for unknown but suspected purposes.

"What do you do, Mister...?" Dad asked. I prepared to jump in and try to prevent Sitri from saying anything too bizarre.

"Please, Mr. Chandler, call me Sitri. I'm a relationship councillor."

"Oh? That must be rewarding work."

"It certainly can be."

Sitri was shovelling pizza in like he was starving. Maybe that was part of the healing process. I manged to eat one slice.

At least I could get Kali on my side again if I handled it carefully.

"How are you feeling now?" I asked Sitri.

"Much better. My nan..."

I cut him off, speaking to the group. "We were retrieving some surveillance equipment this afternoon when Sitri was injured." I looked at Kali when I spoke. She caught the implication.

"You should have said something. Are you all right?"

"Oh yes, I'm fine," I said. "The subject we were trying to surveil surprised us, and I'm afraid I wasn't able to protect him when she went ballistic."

Kali almost choked on her pizza. Okay, poor choice of words.

"You should be more careful," Dad said.

"It turned out to be not that big a deal. His clothes were completely ruined, but his injures turned out to be less extensive than I feared at first."

"You still should have taken him to the hospital," Mum said. *Damn it, Mum, don't be so sensible.*

"I'm afraid that I insisted we not do that, Mrs. Chandler," Sitri said. "As your daughter said, my injuries weren't that serious, and I needed the clothes I'd left here."

"Oh?" Mum said, once again scenting an inconsistency in the story.

"He changed into something more undercover before we went out." I took another piece of pizza that I didn't want, hoping that Mum wouldn't do her Jedi thing and detect that we were lying our asses off.

"Hmm," she said, feeling a disturbance.

"Will you be pressing charges, Mr. Sitri?" Dad asked.

"Soon. Once the case is wrapped up, we can take care of everything at once."

"I'm sure that will be a relief," Mum said.

My sister's concern didn't prevent her from being annoying.

"He's lucky you were around to play doctor," she said with well-feigned innocence. I glared at her and managed not to say anything. Dad laughed too heartily. Mum smiled tightly.

The conversation picked up after that. I could tell that Kali had questions for me about what happened, but she could see that we were both alive and relatively unharmed. She worked with me to put our parents at ease.

Sitri managed not to put his foot in his mouth the whole time. I guess even demons get to experience miracles.

After a while, Mum appeared to have decided that whatever I was doing, I was old enough to decide whether it was a good idea or not. She kept looking at Sitri like she approved of my taste in men. You cannot possibly imagine how weird that made me feel.

"This pizza is marvellous," Dad said. "Where did you get it?" He tried reading a box, but it was all in Italian.

"*Il Pizzaiolo del Presidente.* It's a little place on..."

"Sitri knows an Italian chef who recently moved here. He makes him pizza as a favour."

"I introduced Vincenzo to his wife," Sitri said.

"Do you think I could meet him some time? I have some questions about technique."

"I..." Sitri started to say. Then he caught my eye. "...don't think that will be possible. He's going back to Naples fairly soon." He proudly smiled at me, then looked at the kitchen clock, and rose to his feet.

"Look at the time. I really must be going. It's been a pleasure meeting you all. Veronica, give me a call tomorrow so we can arrange a time to review the surveillance videos."

I rose as well.

"Excellent. I'll see you tomorrow. Thank you for the pizza."

"It was the least I could do."

I escorted him to the door and showed him out.

"He seems like a nice fellow," Dad said once the door was closed.

"He's not *too* bad," Kali agreed.

"*Very* nice," Mum said. There went that weird feeling again. Normally, Mum would never even consider cheating on Dad, but she'd often told me that being on a journey through life with one person doesn't mean you can't enjoy the scenery as you pass by. This wasn't scenery I was comfortable letting her admire.

Mum and Dad decided they needed to go too. That left me alone with Kali.

"What the hell happened?" She said seconds after the door closed. I sat down heavily on the sofa.

"Our killer was waiting for us with her own neutralizer when we went to get the video cameras. The only reason I'm still alive is that Sitri got some kind of warning out of his nanites when she shut them down. He pushed me aside when she tried to skewer me."

I filled her in on the rest of our fun afternoon, including the reason why he was naked when they arrived.

"I'm sorry. I was worried he'd zapped you or something."

"Kali, are you ever going to get over that? Because I have. He's apologized for it a dozen times, and has been nothing but a gentleman during this whole investigation. Cut him some slack."

"I'm just trying to look out for you."

"I appreciate that, but I'm pretty sure I'm in a lot more danger from a homicidal goddess than a perfectly mannered demon." We both paused. "I can't believe what comes out of my mouth these days."

"All right. I'll leave it alone. So what do we do now?"

"If you can make it, I'd like to have you here when we go over the videos tomorrow to see if we can identify Katniss' evil twin. In the meantime, sleep is in order. No matter who she is, things are about to get a lot busier and I'm not feeling all that great."

CHAPTER 11

Light of My Life

S itri impressed me. A month ago he was sociopath living in a culture composed exclusively of sociopaths. Now he was living in a different culture in another universe. He was a good person, and trying hard to get the hang of this etiquette thing. Rather than interrupting my sleep, he waited until I called him at two in the afternoon.

I was finding it increasingly difficult to remember that he was a big, scary demon. It didn't help that he was not only a nice guy, but incredibly hot as well. Just in case I'd missed that point, I had some wonderfully explicit dreams to remind me.

The late start wasn't completely due to me sleeping in. I also had to go to the store to get my telephone replaced. We were also waiting for Kali, who had to attend to her occult shop business in the morning.

It was almost three o'clock before we were all assembled. Kali had brought her laptop with the pictures she'd taken at the ritual site.

Sitri arrived after Kali. She carefully looked at him, trying to see any damage.

"How are you feeling?"

"Not bad. My back itches."

I motioned for him to stand up. "Let's see."

I pulled his shirt up at the back. The skin was red, and there were scabs in places. I ran my hands gently over his skin. It looked like it had been healing for several weeks. My guess was that there wouldn't be any scars.

I let him tuck his shirt back in. "Incredible."

I had some ideas about how to proceed, but I wanted to see if anybody else had suggestions.

"Okay, how do we identify our killer?"

"I can run facial recognition software against Downland databases," Sitri said. "One advantage we have is that she isn't from here. If she's in the database at all she will appear to be the same age."

"What if she isn't in the system?" I asked.

"It would help if we could get a DNA sample."

"You keep everybody's DNA on record?"

"From before the Incident, yes. Even if we can't identify her we may be able to identify her relatives."

"Wonderful. Unfortunately, we didn't have any way of collecting a sample while we had her."

"What about where the two of you came in contact?" Kali said. "Could there be something left behind from the explosion?" She turned to Sitri. "I understand that you were pretty well banged up. It should have done the same to her, shouldn't it?"

"¡Chica inteligente! The only problem will be finding a sample, given that we don't know where she touched," I said.

"That shouldn't be difficult," Sitri said. "Any tissue will retain its Upland charge for a while. All I have to do is run my hands over the area and I should be able to sense anything she left behind. Like with the cedar needles."

"It sounds like we have a plan. We can get the sample tomorrow. Let's see what we have in the way of pictures."

We went through the pictures Kali had taken and picked what we agreed was the best one.

Looking at her, it was difficult to believe that she was a serial killer. She looked more like the pretty girl next door. Sitri seemed quiet.

"It's too bad she's unconscious," I said. "I wanted to look her in the eyes."

"I can fix that," Kali said. She put the computer on her lap and started doing things.

I popped another couple of pain pills. "In the meantime, let's see what we have on the videos."

Sitri and I skimmed through the views from the various cameras. Three were focused on the ritual area. The other three covered the rest of the concrete pad.

The video of the ritual area was nearly useless. Everything had happened so quickly that it was a blur. We could tell that someone had appeared in the triangle before the camera overloaded from the glare of the Downland weapon.

"I meant to ask you. What kind of weapon did you use?"

"It was a directed energy weapon. I haven't studied the detailed physics, so I'm not sure I can explain. I've seen similar things on your television shows, but do you have anything like that in real life here?"

"You mean a laser? You pump energy into something, and it bounces back, and forth until it gets intense enough to burst out."

"Ah, so you do have—lasers. I'm missing some technical vocabulary in English because we never had to discuss things like this with Midlanders before."

"So what about the laser?"

"This one stores energy in an isomerically pure hafnium rod until it's triggered. The effect we saw wasn't the actual beam, which was invisible. It was the result of it ionizing the atmosphere. The main energy output is considerably above the visible spectrum."

That didn't sound good, considering that I'd been less than two metres away when it went off.

"How far above? Ultraviolet? Do I have to worry about my eyes?"

He shook his head. I was trying to remember what was above visible light in the electromagnetic spectrum. I remembered something I'd read about the abandoned U.S. Star Wars program.

"X-rays?"

"Are those the ones you use for medical imaging?"

I started to nod but my head hurt. "Yes."

"The frequency is higher than that."

I'd read enough military science fiction to clue into what he was saying, and it did not fill me with joy.

"Holy shit, you set off a freaking *gamma-ray laser* right beside me? Are you fucking insane?"

"What's the problem? The side leakage would be minimal and—oh."

"Yeah, oh. You forgot I'm not one of you. I don't have any bugs to fix things for me. How much radiation did I get?"

"Not much. I think. Just some from the edges of the beam, and backscatter from it boring through the dirt, concrete, and atmosphere. Maybe a little lower-energy stuff from the ionization."

Kali had put her laptop down. I was yelling loudly enough that the neighbours might hear.

"And how the hell much is *that*?"

"I'd have to find out. Do your doctors have any treatments for exposure to gamma radiation?"

"How the hell should I know? I don't think so. It's not something we usually have to deal with."

"Sitri," Kali said calmly, "get back to Downland, and find out how much radiation Veronica got. And while you are there, find out about any treatments that we might be able to use."

He had the sense to vanish immediately without arguing.

"Well," I said, "isn't this the most fucking wonderful thing in the world? A goddamned gamma-ray laser. No wonder I feel like my insides have been cooked. I wonder if I glow in the dark."

"I can't believe I'm saying this, but it was an accident."

"Yeah, I know. You also know what they say about the road to hell. There's one treatment that would probably work. You could give me your nanites."

"I know. I thought of that right away, but would the first-aid mode be enough? And what about your hormones?"

"What about them?"

"If the nanites keep you the way you are, won't your hormones always be stuck on high?"

"I don't know, but it's probably better to be horny than to be dying of radiation poisoning. At least there's a cure for horniness."

We didn't say anything for a while. What was taking Sitri so long?

"If the bugs keep things the way they are when they're injected, I wonder how they handle radiation damage?"

"I don't know," she said. "Maybe the same way they handle children who are born with genetic problems."

I looked at the kitchen clock. About five minutes had passed.

"What the hell is taking him so long?"

Kali looked scared, which got me thinking of something other than myself. Anyway, I'd had enough of this topic.

"How is the picture coming along?"

She showed me her laptop screen. Our unknown goddess now had open eyes. The effect looked natural.

"How did you do that?"

"I used a picture of my own eyes. She has almost the same coloration as me, so it's a safe bet her eyes are brown."

The woman staring out of the screen at me was pretty and looked sweet. I remembered the fourteen-year old she'd killed. I didn't want her to look sweet.

"I can't wait any longer," Kali said.

She took back her laptop and started doing things. For a while she read silently.

"Have you had any problems with your stomach lately?"

It didn't take a nuclear engineer to figure out why she was asking.

"Yes. After we got home from the ritual site, I threw up a couple of times."

"But you're okay now?"

"Mostly. Still some nausea."

She nodded.

"Have you been having any headaches?"

"Just before you and the parental units came over for dinner. Later. And now."

"Bad?"

"Moderately, but it could be stress or from hitting the concrete wall."

"Do you have any fever or chills?"

"Yes."

"Diarrhea?"

"No."

"Sunburn in unusual places?"

"Maybe. I felt weird just after it happened, like I'd banged my funny bone but all through my body."

"Any unusual bleeding?"

"I've had two nose bleeds. I can't remember hitting my nose, and it doesn't hurt."

"Are you more tired than usual?"

"I got up at noon today."

"So that would be no."

"Very funny," I said, moving around to look at her screen. "What's the verdict?"

She closed the lid before I could read the table she was looking at.

"Wikipedia thinks that you might be okay."

I could tell when Kali was lying.

"Great. My life depends on a Wikipedia article."

I felt like pacing back and forth. That wouldn't solve anything.

I paced back and forth. It kills me to have to wait for something, especially when it's important. This qualified.

If I needed hospital care, how would we explain how I'd been exposed to a gamma radiation source? I could imagine any made-up explanation starting with the involvement of the local police, and rapidly escalating through the RCMP, to CSIS, to a joint task force with Homeland Security. We could say that we had no idea how it had happened, sending them off on a wild goose chase after a non-existent, potential terrorist cell. Or at least one that was far out of their jurisdiction.

That wouldn't work. When they found no other evidence of anyone wandering around with the makings of a nuclear device, they'd start to doubt my innocence and re-examine my life under a microscope. They would probably do that anyway.

Even if the Downlanders had a treatment, I couldn't go to them either. It seemed like a bad idea to put my life in the hands of some doctor who was a known sociopath. Also, whatever treatment they might use probably wouldn't get through my boundary layer thing in time to do any good. Maybe Sitri could bring the treatment here. Assuming that the treatment's boundary layer would let it help me.

Telling the truth wouldn't do us any good either. *So, Ms. Chandler, how were you exposed to radiation? Silly me, I was standing too close to a multi-gigawatt gamma-ray laser my client fired off as a trap for a homicidal goddess from another universe.* Even if they believed it, I was pretty sure that having, let alone using, a laser that powerful went against some kind of regulations. Not to mention being the holy grail for every military in the world. Somebody would undoubtedly end up in long-term custody without benefit of counsel, and I was a prime candidate. At least I couldn't give them the technical information, and they couldn't hold Sitri against his will. If he was as friendly as he seemed, they probably couldn't hold me against my will either. Any outcome led to my life being ruined.

That thought led to another unpleasant one. That beam had gone straight up. I didn't know what the range was, but it went through the cloud layer and kept going. It could have hit, or been seen by, an aircraft or satellites. Were the satellites that kept watch for nuclear tests during the Cold War still active? I had no idea. Nor did I know if they could detect a gamma-ray laser.

The chances were that there were dozens, or hundreds, of satellites overhead that *might* have picked up the beam. They *might* report as soon as they detected something. Immediately afterwards, somebody *might* have ordered satellite surveillance photographs of the area to try to figure out what was happening. It was a miracle that nobody but our Upland friend was there to greet us when we collected the cameras.

Thoroughly depressed, I lay down on the sofa while Kali made me some hot chocolate. At least I now had a good reason for having butterflies in my stomach.

Radioactive ones.

* * *

There was a knock on the door. Kali answered it for me.

"I have both good news and bad news," Sitri said to her.

I sat up slowly, my head pounding again.

"Cut the crap and tell me what's happening."

"It looks like you were exposed to about four Grays. That's 400 rads in older units. I'm not sure which units are more familiar to you." He waited.

"Is that the good news or the bad news?"

"Sort of good. The mortality rate for that dose is only about fifty percent."

Kali slapped him. I was surprised she didn't break her hand.

"You asshole, you screwed up and you expect us to be happy that she only has a one in two chance of dying?"

I was too tired to feel much anger. "Kali, please. Just leave him alone for now. You were the one who said it was an accident."

Sitri just stood there unmomving. I knew the slap hadn't hurt him physically, but he looked for all the world like his chin was quivering, and—holy crap, an actual tear rolled down his cheek.

"I'm sorry," he said. I could hear the catch in his voice. "I didn't mean it that way. I..."

He started crying like a small child lost in the wilderness.

I didn't want to understand Sitri. He'd done bad things to a lot of people over at least the past several hundred years. He'd put me in unnecessary danger of death. He was an ex-sociopath who still had the habit of thinking of himself, and ignoring the needs and feelings of others as inconsequential.

But he was standing in my living room, sobbing with grief, and I understood why.

We were his only friends in two—three—universes, and now he felt like we hated him.

Everybody in his society was as bad as he had been, or much worse. That was okay as long as he was a sociopath and didn't need friends, but he'd come here, and decided to wait until his brain returned to something like normal before approaching me. I was sure that he was truly sorry about what he'd done to me during the Blakeway affair. He was sorry for all the other mistakes he'd made during this case. He was trying so hard to fit in. And now that wasn't enough.

He was scared that we'd abandon him. Not because there was a serial killer after him whom he literally couldn't touch, but because we were the closest things to real friends he'd had in a long time.

We kept thinking of him as a demon, but that was a result of this Incident he kept mentioning. Before that, he was something like my therapist's colleague: Someone who helped people to lead better and happier lives.

Veronica Chandler and Kali Hernández, BFFs to a demon from another universe.

Man, how screwed up was that?

There was only one thing I could do.

I got up, took his hand, and led him back to the sofa. Then I sat him down beside me, and let him cry into my chest while I held him in my arms.

Kali looked at me like I'd gone insane. She started to speak, and I firmly shook my head. I mouthed the words "I'll tell you later" and "chocolate." She shook her head and went into the kitchen.

After a few minutes he stirred, and I let him sit up.

"I'm sorry."

"I know," I said. "I understand."

"You do?"

"Leaving the Downland, and letting yourself feel again must have taken a huge amount of courage. Then we worked together to solve your case, and for the first time in years you found yourself liking somebody for no reason other than friendship."

He sat silently, listening. Kali was in the other room, pretending not to be hanging on every word.

"You want us to like you in return, to be your friends. But you keep making mistakes."

A tear rolled down his cheek again.

"So do I. So does Kali. After Collin Blakeway died, Kali just about strung me up by my thumbs for putting myself at such risk."

"I wouldn't have hurt you."

"I believe you. But we didn't know that at the time. I put her through a hell of worry and anger. Even so, we got through it, and we're still best friends. Now, could we please get back to my radiation sickness?"

"If you recover from the short-term effects there will probably be long-term effects to deal with."

"Such as?" Lately, I was getting far too much practice in appearing more calm than I felt.

"Cancer. In a few weeks you may also have problems with infections."

"I see. Did you find out anything about Downland treatments?"

"Yes. I'm sorry, but the only treatment we have is the medical nanites. They're pretty much a cure-all, so nobody has bothered researching anything else for centuries."

Kali, still pretending not to be listening, brought us mugs of hot chocolate. The smell wafted up. It was rich, spicy, and delicious.

Like the life I might not have anymore.

"Can we use the first-aid mode to fix this?"

"No. First aid is meant for gross trauma. This requires a lot more work."

"If we treat this, how do the bugs know what to fix?"

"Most of your genetic code is still intact. Remember, they go on the basis of majority rule."

Kali cleared her throat. Yeah, I remembered the other point.

"I also have a hormonal problem that is being treated with drugs. Will they fix that or what?"

"That's more complex. What kind of drugs?"

I sighed. I'm not particularly shy, but this wasn't the kind of thing I usually discussed with anyone but family.

"A massively potent birth control pill. The extra estrogen partially counters the other hormones my body produces."

"Is your condition familial?"

"No, nobody else in my family has it."

"Then it's probably an individual mutation. How much do you know about genetics?"

"Not much. Just the basics from high school."

He thought for a moment. "Genes are the codes for building proteins. If the genes aren't turned on, they produce nothing. After conception various genes turn on and off at different times to build the body. In your case it sounds like the genes made part of you too active, so it produces more hormones than usual. Once that structure is built, the genes have no further control over it, just as blueprints have no control over a building once it's constructed. Does that make sense?"

"Yes, for once. I wish all Downland explanations were this clear."

"The nanites can fix the genes that gave you the condition, but not the condition itself. As far as I know, the nanites would think that the hormone levels are normal and maintain them. I doubt that you could ever have children."

Why the hell does life have to be so complex?

"So, you're saying that my choices are cancer and death, raging hormones or sterility?"

"I'm sorry, but yes."

I looked at Kali, who immediately looked away. She wanted me to make up my own mind.

"How long do I have to decide?"

"You shouldn't wait more than a few days."

"Now that's good news. I was afraid you were going to make me decide now."

I picked up the mug and stood.

"I'm going to make supper. I'm tired of pizza." My face smiled.

In the privacy of my mind, a little girl was screaming.

* * *

For some reason I was craving Indian food, so I threw together something tasty but quick: kesar pilau, aloo gobi, and lime-cumin chicken. Cooking helped to take my mind off the decision ahead of me.

"I was wondering about surveillance satellites," I said during dinner. "Won't somebody wonder about the laser?"

"No, unless a satellite was in the path of the beam. It would be almost undetectable from the side. Any satellite in the path would have been vapourized immediately, before it had a chance to report. The back-scatter radiation was only dangerous because you were right beside it. From any reasonable distance it would only be a brief flicker. The visual effects were bright close up, but no more than a twinkle from orbit. Am I right in assuming that your only high energy weapons are nuclear?"

"As far as I know. There was an American program years ago called Star Wars that was supposed to produce x-ray lasers, but as far as we know the weapons never worked."

"Then subsequent surveillance would show no residual radiation and no obvious crater. Even if somebody checked, all they would find would be a small hole. I can patch that as soon as I leave here. If they were particularly diligent, they might detect a slight residue of hafnium, but that was vapourized by the shot and would be scattered over a large area by the wind."

"That's a relief."

After supper, we looked at the video from the three remaining cameras.

I skimmed over the boring part where the goddess was unconscious. When she started to stir, I switched back to normal speed.

She looked like she was groggy, and not at all careful about how she moved. One of the cameras was at just the right angle to solve the archaeological puzzle of whether Bronze Age Greek women wore underwear. Too bad I'd never be able to tell Professor Schliemann. Her clothing was also notable for being knee-length, and leaving one shoulder bare. Both were more typical of men's clothing from that period.

She looked around after standing. When she spotted her weapons and sandal, she staggered over and picked them up. Immediately the bow turned colour. It looked like it had been plated with gold.

"Interesting effect," I said. "More nanites?"

"Without a doubt," Sitri said.

She drew an arrow, which also turned golden, and moved around the area. She moved like a cross between a hunting cat and a member of the police tactical team.

"Probably looking for us," Kali said. "I'm glad we left when we did."

"You and me both."

She examined the pit in the concrete where the laser had been buried. One camera caught a slight smile on her face as she disappeared.

"She must have recognized the weapon and thought it was from the Upland. Maybe she left some kind of alarm behind to tell her if we returned," I said.

"I know who she is," Kali said.

"You do?" Sitri said. He managed to shut himself up before he said anything insulting.

"I remember this from Greek mythology."

"So, who's our serial killer?" I asked.

"She's Artemis, goddess of the hunt."

CHAPTER 12
Broad, Sunlit Upland

I'd been nervous about going to the Downland, but apart from most of the people it turned out to be a nice place. The inhabitants understood that the first person to do something really over the top would set off a chain reaction leading to Armageddon.

The Upland was another matter. Sitri had never been there, and had never spoken with anybody who had. Nobody with superpowers, or even local knowledge, would be going with me. I had no idea what the inhabitants were like, except they thought they were gods. Our only psychological diagnosis was based on how they acted when they visited Midland. That might not be enough to prevent some nasty surprises.

I discovered I had a stupid prejudice that was oddly difficult to shake.

Downland was the home of demons. In most stories, the humans defeat the demon by doing something clever that the demon doesn't expect. The moral of the story is that humans are smarter than demons.

Upland was the home of the gods. Gods smite. Gods, by definition, are smarter than we are. In the stories, the best you can do is to appease them and go along with their plans for you. The worst you can do is to display hubris—considering yourself on their level.

Of course, both the demons and the gods were normal people who had a common origin in a highly technological society that was several hundred years ahead of us. There was nothing supernatural about them; no reason for me to have more than the normal concerns any investigator would have in talking to potential suspects in a criminal case.

So why did I feel like a tiny human who was about to piss off the gods in their own home?

* * *

It had been a week since I'd last seen Sitri. He was giving me the space I needed, which was nicely human of him.

I was also feeling frustrated. I didn't have a current lover so I stopped taking my meds. That way I'd be ready if I decided to get the nanites. Within 24 hours my dreams weren't just erotic, they were wide screen, 3D, with surround sound and virtual reality. Did I want to spend the rest of my life like this?

The alternative was cancer, assuming I didn't just die first of organ failure. There was also the good possibility that I'd get more symptoms in a few weeks. Something called leukopenia where I'd be open to any infection that came along: Effectively, I'd have full-blown AIDS without the HIV virus. Radiation effects depended on so many variables that it was impossible to tell exactly how it would affect me, either in the short term or the long term.

Damn it, this was not fair. A twenty-one-year old shouldn't be in a position where every option would either end her life, or completely screw it up.

Yeah, tell that to the people who grew up in war zones, or places where human-rights violations were the norm.

Normal Canadian problems had solutions. If I married a jerk, I could get a divorce. If he tried to hurt me, I could punch his lights out. If I had a baby, I could keep it or give it up for adoption. If I got into debt, I could declare bankruptcy. Maybe those weren't great options, but at least they would let me continue with my life.

My only options in this situation were telling my parents that I'd be dying sometime soon, or that physically I'd still be twenty-one when they died, hopefully not less than half a century from now.

I went for long walks without my phone. Partially, it was because I wanted to think. I also wanted to be somewhere that Kali couldn't find me for a while. She was coming over every day to see how I was doing. It was sweet, but she was driving me nuts.

There was one issue I could think about and pretend to myself that it only applied to Kali, and had nothing to do with me.

How do you live when you are effectively immortal?

Tolkien's elves have it easy. They have their own culture, and everybody in Middle Earth knows they live forever unless they are killed. There are no nosy neighbours wondering how the same person can have been living in a house next door for the past century without getting any older. Although, come to think of it, something like that did happen to Bilbo Baggins.

In the real world, the best solution I could come up with was that Kali would have to move every twenty years or so, and assume a new identity. That meant finding criminals who could create new identities for her, which would be increasingly difficult as technology advanced. It also meant killing off her old identity, or at least having her pretend to move to some place where her old identity could never be heard from again without anybody asking questions.

That led to more problems. There were fewer and fewer wild places on Earth where a person could disappear. The headwaters of the Amazon were such a place, but it was also an Indigenous reserve that was constantly patrolled by government troops to keep poachers out. In a hundred years there might not be any places left on Earth where she could go to "die."

Maybe she would get lucky, and by then everybody else would live forever too. Or she could invest in space exploration and hope to lose herself on another planet.

I hoped that George wanted to be with her for the long haul. If not, how could we prevent him from leaking the information after she had told him that she would never need a retirement plan?

Her money might be the easiest part of the whole thing. She could set up some kind of charitable foundation that would give money to people who deserved it—all of whom were her. At least it would be easy as long as the financial laws didn't change significantly, or the fund wasn't wiped out by a global economic crisis. Most foundations didn't worry about being around for a thousand years or more.

The whole thing was a freaking mess when I was thinking of it in her terms. It was worse when it applied to me.

Sitri had given me a time limit of several days to make my decision. That had been a week ago. That morning I had noticed sores on my skin that looked like small areas were dissolving.

I picked up the phone and made some calls.

* * *

In deference to Kali and Sitri I made tea. I also made tea biscuits with strawberry jam. If this was going to be the end of my life as I knew it, I wanted to do so with some class and a sense of occasion.

They arrived together. He'd asked her to pick him up from where he was staying in Motel Village. Typically, he hadn't mentioned before that he was living only a few blocks from my apartment.

I spent the first few minutes playing hostess, and my two guests went along with the farce. Both of them ignored the sores on my forearms.

It doesn't take long to serve tea and biscuits. Eventually, I had to say something other than, "cream?"

"I have a question," I said. "Do the nanites work on non-humans?"

Sitri scrunched his mouth before answering. "I don't think anybody has tried it, although there's no reason why I'd have run across the research if they did. They *should* work, although not on anything too different from humans."

"How exactly do you define 'too different'?"

"They certainly wouldn't work on insects or plants. The internal organs are too dissimilar. All mammals have roughly similar bodies and metabolisms. They shouldn't present any difficulties."

"Okay. I've decided that I want you to give me the nanites."

"Are you sure?" Kali asked.

"Hell no, but it's definitely the lesser of multiple evils. I've seen what happens to cancer patients. At least if I'm alive I have options. Besides, over the next few centuries you'll need somebody to keep you out of trouble."

Sitri moved to sit beside me.

"No. Kali is my sister; I want her to do it."

"No way. I don't know how."

"That's why I asked Sitri to be here. He can tell you what to do. It seems like something we'll both have to learn to do eventually."

Kali looked scared.

"Hold hands," Sitri said. I don't know whether he'd finally figured out why this was a big deal for us or not, but at least he was acting like he understood.

"You know there's no going back," Kali said.

I could have said a great many things, but I was literally sick to death of the whole mess. I just wanted it to turn into another mess I might be able to deal with better.

"I know. Do it."

"Visualize your medical nanites waiting for your orders," he said.

I tried to help. "I picture them standing at attention."

"Now think of whatever speaks to you of medical care, flowing down your arm, and out your hands."

"You mean something like a fleet of little ambulances?"

"If that's meaningful to you, yes."

Kali took a big breath and slowly let it out. I didn't feel any different. Really, in movies there would be a helpful eerie glow, or weird things marching down her arms under the skin. At the least there would be dramatic music. Definitely, there should be some kind of dramatic music to mark the occasion. Maybe the theme from *Highlander*.

Get a grip, Veronica. You're starting to freak out.

Sitri put his hand on my wrist. I sat there for what felt like a long time while, apparently, nothing at all happened. Finally, he let go.

"It worked."

I wiggled my fingers. Kali took the hint and stopped squeezing so hard.

"Are you okay?"

It's never too soon after being made immortal to be a smart-ass.

"Does zis mean I haff to call you my sire?" I said in a fake Transylvanian accent. She punched my arm.

"Shut up, Bella."

He frowned. "I don't understand."

* * *

The sores, along with the rest of my symptoms, were gone by the next morning. In the meantime I could have eaten a pony. Seriously, I went through all two and a half kilos of steak in my freezer along with side dishes and all the ice cream. Healing took energy.

The three of us met again that afternoon.

"I've put together a dossier on Artemis," Kali said, pushing her laptop toward me. "Let's hope that the myths have something to do with the reality." I read the file while Sitri hovered over my shoulder, reading along.

If the myths were right, Artemis had no luck at all when it comes to families. It was no wonder that she had issues. Convincing her to give up being a serial killer was not going to be easy. From what Kali had dug up, the only good times in her life were associated with death.

Some of Kali's friends were avid hikers, and they gave her a checklist of things for us to take on an overnight expedition. We'd have to figure out clothing after we determined what the weather would be.

We were not taking local clothes. A full length, woman's chiton was not something you could run in, which was why Artemis had been given permission by her father to wear the shorter male version while hunting. If we scandalized anybody by wearing jeans, that was too bad for them. As long as they didn't haul out the gamma-ray lasers or nuclear bombs, we were literally untouchable.

My plan was to be away for three days to give us a good safety margin. If we didn't find her before then, we'd come back for a couple of days to reset our brains, and then try again. There would be no pizza delivery in the Upland, so I got enough freeze-dried food from Mountain Equipment Co-op to last us. Kali was slightly concerned about the weight of the packs.

"Why don't we just come home in the evenings? Then we don't have to carry all this stuff with us."

"We could, but people act differently at night and that gives us more opportunities to find her. We might miss her because she sees us coming and hides, or we might see her camp fire in the darkness."

She eyed her pack. "I suppose."

We didn't bother with weapons, although we took hunting knives as tools. We had no idea what we'd run into, and at least we'd be able to cut some branches to make a shelter. We didn't need a sharpener: our Midland knives were as just invulnerable as we were.

Okay, I lied. I slipped my baton into my pack for comfort.

By the time the shopping and packing were completed, Sitri had returned from a trip to the Downland.

Kali was going through her pack one more time when there was a knock on my door. I'd already checked my pack four times, and now I just wanted to go. If I'd forgotten anything I'd just have to do without it.

"Welcome back," I said to Sitri. "How's the Downland?"

"The same as ever. I come bearing gifts."

In his hand were two circular medallions. Each was about five centimetres across, and they had stout chains suitable for a dog collar. I hefted one. It wasn't any heavier than a roll of dimes. The chain had no clasp, but it was just long enough that I could slip it over my head. Getting it off again wouldn't be a problem, but losing it accidentally would be almost impossible.

Despite their lack of weight, the medallions appeared to be made of iridescent gold and had a simple design on one side. The lower half circle was black. A square, rotated 45 degrees, was in the middle. Its colours were the opposite: black on top and gold below. It might have been a representation of Downland, Midland and Upland.

"What are these?"

"I assumed you wouldn't want more nanites. These devices allow inter-universal travel and, of course, can be removed at any time."

"I thought we couldn't bring any Downland tech with us?"

" I created these here from Midland matter. Put one on."

I carefully put the chain around my neck. He handed the other one to Kali, who also put hers on.

"I included some simple security. You'll have to program a code phrase before they'll work. That way nobody else can use them, and you won't jump by accident."

"What if we can't speak?" Kali said.

"The code will also work if you say it mentally. To program them, hold the medallion in your hand, and say your code phrase."

It took me a moment to think of something clever.

I grabbed my medallion and said, "beam me up." Kali grabbed hers and said, "there's no place like home."

"Good. You can let go of the medallions. Let's try something simple. Think your code phrase, and picture Kali's living room."

Kali vanished.

"You said that these were for inter-universal travel."

"They are."

"So how come we're going someplace in this universe?"

"That's still inter-universal travel."

"No, that's teleportation. It's not going to another universe."

He looked astonished. "You thought we *teleported* from place to place?"

"Well, yeah."

"Teleportation the way you mean it is impossible. You can't disassemble a person in one place and reassemble them in another. Not and expect them to live. The uncertainty principle by itself will kill you. Kali jumped to the Downland for a few nanoseconds, and then jumped back to her living room. That's much simpler."

As usual, the Downland conceptions of "simple" and "nothing to worry about" were different from mine.

In my head, I said "beam me up," and pictured Kali's living room.

The universe somersaulted.

She was sitting in a chair when I arrived.

"I got out of your way in case we collided."

That was an excellent point. Sitri arrived a moment later.

"What happens if we jump to the same spot?" I said.

"You can't. The exclusion principle forbids it. For the same reason, you can't appear inside a solid object or water. Air, being much less dense than you, get pushed out of the way to make room."

"Cool. Back to my place?"

Sitri vanished. So did Kali. When I jumped into my living room, Sitri was already standing where I'd intended to land. I materialized beside him, slightly off-target with no sense of a collision.

"Now let's try something more difficult," he said. "Key your medallions, and think that you want to follow me."

A moment later we vanished. We re-appeared in an idyllic woodland setting. I immediately recognized the remains of a recent campfire on a rocky ledge. A robin flew by.

"Remember to breathe properly," he said. "In, hold, out."

I turned to Kali. *"Bienvenido al infierno, hermanita."*

* * *

After more practice we returned to my apartment for the final planning. "I did some research, and found Artemis's father," Sitri said. "He was a weather man in Iactupo before the Incident."

"Can you give us co-ordinates or something to get there?"

"They are already loaded. According to your stories, I'd expect Artemis to be somewhere nearby."

"That's a relief," Kali said. "Otherwise, we'd have no idea where to jump in the Upland. We don't have time to search a whole planet."

"We'd still have a problem except that the two worlds have similar geography. At least, they did right after the Incident."

"That seems confusing. If the worlds are identical, how do the medallions know where to send us?"

"Normally, that isn't an issue. For safety, Downland transport nanites are programmed to ignore Upland destinations. Your medallions are based on the original design, before that measure had been programmed in. You'll have to clearly visualize where you want to go to prevent confusion."

"What happens if we make a mistake?"

"For convenience I programmed the medallions to prefer Upland and Midland locations. That's why I had you follow me to Downland instead of doing it yourself. You shouldn't have any difficulties."

If I'd learned one thing from watching Star Trek, you don't want to fool around with things that might confuse your transporter. The results were ugly at best.

"All right, what's next?"

Kali consulted her checklist. "We need to know what kind of weather to expect."

"That's easy," Sitri said. "At this season you can expect Iactupo to be around 30 Celsius during the day and 18 Celsius at night. You might get rain, but it's unlikely."

"If it's raining we probably won't see anybody anyway. We can just come home until the storm has passed. Right?" Kali looked hopeful.

"Right."

"One more thing: When you come back I'd appreciate it if you immediately wash everything that went with you. It would be awkward for me to step on a blob of Upland mud on your carpet."

"Gotcha. What about Upland food and drink?"

"Anything you eat or drink will be isolated inside you while your metabolism breaks it down into molecules. The smaller the piece of foreign matter, the faster the charge dissipates, so by the time I could possibly encounter the molecules they'll have a neutral charge."

Kali grinned. "At least we'll be safe from Downland cannibals." Sitri and I glared at her. "What?"

* * *

It was June eighteenth by the time we were ready. Time sure flies when you are having fun.

We loaded up appropriate clothing for hot weather. Regardless of the terrain, had bare legs and arms couldn't be damaged. It was one of the few times Kali would not be in a Romantigoth gown.

I made sure Sitri had a printed copy of the directions for looking after Yoko Geri while we were gone. To keep out of the neighbours' sight, I told him he should *not* use the door this time.

I could see where this whole *faux*-teleportation thing could be incredibly handy. Unless you had a creepy stalker ex-boyfriend, a vault full of jewels, or a dozen other scenarios where security was an issue. If this tech got out, neutralizers would be a booming business.

"Good hunting," Sitri said as we tightened the straps on our back packs. I held out my hand to Kali, and she took it. We had agreed I'd control the jump this time to make things simpler.

The universe pranced.

* * *

We were in a forest of tall cedars. Through a gap in the trees a mountain was visible several kilometres away. There was a slight breeze but it was still hot—the proverbial ninety in the shade.

"Your dossier said she spends most of her time with her nymphs hunting in the mountains. It looks like we're in the right place."

"Where now?"

I shrugged, then pointed in the direction that led gently upward toward the mountain.

"That-a-way. It's as good as any."

The woods were almost silent as we walked. We listened for any signs of a hunting party, but all we heard was the occasional angry squirrel, and the odd mosquito. Mostly, we were in shade with occasional patches of sunlight reaching the forest floor.

"I wish that Mum was here," Kali said after a while. "She'd enjoy the scenery, and it would be nice to have another police-type for back up."

"Calgary police don't have jurisdiction in the Upland."

"Technically, neither do we."

"Now you are just being picky."

"I wonder if guns work here?"

"Probably. We wouldn't be alive if the laws of physics and chemistry were radically different. At least, I don't think we would. Why?"

"I'm just nervous about being unarmed when we're hunting a serial killer."

"Look at this."

Just as Kali turned to look, I let her have it on the side of her head with a fallen branch the thickness of my wrist and over a metre long. She screamed and tried to cover her head with her arms. By then a third of the club was spinning through the air after breaking across her head.

"What...!"

"Welcome to the League of Extraordinary Women. Sitri hit me with a big rock to convince me that the boundary layer he was talking about exists and actually protects us. Did you feel anything?"

"Panic."

"I meant did you feel anything physically?"

"No, which is weird."

"Exactly. Believe me, guns would be overkill for us here. If necessary, we could wade into a battalion of heavy infantry with just our hunting knives and turn them all into sushi without taking a scratch."

The day had turned hotter, even under the trees. When we stopped for lunch, we also stripped off our t-shirts, leaving us in sport bras and shorts. The good news was that it took time for the heat to leak into our boundary layer. The bad news was that it took just as long to leak out. We would get horribly sweaty if we had to do anything like run for our lives, apart from the problem with sucking in enough oxygen. No wonder demons in stories rarely did anything athletic.

A couple of hours later we found a small stream running down the hillside in a series of cascades. Below one of the falls was a pool. It looked to be maybe a metre deep in the middle.

"Are you thinking what I'm thinking?"

"Oh, yes."

We scouted the area first. Not only were we alone, there were no signs that anybody had ever been here. There weren't even any obvious animal trails or droppings.

Neither of us had ever been skinny dipping before, especially not in an alternate universe. At first, I was nervous, expecting some ranger to pop out at any moment, and arrest us for indecent exposure.

After a while I got into it. There is something liberating about being naked outdoors. In Calgary, there isn't a lot of opportunity to do that without getting hypothermia. Even on a sunny day in high summer day our lakes and rivers are almost all bitterly cold.

We splashed around for a while having fun, then sat by the edge of the pool to dry. After getting dressed, I for one felt much better. Water sucked the heat out of us much more efficiently than the air did. We didn't bother trying to dry ourselves.

That's when we heard the music. Something like a flute was playing in the distance. The music was in an unfamiliar scale, and sounded ancient.

"We have company," I said.

"Maybe we can ask directions."

We followed the tones further up the hill. The musician was sitting on a rock, playing his pipes. All we could see from that angle was the back of his head and shoulders. He was not wearing a shirt. Kali marched straight for him, leaving me to catch up.

"Hi," she said in Kalijiriki. "We're looking for Artemis. Have you seen her?" He stood and turned.

Oh, my. He was a satyr, one of those goat-legged guys with horns who chase nymphs. Since he wasn't wearing a stitch of clothing, it was obvious what he did with them when he caught them. I had a new appreciation for the term satyriasis.

The satyr grinned at her and then played a quick riff on his pipes. His eyes were glued to Kali's bra which was wet and translucent.

"Welcome, sweet ladies. No, I haven't seen her for a while. As usual, she's out hunting." He sighed. "What a waste. All those nymphs sworn to chastity." He pointed off through the trees. "You might try that way, if you will."

"Thank you, kind sir," Kali said. We started off in the indicated direction.

"And thank you for the delightful entertainment you presented earlier," he said as we were walking away. "Would either or both of you glorious ladies be interested in..." He wiggled his hips in an obscenely suggestive display.

"Not right now, thanks," I said, trying to quell my urge to beat him senseless for spying on us skinny dipping. I have to admit that I also wondered if satyrs are good lovers. In one movement Kali turned, curtsied, turned again and kept walking.

"Are you trying to encourage him?" I asked when we were out of sight.

"He should be so lucky. You're the wild one of the family. How often does a girl get to flirt with a satyr in Calgary?"

"Ever been to a club on Saturday night?" I said, too quietly for her to hear.

The sound of pan pipes followed us across the mountain.

CHAPTER 13

Daddy Issues

The cedar forest had almost no undergrowth, which made for easy walking. It was also a bit spooky, like we were in a magical wood where the trees wouldn't allow anything else to live.

The path we were on was faint; more like repeated scuff marks on the ground than an actual game trail. We were following it as it climbed when we found our next clue as to Artemis' whereabouts.

A golden arrow buried itself in the tree directly in front of my face. The colour faded to normal a few seconds after it hit. I automatically tried brushing the tree bark out of my hair, but of course it had just slid off.

Within moments, we were surrounded by a troop of armed wood nymphs who were uniformly dressed in knee-length chitons. Don't ask me where they'd been hiding.

There were a lot of scowls directed at our clothing. I suppose that if showing your calves and shoulders was considered daring for a woman, a sports bra and shorts must have made us looked like prostitutes.

"What do we have here?" Beyond the circle of nymphs stood another woman with a golden bow. She had another arrow nocked and casually ready.

Seeing Artemis unconscious on the ground and seeing her awake and moving were two entirely different things.

She was considerably taller than we were. Her long black hair was held back in a chignon by a gold diadem and pins. Like her nymphs, her chiton was green. Unlike them, her sandals were golden instead of silver.

The picture we had of her with Kali's eyes looked like the cute girl next door. With her own eyes, standing in the forest surrounded by her armed followers, she looked cold, in command, and deadly.

I felt a growing hand pressure on my shoulder. Kali was trying to pull me down with her to kneel before the goddess. If she had an idea of how to handle this I was perfectly willing to let her try.

"Mighty Artemis, Lady of the Wildlands and Mistress of Animals, we have travelled far to ask you for a great gift."

We had?

The nymphs relaxed slightly. Not that their arrows could hurt us, but we had no idea what other abilities our homicidal hostess had. A girl who shot and dressed her own game would not be squeamish about doing whatever it took to maintain her narcissistic self-image in front of her followers.

One of her eyebrows raised slightly. She was looking moderately amused by Kali's speech, which was much better than any of the other possible reactions.

"And what gift would that be?"

"We are from a distant land, Great One. Much of importance has been lost over the years, O Bringer of Light and Comforter of Mothers, and we wish to hear your stories that we may tell them and men might not for-get."

Kali's request was utterly ambiguous, leaving it for Artemis to fill in most of the blanks. It was the perfect approach to take with her. I'm good at getting information from humans, but apparently Kali kicks butt when it comes to mythological beings.

"Is that all?"

"The stories of your deeds are all that we could wish for," Kali said. She sounded so sincere that even I believed her.

Artemis still had her bitch face and didn't move. The nymphs became more tense. I became more tense. Hell, I'll bet that even the trees became more tense.

Then she laughed.

"If it is stories you want, it is stories you shall have. Back to camp; we are done hunting for the day."

The whole troupe of us formed a single line, with Kali and me in the middle and marched through the woods. I kept thinking of Tusken Raid-ers.

The camp was hardly worth the name. True, there was a small stream nearby to provide water, but the camp itself was nothing more than a place where their few possessions were kept while they were out in the woods. There must be shelters available for bad weather, but we couldn't see any. The only particularly camp-like feature was a large fire pit with boulders surrounding it as seats.

A cloth banner with a golden bow on a green field was hanging from a tree. Since no sentries had been left at camp, I imagined that the ban-ner's purpose was to serve as a warning: Artemis owns this stuff. Unless you enjoy extreme acupuncture, leave it alone.

In an amazingly short time, previously killed and hung game was roasting over the fire, and amphorae of wine were brought from where they were cooling in the stream.

I'd expected dinner to be nothing but chunks of roasted meat. Instead, the carcass was seared to remove the hair, then stuffed with herbs, rolled, and bound with gold wire. The skin kept the juices in as it slowly roasted, producing a delicious result similar to porchetta. They kept the roast from burning by occasionally pouring wine over it. Using gold to bind it kept the meat from getting a metallic flavour. It was an elegant solution to *haute cuisine du camp*.

There's nothing like telling a narcissist that you want to hear how fascinating she is to get the party rolling.

While the nymphs took turns preparing dinner, we sat and drank wine with Artemis. There was a lot of wine, but it was cut with water. That made it pretty weak by our standards—probably about five percent alcohol. Still, we both drank cautiously. Neither of us knew how long it took our medical nanites to fix intoxication, or whether they bothered to do so at all.

Since she seemed to have a knack for it, I left most of the conversation to Kali.

"Tell us about your grandparents."

Artemis took a swig from her cup.

"My grandparents were Titans. Mighty gods who ruled before Zeus took over."

"Coeus was my grandfather He's a magnificent theoretical physicist whose work on the ekpyrotic cosmological model led to the development of inter-universal travel after the Event."

It took me a moment to get what she was talking about. She wasn't referring to *some* event, but *the* Event. It was probably the same phenomenon that the demons referred to as the Incident.

"Phoebe, my grandmother, was a brilliant mathematician, specializing in predictive modelling. Her techniques for non-linear modelling of chaotic systems are still the gold standard for precognitive psychotherapy."

I wondered what that was. Predicting that someone would go crazy, or maybe predicting what would make them well?

"Despite their busy careers, they had a wonderful, loving marriage that was blessed with two daughters."

"My aunt Asteria is an astrophysicist who recently solved the problem of creating traversable naked singularities that will lead in the near future to superluminal interstellar travel."

This was a simple country girl? I suspected that, like Sitri, she'd been exposed to their version of basic science courses that were equivalent to our second- or third-year university. I made a mental note not to under-estimate her.

She paused while nymphs refilled her plate and wine goblet. So far everything she'd said fit in with the dossier that Kali had assembled, al-beit from a radically different point of view. Still, I could see how a the-oretical physicist had become the god of intellect, and a mathematical modeller had become the goddess of prophecy.

If I understood the part about her aunt correctly, she was about to create a faster-than-light star ship engine. Holy crap, talk about a high functioning family.

Artemis got more lively as time went on. I wondered how much of that was warming to her story, and how much was due to the wine.

"Their other daughter was my mother, Leto. Now *she's* an awesome woman. She's a doctor who has done astonishing work in obstetrics and fertility. When I choose, I will follow in her footsteps and then surpass her."

That was interesting. Artemis came from a long line of eminent sci-entists, and here she was wandering around the forest taking pot-shots at deer. I could see how being such a relative underachiever would lead to some psychological problems in a narcissist.

Artemis drained her goblet, then held it out to the side. As had been happening all along, a nymph appeared to refill it from a pitcher. I looked around. The nymphs were scattered around us in small groups having their own party. Some of them were making out, proving that their definition of chastity wasn't synonymous with celibacy. Nobody seemed to care if anybody else was watching.

"She is really amazing, like, completely amazing. And really, really, beautiful. Sometimes we go hunting together, you know?"

She was entering the sentimental stage of drunkenness. Kali dug for more information.

"She sounds wonderful. Tell us about your father."

"Zeus," she said, taking another drink. "He's always been nice to me, even when Hera is around. You know, he and Mum got together at a party. She said he couldn't keep his eyes off her. But when she got preg-nant Hera went nuts. Managed to turn off her medical nanites to try to make the birth go wrong. Hera's a bitch."

She had her cup refilled, then held it aloft.

"Here's to Hera, the bitch queen of the universe."

All the nymphs who were still conscious, and not otherwise occupied with each other, repeated the toast. It seemed politically correct for us to do so as well.

"Hera's so stupid, she didn't realize that Mum wouldn't need her nan-ites. I mean, who's so stupid that they think they can prevent the best oste—obstetrician in the world from giving birth. Stupid."

"My mother," she said like she was giving vitally important information, "is the smartest woman in the world. Except me, of course, because I'm her daughter and a MIGHTY GODDESS."

Everybody who was still functional toasted Artemis.

"Anyway, Mum gave birth to me and Apollo before the bitch could do anything about it, or make Daddy even more miserable. You know we're twins, right?"

"How did Hera turn off your mother's nanites?" I asked.

She just shrugged. Since she was trying to take a drink at the same time, wine sloshed down her front. She didn't appear to notice. "Nobody knows."

"How do you get along with your brother?" Kali asked.

"Great! Just great. He's my favourite brother, you know? Mum likes him too. Even Daddy likes him. Everybody likes him. Except Hera. She doesn't like anybody. Especially Daddy, because he can't keep it in his chiton. Of course, if I was married to somebody like her I'd probably cheat too." She looked sad for a moment. "If I had boyfriends. I had one once, not a real one but a boy who was a friend, you know? But I had to kill him."

She said it in a completely matter-of-fact manner that was extremely creepy.

"Who was that?"

"Orion. He seemed different, you know? We hunted a lot together, and he acted nice, but he was in love with one of my nymphs, so of course he had to die." She tried to take another drink, but her cup was empty. A nymph weaved over to refill it, although a considerable amount went on the ground.

That wasn't how Orion died in the dossier. If it was true, I wondered if she'd killed him because he was in love, or because he was in love with somebody else. This girl had more issues than National Geographic.

"You know, I really like Mum and Apollo. Mum is amazing. Sometimes we go hunting as a family: me, and Mum, and Apollo. And me, of course. I'm always there because it's my hunting party. This is my party too."

The last of the nymphs passed out. The next time Artemis needed more wine, Kali sat beside her, and refilled the cup for her. She took another drink, then snuggled into Kali's side, like a little girl with her mother.

"I like you. You're nice," she said. Kali looked uncomfortable, probably wondering if Artemis was going to try to make out with her.

"You sound like you are very happy."

Artemis looked confused for a moment, as if Kali had spoken another language. Then she just looked sad, like a child who has been told that she'll never get the new toy that she wants.

"I'm miserable. I live out in the mountains all the time with a bunch of *stupid nymphs* because Daddy's wife hates me and my brother and my mother and Daddy can't keep his hands off any woman he sees and I want him to love me but the bitch keeps punishing me for stuff he does and I just want Daddy to love me so I promised I'd remain a virgin so I'd always be Daddy's girl and not ever have any other men because they're all pigs just like my father. It's *disgusting*, I mean, he even screwed one of my nymphs and got her *pregnant* and how sick is *that* when she's even younger than I am so I had to punish her but I miss her she was a good friend even if she did break her vow of chastity and that's just wrong because all men are pigs and only want one thing. I *hate* those stupid love gods, always making women fall for men but I can't kill them because then I'll get caught and Hera will punish me again and don't they know that stuff is *wrong.* But I wish my Daddy loved me more and would get rid of that stupid bitch and then Mummy and I could live with him and not get beaten and stuff. You know, the stupid bitch never liked me and she'd beat me, and then I'd cry and go to Daddy, but he'd be all, like, you know, 'go away, I'm busy smiting some Midlander, or figuring out how to screw another nymph, or whatever' and Apollo wasn't any help. I mean, he's okay as a brother and all but he's really into his music and poetry and what I needed was somebody to hold me and tell me that I would be okay and Mummy wasn't around much because that *fucking bitch* blamed her for Daddy getting Mummy pregnant instead of her."

As her speech continued, tears appeared in her eyes. By the end, she had her face buried in Kali's chest and was sobbing. I had to listen carefully to understand any of what she was saying after that.

"I'm so lonely out here but at least nobody's doing anything bad to me except those disgusting Downlanders who just want everybody to get laid and it doesn't even matter if they're married or not so I started making sure that they can't hurt anybody else now that I'm taking care of those stupid, disgusting Midland perverts and I'm so depressed because there are so *fucking many* of them and it'll take forever to kill them all." She sniffed. "I don't get why they do it when it's so *wrong* or at least that's what the *bitch queen* says and why the *fuck* do I care what she thinks." Artemis gulped then burped, her face still buried in Kali's chest. "What does she know about *real* love anyway?"

For a minute she just cried into Kali's cleavage, while Kali, for lack of anything else to do, stroked her hair and looked awkward.

"Mum was never around, and Hera was such a *bitch*, and I just wanted my daddy to love me, you know? I thought that if he was the only man in my life things would be better." She sat up and took another swig of wine, then belched again. It was a startling thing for a goddess to do. One of the nymphs had passed out on the other side of Kali, so she surreptitiously tried to use the hem of her chiton to wipe the snot off her sports bra.

"At least there's a loop hole, so I can give up my virginity if I meet someone nice." She took another swig. "Like that's ever going to happen. What's so great about being a virgin anyway?"

I suddenly had the most incredibly brilliant terrible idea ever. If we were lucky, the world might even survive it. If we were supernaturally lucky, it might work.

"You are such as powerful goddess," I said, "I can't imagine anybody forbidding you anything that you desire."

"Damned right they can't! But all I do is run around all day with a bunch of stupid nymphs. What about what I want? What if I want a husband? Or children?"

"What if you want love?" I said. Artemis burst into tears again, and buried her head in Kali's ample chest. Her voice was muffled, as well as being slurred by alcohol and crying.

"I want somebody to love me, and not just because I'll turn 'em into dog food like I did with Actaeon if they don't." She sniffed again and brought her face up, looking every bit like the forlorn little girl who had crawled into her father's lap looking for approval.

"I know somebody who might be able to help," I said gently. Artemis shook her head hopelessly, her diadem sliding sideways as her chignon came unpinned. She was not a pretty crier.

"Nobody can help me, and nobody wants to. Nobody who isn't already terrified of me, or whom I haven't already turned into something unnatural." She sniffed again. "Curse you, Daddy."

Everything was going according to my cunning plan. I had to be completely out of my tiny Midland mind.

"If I can find a nice man who isn't afraid of you, would you like to go out on a date with him?" I had no idea if gods dated but it was encouraging that there was a Kalijiriki word for it.

"There aren't any men who are that nice. I'm a *mighty goddess, you know.*"

"They might be rare, but I know a few nice men. I've dated some in my time."

"You aren't with them anymore?"

"No."

She gave me a look of professional interest.

"How did they die?"

"They didn't. I let them live."

Artemis looked as incredulous as she could in her advanced state of inebriation. She blinked.

"So you were the one who left all of them?"

"Not all of them. Some of them left me."

"I don't understand. They left you, and you let them live?"

"I didn't have to kill them. Not being in my company was a far worse punishment than death, and it lasts longer."

She nodded her understanding, and the last of her chignon came apart leaving her face framed by long, unruly curls. Some of them were stuck to her face by tears.

"Yeah, make 'em suffer. You would make a great goddess. Maybe almost as great as me. Not that anybody could be as great as me. Except maybe Mummy."

Her rant trailed off as she fell asleep. Kali eased Artemis down onto a blanket, and we tucked the excess around her as she started snoring. It was weird thinking of a goddess snoring.

"That went well," I said.

"What are you up to?" Kali said.

"Don't worry. I have this."

* * *

It was another glorious, sunny morning in the Upland. The trees seemed to be filled to overflowing with birds whose sweet choruses filled the air. A short distance away, the waters of the nearby brook burbled melodiously. The delicious smell of roasted venison still rose from the cooking fire, tinged with the aromatic scent of the cedars.

I loathe camping.

By my reckoning it was shortly after dawn. It should not be a requirement for reasonable people to be functional at such an hour.

None of the nymphs were stirring, which showed how reasonable they were. Either that, or how much wine they'd had. Kali, of course, was up and being productive.

"What are you are doing?"

She waved an empty foil package in my direction.

"Making breakfast. Would you like some scrambled eggs?"

I made a non-committal sound and rolled over in my blanket.

That was when I realized that the wine had caught up with me. I had to pee. It wasn't fair.

I got up. I'd pulled my boots and socks off before passing out for the night. The ground was covered with a layer of moss, so I just went out of sight of camp to do my thing. It wasn't like stepping on a rock was going to hurt my feet.

I had just pulled my shorts up when something jumped me from behind. I fell forward onto the boulder I'd ducked behind, and somebody heavy and strong tried to keep me there.

There was a moment of panic, then I realized I didn't have to limit myself to manoeuvres that would work at home.

I felt my attacker fumbling with my shorts, trying to figure out how to pull them down. I managed to twist to the side so the dirt bag behind me was no longer pushing me into the boulder. Back in my universe it would have hurt like hell to do that, removing chunks of skin against the stone. Here it was the rock that suffered.

He wasn't expecting to lose control like that, and we both fell to the ground. As soon as I could see him, I kicked out with both legs. Happily, I caught him in the stomach and was treated to a satisfying grunt.

It looked like the same satyr we'd met the day before.

From what I'd read of Greek mythology, rape seemed to be a common pastime among the gods, heroes, and especially the satyrs. His trouble was that I wasn't a god, a demigod, a hero, or a nymph. I was the goddess of honey badgers, and he was being a bully.

I was on the ground for maybe a second before I disappeared. He just had time to stand up, and wonder where I'd gone, before he saw my delicate pink toes magically appear between his legs with extreme prejudice. In this universe, they were a lot harder than the boulder.

I'd jumped back to camp, grabbed my baton from my pack, and then jumped back behind him. Damn, I could get used to this technology. I could easily see how the combination of having a quantum boundary layer to make one invulnerable, plus the ability to jump between universes, would make people believe that Uplanders were gods.

He tried to collapse forward, but I put my baton across his throat and pulled back. I discovered that satyrs make an amusing wheezing sound when they are choked.

He tried to head butt me with his horns, kick me, and generally make my life difficult. If we hadn't been in the Upland, some of it might have worked. As it was, I just let him bash his head into my face until he got tired of bloodying himself. I didn't even feel it.

Before his greater strength and weight could make any difference, I planted my knee in the small of his back. He bowed backward, and I pulled down hard on the baton. He landed on his back, on the nice, hard, moss-covered rocks, with the baton still across his throat. When his eyes uncrossed, he was looking up at my upside down face. My arms were straight, and only me supporting most of my weight with my legs and core saved him from instant death.

He tried to grab my arms, but as soon as he moved his hands I leaned forward. The satyr immediately went limp as the steel rod nearly crushed his trachea.

"The penalty for attempting to violate one of Artemis' companions is death," I said quietly.

His eyes were incredibly wide, and he tried to make some kind of in-telligible sound as his hands twitched helplessly at his sides. I smiled at him. From his point of view it was a frown.

"Fortunately, I don't believe in the death penalty."

I gave him about two seconds to get his hopes up.

"Instead, if you ever try anything like this again, *ever*, I'll make sure that you never—quite—die."

Amazingly, his eyes got bigger. Especially when I smiled again. With teeth.

It must have looked really good upside down.

* * *

When I got back to camp, Kali was still the only one awake. She'd missed my brief appearance earlier.

"What do you think of our serial killer?" she said as she handed me a plate of scrambled eggs and bacon.

"I hate to say it, but she's just sad, lonely, and abused. That doesn't excuse what she's done, but if we were in court we could probably make a case for diminished responsibility."

"What do you want to do about it?"

"My gut feeling is that the only way to actually solve the problem is to get her help so she decides to stop killing people. We aren't going to be able to force her without an assassination. I do have an idea on how to get her some help. Just follow my lead."

Before Kali could demand details, Artemis rolled over and groaned. I tried to hand her a cup of water, but she waved it away and stood up. She looked pissed, not drunk.

"I am dishonoured. My nymphs should have been up to see to my guests needs."

"Please, don't blame them. It is our custom to greet the dawn without distraction," Kali said. From behind Artemis, I stuck out my tongue at her.

Artemis began cutting some meat for her breakfast, and reheating it over the small fire Kali had built. Either she had an astounding alcohol tolerance, or her medical nanites had scrubbed her blood for her overnight.

"By the way," Kali said to me, "I heard some kind of fight or some-thing when you were off in the woods. Was it anything we should know about?"

"Just a satyr who was on the wrong path. I corrected him and sent him on his way."

"Was he trying to dishonour you?" Artemis sounded like she was ready to go vengeance goddess on his ass if he had.

"Oh, no. We had a discussion, and he apologized profusely for being a nuisance. You won't have to worry about him again."

Having grown up around satyrs, she looked at me dubiously, but decided not to challenge the word of a guest.

"Do you remember our conversation last night?" I said after a while.

Artemis glanced around. The nymphs were still passed out.

"You will speak of this to no one."

"Of course not," I said. "We only wondered how you wanted us to proceed."

"Proceed?"

"In arranging the date we promised you."

"I don't remember any promises."

"Oh yes," Kali chimed in. "We would be dishonoured forever if we failed you."

"Very well. Produce this man, and we shall see if he is worthy of being in my presence."

"I have an idea," I said. "How about if we arrange a meeting in the Midland? Somewhere beautiful and private, where the two of you can speak without Hera intruding."

"That's an excellent idea," Kali said. "We don't want the evil bitch queen of the universe trying to ruin your life again, do we?"

Kali has her moments, and that was one of them. Mentioning Hera's disapproval guaranteed that Artemis would think that this was a great idea.

"When would this happen?"

"It will take a while to arrange things so that they are suitable for a goddess of your magnificence," Kali said. "We'll let you know."

"So let it be done."

* * *

Artemis and all her nymphs were waving as we hiked away from their camp. Kali waited until we were out of sight before speaking.

"Are you out of your tiny mind?"

"Probably." In the light of day my clever idea seemed a bit less clever.

"You want Artemis to go on a date?"

"If we get her interested in someone, she won't have time to go around killing people. If she has all that free time we can convince her to get into therapy. It's the best solution. Trust me, I have this."

She muttered under her breath, but I still heard her.

"Yeah, if 'this' means mental illness."

The universes did a waltz as we jumped back home.

CHAPTER 14
Physics and Chemistry

The next day we held a working dinner at Kali's house where we brought Sitri up to speed on what we'd discovered.

"Are you serious?" Sitri said. "You actually feel sorry for her after the number of people she's killed?"

"How many people have you killed over the years?" Instead of answering me he just looked terribly uncomfortable. "Before all this, if anybody had told me that a murderer had an abusive childhood I'd have said that it might be a good reason for their behaviour, but there was no way it was an excuse. But Artemis wasn't born with something missing from her brain that makes her a monster. We're talking about a girl who was made crazy by being in the wrong universe, and having the bitch queen of the universe as an evil step-mother. That is curable. You were a sociopathic demon before you spent a few weeks here to give your brain a chance to get back to normal. We need to give her the same chance."

"I believed you were evil when you showed up here," Kali said. "I thought you were trying to get Veronica to lower her guard, so you could do bad things to her."

Sitri looked at the gnocchi on his plate, unwilling to meet her eyes.

"Not too long ago that might have been true," he admitted.

"I was wrong. You are a really nice guy who used to help people. The Incident changed you, and it changed Artemis too. She isn't a born serial killer who gets pleasure from torturing and murdering people. Instead, she's trying to cope with an incredibly abusive and dysfunctional family situation in the only way she can imagine. It's up to us to give her other options."

He took a deep breath, then let it out slowly.

"All right, how do we get her to stop 'coping'? From what you've both said, you wouldn't be in favour of an execution."

"No, we wouldn't. I have a technical question. Is there any way to stop the fireworks when a Downlander touches an Uplander?"

Sitri actually cringed at the thought of such an explosion.

"I've heard that there's been some work done on that, but it's been difficult to test how well it would work in real life. My understanding is that there's a way to siphon off part of the charge into the bulk. The method becomes increasingly inefficient as the charge differential increases."

"¿Que?" Kali asked through a mouthful of gnocchi.

Sitri got that look on his face that meant he was about to explain something complicated.

"Small words," I said.

"The bulk is, um, I guess you'd call it the space between universes."

"Ah, you mean The Void." Kali watches Doctor Who too.

"If that's the term you are familiar with. There's a way of diverting part of the energy there so it won't hurt anything. But if I went to the Upland, the discharge when we met would be almost as great as it would be normally."

"What if you met her here?"

"That's different. Being embedded in a neutral space would buffer the discharge."

"Small words," I said again.

"Being in this universe would let us divert most of the energy. I probably would hardly notice what was left. There would still be some small collateral damage around us, though. Damaged buildings, forest fires, human casualties: that sort of thing."

Different definitions. "We can probably work around that."

"Are you hoping that you can lure her here and then have me ambush her? It would still take a huge amount of energy for me to kill her, and these days I find myself more respectful of life. I don't want to do it if there's any way around it."

I decided that this was an excellent time for me to get back to my dinner before it got cold. He saw I wasn't going to speak with my mouth full and shifted his gaze to Kali.

"The answer is more straight forward than that," she said. "It's just a bit delicate."

"In what way?"

"We need to introduce her to a man who is kind, loving, and can convince her that not all men are cheating asses like her father. Somebody who can teach her that not all love ends in pain, and who makes her feel like she's the most important thing in his world."

Sitri considered the idea for a while.

"That could work, although you'd need someone who wouldn't mind being with a homicidal maniac. Do you have any candidates in mind?"

"Actually," I said casually, "we were hoping that you were up for it."

Regardless of what universe we were in it was a mistake to say something like that to a person with food in his mouth. Kali fetched the paper towels to clean the gnocchi off the wall. I was glad that neither of us were sitting in the line of fire.

"Are you *insane*?"

Kali muttered as she cleaned. "Thank you. That's what I said."

"Not at all. You are the perfect candidate."

Sitri did the last thing in the world that I expected from him. He blushed and played with his food.

"Well?" I asked.

"I—um."

"Come on," Kali said. "We know that you are attracted to her. The way you looked at her picture kind of gives it away. She's a lovely, sweet girl once you get past the godlike narcissism and homicidal rage."

"I don't know. I guess I could bang her a few times, if that would help."

It was my turn to almost choke on my gnocchi.

"That won't work," Kali said firmly. "She's not looking for a one-night stand. She's looking for love. If you agree to date her, you also have to be respectful of her as a woman. You have to be sincere. Otherwise, extremely bad things will happen to all of us. How long will it be before she gets tired of going after your summoners and goes after Downlanders instead?"

Sitri looked miserable. "I don't know if I can fake sincerity."

"I can't think of anybody better for her," I said. You've gotten over being a sociopath. You belong to the same culture, or at least your two cultures have common roots. You know what it feels like to get over the charge thingy playing with your brain, so you can empathize with her situation. Not to mention that you're incredibly sexy."

He blushed again, and it occurred to me that this was probably the first time in the history of the human race that woman my age had made a lust demon blush. I felt kind of proud of myself.

"What's the worst that could happen? She's already on a killing spree."

Sitri mumbled something, then started eating again.

"I'm sorry, what was that?"

He took his time chewing.

"Come on, spit it out."

He looked startled.

"Not literally. I mean, tell us what's wrong."

He blushed again and swallowed. When he spoke, I could barely hear him.

He spoke to his plate. "What if she doesn't like me?"

"You're a stud. What's not to like?"

Kali put her hand on his arm. "Sitri, we know that you are out of practice. We can teach you how to treat a woman on a date. The rest should be easy."

Again, he let out a slow, deep breath.

"This is important," she said. "Just be yourself and remember that underneath it all, Artemis is a nice girl who is fragile. If you don't do this, she'll go thermonuclear on all our asses. The death toll could be in the hundreds of thousands."

"More," I said. "Even if she stays with the Bronze Age technology, she can bring her nymphs here as an army. Imagine them wandering around our world shooting anybody who reminds them of Zeus, Hera, or doesn't conform to her moral expectations. The nymphs are loyal to her and almost as pissed with Hera and Daddy Dearest as she is. Local law enforcement doesn't stand a chance. Even if the military gets involved—how much energy was there in that laser you set off?"

"In the units you tend to use for nuclear bombs it would be about ten megatons."

"Holy crap, didn't you think about the side effects at all?"

"I said I was sorry."

I took a deep breath to calm myself. *Move on, Veronica.*

"You're right, I shouldn't have mentioned it. Anyway, you're saying that just to knock one of them unconscious will take a large nuclear weapon. All they have to do is jump away before it hits. The collateral damage alone would be insane. If we push her too far, she might lose it and invade the Downland after she's done with us. They would be ultimate suicide bombers. None of us can risk it."

Sitri sat looking at his dinner for a moment, then he looked at us.

"You want me to have a blind date with a woman I've never met?"

"Yes."

"One who thinks I represent everything that she considers evil?"

"Yes."

"Who will destroy two universes if I don't get her to fall in love with me. Does that sum it up?"

"Yes."

"No pressure," Kali said.

"All right, I suppose I could try."

I couldn't resist. "No try. Do or do not."

Kali jumped in. "How does the lightning-rod thing work?"

"It would be another kind of nanite so that the charge can be evenly distributed over our bodies. I'll have to manufacture them here, then transfer them to her in some manner."

"Won't that be difficult when you can't touch each other?"

"One of you will have to do it for me."

"What if she catches us?"

"She won't. Just shake her hand or something."

"She doesn't seem like the hand-shaking type. Can you put the nanites in something else that you could hand to her?"

"I suppose. But why would I give her anything?"

"Much to learn about dating you still have, my young padawan."

* * *

George, Kali's long-time boyfriend, would be arriving by the end of the week for his summer stay. Kali was thrilled, but it meant she would be unavailable to work with Sitri for at least several days. We were running out of time before the Downland ministers got bored, and started responding to summonings again. Or Artemis got bored and invaded.

It was up to me to begin Sitri's training.

I gave him a morning's worth of theoretical lectures and pop quizzes, then told him to ask me out on a role-playing date to see if he actually understood the principles.

He told me that he'd pick me up at noon the next day. I had the impression he was planning to take me somewhere nice for lunch. That was a good call. Low key, safe, and a way to get acquainted.

The knock on my apartment door came at exactly noon. I smoothed down the front of my Little Black Dress one last time, and opened the door.

Sitri was wearing a bespoke suit. If a certain famous MI-6 agent had been standing next to him, James would have come off a frumpy second.

"Hi," he said. "I'm Sitri."

"Veronica," I replied. "Please come in."

"I hope I'm not too early."

"No, not at all. You're right on time. I'll get my coat."

"Oh, these are for you."

A bouquet of red, long-stemmed roses appeared in his hand. It looked like two dozen. Sigh.

"Thank you." I found a vase and put them in water.

"Shall we?" He said, extending the crook of his elbow.

I locked the door behind us.

"I hope you like Greek food," he said.

"I love it."

I expected we'd go to one of the excellent Greek restaurants in town. Instead, between steps, the universe decided to practice parkour...

* * *

...and we were walking toward a pale yellow building. The walls around the windows were white and had squared, pseudo-Doric pillars on either side of them. Over the doors was a black canvas awning. A small sign read *The Funky Gourmet.* From the look of the sky and the light hitting the buildings, it was almost sunset.

"Where are we?"

"Athens." Sigh.

Sitri had made reservations, and we were shown to our table by a waiter in a black uniform. The tables were black wood. The chairs were white. Large, modernistic paintings hung on the walls.

"Fancy," I said, switching to Greek because I could.

Another waiter came by and left us with menus.

The food was delicious and highly theatrical. Several of the items were served with dry ice fog cascading from them. It was a combination of *Nouvelle Cuisine* and molecular gastronomy with a Mediterranean flavour.

It was a good thing that the meal was so entertaining. Sitri still hadn't gotten the hang of relational conversation.

"Tell me about yourself," I said between tiny bites of a strange but tasty concoction like a green serpent that trailed across a huge plate. If I'd taken normal-sized bites, it would have been gone in seconds.

"There isn't much to tell," he said. "I was born 176 years ago, went to school, got my degree in counselling, and worked in the field for several years before the Incident. Since then, I've been a member of parliament, and amusing myself by playing demon when Midlanders have summoned me."

Wow, he really sucked at this.

He leaned forward. "So, who is Veronica? Tell me all about her."

I was determined to set a good example, so I told him some stories from my childhood, including the Great Santa Scam and my decision to become a private investigator. At least he appeared to be listening attentively.

After dinner, we took a walk around Athens to see the sights. We stopped by a fountain. We were standing so close that we were almost touching.

"You are beautiful," he said. "Perhaps we should go somewhere less public."

"How about my place?" I said, and the universe Morris danced.

* * *

When we appeared in my living room, he leaned toward me.

I ducked under the attempted kiss and dodged around him. He was disoriented for a moment until he realized I was already in the kitchen behind him filling the tea kettle at the sink.

"Have a seat while I make something to drink."

He cautiously sat on the sofa. "I'm confused."

"No doubt. I'll be there in a minute to explain."

I made us hot chocolate. Maybe it didn't have the same meaning for him, but I needed comfort. He was extremely handsome, and my hormones were at their original pre-prescription level. My resolve not to let him kiss me had been a perilously near thing. I sat in my comfy chair rather than beside him on the sofa.

"Your introduction was great," I said. "Pleasant, and being on time showed respect. However, two dozen roses is too much for a first date. That's either a gift for a long-term girlfriend, or somebody you think you can bribe into sleeping with you. It sends a message that you want things to move faster than Artemis undoubtedly will. Remember, she's a virgin, so everything will be new and scary for her."

He studied the ice cream ball floating in his chocolate. "She isn't the only one."

"Try to relax. You weren't that..."

He was blushing. He wasn't talking about being scared.

"Sitri," I said as gently as I could, "are you telling me you are a virgin?"

He nodded. Wow. This was going to take some serious diplomacy on my part, when all I wanted to do was fall on the floor laughing until I couldn't breathe.

"It's nothing to be ashamed of. Everybody starts out that way."

"I know. It's just—ridiculous."

"I must admit it's a bit surprising. A virgin lust demon does seem slightly incongruous." I caught myself starting to smile and firmly stopped it.

"I told you, I was too busy with my studies and getting my counselling practice going before the Incident to get into any relationships. After that, it became difficult to find somebody I could relate to." He blushed again. "I just never got around to it."

"Well, it looks like we'll be lighting two candles with one match."

He was looking terribly uncomfortable, so I returned to my critique of the date.

"Athens was also too much for the first date."

"You didn't like it?"

"Actually, it was lovely. The problem is that I'm not Artemis. A girl likes to feel that she has some control, and that she's safe. Some women would be excited to jet off to Europe with a guy they'd just met, but most wouldn't. Granted, Artemis can transport herself anywhere she wants, so it isn't like she'd be stranded if the date went badly, but you just need to understand how women feel about these things."

I pulled my medallion out of my purse and dangled it by its chain.

"I could have left at any time, just in case things weren't going well. I almost did during dinner, just to illustrate that there was a problem."

"What was wrong with dinner?"

"Nothing was wrong with the food. It was the conversation. What did I tell you when you asked about me?"

"You told me stories about your past."

"Right. Stories that illustrated who I am, what I like, what shaped me. What did you tell me about yourself?"

He thought for a minute. I could see the light dawn as he figured it out.

"I told you facts."

"Exactly. Including the stuff that Artemis does *not* want to hear from you about being a demon. You want her to feel safe with you, not hear about how you've been forcing people to want sex against their will. She'll immediately think you might do that to her. There's time enough for confessions later, if your relationship gets that far."

"Oh. Okay. I see."

"The last thing was what you said by the fountain. You get points for being subtle, but there usually isn't enough chemistry on a first date for a woman to consider sleeping with you. Even if she wants to, she'll probably say no just to show that she doesn't sleep with every guy she meets. It's that control thing again. It isn't that she wants to control *you*. It's that she wants to know that she has control over the situation if she needs it. That she can say no and you'll respect that. Waiting shows that you are interested in her as a person, and you aren't just a hormone-crazed male who has only one thing on his mind. Remember, that describes her father. With Artemis, you'd be her first lover so she's going to be even more cautious."

Sitri looked frustrated.

"This is so difficult. Can't I just..."

"No. There are no shortcuts in relationships. Think about your counselling experience. I know it's been a while, but if two people come to you for help, you can't just put your whammy on them to love each other again, and expect it to last."

"You're right, of course. I'm just really out of practice talking to an attractive woman."

This time I let the laugh out. "Gee, thanks."

"That wasn't what I meant. Of course you are beautiful, but I think of you as my friend not as a potential lover."

I lost it and nearly spat hot chocolate across the room. "Holy crap, did a lust demon just friend zone me?"

He looked acutely uncomfortable, so I patted his hand.

"Don't worry about it. I actually think it's sweet. That's why we're practising. One other thing. Few women think of themselves as being attractive."

"Now I'm confused again. You don't think you're beautiful?"

"No. The furthest I'm willing to go is mildly cute, and that's only because I have this stupid baby face that makes me look years younger than I am. Artemis will tell you she's beautiful, but that's to keep up her Mighty Goddess persona. Even though she really *is* gorgeous, underneath it all I'm willing to bet she doesn't think she's all that attractive. Calling her beautiful will please the narcissistic goddess, but it will make the woman feel uncomfortable."

He thought about it for a long time.

"You're right. It's been so long since I've done any counselling it never occurred to me that her self-image would be different from her outward presentation. Just for future reference, what should I have said to you?"

"You could have said that you found me attractive, or interesting. Depending on how my hormones were at that moment, you could have just given me that cute boyish smile and let me rip your clothes off. That's a good rule to remember: Always let her do the clothes ripping. That way there's no confusion in her mind about whether she's in the mood."

"Got it. Let her make the first move."

"That also takes the stress off you because you don't have to wonder if your timing is right. Now you just have to work on talking about yourself. Think of some funny stories from your childhood, or school, or whatever. Say nothing about what happened after the Incident. If she asks, tell her that you became someone else, you aren't that person anymore, and you don't feel comfortable talking about it yet."

Yoko Geri jumped into his lap and started purring. Sitri stroked his fur gently. Yoko ate it up.

"See? That's what she wants to know about you. You are a gentle, kind person who loves cats. Not a sociopath who just wants her body so you can stop a nuclear war."

"I understand. I'll do better next time. What should I bring as a gift? Jewellery?"

"Still too much. I have a much better idea. Artemis is going to know that you've either manufactured or stolen whatever you give her. You need to give her something that is uniquely personal. Something that comes from your heart."

He thought for a moment. "Underwear?"

I resisted the urge to laugh again. "Not appropriate either. Among other things, I happen to know that the huntress goes commando."

He looked puzzled. I had a mental picture of gags flying over his head in a V-shape, then one of them peeling off in a missing joke formation.

"In my society, flowers or chocolates are valued because the date has to buy them, which implies both a sacrifice of resources, and a certain amount of success in life to have those resources in the first place. In your society, you just wave your fingers, and things appear."

"We don't need to wave our fingers."

"I wasn't being literal. Giving her jewellery wouldn't mean anything because she can make anything like that for herself for free. So, the question is, what is valued in your culture?"

"Skills, knowledge, and power."

"All right, that's what you should give her. Knowledge is out. Nobody likes a date who is constantly trying to prove that he knows more than you do. We've already talked about power. That leaves skills. You need to have a skill that you can use to impress her. Something that your technology could do, but which you have learned to do yourself to show her that you value her by spending the time and effort needed to make something for her."

Sitri looked like he was mentally going through a list of possible skills.

"How about archery? Wouldn't that give us something in common too?"

"Yes, but how long would it take you to get good with a bow? Also, you don't want to seem to be competing with her."

"What skill could I have that would impress her? I don't think she'd like it if I gave her psychotherapy."

"She's a hunter. I'm going to teach you how to cook."

* * *

Teaching Sitri the kitchen arts was a little like teaching The Hulk how to arrange flowers. With his feet.

"Let's start with a marinated chicken dish. That should be exotic enough to impress her."

Apparently, cooking was a completely lost art in the Downland. Sitri had taken some basic chemistry courses in school, and they had scarred him for life. He had no idea how Vincenzo could have produced a delicious pizza without it being the result of an exact scientific procedure.

The trouble started with the chicken. I brought out a package of boneless thighs.

"Cut these into bite-sized pieces."

I expected to have to show him how to hold a chef's knife, and how to sharpen it with a steel. I didn't expect he'd stand there looking completely helpless. "What's wrong?"

"I'm wondering how to quantify bite-sized. How big is that?"

Fair enough, maybe that was an idiom they didn't use in the Downland.

"Let's say about two centimetre cubes. That's a bit big, but they'll shrink as they cook."

I got the required spice jars out of my cupboard. When I looked at him, he had gotten a ruler from somewhere and was carefully trying to cut the first thigh into an exact, two centimetre strip. I gently took the knife from him. "Like this."

It was a small thigh, so I cut it into two strips lengthwise, and into thirds across its width. He stared at what I'd done.

"None of those pieces is two centimetres in any dimension," he finally said. "Nor are any of the pieces cubical."

"Welcome to the real world," I said. "Real ingredients aren't perfect. Spices are not standardized laboratory reagents. Food isn't about geometry, unless you are constructing a tableau. It's about taking the ingredients as they exist, combining them and preparing them in a way that leads to something creative, visually appealing, nourishing, and delicious."

He looked dubious.

I forced him to cut up the rest of the chicken, occasionally consulting with him about what constituted too small or too large, then we made the marinade.

That was relatively simple. I gave him measurements for the spices, and of course he had to measure them exactly. He spent a good minute making sure that he had exactly 187.5 millilitres of lime juice, and complaining that I didn't have a pipette. I showed him how to add the cumin, coriander, garlic, thyme, whole chilies, and salt. The salt and chilies in particular disturbed him.

"How do you know how many chilies to add?"

"Experience. The ones I buy have a certain amount of heat, and I add enough that it's warm to my taste without causing undue pain."

I grabbed a pinch from the jar of salt in my fingers and simply sprinkled it into the blender.

"But how..."

"If nothing else, get this through your overly literal, scientific head: cooking is an art. The recipe calls for a teaspoon of salt. I added as much as it needed, which was approximately a teaspoon. Embrace the ambiguity, padawan."

I ended the discussion by turning on the blender. It was too loud for us to talk over it. After a while the goop inside looked like brown mayonnaise.

I had him pour the marinade over the bowl of chicken pieces, then stir with a spoon to coat them all. We left the bowl on the counter and went back to the living room with more hot chocolate.

"How long do we let it sit?"

"The longer the better. Usually, I like to make it the day before and let it marinate overnight in the refrigerator. We'll just let it sit until we're ready for supper. Now, tell me about Sitri."

"As I said, there isn't much to tell..."

"Wrong answer. You are 176 years old. Something interesting must have happened to you in all that time. Try again."

It had been decades since anybody had cared enough to ask him personal questions without some kind of ulterior motive. Just for once, I was patient while he struggled to think of something to say.

"I remember playing in a park when I was a child. I was running along a path when I heard two people arguing. There was a man who was speaking like he was quietly furious. He didn't understand why the woman had been with his best friend. I didn't understand the idiom at the time, and I was confused. What was so bad about just being in somebody's company? She was just as angry with him, and told him that if he didn't know what was wrong she wouldn't explain it to him."

"I hid in the bushes, trying to figure out what was going on. I could see that they didn't like each other, but it also seemed like they were a couple. It was so confusing to me."

"When I got home, I asked my father about it. He said that sometimes, even when people are in love with each other, they'll do something that hurts their partner. It can be difficult for them to get over being hurt enough to talk about it and make things better."

"That's when I decided to try to help people like that. That's why I became a relationship counsellor."

"That," I said, "was a beautiful story. It's exactly the kind of thing you should say on a date."

"Really?"

"Really." I looked at the clock. "Let's make the rice now."

I taught him how to make saffron rice *á la* Veronica.

The important part, as far as I was concerned, was the actual cooking of the chicken. He poured off the excess marinade into a bowl, then dumped the chicken into a hot, oiled skillet. I showed him how to flip the pan to turn the meat, and he picked up that skill in a surprisingly short time. He only lost a few pieces on the floor before getting the knack. Yoko Geri didn't mind in the least cleaning up after him.

After the chicken had browned, he added the marinade and turned the heat down to let the sauce reduce.

He seemed to get the idea of cooking until it was done, rather than for a specific, measured length of time. The cook's prerogative of trying the dish to see if it was ready was a big hit with him.

The result was delicious. Okay, so it was my recipe and I'd supervised, but Sitri had done all the actual cooking. He was as proud as a child who has made their first finger painting, and the light of his enthusiasm shone on his face. It made him even more attractive.

It would be easy to fall in love with somebody like him.

I just hoped, when the time came, that Artemis agreed. Because if she didn't go for him, it would not only be disastrous for two universes, I would probably do something embarrassing to get myself out of the friend zone.

CHAPTER 15

No Bikini Atoll

K ali and I were sprawled in her living room after gorging ourselves on fish and chips. It was time for the next step in the plan.

She sipped her tea. "We need a romantic place where they can have their first date. Any ideas?"

"If it was as simple as finding a romantic place for two people to talk over dinner we could reserve a private room at Maison Chandler. Of course, then Sitri wouldn't have a chance to show off his new cooking skills."

"That's not the big problem. If things go badly we need somewhere that's isolated enough that property damage and loss of life aren't issues."

I took a sip from my glass of beer. "An isolated place that's expendable and has a full kitchen. That's a tall order."

"Does it have to be a full kitchen?"

"More or less. The point is for him to cook for her so she knows the food isn't machine made."

"How about this?" She fired up her laptop and looked up "camp kitchens."

"Interesting. If he does most of the prep before the date one of those could work. Add a cooler or two and he'd be all set."

"Great. All we need is an actual location."

"I have an idea."

I borrowed her laptop and Googled "uninhabited islands." After eliminating islands for sale to rich people we zeroed in on actual islands with no inhabitants. Unfortunately, most of them were home to unique species that would be exterminated if their habitat was vapourized. That wasn't acceptable either.

The classic uninhabited island is the Pacific atoll. Possibly the most famous one is Bikini, the site of a couple of dozen nuclear tests almost 70 years ago, and the source of the name of the two-piece bathing suit. I have no idea why somebody thought that a nuclear test site would make a good name for a skimpy bathing suit. Maybe it was a reference to what bikinis did to men's brains at the time.

Bikini is almost deserted because of the lingering radiation. The only people who live there are a few caretakers at the other end of the atoll. After my own brush with radiation sickness, it didn't seem like a particularly good choice for a romantic getaway, even if they were both immune.

Bikini is one of the Marshall Islands, and while looking at the map of that group I noticed one atoll isolated from all the rest.

After a bit of research, we knew that Taongi Atoll is not only uninhabited, but as far as anybody knows, nobody has *ever* lived there. It seemed like a perfect choice.

I hoped that this operation wouldn't screw up like some of my others.

* * *

After a week of intensive training in how to be both a cook and a wonderful date, I don't know which of us was more tired. Sitri was cramming for the test, and I had tried to be a patient teacher. Kali had offered to help, but I told her I had it covered. I suspected she spent most of the week in bed with George while I had a Platonic week with Sitri the Hunk.

Kali and I scheduled the date for a Friday night. Of course, this had no significance to the lucky couple, but it gave us mere mortals the whole weekend to deal with whatever outcome there might be before we had to resume our normal lives.

Whatever normal was. I was beginning to forget.

Although he was unfamiliar with the term, he wanted me there as his wing man. I, in turn, wanted Kali there for back up. I told Kali he'd feel better with his friends around for support. I kept the secret of his virginity.

From our point of view, it was more like a military operation than a date. Sitri had been busy in the kitchen all day, but by six p.m. we were ready to start transporting our gear to the atoll.

Our jump medallions were wonderful devices, but they weren't magical. It took skill and precision to land somewhere that you'd never been before. Since Taongi was a small speck in the middle of a huge expanse of empty ocean, Kali and I let Sitri do the navigating.

There was a lot of equipment. It took several trips to move it all.

Being on the other side of the International Date Line, it was now around noon on the day *after* we'd left Calgary a second ago. With any luck, that was the most confusing thing we would run into.

An hour later, Kali left to fetch Artemis from the Upland. We expected it would take a couple of hours for her to get Artemis over any last minute jitters.

Taongi Atoll was unlike anything I'd imagined. I'd always thought of atolls as a small lagoon surrounded by a ring-shaped island covered with palm trees. Not even close.

I was standing on a white, coral sand beach looking west across an incredibly calm body of water. Eight or nine kilometres in front of me was the far edge of the lagoon, and there was no land on that side. Behind me, the island rose about a metre to a few tufts of bunch grass, and the first stands of beach naupaka. The naupaka bushes were definitely tropical-looking, with clusters of leaves that reminded me strongly of the hen-and-chicks that grew in my mother's rock garden. Their small, lopsided flowers smelled like honey.

I looked at the pile of supplies we'd brought, including the big, heavy containers of drinking water. There was no fresh water anywhere on the atoll, which is why nobody had ever lived there.

"How do you want to set this up?"

Sitri looked down the beach. The island curves inward toward the lagoon, so we could just about see to the south end from where we stood.

"I thought we'd start out walking along the beach," he said. "When we've gotten to the south end of the island it should be about the right time for making supper."

"That's good. She was told not to eat anything for a few hours before getting here, so she should want something by then. Kali and I will camp up here in case you need us. Otherwise, we'll stay out of your way."

I tried not to think about camping for a second time in a week. At least there were no mosquitoes here. In fact, I hadn't seen any insects at all. I wondered how the naupaka were pollinated.

"It should work if we put the kitchen near there."

We jumped the supplies to the far end of Sibylla, the largest islet in the atoll. It was about seven kilometres long, and three hundred metres wide, which gave them a lot of room to walk. I hadn't told him that the south end was a proposed nuclear test site in the 1950s that had never been used. I was hoping that the history didn't turn out to be prophetic.

The inland portion of the south end was mostly flat, with occasional shrubs rooted in coral rubble, and a few small coral boulders thrown up by storms. There were a large variety of birds everywhere, but nesting seemed to be limited to the areas with vegetation. Out in the open we found nothing that could be damaged.

Despite being surrounded by water, Taongi has an arid climate so the chances were overwhelmingly good that it would be a warm, dry, moonlit night. If there was a storm we would cancel everything. The highest point on the island was a whole three metres above sea level. Of course, in an emergency, we could always try to climb one of the tree Helio-tropes. That would get us maybe another five metres of height if they'd take our weight. One thing we didn't dare was to jump home and leave Sitri and Artemis on their own.

We set up the camp kitchen, including the food coolers that contained the only ice within a thousand kilometres. In theory, making dinner for two should be quick and easy. We'd also included a couple of bottles of good wine.

While we were there, I walked across the island to look at the open ocean. A line of breakers about 100 metres from shore showed the edge of the reef. If I had my directions right, the wind was coming in from the northeast. Their hopefully romantic walk would be on the leeward side where they'd just get a mild breeze. Perfect.

I set up our tent while we were waiting for Kali and Artemis to show up. I wasn't sure where she'd gotten it, but it looked new. The instructions were almost clear, and with Sitri's help I set it up on a flat stretch of gravel. We moved the other stuff inside, and that was that.

By my watch there should be at least another hour before Artemis showed up. Sitri was sitting on the beach wearing an open-necked shirt and shorts.

I went into the tent and emerged a few minutes later wearing my bathing suit. I wasn't going to let this opportunity go to waste.

The bottom of the lagoon was mostly covered with living coral. I had to find a place where the beach extended into the water so I didn't hurt anything. The water was warm and completely clear as I waded in.

I hadn't thought much about travel before the Kalevala affair, and here I was swimming in a tropical lagoon in the middle of the Pacific Ocean. I didn't care much that the fate of three universes might be decided in the next few hours when a school of brightly coloured fish swam underneath me.

There was a splash next to me. Sitri had taken his shirt off.

"Try these," he said. He held out a pair of diving goggles to me. I no longer wondered where he got things like that.

The goggles made everything ten times better. Now I could dive and look at the reef from a fish's viewpoint. I promised myself that someday I'd take scuba lessons so I wouldn't have to keep surfacing.

Sitri dove with me for a while, then headed back to the beach. The next time I surfaced, he was back in his clothes and looked completely dry.

I swam for a while longer, then returned to shore. I used a towel to dry myself so I wouldn't be crusted with salt. It was nearly time.

* * *

At three o'clock Kali and Artemis appeared. Artemis looked much as she had when we'd first met, with her hair up in a chignon and wearing a green, knee-length chiton. Surprisingly, Kali was dressed the same way. It seemed that Artemis wanted her own wing woman along. For a moment I worried we'd have to keep Sitri from accidentally touching the dresses but the fabric was moving normally. Artemis must have made them from Midland material.

It was a good thing that I'd dressed before they arrived. I didn't want to have to explain to Artemis why I was wearing next to nothing in front of the man who was going to be her date.

"Artemis," Kali said formally, "I'd like you to meet Sitri. He's the man we told you about."

As we'd planned, Sitri got down on one knee.

"Artemis, goddess of the hunt, of the walnut tree, and friend of young girls, may I present this small token of the great esteem in which I hold you." He had a tiny cooler with him which he opened and brought out a dish filled with ugly, handmade brown spheres.

She frowned as I took them from him, and kneeling, presented them to her. She had no idea what to do with them.

"Taste one," Kali suggested.

Apparently, the concept of having a party in your mouth was previously unknown in the Upland. The look on her face was one of nearly sexual ecstasy.

"What are those?"

"Chocolate truffles with walnuts and Cointreau," I said. "Sitri made them by hand, specially for your enjoyment."

"By hand?" The term itself seemed to confuse her.

"He assembled the ingredients himself, by skill alone, and without any technological help." It was a small white lie, but by her standards chilling them in a refrigerator didn't count.

What she didn't know was that the discharge-dampening nanites were in the truffles. We'd just made it equally possible for her to hold hands with a Downlander, or to strangle him. Time would tell.

"Why don't you two take a walk and get to know one another?" Kali suggested. "We'll wait here in case you need anything."

Sitri held out his hand. Artemis wasn't ready to go that far with a man, especially one she'd just met, no matter how many truffles he gave her. She did consent to walking along the beach in the same direction he was going, with about a meter and a half of space between them. The cooler and truffles went with them.

Kali and I made our way through the bushes to the eastern side of the island. We sat on the sand to listen to the surf and watch the birds.

"Do you think we'll live to see the sunrise?" I asked.

"Do you believe in miracles?" She countered.

I took in the incredible vista in front of us.

"Sitting here, with this view? Yes, I do."

Sunset was at quarter to seven, so we returned to our tent around six o'clock to cook our own supper. That took half an hour. By the time we'd eaten, the sun was touching the horizon across the lagoon.

"I wonder what's happening?" Kali said after we'd finished.

"So far there haven't been any explosions. That has to be good, right?"

We looked off toward the south. Nothing was visible in the darkness.

After another 15 minutes I said, "The suspense is killing me."

Kali stood and brushed the sand off her legs. "Perhaps I'll take a walk," she said casually.

"Perhaps I'll come with you. Just to walk off supper, of course."

"Of course."

She headed north to where our islet was separated from its neighbour by a narrow channel. That way we didn't have to slog through the bushes to get to the other side of Sibylla.

We walked along the beach for a while as the moon rose. The silver trail of moonlight across the ocean, combined with the massive number of stars overhead, was almost overwhelming. It was romantic, but I might have been tempted to ignore the person I was with and just commune with nature. Kali brought my attention back to our unstated objective.

"Let's take a shortcut. You drive."

I took her hand and we jumped close to the south end of the islet.

"It's not like we're spying," she whispered as we made our way through the bushes toward where we'd set up the kitchen.

"Of course not. We're just concerned about them."

The coral crunched underfoot, which made our approach much less stealthy than I'd have preferred. It turned out we needn't have bothered whispering.

There was a brilliant, blue-white flash and a sharp explosion. The concussion knocked us to the ground. A beach naupaka broke Kali's fall. I hit gravel. Purple blotches danced in front of my eyes, rendering me effectively blind, and all I could hear was a high-pitched whistling in my ears. I crawled toward where Kali had been a moment before and found her by touch.

Once I found her, we huddled together under the remains of the bush while the electric-blue discharge continued.

Neither of us said anything. We just clung to each other as more explosions shook the night. They were getting longer, more frequent, and each was followed by a shock wave that made the vegetation shake. We put our fingers in our ears, but that didn't stop the ringing. At least we could shield our eyes from the glare so our sight had more-or-less returned to normal. The explosions were coming from just ahead.

"We have to do something," Kali yelled in my ear after the fourth explosion in half as many minutes. I nodded to let her know I'd understood and started crawling in the direction of the detonations. I didn't know how we could stop a goddess and a demon from fighting to the death, but we had to try.

We moved from bush to bush, hoping to keep out of the line of fire until we knew what was going on. When we got to a bush about fifty metres away, we stopped.

"Wow," Kali yelled in my ear, "That's never happened to me."

The discharges didn't act like normal electricity. Instead of one quick spark when their two bodies touched, each point of contact created a new energy surge so they looked like they were covered in lightning.

They were lying on the charred remains of the blanket we'd spread near the camp kitchen. At some point Sitri had lost his shirt, and Artemis was running her hands over his chest. Her fingers left trails of ionized air and more lightning behind them.

The real fireworks were happening further up. Every time they kissed, a blue bolt of energy leaped between them, causing the concussion wave. It didn't seem to hurt them but we had to shield our eyes as their lips met.

His hand was on her calf, also leaving ionization trails, and slowly moving upward toward what remained of her chiton.

"I wonder which base he'll get to?" Kali said during a lull when they were just running their hands over each other and gazing fondly into each others eyes through the lightning.

Oh, oh.

"Run," I yelled. I sprinted as fast as I could while bent over double. Kali was close behind.

"What's wrong? Don't you want to see what happens?"

"Stay if you want to, pervert, but if that's what a kiss is like, I want to be at minimum safe distance when somebody has an orgasm."

Kali jumped. In the excitement I'd forgotten about our medallions. It would have been funny if it hadn't almost gotten me killed.

* * *

She was back at camp when I arrived a second later. The flashes from the south end of the island were lasting longer and becoming more spectacular. Each one was followed about 20 seconds later by the crack of the detonation. My ears were recovering. My medical nanites must be on the job.

"Do you think we'll be safe here?"

"We should be. This is about where the observation post would have been built when they were going to set off a nuke on this island."

Kali and I sat on the beach and watched the fireworks.

Half an hour later there was a much larger flash that lit up most of the lagoon. I didn't wait for the concussion.

"My place," I said, grabbing her hand.

We appeared in my living room. Yoko Geri was standing sideways with his back arched, and staring at us. I approached him slowly, and he calmed down as I petted him.

"Sorry, fur face. We didn't mean to startle you."

According to the clock it was about two in the morning.

I picked some naupaka leaves out of my hair. "I doubt that either of them will miss us until at least sunrise. We should spend the night here so we can move out at first light."

"Sounds good. That would be just about noon Calgary time."

"A sensible time to get up."

* * *

We got up earlier, but not much. After an early lunch we jumped back to the atoll. The sun still hadn't made an appearance. As far as we could see, the north end of the island was still intact, although small branches and leaves dotted the ground.

"Should we just wait here for them?"

"I was thinking about that. We should see how much damage they did during the night. It'll give us an idea of what to expect in the future."

"Do you think this will turn into more than a one-night stand?"

"Neither of them strike me as casual sex types. Whether the relationship lasts or not is a different question."

We walked south along the beach. The full moon was still up, although skimming the western horizon. I'd never seen a moon set over the ocean before. It was incredibly beautiful.

So far everything looked normal.

"Gods, we're stupid," Kali said suddenly. "If we walk on the east side, we can see the sunrise."

The sky was beginning to lighten in the east. The breakers a hundred metres from shore were audible but barely visible. The water was gently lapping on the coral sands at our feet. A deep orange glow was illuminating the bottoms of some scattered clouds.

One spot on the horizon was brighter than the rest. Gradually the orange turned to yellow and then a brilliant spot appeared as the sun came into view. The sky slowly turned blue.

It was terribly romantic. I was glad to share the experience with my best friend, but I really wished that...

"I wish George was here," Kali said, hugging me. It looked like I wasn't the only one who wished that the nearest unoccupied male was closer than 560 kilometres away. At least we'd chosen a good place for a date.

After watching the sunrise we resumed our walk along the beach.

"Do you want to jump closer?" Kali asked.

"No. We don't know what shape the end of the island is in. I'd hate to jump onto a bed of molten rock or something."

We didn't see any blast damage until we were almost at the south end. It was slight, considering. There were a lot of leaves on the ground. The area where things were obliterated wasn't much more than fifteen metres across. Score one for the nanites.

We found the happy couple wrapped in each other. The blanket was completely incinerated. In the morning light, the glow surrounding them was bearable. The remains of their clothes were scattered around the area as a few smouldering, charred rags. Two of the wine bottles were empty and lying, partially melted, in the sand beside them.

The crunching of our footsteps in the gravel woke Sitri, who raised his head to see what was happening.

"Oh," he said. "Hi."

"Have a nice time?" Kali said. I poked her in the ribs.

"Yes, thank you." He looked around and realized he had nothing wearable. "Um, I need new clothes."

"I'm on it," Kali said. She vanished.

Artemis opened her eyes and gave Sitri a sleepy smile.

"More?" She stretched, and her bare feet popped out from beneath his leg as she wiggled her toes. The lightning was tolerable.

"We have company."

She turned, saw me, and gave a little shriek.

"What are you doing here? Where's Kali?"

"We were just making sure you were all right. Kali went off to get new clothes for both of you."

Artemis blushed all the way down to her navel, which set Sitri off as well.

"I'll leave you two alone."

Kali reappeared in different clothes, a shirt and shorts draped over one arm, and the chiton she'd been wearing draped over the other. I took them from her and put them on one of the coolers that was still intact.

"We'll be back at our camp. Try not to destroy these clothes too."

Kali wanted to stay, but I pulled her away from the love nest so we could walk back to our camp.

"I thought I was the pervert of the family," I said as we walked along the wet sand by the lagoon.

"I'm not a pervert. I'm just curious. Nobody's ever studied the mating habits of demons and gods before."

She was the mythology expert. I'd take her word for it.

As we walked we heard faint laughter carried by the breeze, and two naked people ran across the beach. I noticed that the one with flowing black hair was doing the chasing as they threw themselves into the water.

"I don't think we have to worry about them fighting," Kali said. From that distance they were tiny. Detail was lacking, but after splashing around for a while the two tiny figures merged into one. There was a definite blue sparkle around them in the water that was a lot less noticeable in the sunlight. There was a haze over the surface like steam. It looked like water didn't ground the discharge.

"No, I'm pretty sure that fighting isn't what they are thinking about. I'm surprised that Artemis was willing to move that fast."

"I'm not," Kali said. "When I went to get her yesterday, I found she'd had a revelation since we last saw her. The key was you telling her that nobody could prevent a goddess like her from doing what she wanted. Her narcissism actually allowed her to overcome her fear of Hera, and her anger with her father. She decided that if the date we'd lined up for her was as decent as we said, she'd pretty much throw herself at him to spite her parents. She was tired of waiting, and trying to satisfy other people's desires. I bet you that with him acting like a gentleman instead of the typical gods and satyrs she's used to, he had her at the truffles, and definitely with dinner."

Shortly after we got back to our camp, a sharp detonation rolled down the beach toward us. The two love birds had left the water and were doing something on the beach. At least, that's where the speck of sun-bright glow was. It didn't take any imagination to guess what was happening.

"I believe our work here is done," I said.

We packed up our camping gear and transported it back to Kali's place in three trips. One of the reasons why I don't like camping is that you have to do a lot of packing, unpacking, and transporting. It seems like a lot of effort.

Kali found a piece of cardboard, a marker pen, and some butcher twine. I wrote a short note to the happy couple, and jumped back to the atoll to tie the sign to a bush where they would see it.

Gone home to give you some privacy. Let us know when you get back. P.S. - No littering. Bring the sign and everything else back with you.

I'd gone way over the 30 hours covered by my retainer, so now all I had to do was to bill my client, and hope like hell that Sitri could keep Artemis too busy to destroy the world.

I also had to get over a vague feeling of jealousy that I wasn't the one having Sitri ring my chimes. Stupid of me, I know, but hormones have no conscience.

Ain't love grand?

CHAPTER 16

Going to Bat for a Loved One

I felt like I'd hit the bottom of a long, terrifying water slide. The blind date on Taongi Atoll made a big splash followed by sudden deceleration and then—calm.

We'd found the killer, and she'd been, if not punished, at least stopped. The image of fourteen-year old Eric haunted me, but there was no court that was competent to try Artemis, even if she agreed to abide by its decision. I decided to take the win and be done with it.

Minus the retainer, Sitri owed me 139,000 dollars. To make myself feel better I asked him not to counterfeit gold coins on his next trip to Nigeria. It turned out he only did that because he needed the money in a hurry and had to chase the banking hours across several time zones. He assured me that, in the future, he would make a variety of raw nuggets of several metals and spread them out over different markets.

He even returned the kitchen equipment he'd borrowed, apologized for the damage, and replaced the items that had been melted or charred during his hot date rather than waiting for me to bill him for them. His social skills were improving.

The next surprise was one that I hadn't expected for at least several months.

"Do you know a good psychologist?"

"Several. Why?"

He looked bashful, like a young boy who is about to confess that he likes a cute girl in his class.

"Artemis and I want to stay in Midland, and it would help if she could get some counselling for what she's been through."

"Wow, that's some turn around. Is she starting to get over her narcissism?"

"That's something else unusual. She's already over it."

"What? It's only been two days."

"As nearly as I can tell, the—um—multiple discharges normalized her brain a lot faster than if she'd just waited here like I did. That was completely unexpected."

I'm an evil person. "You're saying that screwing her brains out has screwed her brains in?"

He thought for a moment, probably trying to parse the idioms and decide if the statement was true. He blushed when he got it.

"Yes, " he said. "I feel better too."

"I'll bet you do."

He blushed again. A lust demon blushing over a pretty girl: that will never get old for me.

"I believe I had some residual sociopathy that has now been resolved," he said formally.

"All right, but I'll have to prepare the psychologist so she doesn't automatically assume that Artemis is delusional. You and I will probably have to do that together."

"Whatever you need. I just want her to be happy."

"That's a good sign for both of you."

This was going to be extremely interesting.

* * *

I called that afternoon. "Hi Trinity. It's Veronica Chandler."

"This is an unexpected pleasure. What have you been up to?"

I couldn't help it. I burst into laughter at the unintentionally loaded question.

"That's a long story that you need to hear. Right now, I know someone who needs a psychologist who is willing to treat an unusual client with a unique background. This is a particularly sensitive situation, and you'll want me to explain it to you in person."

"I see. Given several of the other clients you've directed to me, this one must be *quite* unusual. Can you give me a hint?"

"The client is a woman with a long history of an abusive family. It's her situation that makes it complicated."

"I prefer to ask the client about her situation myself."

"I hate to be mysterious, but trust me, you'll want a separate explanation before you see her so you can put her in context."

"All right, I'll trust your judgment. When did you have in mind?"

"As soon as you are free. The sooner she's in therapy, the sounder I'll sleep."

"Why? Is she prone to violent episodes?"

My mind went back to the *faux*-lightning on Taongi Atoll, and a teenage boy slumped on his bedroom floor.

"Definitely."

There was a pause. I assumed she was consulting her calendar.

"How long do you think this briefing will take?"

That was a hell of a question too.

"At a minimum, let's say three hours."

"That definitely qualifies as a long story. Tomorrow morning, seven o'clock, my office. My first scheduled appointment is at ten so we can't go overtime."

"Done."

"This patient had better be worth it."

"She is, in both senses. I'm not worried in the least about disappointing you, nor is this case *pro bono*."

She must have heard something in my voice.

"Then what is worrying you?"

"That we'll all end up in the psych ward together."

* * *

The next morning I collected Sitri at an unholy hour, and we drove to Trinity's office. It felt odd to be driving after all the jumping around I'd been doing. I suppose we could have jumped, just to give her one more piece of "context," but I didn't want to risk giving her a heart attack. I also didn't want to be seen by anyone else.

Her office was in a normal house in a residential neighbourhood. There was no identifying sign out front.

She was surprised that I had someone with me.

"Is this the person you were telling me about?" She asked.

"No, this is the client's boyfriend, Sitri. He's here to help with the explanations."

Sitri was wearing his suit, which made him look both reputable and dashing. He shook her hand. "I'm happy to meet you, Doctor."

She pointedly looked at what I had in my hand.

"Why are you carrying a baseball bat?"

"That's part of the explanation."

She raised one eyebrow. Spock could not have done it better.

"Then we'd better get to it."

We went to her office and she closed the door. I opted for the "rip the bandage off quickly" method. It seemed easier and faster than trying to convince her of all the weirdness one piece at a time.

"Firstly, would you please examine the bat?"

I handed it to her, and she looked it over.

"It's a baseball bat. What am I looking for?" She handed it back.

"Sitri is a demon. He recently met a nice goddess who had an abusive childhood, and she wants to get over it so they can continue their relationship."

She didn't even pause. "I see. May I assume that you are speaking metaphorically again?"

"No, literally. And our sessions never were metaphorical."

I stood up and swung the bat as hard as I could at Sitri's head. It bounced off with a metallic clank. The vibration nearly made me drop it. Ow. Despite that, I brought it down again on top of his head.

Trinity was out of her chair almost as fast as I was. While I shook my hand to get some feeling back in it, I saw her staring at Sitri who, of course, was sitting calmly in his chair, very much alive and unharmed.

"What do you think you are doing?"

I sat down again, and handed her the bat, handle first.

"We could spend a lot of time trying to convince you that we aren't crazy or lying. That Sitri is literally a demon. That his girlfriend is literally a goddess, and that she's desperately in need of therapy. This seemed like the easiest way to convince you that we aren't dealing in metaphors."

Trinity carefully took the dented baseball bat from me. She examined it and then put it aside well out of reach of either Sitri or me.

"Are you sure you are all right?" She asked Sitri.

"Never better. It would take a nuclear weapon to hurt me."

"Are you being literal again?"

He smiled. "I'm told that it's one of my failings."

She looked thoughtful for a moment, then picked up a notebook and pen.

"I must say, Veronica, you certainly make my life interesting. All right, which goddess?"

Explanations took all three hours, and she still had questions.

"So these nanites allow you to speak any language?"

"Not any language. Just the top five thousand or so."

She expressed her doubt in Hindi. I told her that we didn't have time for this in the same language. She told me not to be impertinent in Irish. Sounding like I'd been raised in Dublin, I told her that we weren't being impertinent, and she needed to believe us.

She put her pen away and closed her notebook.

"Very well," she said. "You were right. I'm not disappointed by your judgment as to what constitutes unusual or unique. I'll clear some time in my schedule and handle the case myself."

"I know you are trained not to freak out when a client tells you something shocking, but even so, you are taking this surprisingly well," I said.

"Blame my upbringing. What you have been calling demons seem more like the *asuras* of Hinduism, who can be either good or evil, and are half brothers to the *devas*, or gods, who are also more complex than Western ideas of divinity. The concepts that we've covered today aren't as unfamiliar to me as you might think."

"Thank you, Doctor MacMillan," Sitri said. "Your help means a lot to me." He offered her his hand. There was the slightest delay before she shook it.

"Don't thank me yet. Long-term abuse can be nearly impossible to treat, but I'll do my best. The fact that Artemis actually wants help is a big step forward."

We rose to go, and Sitri reached into his jacket and handed her a bundle.

"I almost forgot, Artemis is new here, so I'll be paying for her sessions. Please let me know when you need more."

She looked at the stack of hundred dollar bills, neatly bound with an official Bank of Canada band.

I found her stunned look amusing. "I told you this case wasn't *pro bono.* And before you ask, the money is real and was gotten more or less legitimately."

She riffled through the bills. "Is this *ten thousand* dollars?"

Sitri pulled out another bundle. "Isn't it enough?"

"Yes, it's entirely enough for now. Thank you."

CHAPTER 17

Ethics

I was sitting in my comfy chair with my legs up on the coffee table. Yoko Geri was sitting in the trough between them, looking at me with his big eyes and purring as I scratched the side of his neck.

I had several decisions to make. None of them were at all easy. My last demon-infested case had required me to tamper with a witness' memories so I could introduce evidence that saved three lives. Maybe the ends justified the means, but that wasn't who I wanted to be. I was determined to make the right choices this time.

I'd gotten more information about the medical nanites by having Sitri retrieve the full technical specification and user manual from the Downland. It took me a long time to wade through all the material, especially since there were a lot of technical terms that didn't exist in English.

The nanites full capabilities were startling to say the least.

Once they were in a healthy body they reproduced until there was at least one in every cell. That took a while, and the person had to eat a lot during that phase.

Once there were enough of them, they fixed every known genetic disorder. If I'd ever had the genes responsible for Huntington's disease, cystic fibrosis or breast cancer they were gone. I could no longer pass on anything bad I'd inherited. The list of repairs was impressively long.

Several of them were unknown in Midland because we hadn't figured out what caused aging yet.

The nanites did far more than just repair wear and tear on the body. They mended a lot of small genetic problems that evolution can't get rid of because they don't become serious until after the age when most people have already passed them on to their children.

The nanites fixed them. All the accumulated mistakes in our genes that fail to maintain our bodies properly as we get older. Gone.

Once that phase was complete, the nanites recorded the repaired genome so they could fix any future mutations. That just happened to prevent any environmentally caused cancers as well.

The nanites didn't try to fix existing structural problems unless they were associated with trauma. If I'd broken my arm before getting them and it was set improperly, they wouldn't straighten it. If I broke my arm *while* I had them they'd make it good as new. The manual didn't say exactly how they straightened the bones, and I wasn't sure I wanted to know.

There was a reference to getting such things repaired before giving a person the nanites, as if all structural problems could be cured by one treatment. The manual's author must have considered the treatment so common and obvious that it wasn't worth mentioning in detail.

If I could find out what was involved, I might be able to solve my hormone problem.

As I'd been told, we could still be killed by inflicting enough damage that critical organs would die before the nanites could make repairs. In practice that meant something like a bullet to the brain, or being completely incinerated. Being shot multiple times anywhere in the body probably wouldn't do it unless there were enough bullets of large enough calibre to make the body into hamburger.

We could be starved or asphyxiated, but the nanites would still try their best to keep us alive for as long as possible by putting us in what amounted to suspended animation. Nobody had actually tried it, but calculations indicated that starving to death would take about five years.

Even a bullet through the heart wasn't necessarily fatal. The nanites would immediately induce suspended animation, stop the bleeding, and bind together to create a mechanical pump to keep blood circulating. The suspended animation meant the pump didn't need to be as big as a real heart. While that was going on, the heart tissue would be repaired at much faster than normal rate.

Cuts or punctures would stop bleeding within seconds and heal within hours if the nanites were present in the normal numbers. Kali's stab wound had taken days to heal because Beleth had just given her a portion of her nanites and there weren't enough for instant healing. Still, the bleeding had stopped within seconds. If the same thing happened now, she wouldn't even need to miss work the next day.

If I lost a leg it could be reattached simply by holding the two stumps together. The nanites in the leg itself would put it into suspended animation to keep it alive while those in the body recreated the blood vessel connections. Others would repair the bone, muscle, and nerves. I'd be able to walk on the leg within a day or two, assuming that I ate enough food to fuel the reconstruction.

I already knew that the nanites would attack any invading organism, from viruses to parasites. Screwy proteins fell into that class, so I was also immune to prion diseases and something called advanced glycation end-products that caused skin wrinkles and macular degeneration. Likewise with poisons, unless it was a massive dose of something that acted almost instantly. By massive they meant chugging a litre of cyanide, or breathing an atmosphere that was pure hydrogen sulphide for an extended period.

Metabolic garbage, both inside and outside my cells, that couldn't be handled by normal body processes was broken down and used as fuel.

The nanites would even block pain impulses if asked to do so. They would also act automatically if there was trauma so the person could ignore the wound while getting away from, or dealing with, the cause. The pain would last just long enough to let you know that you were hurt. Belphegor had only hurt for a moment when he punched me, but he still had to be careful of his broken hand. If he'd tried to use it, the nanites would have given him another jolt of pain to remind him.

Kali and I were, for most definitions of the word, immortal. That introduced some incredibly difficult problems into our lives.

Right now I was just concentrating on one of the small ones. If I could solve that one then maybe the others would look less intimidating.

Yoko slowly closed his eyes, enjoying the petting.

He was now two and a half years old, which was the equivalent of about 26 in human terms. According to his vet he could expect an average life span of 12 to 15 years, although a lot of cats were around longer. One of the vet's patients was 25.

I'd always intended to take care of him for the rest of his life; this was his Forever Home. Intellectually I knew that I'd live longer than he would, but now I was forced to consider that I'd live longer than hundreds of cats. Maybe millions.

The manual said that the nanites were optimized for human bodies, but should work on anything with a similar physiology. A crab or snake would be poor candidates but they would work on a cat.

If they did, Yoko Geri wouldn't have to die. We could be together, if not forever, then at least for a very long time.

The same thing applied to friends and family, of course. The difference was that they were independent, sentient creatures who could give informed consent. A cat couldn't.

Or could he? Hell, my life lately was defined by miracles.

I picked up my phone and made a call.

Sitri had moved out of his motel and gotten an apartment with Artemis, so I wasn't sure who would answer.

"Hello?" There was static on the phone and feminine giggling in the background. Shit.

"Hi Sitri. I'm sorry, did I catch you at a bad time? I can call back later."

"No, it's okay. We were just, um, finishing up." I heard outright laughter in the background. Also bird song and wind. Were they outdoors?

"Can I borrow you for an hour or so? I need to ask you some—"

There was a burst of static on the phone. "Stop that! I'm trying to talk!"

"—questions. Are you sure you're available?"

"Yes, I can be there in a few minutes if you wish."

"Thanks. Just pop into the living room."

"Do you mind if Artemis comes too?" She started laughing again. I heard Sitri speak away from the phone, "I didn't mean it that way!"

"Sure, bring her along. I'll make hot chocolate."

They arrived 15 minutes later, which I assumed was just enough time for a quick shower and putting on some clothes. Artemis was making up for lost time, and some days I suspected her libido made me look like a nun.

I got them installed on the sofa and brought out the chocolate. Artemis liked it even more than Midland wines.

They sat at opposite ends of the sofa so there wouldn't be any accidents requiring me to get a new sofa or apartment.

She looked adorable with a foam moustache. "What's up?"

"I've been thinking about the translator nanites."

Sitri looked puzzled. "Okay."

"As I understand it, when I try to speak they process brain activity associated with language, and then hijack the muscles that would have spoken in the original language."

"That's right."

"And when I hear another language they guess which one it is and hijack the nerve impulses from the ears so I hear English."

"Not quite. You have probably noticed that you still hear the other language faintly. The hijacking, as you call it, takes place in the language centre itself."

"Okay, great. What do you know about sign language?"

Artemis licked the chocolate off her lips and frowned. "The language of signs?"

"No, it's a language made of symbolic gestures used by deaf people so they can communicate without writing things down."

They both looked blank, so I fired up my laptop and showed them a YouTube video of a person demonstrating American Sign Language.

"That's a fascinating solution. We don't have anything like that, of course. Nobody in Downland is deaf."

"Upland either."

"Would it be possible to modify the translators to handle a language like that?"

"I don't see why not. The person's brain is undoubtedly processing the signs through their language centre. In principle, it should be no different from reading another language by looking at a page of symbols."

"We could find somebody to make the modifications if you want to be able to understand sign language," Artemis said.

"I had something else in mind. I want to be able to ask Yoko Geri a question and get his answer. We suspect cats communicate by a combination of vocalizations, smell, and body language."

The goddess and the demon both looked stunned.

"I don't think anybody's ever tried anything like that before," he said.

"Can it be done?"

"We'll have to get back to you."

* * *

It was almost three weeks before Sitri called back.

"I have an answer for you. It's possible, but not the way we expected. The translators can't handle what you want."

"Why not?"

"Think of it this way. If you purposely made a sign language gesture, it would go through your brain's language centre. If you waved your hand similarly for another reason, it wouldn't. The translator software can easily be modified to handle sign language because it is intentional. You *intend* to communicate in that way."

"I understand. I read that cats will sometimes wash to relieve stress, but the nanites can't tell the difference between normal washing for cleanliness and an instinctive response that means 'I'm stressed.' Am I right?"

"Something like that. However, there's another way of handling this. Imagine that we don't have a language in common. If I say something you may be able to guess what I mean. When you get it, I confirm that you are right, and we both feel satisfaction that we've successfully communicated. That goes both ways, of course."

"How does that help me?"

"We can set up a learning loop so that his brain activity is transmitted to you. Your degree of understanding is fed back to him and when you understand his concept the nanites will learn to associate the activity with the concept. The reverse happens as well, so eventually you and your cat will learn to understand the internal languages. As a beneficial side effect you'll be able to understand each others emotions. "

I had to process that for a minute.

"Are you telling me that you can put me in telepathic communication with Yoko Geri?"

"Effectively, yes."

"Holy crap. Will it work with others?"

"Yes and no. You'd have to give the nanites to the other person, and you'd also have to learn the internal language of each individual person you wanted to communicate with. Each individual would require nanites on different communication channels or the whole system would become terribly confused. It should be easier with your cat, assuming that they don't have the same variety of concepts that we do. Of course, if it's just you and Yoko Geri you won't need multiple channels."

"How long will it take to learn to talk to each other?"

"Nobody is sure. If you are diligent, maybe a few weeks. This has never been done with a cat before. The only research was originally used with dolphins."

"You guys can talk to *dolphins*?"

"Before the Incident, yes. Afterwards, they lost interest in the project. Their language is acoustic, so it was a much simpler problem."

"Is there any risk involved?"

"Not much. We have no idea what a cat's mind is like, but you can turn off the link as easily as you can turn off your translators. The only risk is that you might be overwhelmed by the alien thoughts and be unable to remember how to turn them off. For that reason I had the technicians include a fail-safe that cuts the link after a short time if you fail to respond. Nobody knows how much of a risk that is, but in theory it shouldn't be much of a problem. If you are thinking of getting dressed, you know those are your thoughts because cats don't wear clothes."

"Okay. That makes sense."

"But if you are feeling hungry, is it your thought or the cat's? The source of any concepts you have in common might become confused. For example, you might feel hungry right after a meal."

"The safety cut-out would terminate the link if I get confused?"

"Yes. It might not happen at all, but I wanted to make sure you are as safe as possible. Are you sure you want to do this?"

I could feel my stubbornness rising. I would be damned if I'd make a decision on immortality for anybody without their informed consent. When I was this close I wasn't going to back away. Otherwise, I'd spend the rest of my long life wondering if I'd done the right thing.

"Yes, I'm sure. When can we do it?"

"Now, if you wish."

"All right, come over. Let's get this over with."

When Sitri appeared, I was sitting on the sofa with Yoko Geri. He sensed something was going on, and wasn't happy that I was trying to hold him. I wondered what cues I was giving off to make him feel that way. I'd know soon enough.

"One last question: if I break the link does he have any residual weirdness going on in his brain? I mean, he won't still be aware of being connected to a human, will he?"

"No, he shouldn't feel any differently than he does now. After the mistakes I've made, I also had the technicians include an external shutdown command. If things don't go as planned and the automatic shut-off doesn't work, I can deactivate the nanites for both of you."

It was astonishing how much trust had developed in our friendship compared with when we first met. I took a deep breath and let it out. "All right, let's do this."

He took a small box from his pocket. Inside were two tiny pills. They weren't red or blue, but an unappetizing dull grey. I got a blob of Yoko's favourite cat food, which interested him greatly, and put one pill inside it. He ate it without any difficulty. I took my pill at the same time.

I waited until he was finished eating. "I don't feel anything."

"Give it a few minutes. They have to figure out what they're doing."

I sat on the sofa. A minute later Yoko sauntered out of the kitchen licking his lips. This time he wanted to be on my lap, and I wondered if this was the last time his motivations would be mysterious to me.

I scratched him gently between his ears, and felt something in my own head. It was like hearing an unfamiliar word, except that whatever it was, it wasn't pronounceable.

Pleasure?

"How do you feel?"

Sitri's words startled me. "I'm okay. I think I just learned my first word of Cat."

I had the sensation of hearing two unknown words, and now one of them was replaced by "pleasure." That probably made sense if Yoko was thinking two things at once.

Happiness? No. *Contentment?* Yes. Pleasure-contentment.

He looked directly at me, his purr vibrating my legs. He slowly closed his eyes, and just as slowly opened them.

Trust.

* * *

Over the next several weeks, I worked on my telepathic connection with Yoko Geri. It was an unbelievable experience. There's a big difference between getting to know someone and literally getting inside their head. Especially when that someone isn't human.

We started with concepts. Pleasure, contentment, trust, hunger, love, annoyance. These led to comparisons: politely interested in a snack versus starving.

Of course cats don't use English grammar. The software was good at filling in the blanks, so after a while what I heard in my head was more-or-less proper English. A lot things that require humans to use grammar were implied when cats communicated. The flick of a tail would literally mean *not-care,* with the subject and object implied by it being *his* tail and *you* being the only other person present. Humans needed to say. "I don't care what you think." I have no idea what my sentences sounded like at his end of the conversation.

We settled one long-standing question pretty quickly: Do cats love us or are we just warm furniture with opposable thumbs?

Yoko Geri loved me. Partially because I was warm, soft, fed him, cleaned his litter box, and stroked his fur. That might sound mercenary, but I loved him because he was warm, soft, soothed me with his purr, and kept me company at night.

He also loved me for a reason that wasn't terribly complimentary.

I was his kitten-mother. I took care of him like an incompetent mother who didn't know how to wash him properly, but I was also an over-sized, incompetent kitten. He liked to think that he was taking care of me. Cats take things as they are, rather than wishing they were different, so although I wasn't a terribly smart kitten, he still loved me and appreciated my occasional cleverness. Imagine using a bathtub full of water instead of a tongue to wash oneself! I found that out when he was watching me soak in the tub. He didn't care for it himself, but he was still proud of me for overcoming my seeming disability of being unable to lick my own butt.

He had even learned to appreciate my habit of using my paws to wash him instead of using my tongue. That was how he interpreted me stroking his fur, which in itself was an act of affection showing that I recognized him as the dominant cat.

It also turned out that cats are, in general, inherently more sensible than we are. Rather than using words or actions that might be misinterpreted, they granted consent by sticking around. If he didn't want attention, he would simply leave. It's their equivalent of saying no. If the other cat still tries to do the rejected thing, lack of consent is enforced with an angry hiss, and ultimately with teeth and claws.

That humans find this difficult to understand is just another way in which we are unskilled kittens.

Like most people owned by cats, I had sometimes wondered how to get away if Yoko was sitting on me when I needed to go somewhere. The answer, in his terms, was obvious. If I didn't want to be there, I should just move. It was what was expected. He wouldn't be offended.

My first mistake was in trying to pose my question to him the way I would have asked another human. *"Would you like to live forever?"*

He seemed confused by that. *"I will live forever."*

Now it was my turn to be confused. *"Nobody lives forever. Except Kali and me. You can live forever too."*

"I will live forever." We still weren't communicating. He was just agreeing with me, as if I'd said that Chicken Feast is tasty.

It took a while for me to understand that the problem with my question was that there was no way for him to answer it. It made no sense to a cat's conceptions of life and time.

Humans live in a large community, and we are constantly communicating to each other the news that other people die. It's part of almost every story we tell each other. We also keep track of history, so we know that people used to live long ago and are now dead. If only as an intellectual exercise, humans know that they will die someday, and their ability to create the mathematical concept of an average life span means they can even guess approximately when. The statistics said I should live to 82, which meant I would have died somewhere around 2076 if I'd never gotten my nanites.

Except for a few weeks at the Humane Society, Yoko had spent his entire life in my apartment. The only cats he knew were humans, or strangers he could see wandering by outside. Nobody in his world had ever died, so the concept wasn't one he could take seriously. Empathy with another creature's death is not a useful thing for a predator to have. Cats had never thought to look at a formerly-alive mouse and think *there but for the grace of Bast go I*. Prey was alive, and then it was food.

It was difficult to explain death. The lie that it's like "sleeping but you never wake up" that adults tell human children made no sense to him at all. You sleep, then you wake up. Most often you are just dozing, and the slightest thing will wake you. He thought that not waking up sounded like something incompetent kittens might do if they were really stupid.

That something might consider *him* as prey and turn him into food simply didn't occur to Yoko. When a mouse somehow got into the apartment it was up to him to catch it. To his knowledge, there was no mightier killer in the world than him. Except, possibly, me. After all, despite an apparently complete lack of hunting skills, I somehow managed to bring home enough food for the two of us. Especially that scrumptious Chicken Feast that I occasionally caught.

The other concept that was different for cats was time.

Cats don't look at the clock and say to themselves, "it's about three hours until supper time." They just cruise along doing cat things until they either realize their stomach is loudly hinting or until somebody goes to the kitchen, uses the can opener, or otherwise makes a pointed reference to food.

If the human goes away on a trip, they do cat things until you come home. Then it's either *"oh, you've been away for a while. Hi,"* or *"oh, it's you. You abandoned me, and I'm going to snub you for a while."* They are as much individuals as we are, and it's ridiculous to think that cats, as a class, act in only certain ways.

Cats are aware of the passing of time, but they don't mark it. They also don't assume. Cold-time came last year and the year before, but that doesn't mean it will come this year. They don't think about the coming winter until it arrives. There would be no point to it.

"To every thing there is a season, and a time to every purpose under the heaven" could have been written by a cat, but not as a statement of philosophy. It was a statement of fact that was too obvious to need a comment.

Any time beyond a small, sliding window centred on now was "forever."

How long had Yoko Geri been living with me? He was too young to have memories of his life before I brought him home, so the answer was "forever."

How long would he live? He had never seen another cat die, and I wasn't sure that he would apply such knowledge to himself anyway. He was the apex predator in the house—in principle I could attack him, but I never had despite many opportunities. The world didn't exist before him, and the world would not exist after him. He would live forever.

I couldn't explain what my question meant, so he eventually dismissed it as something only a foolish kitten would think. I needed another way to express my question.

"Do you remember when I went away and Kali was feeding you?" Bear in mind that when I pictured "Kali," he thought something like "female-big-kitten-long-fur-<her smell>." Mercifully, the nanites translated such things for me.

"Yes."

"How would you feel if I'd never come back?"

That was a bit abstract for him, but he finally answered. *"I would be sad. You are good to sleep with."* There was a pause while he though further. *"Kali would live here and bring food."*

"Would you like it if I made sure that I always come back?"

"You always come back."

"I might not."

"You do."

That was another difference between humans and cats. Cats don't worry about little things. If somebody is in your way you don't get upset, you just go around them. If somebody is in your favourite spot you either sit elsewhere, or you get them to move. It depends on your relative social ranks and your whim at that moment. If your food bowl is empty you either wait until your kitten notices, or tell them to fill it. In no case do you hold a grudge unless somebody hurts you.

Hypothetical cases like my question count as little things. I'd have to make this more immediate.

"Something might eat me while I'm away. Or it might eat you."

He snapped to full attention and his fur bristled. *"What?"*

"I don't know. Something like the animals on TV."

He relaxed. *"They are all too small to hunt us."*

Another conceptual problem: He didn't see images as symbolic reproductions. A picture of a tiger didn't represent a fully-sized tiger. It couldn't be: it didn't smell real, and his eyesight was different from ours, so what we saw as a tiger on TV didn't look right to him. We speak of pictures being photo-realistic. To him, a photograph was *never* realistic. The images on TV were interesting because they moved, and they were small enough to count as prey. They were made up of small dots of light, so they were not much different from a laser pointer. He just didn't get the idea that you could make a representation of an animal at a size other than real life. Elephants were no bigger than he was. No amount of arguing would convince him otherwise unless we went to the zoo. Even then, he'd probably think the TV-elephants were a different species than zoo-elephants.

It was exactly the point made by René Magritte in his famous painting *The Treachery of Images.* That's the one that's a picture of a pipe with the caption, *"ceci ne pas une pipe."* This is not a pipe.

All of this thinking about thinking finally came down to one simple concept. *"Do you want to live with me forever?"*

"Yes." He gave me a slow blink. *"I love you."*

As informed consent went, that was as good as it was getting.

I put my finger tip on his nose, and gave him my nanites before he could protest the personal intrusion. I didn't know if putting them on his fur would be good enough.

He pulled his nose back and licked it. *"That was annoying."*

"Sorry." I hugged him.

Whatever life brought me from now on, at least I had an immortal cat for company.

An immortal *talking* cat, made possible by my friend the demon prince who was a really nice guy.

My life was seriously weird.

CHAPTER 18

The Secret

K ali and I were having home-made lasagna at her place. Watching her in the kitchen, I was sad that her mother hadn't lived to see her improved cooking skills.

"How's life? Any new men?"

I sighed. "No. Although there is an interesting guy I've been talking to lately."

"Details. Now."

"I asked Sitri to look into some Downland technology for me. Yoko Geri and I can now talk to each other."

"What? Seriously?"

"It took a while to learn the way he thinks. It's—different."

"Say something in Cat."

"That's not how it works. It's more like telepathy."

"Wow. Can you read anybody else's mind?"

"No, just his. Sitri says everybody's brain encodes their thoughts differently. Someone else would have to be given the nanites, and it would take weeks or months to learn to understand each other."

"That's unbelievably cool. You literally have your own familiar. Maybe you should take up Wicca again."

"I didn't just do it for fun. I had a question I needed him to answer."

"Which is?"

"Whether he wanted to live forever."

"You wanted to give him your health nanites? Why ask?"

"I needed his consent. While I was in Europe, I did some things that saved lives but were not at all ethical. If, for any reason, Yoko didn't want a long life I wasn't going to force it on him."

"Will our nanites work on him?"

"They already have. I'm the proud room-mate of the world's first immortal cat."

She didn't answer. We ate in silence for a while.

Finally, she spoke. "That brings up other questions."

"I know."

"Big ones."

"I *know*. I just don't know how to answer most of them."

We finished the lasagna and went into her living room. She poured us two glasses of what looked like white wine.

"Try this. You'll like it."

I sniffed. The bouquet was definitely floral. "What is it?"

"Mead. I got it from Cathie, the woman who does custom ritual robes for me."

I took a sip. It was delicious.

"Wow, I could get used to this."

We sat for a while, ignoring the problems Kali had brought up. That didn't last long.

"You and George are pretty serious. Would he want to be immortal?" I asked.

"We're getting married when he graduates."

I put my glass down and wrapped my arms around her. "I knew it! One time when I was over at your store you had a wedding planner website open on your computer."

"I wondered if you'd seen that."

"You could have mentioned something."

"Back then it was just a fantasy. Now it's not."

"Are you sure you want to be with him for the rest of your life? With the emphasis on *your*."

"Yes. I'm sure."

"Have you told him about our health condition?"

She let a breath out slowly. "Yes. We also talked about the problems it will cause."

"And?"

"He's decided that he wants to be part of the club." She paused again. "And that he isn't going to tell his parents."

"Ouch."

"You've met them. They're religious bigots who want George to get a nice *white* girlfriend who would never dream of sleeping with him for fun, let alone before marriage."

I was about to say something trite, but everything she said was true. They had forbidden their son to date Kali for exactly the reasons she'd given. He'd responded by telling them that he had to stay in Toronto to work during the summer breaks from university. Instead, each year he flew back to Calgary and he worked here while they lived together.

He hadn't seen them in two years. He didn't like that, but their own actions made the choice between them and Kali inevitable.

My parents were cool, and I had trouble wrapping my head around dysfunctional family like his. Having met them, I could understand why he didn't want them around forever. I just hoped he didn't regret it later.

"What about his friends and other family?"

"The rest of his family are a lot like his parents. He hasn't made any close friends other than us, so that's not a problem for him."

"When are you going to do it?"

"I'll give him my nanites on our wedding day."

I laughed. "I'm glad you're saving yourself for marriage."

She smiled, then it faded. "What about Mum and Dad?"

I downed the remainder of the mead.

"It's tricky. I want to tell them, but it's all mixed up with the demon business and everything else. I don't know how they'll take it."

"Yes, you do," she said while refilling my glass. "Mum will be calm and professional about it when you give her proof that it's all real, and Dad will flip out about his princesses getting into dangerous situations."

"Yeah. That's what I'm afraid of."

* * *

The pretense of a family dinner for springing the news didn't appeal to either of us. For one thing, I was sure I'd be too nervous to eat anything. For another, the suspense of waiting to start the conversation would kill me. Instead, I just arranged for Kali and I to meet with Mum and Dad at my apartment on Sunday.

They arrived right on time, at one p.m. Kali had come early to help me to rehearse the story.

I got everybody something to drink and sat in my comfy chair. Kali was in a new chair I'd bought a month before. Mum and Dad were on the sofa.

"I suppose you are wondering why I called you all here," I began. Dad smiled. Mum and Kali didn't appreciate the joke. I took a sip of my coffee.

"I—we—Kali and I—have a story to tell you. I know you'll have a lot of questions, but please try to save them until we're finished."

"What's wrong?" Dad said. "Whatever it is…"

"There you go, asking questions." He shut up and I cleared my throat. "This whole situation started just after I began working as a P.I. Mum, do you remember me asking you for information about a woman named Beleth?"

"Yes. As I recall, you said she was living in an empty house somewhere in the North-east. She's also the woman your father and I met in Ireland."

"That's the one. She was training one client's husband and another client's boyfriend as a dressage horses."

"You asked me to put you in touch with somebody from vice. Peggy, if I remember correctly."

"Yes. My theory was that I was dealing with a scam artist who was pretending to be a demon."

Dad was listening with a bit of a deer-in-the-headlights expression. This was the first time he'd heard anything about my cases. Mum just looked uncertain. "I'm not sure where this is going."

"She isn't a scam artist. At least, not in that way. She really is a demon."

"As in—what? A psychopath in a religious cult?"

"No, a real demon. She lives in another universe called the Downland. Most of it doesn't actually look like Hell, though."

I felt myself founder. Kali jumped in. "What Veronica means is that Beleth belongs to a race that humans have been calling demons. They live in another universe, and some of them come to Earth for entertainment."

Our parents looked at each other.

"Okay, I thought we had figured out how to tell you, but we're just confusing things." I fingered the medallion I was wearing under my shirt.

"The Downlanders have advanced technology. Like this." From their point of view, I vanished.

From my own, I appeared in the hallway outside my apartment. I stumbled backwards as my support disappeared. I forced myself to wait for a count of five, then started to sit and jumped back to my chair.

In the meantime, Mum had gotten up and was examining the chair. Dad was sitting stiffly upright with a shocked look. Both of them jumped when I reappeared and dropped into my seat.

"How did you do that?" Mum demanded.

"Remember the naked man who was here when you came over for supper?"

"How could we forget?" She sat down beside Dad.

"He's another demon. He hired me to find out who was killing the people who were summoning him." I pulled the locket out. "This is the device he gave us so we could travel from here to Downland and back. The day you met him we'd had an encounter with the killer and he was injured. That's why he was bandaged."

Dad couldn't stand it any longer. "My God, Veronica! I had no idea your cases were so dangerous."

"Dad, it's okay. I'm more than capable of taking care of myself."

"I know, but this isn't a mugger with a knife we're talking about..."

"Dad," I said the same way Mum would have, "drop it. Please."

"Why didn't you take him to the hospital?" She paused. "I suppose that would have led to too many questions." She smiled mirthlessly. "I assume he doesn't have an Alberta Health Care card or travel insurance."

"More questions than you think." I looked at Kali. "I suppose we should give a demonstration. Can you call them?" She pulled out her phone.

Dad was still trying to make sense of things. "Call who?"

"Sitri and Artemis. They're a couple now, living in an apartment up by Nose Hill. He's a demon, and she's a goddess."

"Veronica," Mum said, "you're scaring me. Do you actually believe this story of yours? I'll admit that your vanishing trick was impressive, but..."

"They'll be here in a few moments," Kali said as she put her phone away.

There was a knock on the door. Kali got up to answer it.

"Hi, guys. Sitri, you've met our parents. Mum, Dad, may I present Artemis, goddess of the hunt."

Today she was wearing her hair down and a blue chiton with gold trim. It looked spectacular against her darker skin.

"Mrs. Chandler," she said as she held out her hand. "I'm pleased to meet you."

Dad rose and held out his hand. She hesitated, as though she didn't know what to do, then shook his hand briefly. Dad looked her in surprise.

"Firm grip?" I asked him.

"Um, yes. You must work out a lot."

She and Sitri blushed. Dad seemed to have missed the implication. Kali snorted.

I got my tactical baton from the shelf and opened it with a snap.

"Hold your arm out," I said to Artemis.

"Wait just a minute," Mum said, rising from the sofa. Before she was fully standing I brought the baton down on Artemis' slender forearm so hard it whooshed.

Instead of a sickening thump and the crack of breaking bone, the baton made about the same sound as if it had hit a concrete wall. Her smile never wavered. Her arm didn't move.

Mum was furious. "You could have badly hurt her!"

I handed her the baton. "Try it yourself. You can't hurt either of them."

"Like hell I will. I don't know what you and your friends are playing at, but I'm not going to hit anyone."

"Okay. How about this?" I grabbed a knife off the kitchen counter and stabbed Sitri in the head. I didn't want to ruin his clothes.

The knife was an old one I didn't mind losing. That was good, because it hit his skin and the point snapped off.

"We can keep this up all day, Mum. Or you can believe your own eyes. If you'd brought your Glock, you could bounce bullets off them. Or we could try running them over with your car, if you don't mind the repair bills."

Mum was silent. I could almost see the thoughts bumping into each other in her head.

Dad managed to drain his coffee even though his hand was shaking. "Veronica, I don't know how this is possible, but I do know my daughters. Neither of you have ever liked practical jokes, so you must be serious." He looked at Artemis, then at Sitri. They both tried reassuring smiles. I don't think it worked very well.

"This is the first I've heard of this, so let me get this straight. Your first cases involved real demons?"

"Yes."

"And Sitri is a demon?"

"Yes."

"But he's also a friend of yours and living in Calgary?"

"Yes."

"With his girlfriend. Who's a goddess. And killed people."

"Yes."

"Artemis. *The* Artemis."

"Yes, *the* Artemis. Daughter of Zeus, expert hunter, runs around in the woods. *The* Artemis. If it helps any, they don't have any magical powers. Think of her and Sitri as aliens with advanced technology."

"All right. What about this Beleth person?"

"She's a bit of a wild card. She's a member of the Downland parliament and seems to be a real nut case, although sometimes I wonder if it's an act."

"Does she live around here too?"

"No, as far as we know she still lives in Downland. She does have one —two—redeeming qualities so far. She saved Kali's life. And the lives of three women in Sweden."

"She...what?"

"I went with Veronica to see one of her clients," Kali said. "A human client, that is. We tried to talk her down, but she went for Veronica with a knife and stabbed me instead. I don't remember much after that."

"Kali was bleeding out. Beleth was there, and she stopped the bleeding. That was a few days before you got back from your trip to Ireland."

"A few days?" Mum said. "How is that possible?"

"I'm a fast healer," Kali said. "And that brings us to the real reason we asked you here. Sitri, Artemis, would you mind sticking around? Mum and Dad might have some questions we can't answer."

"Sure, whatever you need," Sitri said. "I'll just get more chairs." Mum and Dad were startled when he held out his hands and two dining room chairs appeared in them.

"Everybody in both the Upland and Downland have these nano-machines in them that keep them healthy," I said. "Sitri, how old are you at home?"

"One hundred seventy-six years."

"Artemis?"

"I'm only a bit over one hundred."

"In almost four centuries since the medical nanites were created, I'm told that the only people who have died were victims of injuries so severe that the nanites couldn't heal them in time."

"How severe an injury are we talking about?" Dad asked.

We told them. We also told them about the rest of the features.

"That's amazing, but I'm not sure where you're going with this."

"Beleth saved Kali's life by transferring a portion of her medical nanites to her to heal her wound. Everything I just said about the demons and gods now also applies to her."

Kali reached over and grabbed my broken knife. She made a face like she expected it to hurt, and sliced her forearm.

Mum and Dad just stared. I think we'd overloaded them.

Kali held the edges of the cut together for a few seconds. When she let go, the wound was sealed and barely visible.

Mum and Dad looked—I wasn't sure what. Probably a mixture of shocked, concerned, and confused. Dad finally spoke.

"So Kali is…?"

"Effectively immortal," she said. "Yes. The Downland only have clinical data for 400 years, but the nanites are self-renewing and expected to function for thousands, if not millions of years." I saw her shiver slightly as she said it and I felt a pulse of adrenaline myself. Saying it out loud it made it feel more real.

"That's not all." I told them about the gamma-ray laser accident while trying to downplay the exact details as much as possible.

"I would probably have died from acute radiation syndrome if Kali hadn't given me a portion of her medical nanites. There wasn't any other choice. I'm immortal too."

Mum seemed almost frightened. "The nanites can't be removed?"

"No. The developers never thought anybody would want to."

"I don't know what to say."

"We're still the same people we were. You could think of it as being vaccinated against death. It's just technology."

"We have an offer for you," Kali said. "Giving you our nanites is as easy as shaking hands. You can be immortal too."

They were both silent.

"Mum? Dad?"

Dad cleared his throat. "I don't know what to say. It's overwhelming."

"I know. But think of it this way: you can spend as long as you want learning about the cuisines of every culture. Not only that, but you can learn about the foods of two other worlds as well."

"Mum, you can do anything you want. Travel anywhere, take courses, learn more than the greatest detectives have ever known."

They asked a lot more questions, and the four of us did our best to answer them. Mum in particular wanted more details of how this had all come about, and what the Uplanders and Downlanders were doing in our world.

I had to be clear that there was no possible way for anybody to arrest somebody from either place if they committed a crime here. Even if they did allow themselves to be arrested they couldn't be prosecuted without causing a global panic and economic crash. And good luck trying to imprison them without Downland police equipment.

Sitri popped out—literally—to get pizza from Naples for supper. This time we told Dad the truth about Vincenzo. By the time we'd finished answering questions, it was almost ten p.m.

"Well?" Kali said. Yoko Geri had come out of my bedroom and was lying in her lap, looking at Mum and Dad with great interest. He chirped. *"Why are they upset?"*

I wasn't sure how to explain it to him. "We asked them if they want to live with us forever. Like I did with you. They aren't sure of their answer." He hopped down and bunted Mum's legs, then leaped onto Dad's lap and started purring. *"They should say yes. I love them too."*

"Who are you talking to?" Dad said. That's when I realized I'd spoken out loud. Crap.

"I suppose we should have mentioned that too. Yoko Geri is immortal too. And he and I can speak with each other telepathically."

"You're telepathic?" Dad asked.

"Only with my cat."

"More demonic technology?"

"Yes."

"I see."

There was a pause while Yoko suggested that Dad pet him by bunting his hand. Dad didn't need telepathy to get the message.

"Your mother and I will have to discuss this. There's a lot to take in, and it's a big decision."

I couldn't blame them for wanting to be cautious, but I wished they would make up their minds. I hate waiting.

"Don't forget that this is all top secret."

Dad smiled wistfully. "Who would believe us?"

By 10:30 everybody had gone home, leaving Yoko Geri and I alone. I was exhausted. It didn't take long for his purring to put me to sleep.

CHAPTER 19

The Dinner Party

Two months had passed since Artemis and Sitri had become a couple. To nobody's surprise, we didn't see much of either of them during that time. Sitri called every few weeks to let me know how Artemis was doing with her therapy.

George and Kali were, as usual, inseparable during the summer. I occasionally saw them.

My own love life consisted of me being left to my own devices. In an effort to be both green and economical, I switched to rechargeable batteries.

Once a week I tried to make time to have nice, normal dinners with our parents. I also tried, mostly successfully, not to bug them about making their decision about immortality.

I had a few normal cases to keep me busy, one of which involved tracking a missing fifteen-year old girl who had run away from home.

When I located her in an ill-kept house in a bad neighbourhood, she was working as an unpaid intern for an unsavoury group of entrepreneurs.

I politely informed them that she would be coming with me so I could return her to her loving home, an offer to which she immediately and enthusiastically agreed.

They suggested that the matter was none of my business and that if I didn't want to increase the burden on our health care system, I should find something else to occupy me. One of them offered me an entry-level position within their enterprise, which in turn led to further discussions.

I explained my position, using my baton to illustrate the major points in my argument. I stated I was already employed, that the whole matter certainly *was* my business, and that the young lady would much rather be in my company than theirs. They disagreed.

They forcefully presented their counter-arguments with the help of fists, beer bottles, and several knives. It felt good to be able to use my Krav Maga skills for something positive. Only one of them managed to connect with his knife: a slash across the side of my abdomen. He seemed quite upset when I didn't appear to notice his efforts and only bled for a few moments.

After a while they ran out of arguments, and we eventually settled our differences when I called in the Calgary Police and EMS for some binding arbitration. The whole affair resulted in a lot of paperwork.

There were also several pairs of incredibly grateful parents and a handful of deeply thankful girls who had been locked in the basement. They'd gotten in far over their heads, and had no idea how to get out.

There were also four gentlemen who would be taking an extended vacation from their business pursuits. That was probably for the best. It would have been difficult for them to adequately supervise a teen prostitution ring while wearing casts. Their impassioned warnings to the officers that I was a demon in disguise went largely unheeded.

By the time EMS got around to looking at my wound, it was merely a shallow nick that wasn't enough to warrant a bandage. The nice paramedic commented that I was lucky the knife had only scratched me.

I like mostly normal cases. Especially ones with happy endings.

* * *

Yoko Geri was sitting on my lap, and I was stroking him gently, trying to decide what to make for supper, when my phone rang.

"Hi, Veronica," the cheerful voice said, "am I interrupting anything?"

"Sitri, how are you? I'm just sitting around petting my cat."

There was a pause. "Is that a metaphor? Should I call back later?"

"No. I'm being literal. Yoko Geri is sitting on my lap."

"Oh, good. We know this isn't much notice, but we were wondering if you would like to come to our new place for dinner tomorrow."

"Come over where?"

"Artemis and I bought a house."

Holy crap, things certainly had changed. He sounded proud of himself, as well he should.

"That's amazing. I'm happy for you both." Not to mention the rest of the universe.

"Thank you. Kali said you would be."

"You asked her too?"

"Artemis did. She and George suggested six o'clock."

"Tomorrow?"

"Yes. Feel free to bring a plus one if you wish."

"I'll be there. Where exactly is there, by the way?"

"Outside Cochrane. We have a place out in the country so we don't disturb any neighbours." *Oh yeah, I'll bet.* "I can e-mail you a map for getting here."

"Great. I'll see you then."

After he hung up, I wondered how normal this dinner party would be. This could be interesting—in the same sense as the famous Chinese curse.

* * *

"Come on, it'll be fun."

We were in Kali's bedroom, trying on outfits. She received my best, dubious look.

"What part of going to dinner with a demon and a goddess is fun?"

"What happened to Veronica the Sympathetic? You were the one who convinced me that Sitri is a nice guy once he got over being a sociopath, and Artemis was really sweet once she stopped killing everybody who offended her."

"Well, they are. It's just that I don't know what we have to talk about now that he's no longer a client, and she's no longer a person of interest."

She tried holding another dress in front of herself, and studying the result in the mirror. She made a moue and put it down.

"We should make it formal. After all, this is a housewarming party."

"Are you listening to me at all?"

"No. We'll talk about the things you talk about with any new couple. How they like their new place. How many rooms they've had sex in so far. How many neighbours have complained about the explosions."

"Gak! Tell me again, which one of us is the sexual conservative?"

"It'll be fun, trust me."

"Yes, it'll be so much fun being a fifth wheel."

"You could invite Stan as your plus one."

That wasn't a bad idea. Stan was a good friend, so he was safe. More importantly, he knew about Sitri and the Downland. It wouldn't be like throwing a novice to the wolves.

"It's short notice. Maybe he isn't free."

"Don't be so negative. This is going to be so much fun."

My sister is insane.

* * *

Binky was in the shop getting his yearly tune up, so we all took Kali's car. I sat in the back with Stan and the big box, while George rode shotgun to navigate.

We drove out to Cochrane, turned north for several kilometres, then west. We found the house at the end of a gravel road. Artemis' banner was flying from the mail box so we knew we were in the right place.

The front door opened as soon as we got out of the car. Sitri was wearing an apron over dress trousers and shirt.

"Hi guys," he said.

"So this is your new place," Kali said as she swept toward him in her finest red gown, with George behind her in a three-piece suit. I brought up the rear in a new, navy-blue dress that Kali had insisted I buy for the occasion, thus doubling my girly wardrobe. Stan was also in a suit, and had been voluntold to carry the big, wrapped box. I was good with that. It was a lot heavier than it looked.

The entry hall was magnificent, with a marble floor and oak panelled walls.

"This is for the two of you," Kali said. Stan offered the box to Sitri before his knees gave out.

"Why, thank you," he said. "What do I do with it?"

"It's a housewarming gift," she said. "It's something useful that, hopefully, you don't already have. Generally, you and Artemis open it together."

"She's getting dressed right now. Can we do that later?"

"Perfect."

I was about to introduce Stan when a voice interrupted from the stairs.

"Kali! Veronica!"

Artemis was making a grand entrance at the top of the stairs. Nobody looking at her would have mistaken her for anything other than a goddess. Her luxurious black hair, though styled in ringlets, was still long enough to flow down to her lower back. The short, translucent, emerald-green silk chiton complemented her Mediterranean complexion perfectly. Her belt was gold, worked into the form of linked grape leaves, and accented with cut rubies the size of Sitri's thumb nail. I would not have bet on them being fake. It circled her torso just below her breasts. It was the kind of dress that gets daughters grounded for life by overly protective fathers.

Fortunately for everyone, her father was in another universe.

Despite the new dress, and fancy hair-do that Kali had put up for me, I felt like a lump of mud amid diamonds. George just looked uncomfortable. At least, as a constable, Stan was used to meeting a lot of new and interesting people who might want to kill him.

Artemis reached the bottom of the stairs. She hugged Kali like a long-lost sister, then gave me the same. She smelled like lily-of-the-valley. She looked at George and Stan like she wasn't sure what they were.

"Artemis, this is my boyfriend, George."

"Kali says that you are a good and decent man," she said.

"Um, yes, ma'am. Kali deserves no less. I try."

"Good. You'd better. Or else." None of us were sure if she was kidding.

"And my friend Stan," I said.

"A pleasure," he said, holding his hand out to her. She looked at it du-biously, then shook it perfunctorily.

"Excuse me," Sitri said. "I have to attend to supper."

Artemis held out her hands to Kali and me, and led us into the living room, leaving George and Stan to follow if they wished. Her relationship with Sitri hadn't yet led her to accepting men in general. At least she was being tolerant.

"I haven't seen you for months. How have you been?"

"Happy," Kali said, like she'd just bitten into a chocolate soufflé. "George and I have been spending a lot of time together this summer." Kali held his hand.

"His parents still don't know that he's coming back to Calgary during the summers?"

"Not yet. We know we'll have to tell them some time, but neither of us is in any hurry."

"If you like, I could solve the problem by killing them for you."

There was a dead silence that was broken only by the sound of a pot lid rattling in the kitchen.

"I'm kidding," she said. "Dr. MacMillan has led me to understand why killing people who annoy me is self-defeating. Mostly."

George looked even more uncomfortable. So did Stan.

Stan had gotten an expanded explanation of the whole mess from me so he understood that, whatever the happy couple might do to offend his policeman's sensibilities, they were beyond his jurisdiction. Neither of us had to like it. We just had to accept it.

"I'll see if Sitri needs any help," I said.

* * *

The kitchen had huge, west-facing windows, which made it wonderfully light, and gave an incredible view of the mountains.

"Need a hand?"

"No, thanks. Everything is under control." He was stirring a large pot full of something that smelled delicious.

"Have you been doing much cooking?"

"Every day," he said proudly. "Before meeting you, I would never have believed how satisfying it is to cook my own meals. Artemis loves it as well."

"She cooks too?"

"No, she leave that to me. But she tells me how well I cook. I'm on a mission to try everything in this world. She does come shopping with me. Sometimes we make it a day-long adventure."

"That should keep you busy for a while. What are we having tonight?"

"A surprise," he said, putting the lid on the pot before I could move closer.

He took the lid off another pot and briefly stirred the contents.

"If you could let everyone know, supper will be served in about five minutes." He took off his apron. It disappeared from his hand before it could drop.

The dining room table had room to expand out to twelve seats once the leaves had been put in. Currently, it was perfectly sized for six.

Sitri came into the room just as we were milling around. He had changed into a bespoke tuxedo that must have cost several thousand, and would have had 007 weeping with envy.

"Veronica, please sit here." He seated me to the right of the head of the table with Stan beside me.

"Kali." She went on the left side with George beside her.

He then made a big production out of seating Artemis at the far end. Their proximity, especially when she had that much bare skin showing, made me nervous.

"I'll be back in a moment."

He went into the kitchen and returned a few moments later with an antique trolley with several chafing dishes and utensils. It was an impressive set up.

He served us as we passed our plates up to him. The meal itself was simple enough: three dishes plus a huge bowl of freshly made tea biscuits. After we had our plates back, he circled the table pouring a Cabernet Sauvignon into our glasses. When he returned to his seat, he raised his glass.

"To friends, new beginnings, and the most beautiful women in three universes." Artemis blushed down to her neckline. George and Stan toasted enthusiastically.

The meal wasn't extraordinarily fancy, but it was definitely delicious, and an amazing achievement for somebody who had learned to hold a chef's knife only a few months previously.

"Are you familiar with Brazilian food?" Sitri asked me.

"Not as much as I'd like to be. Most of the South American dishes I've cooked have been Colombian."

"As well they should be," Kali said. George snorted.

"The stew is *feijoada*, the national dish of Brazil. Beside it is *farofa*, which is fried manioc flour with eggs, onion, bacon, and butter. The rice is..."

"*Arroz amarillo*, rice cooked with ground *achiote* seeds. It's also served in Colombia. Where did you find manioc flour in Calgary?"

"I didn't. I got it from a shop in Florianopolis."

"When were you in Floripa?" Stan asked.

"This morning, when I went to shop for supper. You've been there?"

Stan didn't miss a beat. "A few years ago for a police conference. I was with West Yorkshire at the time."

We all had seconds. Dessert, rather than something Brazilian, was *crème brûlée*. Apparently it was one of Artemis' favourites.

After supper, we went back to the living room for cocktails and conversation. This was the part I had been dreading.

* * *

"What have you two been up to lately?" Kali asked, sipping her cocktail. In keeping with the Brazilian cuisine, Sitri had made caipirinhas. As our designated driver, Kali's was made with sparkling water instead of the alcoholic *cachaça*.

Kali and George were sitting on a sofa with their arms around each other, while Stan and I were in separate arm chairs. Artemis and Sitri were sitting beside each other on a love seat, which I was pretty sure violated their unique requirements for safe sex. At least, safe for us. Artemis downed the last of her caipirinha.

"Apart from buying the house, we've been getting all the other things we need," Sitri said. "It's amazing how much stuff you need in this world." He turned to Artemis. "That reminds me; our guests brought us a gift."

"I'll get it," Stan said.

He brought the box from where it had been left in the front hall, and they opened it on their laps.

"We thought it was something you could both enjoy," I said.

Sitri was ecstatic. "A stand mixer! I've been researching which one to buy. Now I can make even more things for you!"

For a moment, he looked like he was going to kiss her. Before I could dive for cover, he hugged her instead. I still expected to be blasted out of existence, but there were just some harmless sparks.

"I don't want to spoil the moment, but why aren't the rest of us dead right now?"

"Artemis went back home for a short visit," he said while she drained her glass again. "The Upland has developed a more efficient design for the charge diverter than we did, so we can touch each other with only a slight coronal discharge. Kissing can still be hazardous to any Midlander within a couple of metres."

"We'll have to wait a while before we host any orgies," she said happily, then drained her glass again. This time when she put her glass down, I noticed it was full again. Oh, oh. She was still getting used to

Midland liquors, and for someone who had grown up drinking watered wine, she was a cheap drunk. Fortunately, she was also a happy one.

"How's your shop doing?" Sitri asked.

"Great," Kali said. "There's a real upswing in interest about the occult lately. I'm thinking of holding some introductory classes in the evenings. I just have to rework some parts of the traditional material in light of recent events. That's the hard part."

"That sounds like fun," Artemis said. "We could teach classes too."

Sitri waved his free hand in front of him as if outlining a marquee. "Absolutely. How to Observe Heavenly Bodies." He leered at Artemis' rather revealing bodice. Some things transcend universal boundaries.

"You men are such pigs," I said.

He gave me a devilish grin.

"I've turned men into pigs," Artemis said happily.

"There's something that I've been wondering about..."

Artemis giggled and blushed. "My safe word is pomegranate." I got up and took her cocktail glass away from her. It was time to cut her off.

"There's a couple of megawatts worth of lightning every time you kiss," Kali said, "and that doesn't hurt you. Why would you need a safe word?"

"That *wasn't* what I was going to ask either," I interrupted. There are some cosmic mysteries we were not meant to know. "I've lived in Calgary my whole life, and never seen anything weird. Well, except for the Buck Shot Show." Damn, Artemis wasn't the only one who should stop drinking. "Why has all this occult stuff started happening in the past few years?"

Artemis clapped her hands together. "Oo, story time!" A fresh cocktail glass appeared in her hand. So much for cutting her off.

"It might be a bit technical," Sitri said.

"When isn't it? Go for it."

"All right. This one time, in Downland..."

CHAPTER 20

Sitri's Tale

Sometimes, tradition outweighs common sense. True, making marks on clay tablets had given way to marking certain types of bark, then uniform sheets made from plant fibres. These things created more-or-less permanent records.

But teachers needed a means of displaying temporary data for students. Their first attempt was to use wet sand and a sharpened stick, then smooth stone surfaces marked by a piece of much softer stone. These gave way to polymer surfaces, markers that left pigments behind that dried almost instantly, virtual surfaces that displayed digital information, and then holographic technology.

Theorists and researchers also needed a means of making temporary notes; doodling their ideas in a form that could be easily changed as the ideas and designs evolved.

Almost none of them used the modern technologies. From ancient tradition, they considered the stone surface marked by softer stone to be a symbol of their profession. Every laboratory had at least one wall sheathed in black stone, covered with equations and diagrams in white from the streaks left by the softer stone rods. Even the white dust left behind on clothing after markings were erased became a matter of pride in one's profession.

People, no matter what universe they come from, are strange creatures.

On the morning in question, the head of the Institute for Advanced Enquiry was standing in front of his stoneboard, pondering a set of complex equations with his beady, black eyes.

He was vaguely aware of the tapping sound of hooves on the tile floor, as his research assistant entered the room with his head carefully cocked to one side. He had occasionally been known to catch his horns on door frames when he was in a hurry. Whether it was the door or his head was damaged more was a matter for debate among the staff.

"What's up, Thoth?" Morax asked as he trotted into the laboratory. His tail swished from side to side. Thoth had always found that annoying, even when Morax didn't get too close to a desk and scatter papers everywhere.

"I've found a practical way to prove M-theory."

Morax snorted. "I keep telling you, nobody is going to take a theory seriously if you name it after your wife."

Thoth sniffed dismissively. Not easy to do when you have the head of an ibis.

"Besides, M-theory isn't testable in the lab. The energies required are too high."

"They were. This new transformation should require far less energy to test. That should put the dissenters in their place. "

Morax tapped over to stand beside Thoth, and studied his boss's equations.

"Hmm. Maybe. You'll need to get clearance from the Ethics Board. It looks like you could destabilize spacetime and cause an ekpyrotic cascade unless you are careful."

"It's a small risk. Tiny. Not even a real possibility. It doesn't matter anyway. Isfet is so disorganized she rubber-stamps everything that comes across her desk. It won't be a problem getting permission."

Morax looked at the equations again and frowned.

"Yeah, that's what I'm afraid of."

* * *

Thoth was actually bouncing when he arrived the next morning.

"You look perky," Morax said. "Did you get some last night?"

"Yes, not that it's any of your business. I also have some news. Isfet is out. Ma'at has been named the new head of Ethics."

"Isn't that a conflict of interest, having your wife review your applications?"

"Like that would sway her. You know how passionate she is about fairness."

"Yes, I do. Don't get your hopes up."

Thoth harrumphed and went into his office.

Two days later, Thoth was standing in his wife's office. He was not a happy physicist.

"What do you mean, my application has been denied?"

"The risk is too great," Ma'at said calmly. "Your proposed experiment could cause the universe to fracture."

"That's extremely unlikely! I only mentioned the possibility as due diligence."

"Still, after reviewing the evidence and consulting with your colleagues, I can't in good conscience give my approval."

"Who did you consult with?"

"Morax."

"That's absurd. Whatever he said is bull!"

"Dear, that's racist. How would you like it if somebody said that M-theory is for the birds?"

Thoth gritted his teeth. Again, not easy to do with the head of an ibis.

For the sake of marital harmony, he decided not to press the matter at that moment. He left her office, closing the door quietly behind him.

He had not spent six years of his career developing M-theory just to have a short-sighted bureaucrat stop him in his moment of triumph, even if that bureaucrat was his wife. This wasn't fair. This wasn't just.

This wasn't over.

* * *

As high-energy quantum experiments go, this one was cheap and simple.

It was cheap enough that he got around leaving a documentation trail by scrounging and borrowing equipment. It was simple enough that he could put it together himself in his private laboratory. There was no need to involve that traitor Morax, or jeopardize the project by mentioning it to any of his other researchers. This close to the finish line, he wasn't going to risk that they might talk.

Instead, he told them he was working on something new, and locked himself away. He'd done it before, and nobody thought that anything was amiss.

A few weeks later he took a deep breath and closed the switch. Apart from a glowing power indicator, nothing happened.

This was as he expected. The energy needed for the experiment was manageable but still considerable. In order to accumulate it without anybody noticing a sudden drain on the Institute's power systems, the equipment would be storing energy for several weeks before the experiment itself could begin.

Then they would see. His name would be famous, and his detractors would have to apologize.

As far as he was concerned, the outcome of the experiment was a foregone conclusion. He didn't even bother to be in his lab when the energy intake was finished. The actual experiment, during which the energy would be dumped into a tiny volume of space, and create a microscopic spacetime bubble, would last for a few microseconds. His instruments were the only competent observers, and he could review the data the next day as easily as he could that evening. There was no reason for him to lose sleep over it.

He left the laboratory in the late afternoon, telling his researchers that he was going home to spend a restful evening with his wife.

* * *

After the fact, all of these events became matters of public record. Most of them were reconstructed from Thoth's laboratory notes and of course, the apparatus itself.

Needless to say, I knew nothing about them at the time. I was driving home from a late evening at my clinic when the experiment became a matter of personal interest to me.

At that time, we still used roads and vehicles for transportation. As the highway passed over the shoulder of a hill I could see the lights of the valley spread out below me like a field of stars on the ground. It was my favourite part of the trip.

I was just passing the summit when large patches of lights went out. The dark areas appeared to be more or less circular, and of various sizes. There was no discernible pattern.

From what I know of Midland technology, electricity is distributed from central stations. This almost guarantees occasional power outages. In our world, each building has its own power system. There is nothing short of a bombing attack that could have disrupted the power in the way I was seeing, and there was no evidence of any explosions.

While I was wondering what had happened in the valley, I noticed that there was a sudden gap in the oncoming traffic. A big gap. It looked like the highway had been blocked up ahead, and no vehicles were getting through. After a minute, I saw one set of lights coming toward me. That was good. I just needed to get to the next exit in order to go home, and the one oncoming driver meant that the blockage must be beyond that. The sudden blackouts, plus the road blockage, was unnerving. Like stepping off a dais when one thought the floor was level.

I made it to the exit and turned east. Just to the north of the secondary highway, one of the blacked out areas was coming up.

There were no vehicles behind me when I got to the dark area. That was fortunate, because what I saw made me slam my vehicle to a halt and stare.

The entire subdivision was missing. Not destroyed, but missing. There was nothing but the fields and forest that must have existed before the houses, streets, and schools had been built.

Whatever had done this seemed to have taken a circular chunk out of the area, including a small portion of the road itself. I pulled over, got out, and looked at the edge of the pavement. The missing pavement had been replaced by undisturbed meadow grass and wild flowers, as if that section of road had never existed.

I hiked across the field. There was enough light in the sky that I could see a few houses on the edge of the phenomenon.

Only one of them was whole, and the remains looked for all the world like a giant blade had cleanly sliced through them. Two of the houses had remaining bedrooms and I found people huddled in what was left of their homes.

I called emergency services several times. I couldn't get through, which in itself was frightening. I'd never heard of all the communication channels being in use at once.

The house that was still intact was empty. I made a decision and broke in so the survivors would have a place to stay until they could get help. If the owners objected they could complain.

My house was, fortunately, one of those that was still in place. I let my computer scan for news about blackouts and disappearing buildings. The only local news item I could find was that the highway was blocked because part of it had disappeared, just like the subdivision I'd passed.

Ours was a safe society. A natural disaster even a fraction this bad had not happened for at least two hundred years. To say that I was terrified would be a gross understatement.

* * *

"We have to figure out exactly what happened, and how to reverse it." Morax said at a staff meeting the next day.

Thoth wasn't there. Thoth wasn't anywhere. Neither was Ma'at, their house, the neighbourhood where they'd lived, and approximately half of the world's population. It hadn't taken Morax long to suspect what might be going on. After breaking into his boss's laboratory, he was almost certain he knew.

"I have some good people analyzing the equipment in Thoth's lab. We're still going through his lab notes."

"What do we do in the meantime?" Gamigin said. He shook his head and his mane whipped back and forth while his hooves tap danced nervously.

"Calm down. We can't do anything until we understand exactly how the equipment works."

"We have to do something," Gamigin said.

"We *are* doing something. If you don't have something productive to add then shut up," Marbas roared.

Morax let out a long breath. If you think your proverbial lions and lambs have problems co-operating, try a literal lion in the same department as a donkey. "Don't be an ass," Morax said.

"Watch it!" Gamigin snapped, baring his teeth.

Everybody was on edge. Most had lost at least one friend or relative to whatever had happened. The good news was that, if the equations he'd seen a couple of weeks ago were responsible, most or all of the missing people should still be alive. They just had to figure out how to get them back. *This is going to be a very long day*, Morax thought. *Probably to be followed by a very long string of very long days.*

* * *

Time passed. After three weeks everybody was—different. I no longer cared about my clients' problems. If I had, I'd have had more work than I could handle, as people came to find out why they no longer cared about their family members. The only problems I worried about were my own. For a while I still saw clients. Rather than trying to determine what they needed, I started manipulating them into doing what I wanted them to. In retrospect, it was a black time for me. At the time, of course, I saw it as being fun.

The biggest change in the world as a whole was that a former minister named Belphegor staged a coup to overthrow our constitutional monarchy and name himself prime minister. The royal family was assassinated, as were a lot of the ministers who were loyalists. That left a large gap in the power structure that had to be filled.

Most people didn't care. It didn't directly impact their lives.

I knew some people who had to do favours for me or face the consequences, and I remember thinking that being a minister was my right. After some political manipulation, I joined the new parliament a year after the Incident that changed the world.

* * *

Morax made his way through the formal gardens to the Parliament building. He carefully walked up the marble steps and entered the inner chamber through the colonnade. Inside were the 71 other ministers. As they noticed him, they took their seats to hear his report. Belphegor, of course, was seated on the dais previously occupied by King Iblis.

Morax began his report. "In the past two years, we have gained a basic understanding of our situation. Thoth's experiment caused an ekpyrotic cascade that literally ripped our universe apart."

"Question," Buer asked from his seat. "For those of us who are not physicists, what exactly does that mean?"

Morax sighed. People always expected theoretical physicists to explain the grand richness of reality in language fit for babies.

"A membrane is a two-dimensional surface in a three-dimensional space. Is that clear so far?"

The ministers nodded, some less surely than others.

"We physicists generalize the term by referring to a membrane as a two-brane. That's a two-dimensional surface in a three-dimensional space. We can then talk about higher dimensional branes in the eleven-dimensional space required by Thoth's M-Theory."

Fewer ministers nodded. He'd have to simplify the explanation even more. Morax bulled ahead.

"Our universe is embedded in what we call the bulk. That's the emptiness between universes. Thoth's equipment formed a tiny spacetime bubble that inflated until it wedged our universe apart. It was like inflating a balloon in the middle of a pastry It pried the layers apart, except that each half is the same size as the whole."

"Just like a splitting pastry, some tiny flakes from one side stuck to the other side during the Incident. The pieces that were torn away from here are embedded in the copy, and were replaced by what would have been here had those pieces never existed."

"Hence the missing areas here being filled in by primordial landscape," Beleth said.

Morax was relieved. At least one other minister had a brain. "Precisely. The copy universe, along with roughly half our population, will continue to move away from us in the bulk until it collides with another brane. At that time a new universe will be formed from the energy released by that collision."

He looked around. A few ministers were nodding. Most still looked confused.

"Don't think of that collision as violent. From inside, nobody will feel a thing."

"How do we get them back?" the Prime Minister said. "I need some of those who are missing."

"That's the difficult part. They are now in their own universe. We're developing technology to detect their location—location is an inexact word, of course—and to allow travel between the two universes. The big problem is the energy required, but we have some ideas about that. Give us another few months, and we should have more news."

* * *

Marbas attentively listened to the report. "Are you sure?"

"Yes," Bathin said, his scaly tail slowly moving behind him. He was now second in command of the facility after Marbas. "We expected a third universe to form on the far side of our copy, where the collision occurred. Instead, the energy was transferred to *this* side, just as a brain concussion sometimes occurs on the opposite side of the head to the one that was struck. We didn't anticipate that. We can't travel directly to our copy without going through the new universe in between."

"And that is possible?"

"Again, yes. My team is making excellent progress. The only difficulty with the intervening universe is that its time rate is a lot faster than ours. Our best theories indicate that an object from this universe will retain its characteristics when it travels there. Since power equals energy over time, it will be difficult to generate enough power to do anything substantial in the middle world. Its only use to us is as a way station."

"How soon before we can try it?"

Bathin looked thoughtful. His tail twitched.

"Give us a few weeks for tests. We want to be sure we won't cause another split."

* * *

"That's the current state of our research," Marbas said to parliament. "There is one other thing, though. The travel technology will revolutionize our world."

"How so?"

"Once the bugs are out of the inter-universal travel modules, vehicles and roads will become obsolete overnight. We can transfer a person from here, in this universe, to a spot in the middle universe for a tiny fraction of a second, and then back to some other point in this universe."

"You're talking about teleportation," Belphegor said.

"Effectively, although not technically. Emergency services will be changed as well. After all, if you can jump from an accident site to some arbitrary location, hospitals don't need to be close to anywhere in particular."

"Interesting," Belphegor said from his throne. "I'm not sure I want the general masses of people popping over to another universe. It could set a bad precedent for dissidents. Especially if they get it into their minds that it would make a good base for a counter-coup."

"We can set limits on the hardware so that a traveller will only stay in the middle universe long enough to jump back."

Belphegor looked thoughtful.

"Can you remove that restriction for members of parliament?"

"Of course."

"Then do so. There's no point to being in power if you don't have privileges."

Parliament echoed to thunderous applause and cheering.

* * *

The test took place just over a month later. All the ministers were there as observers. Just for the sake of paranoia, Flauros was dressed in a protective suit that would stop heat and radiation, as well as give him breathable air.

"Remember," Marbas said to him. "Jump to the middle universe, then immediately onwards to our copy. Make contact with somebody in authority. Let them know that we can bring them home, and then return."

"Got it," he said with a smile. He held the medallion hanging around his neck in one hand, waved to the crowd with the other one, and disappeared.

They expected him to be gone for a day or two. Surely it couldn't take any longer than that to find someone in charge.

Over a month passed before they saw Flauros again. He was no longer smiling.

He was almost naked, covered only by charred shreds of his suit. Flauros didn't look any better than his suit. His whole body was covered with burns and he was near death, despite his medical nanites doing their best to keep him alive. Whatever he'd been through must have been terrible.

When he managed to speak, they learned that the reality was worse than they had thought.

Flauros had gone off script as soon as he jumped to the middle world.

He found himself in a quiet forest. The water table must be high, because there were a lot of small pools scattered between the trees. Nothing appeared to be immediately dangerous, so he sat down and took a device of his own design from an inside pocket.

Despite his mission briefing, he wasn't going to look for anyone in authority. As a sociopath, Flauros had no interest at all in authorities. What he did care about was his wife, Anyanwu. He hadn't seen her since the Incident. He had the signature of her medical nanites, and he managed to get an approximate location for her. That was all that was possible from this universe. He programmed his jump to come out as close to her as he could.

The copy didn't look like another universe, any more than the intermediate universe had. Ahead of him was a clearing and a small, grass-hut village.

The people stared at him oddly as he approached. He assumed it was just because he was in an isolation suit until he looked behind him. He was trailing a stream of glowing gas from his back as he walked. When he stopped, the glow enveloped him, almost as if he was ionizing the atmosphere slightly. The glow followed his hand as he waved it slowly in front of him. It was a curious effect but seemed harmless.

"Anyanwu!" He called. He heard a slight noise, and a woman emerged from one of the huts. A radiant smile shone from her black face.

"Flauros!" She shouted and ran toward him. He held out his arms to hold her and...

"And?" Marbas asked. It was two months after Flauros' return.

Flauros would be a long time recovering. His medical nanites had been damaged and new ones would have to be carefully created to try to restore his body to its original condition.

"I woke up a long time later. My jump medallion was damaged, but it worked well enough to bring me back. I don't remember anything else until I woke up here," Flauros mumbled. He couldn't speak properly. His mouth and jaw were too badly burned.

* * *

"Our analysis was completed yesterday," Marbas said to the assembled ministers. "Flauros will survive his injuries, but his medical nanites were badly damaged, and they no longer understand what his original state was. As a result he'll always have scars."

"Enough about him. What happened?" Belphegor said.

"According to the message we found embedded in his medallion, there were two explosions. Our counterparts found him lying in a crater that used to be a village. The first blast was what brought the rescue workers. The second explosion occurred when a worker tried to move him. Unless and until we solve the problem of opposing charges, we don't dare travel to the copy universe, nor they to ours."

"How big an explosion?"

"Our message left by our counterparts estimate that both blasts were around 70 megatons. The blast radius was around 19 kilometres. People died from burns as far away as 57 kilometres. The resulting crater was four kilometres in diameter and almost half a kilometre deep."

"The area was only lightly settled, so the casualty estimate is that more than three thousand people were killed in the original blast, with another hundred or so dying when they tried to rescue him."

There was complete silence as the ministers tried to digest the scale of the catastrophe, and imagined it happening in their own back yard. Belphegor broke the silence.

"Is there no way around that?"

"We're looking into some theoretical possibilities for draining off the discharge into the bulk. It will be several years before we know if it's feasible for people from the home universe and copy universe to meet."

"I'm getting tired of the awkward descriptions. We need simple names for the universes."

"At the Institute, we are using designations based on relative charge," Marbas said. "Our charge is negative with respect to the other two. The intervening universe appears to have a neutral charge, and our copy is positive. We propose Downland, Midland, and Upland, respectively."

"That isn't terribly complimentary to us," Beleth said.

"It is, however, a more or less accurate description of the physics as we understand it and it's not difficult to remember."

"Very well. What about this Midland?"

"There seems to have been a dimensional phenomenon similar in some ways to the elastic collision between table balls that causes them to spin when struck. That's very inexact, of course, but the result is that Midland's time rate is currently about 200 times faster than ours. Performing any kind of action would take so long, from our point of view, as to be worthless. At best, we can appear as flickering shadows to them. However, there also appears to be a process analogous to friction at work. Their time rate is gradually slowing and should synchronize with ours fairly soon. We won't be able to do much until the situation stabilizes."

"How long until that happens?" Belphegor asked.

"About 95 years, our time. Two hundred thousand years, Midland time."

"That isn't too bad," Beleth said. "We have research studies that will take longer than that. Does Midland have any indigenous population?"

"Yes. They look very similar to us, so we're unsure about whether this is a truly separate universe or another, distorted copy of ours."

"It should be fun playing with them," I said. "The possibilities are endless."

That got me an ovation from the ministers. I thought at the time that Beleth seemed entirely too cheerful about the whole disaster, even for a sociopath.

I could never prove anything, so I let the matter drop.

CHAPTER 21
Artemis' Tale

We were all quiet for a while after Sitri had finished his story. The magnitude of it was hard to take in.

"All of this was an accident," I said. "Our entire universe."

"I'm afraid so," Sitri said. "We could visit Midland to gather data, but it took major effort to actually do anything physical. Swapping information was easier, of course. For thousands of your years, we were nothing but vague impressions to your people. Some decided to create groups in Midland after their own image, which is why there are more or less distorted echoes of our stories throughout your mythologies. The effect of your slowing time rate became significant in your fifteen hundreds, give or take a century, and lately it's become exponential. Within the past two years, the time rates have synchronized."

"That explains what happened in Downland. What about Upland?" Kali said, swirling the ice cubes in her glass. She seemed to be taking this better than I was. An Egyptian god who was really a self-centred physicist had said, "let there be fame," and there was light. Shit.

Sitri stroked Artemis' head. Sparkles of light played through her dark hair attended by the crackle of discharges.

"Sweetie?"

"What?" she said vaguely, her words slightly slurred. "I was very young when the Event happened, but I remember some of it. And like the Downland, much of what happened then is now public record."

* * *

"Honey, I'm home," Thoth called as he tossed his keys into the basket by the door.

"I'm in my library," Ma'at called back. She had spent the past several hours experimenting with arranging her books in strict alphabetical order with all the spine titles facing the same way, even if the book itself had to be upside down to do so. When Thoth entered, she was measuring to ensure that all the books were exactly the same distance from the front edges of the shelves.

Thoth sighed. As far as he knew, everybody else in the world used electronic storage for information sources. Only his wife was—he supposed *dedicated* was a polite word—enough to have a collection of actual hard copy books. He'd tried to convince her that a data core was a better use of the space in their house, but it was like trying to change the mind of a cosmic force.

In any case, she'd have just pointed out that if she had to get rid of her books, it was only fair that he replace his stoneboards with holographic displays. The argument wasn't worth it.

Last month, the books were in order by subject. He wondered how many more times she would keep rearranging them. Maybe next month she would sort them by colour, or cover texture.

"How was work?" She remained absorbed in her task.

"I've found a way to test M-theory. All I need is for Isfet to approve the experiment."

Ma'at turned to face her husband. Her hand went up to touch the feather she habitually wore in her hair. It drove her nuts if it was out of place.

"Isfet won't be reviewing your application," she said.

Thoth blinked and tilted his head to one side to indicate puzzlement. "Why not?"

"I've been named as the new head of the Ethics Division."

He hugged her, being careful not to nudge the books behind her with the end of his beak. "That's marvellous news! Congratulations! It will be so wonderful working with you."

They spent a pleasant and restful evening together. They even made love, although he had to revert back to his natural form for that. There are some things you cannot do with the head of an ibis, especially if you want to remain on good terms with your partner.

* * *

Of course, having Ma'at as head of Ethics didn't work out for him as he'd planned. Still, Thoth remained on good terms with her even after she refused to approve his experiment. After all, from his point of view, her ruling hadn't really changed anything, and he knew she'd eventually come around when everything worked out.

Unfortunately, he didn't know his wife as well as he thought. She was not happy with Thoth ignoring her authority. She left him soon after, and she moved in with, of all people, Isfet.

Once people had figured out what had happened, Thoth was offered a deal. He was placed under house arrest with a duplicate of his laboratory where he was to work exclusively on getting us home. If he did so, the deal was that he would not be imprisoned for life.

After a while people noticed that something weird was going on. Take my father for example. Mum had talked to people who knew him before the Event. He was a second-rate meteorologist, and happily married to Hera. She was a bit strict, but there was no hint of infidelity on either of their parts, and she wasn't the harridan she became.

After the Event, he started getting these delusions of grandeur. He began lording it over people. Then his sex addiction started. The funny thing is that a lot of others in his circle went along with him being in charge. However, most others didn't think he made a particularly good ruler and started their own groups. After a while there was a lot of not-talking going on between the factions.

"Wait a minute," I said, "let me get this straight. Each of what we'd call pantheons is living in its own group, doing its own thing but not talking to anyone else?"

"Exactly, although some of us get along with our counterparts on an individual basis. I've been hunting with Diana lots of times. Eris and Loki have been doing a sort of Bonnie and Clyde thing together. I can under-stand her fascination with bad boys."

She looked fondly at Sitri for a moment, then her smile faded com-pletely.

"Instead of a unified government, we now had dozens of cliques, each of which believes that it has the only true mandate to rule. From what I've read of your political units, ours is an entire world of countries like North Korea. The only reason it works is that our technology is high enough that each can ignore everybody else."

"Then, one day, everything changed."

* * *

The village of Onicha was a peaceful place. Its main claim to fame was as a minor trading centre for the area. The residents saw the Event as a sign that modern technology was out of hand, so they tried to live simply.

Other factions, of course, distrusted them for this, and kept close watch on them in case their alleged lifestyle was a mask for some sort of power play. That didn't have to make real sense. It was just how most people thought. At least it meant we had a detailed record of what happened.

When a stranger from nowhere arrived in the village, everybody was curious. The satellite images clearly show a man in a protective suit en-tering the village trailing an ionization cloud behind him.

A moment later, a woman ran toward him, obviously glad to see him.

As they touched, a brilliant flash overwhelmed the cameras. When they recovered, there was a mushroom-shaped cloud towering 40 kilometres over the area.

The explosions were terrible. At first, we thought nuclear weapons had been detonated. This was disproved when no radiation could be detected. We assumed that some faction was mounting an attack, but nobody claimed responsibility and there were no further incidents.

Since there was no fallout or radiation, rescue teams entered the area as soon as it was cool enough for their armour to handle. It was one of the few instances where the various factions pulled together for disaster relief, although there was intense bickering about who should be in charge, and what exactly should be done.

I've seen the crater. It's a monument where children are taken so that the explanation of why the Upland and Downland can never meet makes sense to them.

You asked why I'd need a safe word. The answer is simple. We are all terrified of something like that happening to us. I don't think that Sitri and I could ever be that—overly enthusiastic--with each other, but there's no sense in taking chances. The knowledge of the physics of inter-universal travel isn't complete, and we aren't sure where the gaps are in what we know. So far the diverters work properly, and even the most passionate sex only produces a tingle. Apart from the *other* tingle, that is.

When I tried to attack you in that place with the concrete room the door between us absorbed the discharge and acted as a fuse. We were thrown apart by the explosion as the metal vapourized before the energy could build to maximum. Even that wouldn't have been enough if we'd been in our own universes. You can be thankful that our first meeting was here in Midland. Otherwise, we'd have made a similar crater.

The rescue workers found Flauros lying embedded in the crater floor. At first, they thought he was dead. When he moved the workers touched him to put him on life support there was another explosion that killed a hundred rescue workers in the area.

By the time the next set of investigators went in, Flauros was the only thing left living. Nobody dared to touch him. By then his medical nanites had at least stabilized his condition, and he was identified from instrument readings of his technology. Thoth was consulted and determined that Flauros had to have come from the Downland.

There was talk of retaliation, but even the most militant factions realized it would be a bad idea. Neither side would need actual weapons. Any rock could be jumped to any location in the other universe, and in any number. Each would be equivalent to a nuclear bomb. There was no conceivable scenario where anybody could survive, let alone win.

His medallion, being a prototype, could be remotely programmed. A warning message to the Downlanders was uploaded to a section of unused memory. Nothing material could be sent with him.

When we sent him back, he was barely conscious enough to trigger the device. But we didn't dare wait any longer.

* * *

"Now you know why all of us you've met are more familiar with advanced physics than you might expect," Artemis said. "If we weren't it would be like one of you growing up without knowing how to cross a street safely, or what areas of the city to avoid after dark." She smiled wistfully. "The youngest wood nymph could probably teach your Stephen Hawking a few things."

"It's horrible," I said, "that none of you can ever be reunited with your loved ones in the other world."

"Well, it turns out that's not true," Sitri said.

"Well, no. Obviously you and Artemis got together, even if you didn't know each other before."

"That's the problem," she said.

"I don't get why—oh, crap."

"Yeah. We can be reunited if we're careful and we move to your world."

"How many of you are we talking about?" Kali asked.

"In Downland?" Sitri said. "When you eliminate those who are content to stay where they are, who have no families on the other side, there are probably several tens of thousands of potential immigrants."

CHAPTER 22
We Have a Problem

I was stunned. "Holy crap. I thought we were talking about maybe a few hundreds."

"Right now, only the parliamentary ministers have privilege of coming here unless they explicitly send an underling. Most Downlanders think of Midland as a primitive universe with nothing of interest apart from entertainment for the elite. Once our situation becomes known, it will be almost impossible to enforce the travel ban. Bootleg technology has a way of becoming available when it's in demand, and it will be easier to remove the code from the nanites that prevents people from choosing to travel here than it was to install it."

"The numbers are higher for us," Artemis said, "although we never limited who could interact with Midland. My guess is that about five thousand have been here overall. Double that for the number who might choose to move here."

This wasn't the kind of uncomfortable conversation I'd feared, but it would certainly do. "Tens of thousands of gods and demons wanting to immigrate to Earth. That makes any normal refugee operation look like child's play. I don't suppose that anybody has any kind of plan to control this situation?"

"No," Artemis said. "Historically, none of the factions have ever agreed on much. The ban against travelling to Downland is about the only one I can think of. Right now my nymphs are the only ones who know that I'm living here with a Downlander, but even though they are loyal to me word will eventually get out. I can just imagine my father demanding to settle on your Mount Olympus with his people and start directing human affairs."

"Apart from the obvious political issues, that's not going to go over well with any of the major religions," Kali said. "If we can't stop this before it starts it'll be a real mess."

"It's a complex situation, and it's going to take a long time to figure out any kind of reasonable solution." Sitri said, "let alone one that everybody will agree to. I'm sorry. We didn't intent to cause any problems for you."

Nobody spoke after that, and the only sound was the ticking of a mantle clock over the gas fireplace. The silence became uncomfortable.

Stan had been nursing one cocktail all evening. He put his glass on the table and cleared his throat. "If you don't mind, I'd like to call it an evening. I have to work tomorrow morning."

"I guess that means we're leaving," Kali said. "Thank you both for a lovely evening."

We made our way to the door, with further choruses of "thank you," and "we had fun." Artemis hugged Kali and myself. Sitri hugged everybody. It might have been my imagination, but they felt different. Softer, somehow.

* * *

As we left Cochrane everybody was quiet. Maybe they were thinking about Sitri and Artemis' stories. I certainly was.

The idea that our entire universe was an accident by some bird brain who didn't double-check his work took some getting used to. I suppose it didn't make any real difference to me as a person, just as it wouldn't make any difference whether my parents planned my birth or not. But at least my parents didn't have sex with the intention of winning a Nobel Prize and were surprised when they had an unwanted baby instead.

We'd reached the Calgary ring road before anyone spoke.

"Well," George said. He didn't seem to know what to say next.

"Yeah," Stan said.

"This is a disaster," Kali said. "Tens of thousands of immigrants, all of whom are immortal, invulnerable, and mentally ill. How the hell do we fix this? They'd need to be segregated somewhere until their brains heal, then go through counselling. Just the counselling would cost tens of millions of dollars."

I cleared my throat. "I don't think fixing this is up to us. So far we've been stumbling along, dealing with things as they come. Maybe it's time we contacted somebody official and let them handle it."

Stan snorted. "That will end well."

"We can't afford to be cynical," I said. "So far we've been handling the whole Upland-Downland thing like we're the Scooby Gang. We don't have the resources to do this on our own. It's time to pass it on to people who cope with emergencies for a living."

Kali glanced at me in the rear view mirror. "What do you suggest?"

I looked out the window at the passing lights. "I have no idea. Yet."

"Don't do anything without talking to us. We only have one chance to get this right."

"I'm not stupid. I wouldn't do anything without a lot of research any-way."

"I didn't say you're stupid. It's just that you can sometimes be impa-tient."

I crossed my arms and looked out the window. The men were wisely silent.

* * *

The next day I woke up with fur caressing my nose. Yoko Geri was sleep-ing draped across my neck with his head against my cheek. He'd never done that before.

I couldn't speak clearly with the weight of his body against my mouth, but that didn't stop our telepathy. *"What are you doing?"*

"You were scared." He'd picked up my concern from the night before and was comforting me. Why couldn't I find a human like him?

I drew him even closer with one arm and kissed the top of his head just to feel his soft fur against my lips and to breathe in his furry scent.

"I love you."

He stretched, and I could feel him yawn.

"I know."

After a shower for me and breakfast for us, we sat together on the sofa. I was thinking. The fur ball sprawled beside me was just hanging out with his favourite kitten.

It didn't take me long to decide that if I was going to contact the gov-ernment I'd need to know what they'd do with the information. The good news was we'd had a federal election not too long before, and the new government had to be more sensible than the old one. Frankly, I wouldn't have trusted the old Prime Minister with this situation as far as I could comfortably spit a fully grown moose.

What I needed to do was to talk to somebody high enough in the gov-ernment to have the answers I needed without immediately giving away the real situation in case those answers weren't acceptable.

Crap. Even when I was trying to pass the mess on to somebody official I found myself trying to be in control. Couldn't I just dump the whole thing on somebody's desk and walk away?

The answer was obvious, at least to me: hell no.

That might work if it was the right somebody, but if it wasn't, Canada could find itself at war with two other universes, both of which had much better technology than we did. I could just picture Sitri's gamma laser anti-personnel mine turned on its side. It wouldn't surprise me if it could burn through an entire column of tanks. Or take down a satellite.

Our military would be in big trouble with no GPS or satellite imaging.

Of course surveillance satellites were pointless anyway. Our opponents could just jump in, nuke a target, and jump out again within seconds. Photos of troop movements older than five seconds would be pointless, assuming they bothered with ground troops.

Then there were the surveillance nanites. Sitri said they were everywhere, and I wondered what else they could be programmed to do. It might not be possible for us to hide targets.

The other side of it was that anybody we sent into the Upland or Downland would be invincible. What would one of our small nukes do in the Downland? There would be no way to knock it out before it detonated. That assumed that Kali and I gave our side the jump medallions, and that Midland had the technology to reproduce them.

Would we do that if it meant saving our world at the expense of two others?

No, the one thing I couldn't do was to blindly trust any government to handle this properly. I would have to do my homework.

Why did I always find myself having to be an expert in things that nobody should ever have to be an expert in?

I did have a starting point. There was a librarian who had helped me before with investigations. Despite what a lot of people my age thought, not every research asset is online and freely available.

The difficult part of that was figuring out exactly what I was going to ask her.

* * *

Several days later I made the call.

"Calgary Public Library. Tereasa speaking."

"Hi Tereasa, it's Veronica Chandler."

"What can I do for you today?"

"I have some questions about federal government policies on handling emergencies."

"What kind of emergencies do you have in mind?"

"Low probability things that somebody must have thought about even if it's not public. Something like alien invasions."

I swear, I could *hear* her eyebrow go up. "I assume you aren't talking about immigration policy?"

"No, nothing like that. How would the government handle it if a spaceship landed on the lawn in front of the Parliament Building?"

"That's an interesting question. When do you need an answer?"

"Sooner would be better. How long do you think it would take to research?" There was no answer. "Hello?"

"Sorry, I just had an idea. Can I call you back in a while?"

"Of course. I'll be near my phone all day."

Her call came an hour later while I was struggling to read a novel called *The Broken Shield* by Timothy Reynolds. My struggle wasn't with the book itself, which was really good. Any other time I'd have zoomed through it in one sitting, but I was identifying entirely too much with the protagonist. Among other problems, he had to wage a mostly solo fight against demons (or at least their agents) who could teleport from place to place. He even had an animal sidekick, although his was a dog smaller than Yoko Geri. According to his biography, Reynolds lived in Calgary, which meant there was a disturbingly real possibility that his story was at least partially based on true events. I wondered if I should contact him for moral support. Maybe when the current crisis was over.

Tereasa sounded happy when she called back. "I haven't found a documented answer for you yet, but I do have a possible source if you're interested in going to Edmonton for the weekend."

"What kind of source?"

I swear I could hear her smile over the phone. "How about a cabinet minister?"

"Sure, an Alberta MLA sounds like a good start. Maybe they can put me onto a federal source."

"No, I mean a federal cabinet minister. Susan Goodrunning."

"I'm not sure I've ever heard of her."

"Then you'll want to do some research of your own before the weekend, assuming you want to meet her. She boarded with my family when she was in university and we've been friends for years. She'll be in Edmonton this week and my brother invited me up to visit on Saturday. You are welcome to join us."

"Sounds good. Will I need a hotel room?"

"No. My brother has room for both of us."

"Cool. When do you want to leave?"

"We can go up early if you want. Edmonton has a lot of book stores."

"You tempter. That would be great."

We worked out a few more details, such as times and places. After we rang off I researched Goodrunning.

She was famous in Canadian politics. How had I not heard of her before?

Goodrunning would be ideal for what I needed, as long as I could keep the conversation hypothetical. She was the Minister of Public Safety and Emergency Preparedness, which sounded harmless enough. It wasn't. Her responsibilities included the Solicitor General, the federal prison system, the Royal Canadian Mounted Police, the Parole Board of Canada, the Canadian Security Intelligence Service, and the Border Services Agency.

If anybody knew about secret government plans for dealing with alien invaders, it would be her. Whether she'd talk about any of it with me might be another matter.

Her background was one of those depressingly inspirational things you find in Readers Digest. She'd grown up on a reservation in Northern Alberta, and at the age of seventeen she'd been attacked while walking home from a friend's house.

The three white guys in a pickup truck were cruising that crappy dirt road specifically to "have fun with an Indian," as they told the terrified girl. They had chased her down, raped her and then slammed the truck door on her arm repeatedly just to hear her scream before throwing her into a water-filled ditch. Her injuries were so severe that her lower arm had to be amputated.

The men were never caught. Most people in the area were philosophical about it. Canada did not have the best record in solving the problems of our Indigenous population and this was just another one of those things, like the crappy road to the reservation and the bad water supply.

My reaction was more active. I was outraged that something like this could happen in my country, and for once my lack of patience was good for something. I wrote a scathing letter to my MLA, another to my Member of Parliament, and sent a copy to the Prime Minister's Office. I also promised myself I'd go up there, after this case was resolved and investigate it myself. Nobody should get away with something like that.

I didn't know if any of that would do any good. The case was twenty years cold, but I had to do *something*.

I *really* hate bullies.

After lunch, I went back to reading about Goodrunning. She was famous for not using any kind of prosthetic, and wearing only short-sleeved tops so nobody could miss what was done to her. In winter, she wore a coat with one sleeve shorter than the other, the shorter one being sewn closed. She was also famous for constantly championing better conditions for Canada's Aboriginal people, for pushing for better rape crisis counselling, and fighting for rights for the disabled.

After high school she went to university in Edmonton where she got her degree in law. Then she started going after people, companies, and governments who weren't giving our Native peoples a fair deal.

In other words, she was another honey badger. This was going to be an interesting trip, in some sense or another.

* * *

Edmonton is a three-hour drive north of Calgary, and I've always found the prairie scenery boring. Oh look, a wheat field. Oh look, another wheat field. Having Tereasa along made it a lot more fun. It turned out that she was also a Nightwish fan, so we played music when we weren't talking about books.

Her brother, Christopher, made me feel at home and showed me to the guest room so I could get settled. He lived by himself in the house where they had grown up, so there were three bedrooms. Their parents had moved to a condo once the nest was empty.

Tereasa and I headed out to start our tour of bookstores. One of them was the Chapters on Whyte Avenue.

I was on the second floor, looking at the cookbooks when I spotted a pretty, black-clad woman with red hair cruising up to a nearby table where an author was doing book signings. She was in a powered wheelchair and somehow looked familiar. I just couldn't place her.

I hovered nearby until she'd gotten her books signed.

"Excuse me. I know this sounds stupid, but have we met? I just can't remember where."

Her chair turned to face me. Up close, I was certain we'd met. She gave me a dazzlingly beautiful smile, and that's what did it. "You were in Finland."

"At the concert in Joensuu," she said. "You're the private investigator. Vanessa?"

"Veronica. I never thought we'd meet again." My brain finally put the last pieces in place. "Bailey Dawn."

She spoke over my shoulder. "Look who I found."

The man behind me was her husband who had also been at the concert. Daniel.

"Hi. Are you sure you aren't following us?"

"Pretty sure. I'm just here for the weekend. You'll be glad to know that your concert made me into a Nightwish fan."

"Great! Will you be coming back to Finland next year?"

I had some momentary flashbacks to the grim parts of that case. I mostly succeeded in overlaying them with the wonderful memory of Finland and the concert.

"Not for a while, at least. How have you been?"

We chatted for about 15 minutes before they had to leave to meet a friend.

Sometimes, my life is one long string of weird occurrences and fantastic coincidences. At least this one was pleasant.

* * *

We made it back in plenty of time for dinner. I had a moderately ludicrous pile of books with me, including three by the author who'd been doing the signings. Daniel had recommended them.

About half an hour later the doorbell rang.

The Honourable Susan Goodrunning was about my height, and in her late thirties. Her long black pony tail was sprinkled with glints of silver, and went nicely with her black suit and navy blue blouse. I was prepared. I knew her story, and it would have been rude to stare at the remains of her left arm. I stepped forward as I was introduced.

As we shook hands, I realized that, despite my best intentions, I was staring at her arm. Immediately I could feel my face heat up, which made it far worse. She said nothing, but she noticed.

Good first impression, Veronica.

"Tereasa tells me you have some questions about government policy."

That was safe enough. "Yes, if you don't mind, Ms. Goodrunning."

"Not at all. We can talk after supper. And call me Susan."

Over the objections of my hosts, I helped clear the table after the meal. After that, there were no more reasons for putting off my discussion with Susan. I had a feeling that I'd let my impatience goad me into doing something stupid again.

I was sitting in the kitchen polling the butterfly collection in my stomach for the best approach to the upcoming talk when she came in.

"Are you busy?"

"Not at all. Just thinking about what I wanted to ask you."

"Go ahead."

"It's a rather unusual question. Would you mind if we went for a walk?"

She laughed. "Have you ever watched question time in parliament?"

"No."

"If you had, you'd know that we have to be able to answer just about anything. But we can go for a walk if you like."

That relieved some of my anxiety. At least I wouldn't have to worry about Tereasa and her family listening to us.

We were putting on our shoes when Tereasa wanted to know where we were going. I had this terrible teen urge to say, "out."

"Just for a walk."

"Mind if I come with you?"

Shit. There was no reasonable way I could say no.

"Sure, if you like."

We left the house and I randomly turned left. I assumed that the others would be able to get us back if I got lost. We'd been walking for about five minutes when Susan prompted me again.

"So, what was your question?"

I figured might as well dive in head first.

"What is the government policy on alien invasions?"

"What do you mean by alien?"

"You know, creatures from outer space." At this point I wasn't going to quibble about a difference between *outer* and *other*.

"You win. That's the most unusual question I've ever been asked. I'm curious; why do you want to know?"

"I have a friend who's a writer. It's research for a novel."

"That's good. If there was a real invasion, we'd have to see how well our policy worked, and I'd hate to have to do that."

"Why is that?"

"Canada's policy on alien invasion is nonexistent. That's why I'd hate to have to test it." She laughed again. "I asked the same question when I became an MP."

Tereasa was fascinated. "Really? Why?" Susan gave her a *seriously?* look. "Oh, right. Babylon 5."

I was missing something. "What?"

"It was my favourite TV show while I was in university," Susan said. "Tereasa and I used to watch it together. Spaceships, lots of interesting aliens, and tons of political issues. Conspiracy theorists and movie makers always assume that governments, the U.S. government at least, have some secret plans for handling an alien landing. I was disappointed to learn that they don't."

"You mean there's nothing at all?"

"Not about landings. There are UN treaties outlining a procedure for handling radio communications. Nobody seriously believes that aliens will physically come here except for one or two oddballs."

"That seems weird to me. I mean, if you expect a radio message why not a landing?"

"It's mostly SETI researchers who put the guidelines together. The UN General Assembly is supposed to make the final decision on whether we answer any communication, and how. One thing your friend might find interesting is that telling the public is part of the protocol."

Friend? Oh, right. "What about causing mass panic? Every movie I've ever seen mentions that."

"There was a meteorite found in Antarctica several years ago. For a while the scientists studying it thought they'd found a fossil alien bacterium. It was in the news for a week or two as various religious leaders were interviewed and viewed the whole situation with alarm. Then the story died out. If there's no widespread panic from a Martian germ, it's unlikely that a radio message from several dozen light years away would cause much more than a big argument on the internet."

"What happened with the fossil?"

"It turned out to be a false alarm. But that was after it was old news. Few people cared by that point."

"What *would* Ottawa do if aliens physically landed on Parliament Hill?"

"That's a good question. As long as they didn't land shooting, I suspect that somebody's old anthropology or linguistics professor would get a quick phone call to come deal with it. Depending on who was in power it might also be seen as a photo op."

"What about the military?" Tereasa asked.

Susan shrugged like a Québécoise. "I don't see that they'd have much of a role. If the aliens were hostile it likely would be all over by the time we could get troops into the city, and bombing our own government and civilians seems like a self-defeating response. I can't see a huge mob of Canadians converging to attack the aliens, so they wouldn't be needed to defend the aliens either. We don't have any sensible response to invaders in orbit unless their detection systems are worse than ours. ICBMs might be able to reach them if they aren't shot down first."

Her response seemed so rational that I was tempted to take it at face value. I very, very badly wanted someone to take this whole mess out of my hands. Of course, you never really know how someone is going to react until the situation is real. This could still be a disaster. I was getting nervous again. There was only one way to tell if her answer was genuine.

"I must admit that I have an ulterior motive," I said. "I don't really have a writer friend. Well, I do, but he doesn't have anything to do with my question."

Susan stopped walking, which meant Tereasa and I had to as well. "I see. I can understand you being nervous about asking for yourself. Writing is a nerve-wracking experience, but don't appreciate being lied to, regardless of the reason."

Shit. I needed to salvage this.

"Look, I didn't mean to lie. It's just that there's a delicate situation, and I needed to know how the government would handle it before I gave you the whole story."

"*What* whole story? This isn't for something you are writing?"

"No. It's—complicated. It would be easier to show you, if you don't mind."

A series of expressions ran over her face. Mostly annoyance and caution. "We were talking about alien contact. How could you 'show me'? Do you have physical proof?"

"Again, that's difficult to explain." I got out my phone and dialed. Fortunately I'd more-or-less prepared for this beforehand.

"Veronica, what are you doing?" Tereasa asked. I put one finger up.

"Hi. Are you busy? I need your help. No, just come to me."

Tereasa had time to say, "Who was that?" before Artemis appeared in front of us. She took a quick look at the other two women who were temporarily frozen with shock.

"Hi, Veronica. Who are your friends?"

"Tereasa's a librarian who helps me with research. Susan is a minister in our parliament. I was trying to find out how our government would respond to our immigration problem."

"Who the hell are you?" Tereasa had finally found her voice.

Artemis spoke to me. "I assume you want me to explain the situation?"

Before I could answer, a car turned onto the street and came toward us. The brilliance of its headlights made us all turn away.

"We should continue this conversation in private."

"No, wait!"

Artemis put her hand on Susan. As Tereasa leaned forward to defend her friend, Artemis grabbed her by her wrist. I tried to intervene just as the universe gracefully pirouetted, and fell on its ass.

* * *

We appeared in a cedar forest on the gentle side of a hill. From the quality of the light, it was either dawn or sunset. From the terrain, it had to be Upland near where Kali and I had first found Artemis.

In my career I'd had some plans go terribly wrong. This was at or near the top of the list.

When we jumped we were all in motion on a flat, level concrete surface. That was no longer true.

I stumbled forward into Artemis, which knocked her off balance on the uneven ground. The other two women fell as their footing changed. Susan rolled downhill, and I tried to stop her. On the other side Tereasa flailed, grabbing at me to stop herself from falling.

From the outside, the result must have looked like slapstick comedy. Susan tumbled down the slope and fetched up sitting against a tree. Artemis was pulled off balance and sat down heavily on an outcrop of small rocks. Tereasa pulled me backward and we both toppled down the hill. We didn't hit anything for several metres.

I discovered something new. When two Midlanders collide in the Upland, it hurts just as much as it would at home. Our boundary layers didn't protect us from each other.

Tereasa got the air knocked out of her. I cracked the side of my head against her forehead. Neither of us were happy.

It didn't help that the ground here was covered with leaf litter that was soaking wet from a storm so recent that I could hear the grumble of thunder just over the hill. Water dripped from the trees overhead, and slowly penetrated my clothing and hair.

It wasn't the dramatic revelation I'd hoped for.

"What the hell just happened?" Susan said, huddled by the tree. She made no attempt to get up. "Where are we?"

Tereasa managed to sit up. She was still gasping from me landing on her stomach, and her hands were buried in the leaf mould as if she expected the ground to disappear.

Artemis got up slowly. Despite her nanites, those rocks wouldn't do anybody's butt any good.

"My apologies. That wasn't how I expected the jump to go."

I got up somewhat unsteadily and climbed up to where Susan was still sitting. I offered her my hand, which she looked at disdainfully. Instead, she used the tree to pull herself up with her one hand.

"I have to apologize too," I said to the others. "This *really* isn't what I wanted to happen." I took several deep breaths.

"I can't breathe," Tereasa said, panic edging into her voice.

"Draw in a breath, hold it for a moment, then let it out. You'll be all right," Artemis said. Now that she was in her home environment she was reverting a bit to her Mighty Goddess persona.

I tried to explain better. "The air is—thinner—than we're used to. You'll be okay if we do as she says." Technical explanations could wait until later.

"My camp is nearby. There will be a fire where we can dry ourselves."

Without waiting for a reply she turned and hiked off through the trees. I made sure the other two were stable on their feet, then followed her. Having screwed up the entire proceeding I wanted to postpone the next argument.

The camp was only a hundred metres or so. It looked much as it had the last time I'd seen it.

As soon as we arrived, the nymphs scurried around getting things for us.

We sat by the fire, and waited while the nymphs distributed blankets and wine. Having just had supper the three of us declined the roasted venison.

Susan refused the wine as well. She insisted on draping the blanket herself. "Am I a prisoner?"

Artemis raised an eyebrow. "Not at all. You are my guests. There's no need to be afraid. Nothing can hurt you."

"Do you have any idea what the penalty is for kidnapping a Cabinet Minister?"

"Nobody has been kidnapped."

"Then take us back where you found us. Now."

Artemis looked to me. "Veronica?"

"I'm sorry, Susan. This isn't the way I wanted... Okay, let's again start from the beginning. I was asking you about government policy on aliens because I wanted to know if it would be safe to get your help with a developing situation. I didn't expect Artemis to whisk us away to her home before we could explain things to you. I'm sorry."

"You should have been clearer," Artemis said.

"Are you telling me that this—these women are aliens?"

"In a sense. They are from another universe. rather than outer space, but yes."

"You're completely mad."

I sighed and held my temper—barely. "You sound like every badly written TV show. Why does everybody say, 'you're insane' when they hear something that challenges their world view? If I'm insane, then you're stupid for antagonizing me. If I'm not, then you're stupid for not listening to what I have to say. Which is it?"

I could see the anger rise, and then be forcibly dragged back. Whatever else, Susan was good at controlling her feelings. "All right, convince me."

"We're in another universe. One with different properties than our own. For that reason, the three of us are invulnerable here, just as Artemis' people are invulnerable in our world." I turned to our hostess. "Would you shoot me, please?"

Artemis only hesitated for a moment before grabbing her bow and an arrow, both of which became golden at her touch. She then backed off two or three paces so she wouldn't be hit by shrapnel while the nymphs dove for cover.

I sat calmly while the arrow struck me dead-centre on my chest. The bronze head bent and broke. The cedar shaft snapped and splintered. For a moment nobody said anything.

"That proves nothing. The arrow could have been a fake, or prepared in some way."

"Wow. Tough room. Okay, let's get personal. One of you find a rock. Any rock. The bigger the better as long as you can lift it."

"Why?"

"Just humour me. Please. I'm trying to give you the proof you asked for."

Tereasa got up and purposely ignored a pile of stones that had been moved to make the ground more level. She patted the undisturbed moss at the edge of the fire light, then dug out a rock about the size of a cantaloupe.

"Hit me with it."

"Forget it. I'm not going to do that."

"Fine, then. Throw it up in the air. Nice and high."

She held it in both hands and threw it as high as she could, which given that it must have weighed ten kilos wasn't far. Regardless, I managed to get under it and bunted it with my head like a soccer player. There was a thud as we connected and the rock tumbled off into the night. The collision staggered me slightly, but of course I was unhurt. Both Midland women gasped.

"You could have been killed!" Tereasa said, more with anger than concern.

"No, I couldn't. It would literally take a large nuke to hurt us here. When Artemis or any of the others are on Earth the same thing is true of them."

"All right," Susan said, "I'll believe you for now. What do you want?"

"I just wanted to convince you that there are aliens among us, and that the situation needs to be handled properly." I explained about the impending flood of immigrants, with Artemis throwing in some bits to clarify.

Susan the politician was not happy. "You've known about this situation for years, and you're only telling someone now?"

"I've known about *demons* for a few years, but I've only known the true situation for several months. The whole immigration thing only came up a few days ago."

Susan blew out a big breath while staring at the fire.

"I'll have to inform the PM. Can your—friend—show up in Ottawa? I doubt that anybody will believe this without absolute proof."

"No problem," Artemis said. "Just tell me where and when."

"Until I say otherwise, this whole matter is confidential. Do you understand?"

Tereasa and I agreed.

"Fine. We need to get back before we are missed."

I had Artemis drop us off just out of sight of Christopher's house in case anybody was watching. This time we all held hands to jump and started from flat ground. It worked much more smoothly.

* * *

"There you are!" Tereasa and Christopher's mother said as we entered the kitchen. "Would you like some tea?"

"No, thanks, Mrs. Shepherd." I tried to get to my room as fast as possible before she asked too many questions.

"Where did you go?"

Crap.

"We were just walking. I wanted to ask Susan some questions, and Tereasa came along to keep us company."

Susan let me spin the story. Tereasa was either willing to go along with it or wanted to see if I could get around her mother.

"That's nice. So many young people these days don't seem to care about how our government works. Why do you all smell like smoke?"

This was almost as bad as trying to hide something from my mother.

"Somebody was burning bushes or something." I had enough sense not to say barbecue.

"That's odd. It smells like cedar. I didn't know that there were any cedars around here."

"Maybe somebody was burning scrap lumber from building a deck."

"Hmm. Maybe. Funny time for it."

I didn't know what to say to that, so I said my good nights and went to my room. It was only 9:30, but I had a lot of new books I could read.

A few minutes later there was a knock on the door followed by Susan's voice.

"May I come in?"

I hadn't gotten undressed yet, so I opened the door for her. I perched on the bed.

She sat in the make-up chair. "I wanted to know if we're good."

"Of course. I'm surprised, though. I'm the one who lied to you and got you thrown down a hill."

"Yes, and now I understand why. I'd have been equally cautious if I was in your place. In fact that good judgment is why I'd like to offer you the chance to be the government's resident expert on these matters. We'll need someone to advise us on policy no matter how this plays out."

"Wow. Um, okay. But wouldn't it be better for Artemis or someone else from their people to advise you?"

"She isn't a Canadian citizen, and in fact is, if I understand correctly, an illegal immigrant with a personal stake in the matter. As far as I know you are our only home-grown expert in inter-universal politics."

Oh, crap. The universes were doing it to me again. Once more, I was the only logical candidate for something I had little interest in doing. Sure, it would be cool to be a government expert, but I still wanted to be a normal private investigator. I *liked* normal cases like catching insurance cheaters. Besides, it wasn't likely that I could brag about my new position to anyone.

But if the people who had become my friends were to have a chance at being allowed to stay, and a war bigger than any in history was to be avoided, I didn't have a choice.

Shit. Again.

"All right, I'll do it. But believe me when I say that if I tell you that something is impossible, or imperative, you'd better not send it to a committee for debate. We're dealing with a situation that nobody in the diplomatic corps has ever dreamed of, and certainly never been trained for."

"From what I've seen, you are right. I'll back you as much as I can."

She left soon after to go back to her hotel. She had government business early the next morning.

I managed to read for a while, but thoughts of what I'd started kept distracting me.

Veronica Chandler, advisor to the federal Cabinet on extremely foreign affairs. As long as everything went well, this could be the beginning of a new and glorious age for Canada, the world, and even myself.

As long as everything went well.

I suddenly realized that events had gotten away from me and I'd broken my promise to consult with Kali and Stan before doing anything.

I got very little sleep that night.

CHAPTER 23

O Canada

Despite the broken promise, my most outstanding feeling was over-whelming relief. I'd told somebody about a secret I'd been hiding for three years, and now it was their problem instead of mine.

Susan would be heading back to Ottawa in a few days. She'd told me that she didn't want to discuss the matter with anyone there until they could meet face-to-face. That sounded sensible to me.

Tereasa was angry with me for using her to get to her friend. She was also excited that she was involved in the start of the biggest story in human history, and afraid of the possible outcome. It made for a somewhat strained trip back to Calgary.

Kali and I hadn't seen each other since the night of the dinner party two weeks ago, so as soon as I got back I texted her to see if she wanted to get together. I needed to see a friendly face.

I also needed to grovel for forgiveness.

* * *

The next day I still hadn't heard from her, so I called George.

"Hi. Is Kali around?"

"No," he said. "Can I take a message?"

What the hell? "Where is she?"

He paused. "I don't know."

"What do you mean you don't know? Is everything okay?"

"Yeah. Fine. I have to go."

Again what the hell? Kali and George were practically glued to each other when he came home. It was time for some investigation.

Twenty minutes later I was at her front door. Not knowing what was going on, I used my key rather than ringing the doorbell. I also had one hand on my baton just in case something bad was going on.

George dashed out of the kitchen like an abandoned puppy when he heard the door open. He looked surprised and disappointed to see me.

"Oh. Hi." This was completely unlike him.

"All right, what's wrong? Where's Kali?" I said as I closed the door.

"She's... I don't know." He flumped on the sofa. "She left a note for me two days after the dinner party saying that she was going away on a business trip and I should pretend like everything is normal if anybody asked."

"Anybody, meaning me."

"She didn't say that. Just anybody."

"Do you have any idea where she went?"

He shook his head.

"Did she take her car?"

"No, it's still in the garage."

"Did she take anything with her?"

"I don't know."

Men.

"I'm going to look."

He trailed behind me as I headed for the bedroom. It was probably more for companionship than to keep an eye on me.

Kali's—their—bedroom was much like I remembered it from when I lived with her. The Romantigoth band posters were still on the walls. While she kept the downstairs spotless, she was more relaxed about housekeeping up here.

The first place I checked was her jewellery box. That's where she kept all her valuables, including her passport. It was missing. Her jump medallion was also gone, but that didn't mean much. She could have been going to Edmonton for all I knew, and cutting out the three-hour drive would be worth it. That didn't explain the passport, though.

Jumping to the Upland or Downland wouldn't explain it either. In theory, she could have jumped to another country, but any activity that required a passport would also trigger questions about when and how she got there.

Her closet contained her usual assortment of gowns, plus some other clothes. The only thing I noticed missing was a blouse. That was odd. Her combat boots were there, but her dress flats were missing. Rooting further into the closet, her black dress slacks were also missing.

Where could she have gone without telling George or me? Especially dressed in a business casual suit with a passport and her jump medallion.

* * *

She still hadn't shown up four days later when I got a call from Susan.

"Can you come to Ottawa for a few days?"

"Sure. I don't have any cases right now. How does this work? Do I buy my ticket, and you'll reimburse me, or what?"

"Don't bother. We'll send somebody to pick you up in two hours. A plane will be waiting for you at the airport."

I could have used my jump medallion and been there immediately, but I still wasn't completely convinced I was doing the right thing by involving the government. I wanted to keep my medallion private for now.

I put clothes and stuff for at least a week in my backpack. I also called Mum.

"I'm going out of town. Can you look after Yoko Geri for me?"

"Certainly. Where are you going?"

"Ottawa. I have a new client."

"Good. We all need more normalcy in our lives. By the way, have you heard from Kali lately?"

"No, I haven't. George said she's out of town, but he says he doesn't know where she went. I'm worried."

"That doesn't sound like her."

"That's why I'm worried."

"I'll see what I can find out. She's a big girl. I'm sure she's all right."

"Probably. Let me know if you find her."

The door intercom buzzed. The security camera showed two men in suits and sunglasses. To someone who'd spent as much time as I had around police, they almost screamed plainclothes. My bet was RCMP.

"I have to go now. My ride to the airport is here."

"Have a good trip. I love you."

"Love you too, Mum. I'll give you a call when I'm on my way back."

I opened the door just as one of them was about to knock.

"Veronica Chandler?"

"Who's asking?"

I was right. They showed me RCMP credentials. I wasn't above making one of them carry my luggage.

Their car was, of course, black, unmarked, and obviously official. It made the whole thing seem even more cloak and dagger.

Thoughts nagged me as we wound our way to Calgary International. This was it. I was going to meet with Cabinet Ministers in Ottawa to advise them about an alien invasion. The unreality of the whole situation was topped only by the absurdity of me being involved in interuniversal politics. I was really beginning to freak the hell out by the time we turned off onto an airport access road I didn't know existed and were cleared through a checkpoint.

Rather than going through the terminal, we drove out to my plane and I boarded on one of those mobile stairs. My RCMP escort and I had an entire Gulfstream 280 to ourselves for the three-hour flight to Ottawa.

It's a good thing my seat had its own TV screen so I could watch movies. The two men were not big on conversation.

* * *

In person, Prime Minister Adley Thorson was even more handsome than he was on TV. I know that sounds shallow, given that we should be judging politicians on their deeds, not their dimpled chins, but this is me we're talking about. At least I didn't drool on him.

Susan and I were in his office. It was smaller than I expected, with a gorgeous white plaster ceiling and oak panelling everywhere else. Even the windows had louvred oak shutters. Susan and I sat on the sofa while he sat in a matching chair across the coffee table from us. "I'm happy to meet you, Ms. Chandler. Would you like anything? Coffee? Tea? Water?"

I was my usual suave and charming self. "What? Um, uh, no. Thank you."

"Susan has told us some extraordinary things about you and the current situation. I've known her for years. I find it impossible to believe that she's lying, and only slightly less possible that she's made a mistake. That's why I wanted to meet with you. I'm sure you understand that we can't proceed without proof."

"Um, sure. What do you need? Proof of the political situation or just proof that the Downland and Upland exist?"

"I believe we can assume for now that if these other worlds exist, then the rest of the story is true. I must caution you, however, that these gentlemen will not take it well if you try to abduct me. For that matter, neither will I."

Glancing at my two RCMP escorts who were standing across the room near the desk, I noticed they both had clear lines of fire on me that would miss the PM and Susan.

I sat even further back in the couch. Just because I was immortal didn't mean I wanted to prove it by taking some bullets.

"How about if I show you something harmless but impossible?"

He sat back in his wing-back chair to watch, like a skeptic at a magic show.

Sitri or Artemis could have just called an object to them, but I wasn't that good yet. I jumped to the Downland, found a dead branch on a pine, snapped it off, and jumped back with it. I was gone for not more than five seconds.

In that time the guards had moved from their posts to the Prime Minister's chair, where one of them was hauling him from his seat. Their guns snapped around to cover me as I reappeared.

"It's okay, it's just a stick," I said, raising my hands slowly. They didn't look like they believed me.

Susan reached over and took the branch from my hand.

"That's from the Downland," I said as non-threateningly as possible. "Try to break it."

The branch was less than the thickness of a pencil. Anybody old enough for kindergarten should at least able to bend it.

By then one guard was standing in front of the PM. Susan handed it to the other one for examination. He took it like it might be a venomous snake.

"It's all right," Thorson said. "I doubt that any of us would be alive if she intended any harm."

The man holstered his pistol and tried to bend the twig. He showed astonishment when it didn't work. He tried harder. We could all see his arms shaking with the effort. Even if it had been a steel rod, he should have been able to bend it.

When he gave up, his boss held his hand out. He tried to mark the wood with his thumbnail, then with a letter opener from his desk. He even tried flexing it and had no more luck than his guard.

"Remarkable. And this is...?"

"Exactly what it looks like. A twig from a pine tree. If you put it under pressure for a few days it will eventually bend, but the more force you use the more it resists."

"Fascinating. Let's try an experiment. Give me a hand." He put a marble pen holder on the floor by the leg of his desk. The two guards lifted the corner, and the PM put the stick under the leg with one end resting on the marble. It didn't move.

"Huh," he said, motioning us back to our positions.

"Susan told me that the ability to travel between worlds is something only the inhabitants of the other worlds have."

"Yes, much of their technology is based on nanites they carry inside them. Those are..."

"I'm familiar with nanites," he said. "How did you get them?"

Well, Veronica, that was stupid. The cat was out of the bag now. "I didn't." I pulled the medallion from my shirt, and one of the guards almost went for his gun again. My vanishing act had them spooked. "This does the same thing, but it's based on older technology and lets me go to either the Upland or Downland."

"Saying 'Upland and Downland' all the time is getting tedious. Is there a collective term for the two other worlds?"

"Not that I know of. How about Otherland? I'm pretty sure Outland is taken."

He smiled. "So is Otherland, but we'll use it. Now that we've settled that important point of grammar, shall we move on to the matter of whether Canada is in danger from an alien invasion? And how we're going to protect it if we are?"

* * *

I spent the next week and a half sequestered with the Cabinet. A few Ministers weren't able to be there, or had to leave for other duties, but the room was still almost full.

The Opposition must have caught wind of something, because there were always journalists outside waiting to accost the ministers. Mostly the questions concerned various conspiracy theories: Adley Thorson was ill, despite the recesses we took so they could attend Parliament. The Cabinet was going to quit. The Cabinet had been fired. The Prime Minister was going to announce some new program. It was an obvious fishing expedition.

The press never saw me. I jumped from my hotel room to the Cabinet meeting room in the Centre Block and back again. If we worked through a meal it was brought in while I hid in my hotel room. The ministers were as anxious to keep my name and face out of the press as I was.

The morning of the first day was taken up with convincing everybody that the three of us weren't insane. That was made much harder by an ex-minister who had made extensive claims about aliens living among us. He never offered any actual proof, so most people thought he was a crackpot. I wondered if he knew something they didn't.

The PM brought the pine twig for the Ministers to examine. After a day under his desk it had a distinct curve in it, but it still couldn't be bent or snapped by hand. That wasn't enough, so I had to demonstrate the reality of the Otherlands again. A few ministers wouldn't believe even after I'd disappeared and reappeared, but a short trip to Upland with ministerial approval settled the matter.

Our Prime Minister was smart enough to know that he needed as many opinions as possible to make an intelligent decision about this. I approved of Thorson's collegial approach. I sure as hell wouldn't want to make decisions this far-reaching by myself.

The whole thing was exhausting. Maybe you needed to be a politician to build up stamina for all-day meetings. I talked myself hoarse trying to convince the ministers that this was a political situation that nobody had ever encountered before, and that standard solutions wouldn't work. This wasn't a psychotic head of state they were dealing with. It was two entire worlds of psychos.

A team from the Office of Protocol was brought in on day three. Once more I had to convince people who thought they knew more than I did that Weird Stuff Is Going On.

"If there are illegal aliens in the country we can just arrest them."

The PM and I had discussed this situation, so I pulled out my phone and dialled. "Okay, try it."

"I'm sorry. What do you mean, "try it? The RCMP should certainly be able to..."

As arranged, Artemis appeared just behind my chair. There was chaos for a minute until the PM calmed them down.

"This is a friend of mine who also happens to be from the Upland. Try to arrest her."

Artemis smiled, intending to put people at ease. It didn't.

"I don't think..."

"Oh, for heaven's sake." I went to the door. Outside a constable was guarding the door.

"Could you come in for a minute? We'd like you to arrest this woman."

He looked at Artemis, then at his boss. The PM nodded.

"Don't worry, I won't hurt you," Artemis said kindly.

He approached her warily, fishing the cuffs from his duty belt as he came. She held her wrists out and he put the cuffs on.

As soon as he let go they fell to the floor at his feet. Artemis was standing by the door.

The constable didn't know what had happened, but he wasn't about to fail in his duty. He launched himself at the woman who had evaded him.

She let him throw her to the floor, then vanished. The unexpected drop knocked the breath out of him. As he knelt on the carpet she put her hand on his shoulder from behind.

"Are you all right?"

"Enough," the Prime Minister said. "Thank you, constable. You may return to your post. Everything you've seen in this room is to be held in the strictest confidence."

"Do you need another demonstration, or have I made my point?" I said as the door closed. "None of the people who will be coming here can be arrested. Unlike me, bullets will bounce off them, as will tactical batons, tasers, and anything else you can think of. If you did manage to arrest them, they would disappear from where ever you tried to hold them."

Artemis, of course, didn't even had a hair out of place. "Do you need me for anything else?"

"No, thanks. Give Sitri a hug for me." She vanished amid further pandemonium.

*　*　*

The next argument consisted trying to decide who would be the best person to appoint as the ambassador to the Otherlands.

"I don't think we want..." I started.

One of the men from Protocol cut me off. "What about Antoine Petard? He has experience in war zones."

"I believe Veronica was about to make a point," Susan said, her voice filling the room. Damn, that woman had lungs on her.

"Thank you. We don't want one ambassador. We want several for each of the Otherlands."

"That isn't how things are done," said the loudmouth. "The ambassador will have a staff, but it is usual for a new embassy to have only one accredited envoy at a time."

"Let her speak," said one of the other female Ministers. He shut up.

"If you have only one ambassador, he or she will have to stay in-universe for some time. That will be extremely bad for their mental health. If you appoint a team of ambassadors, they can rotate through weekly. Trust me, you don't want a sociopathic or narcissistic ambassador looking after your interests."

There was a brief pause.

"Veronica makes a good point," the PM said, "and we'd be foolish not to take her advice. Regardless of what current protocols are, we should adopt her suggestion. Not only is Veronica our expert on Otherland affairs, she'll also be a *de facto* member of whatever missions we send out. Unless anyone else here can travel between universes?"

"Why don't we build more of those pendant things? We'll need them if things go badly."

"You mean for troops," I said. "You want to invade two universes with, what, a hundred thousand soldiers?"

"From what you've said, a hundred thousand soldiers who are impervious to any weapon."

"I did *not* say that. I said they'd be immune to most injury. I personally know of two weapons the Otherlands have that would cause problems for an invading force: nukes and portable gamma-ray lasers."

"I did actually think to ask about that," the PM interrupted. "Her medallion was built with techniques that we probably won't be able to match for a century. Veronica was kind enough to loan us her device while scientists at the NRC looked it over. None of the scanning technologies we have showed any obvious internal structure, and nobody can figure out what powers it. A surface sample showed it to be completely coated with silicon carbide, but the scratch made to confirm that healed itself within moments. Ms. Chandler has seen similar technology and is certain that even if we managed to break open the device it would heal itself. It's not something we have any hope of reproducing right now."

"In other words," I said, "the only way to get more medallions is to trade for them with the Otherlands. If they catch any hint we want to weaponize them, I doubt that would work out well."

* * *

After a while they ran out of steam with the immediate problems, and I was sent back to Calgary by commercial flight. I was getting a consulting fee for my time as well as transportation costs. The best part of that was I hadn't lied to my mother—I really did have a paying client in Ottawa.

I texted everybody in my family to let them know I was coming home, then slept the whole way back.

CHAPTER 24

Trouble in Paradise

My father was waiting to pick me up in Calgary. He was alone, which bothered me. We gave each other big hugs before heading for his car.

"Where is everybody?"

"Your mother has a new case and had to work. Kali still isn't back from where ever she went, and George doesn't want to leave home in case she returns."

"I'm really getting worried."

"So are we. None of us have heard from her in weeks. She hasn't even contacted Keith at her shop. He needs her to sign off on some things."

This had gone on long enough. "Don't worry, Dad. I'll find her." I squeezed his hand and wondered if I could actually deliver.

* * *

As soon as I got home I put my travel clothes in the hamper, gave Yoko Geri a hug, and retrieved my red phone from my night stand. I hadn't taken it with me to Ottawa in case things had been less straight-forward than I'd expected.

The phone was a high security, encrypted model that connected me with the BSI, an organization that provided forensic and other services to law enforcement agencies worldwide. Their methods were intended to get results rather than produce legal, court-admissible evidence, so they operated in secret. If anybody could find Kali, they could.

The text I sent was short: *Need to locate a missing person: Liliana Marina Hernández Rojas. Goes by the name Kali. Owner of Bhadrakali Occult in Calgary. No word from her for at least three weeks.* I attached a picture of her.

A few moments later a text came back. *Urgency?*

I wasn't sure what formal rating system the BSI used, and resisted the urge to say something emotional. After some thought I settled on *8/10.*

Do you have any idea where she might be?

No. She took her passport but told no one her destination.

A few minutes later the BSI phone chimed and a Be On The Look Out appeared along with Kali's picture and description. I'd seen these before, and they gave no indication of who was looking for the person or why.

You can imagine how patiently I waited.

Two weeks later my BSI phone chimed again. I had a new message.

Subject Liliana Rojas checked into Marshall Islands Resort, Majuro, Marshall Islands.

I sent back a *thank you* text and thought about what I'd learned.

What was she doing out in the middle of the Pacific Ocean for over a month and why didn't she tell anybody?

* * *

Majuro, the capital of the Republic of the Marshall Islands, has a population of 28,000. That makes it their largest city.

It was now ten a.m. on Monday in Calgary which was just before sunrise on Tuesday in Majuro. I did a bit of research, put on a t-shirt, shorts, and running shoes, my medallion, and jumped.

I still wasn't completely confident of my accuracy when jumping to new places, so I shot for the open plaza in front of their government complex. The sun was up but hidden by the building. The air temperature wasn't too bad—about like Calgary on a warm day. I used the map on my phone to orient myself and started walking.

The resort was less than a kilometre west along Lagoon Road. That was their version of the Trans-Canada Highway running the length of the main island—about 50 kilometres long and one lane either way. There were a few side streets here and there, but in most places the land was too narrow for anything but the highway and some buildings on one or both sides.

People were already moving around getting their errands done before the sun got too hot. Most women were wearing more than me, but nobody seemed offended by my clothes, probably because I was clearly a tourist and didn't know better.

Kali should be easy to find. Almost all the city's inhabitants were Marshallese. Despite Kali's *mestizo* colouration, she would stand out almost as much as me.

Land was too precious to waste on sidewalks, so everybody either walked on the road or, if there was room, beside it. The drivers were used to avoiding the pedestrians and the speed limit was low.

The resort was a half dozen, robin's egg blue buildings linked by walkways with the main entrance in the centre one. I entered the lobby, and it was immediately cooler.

The staff behind the desk were both wearing white uniform shirts with a diagonal blue flower pattern. The man at the far end was sorting through some papers, so it was the woman who said, "may I help you?"

"Yes, I'm looking for Kali." I hoped that was the name she'd checked in under.

The clerk consulted her computer, then put her hand on a telephone handset. "Who may I tell her is here?"

I waved my hand. "Don't bother. We're supposed to meet for breakfast and she probably isn't out of bed yet. When she shows up please tell her that her sister is outside looking at the view."

If Kali was avoiding people she might slip out the back, so I headed west to the end of the resort. The doors on the street side were all closed and draped. Nobody was visible.

The lagoon side of the resort was about the same. Every suite had a sliding glass door and even on the upper floors most of the drapes were drawn. Of course, I couldn't see into their windows anyway. One set of ground level drapes was partially open and I could see into the room.

I wish I hadn't.

Through the glass I could see Kali, naked and kneeling on the bed as she bounced up and down. Her long hair was bouncing along with her, creating a cloud around her face. An equally naked Marshallese man was lying under her.

There were plenty of chairs on the terrace, and I stumbled into one. I couldn't believe what I was seeing. Twenty minutes later the sliding door opened and the man, wearing only knee-length shorts, came out and headed along the terrace to the east.

He passed another man walking toward me who reached the door before I could. Kali, still naked, met him at the door and gave him a kiss that should have melted the glass.

"Kali!"

Her eyes locked onto me as I approached. She showed no surprise.

"What are you doing here?"

"I'm looking for you. We've been worried sick that something happened to you."

"As you can see, I'm just fine."

"Like hell you are! What do you think you are doing?"

"Nothing that's any of your business." She seemed to realize that she was still holding the man in her arms. She pushed him away. "Come back later."

For a moment he looked like he'd argue, but then left without a word.

"Kali, what's going on? This isn't like you."

I followed as she headed back into her room. "You have sex with any number of men you want. I'm just doing the same."

"No, you aren't. I've never done anything like this. What about George?"

She shrugged. "He isn't losing anything. I'll let him have plenty when I get home."

"Do you hear yourself? You're the one who was always about monogamy, and who waited until you were sure you were in love with somebody worthy of you. What's gotten into you?"

She laughed. "So far Benson, Peter, and Samuel. And James, if you hadn't interrupted."

"You've been sleeping with *four men?*"

"Not all at once, and there hasn't been much sleeping involved."

"I don't understand. How could you cheat on George like this?"

She shrugged. "It's easy. Men screw around all the time. So do you. Maybe I woke up. It's not your concern."

"Damn it, you're planning to marry George! How could you run off for a month without telling anybody where you were? Are you planning to stay here?"

"I don't owe you or anyone else an explanation. As you can see I'm perfectly fine. If you want to worry about it that's your problem. And you will *not* mention this to anyone else."

"*Hermanita,* you're scaring me. Whatever you think, this isn't at all like you."

For the first time in my life, I felt uncomfortable in her presence. Part of it was that she was a naked mess after what I assumed had been a long night of passion, but more than that it was the way she looked at me. It was hard to say exactly what was wrong, but it was like being watched by a manikin.

"Are you on drugs? You're acting like you're stoned or something."

"Don't be ridiculous. My mind has never been clearer."

"Are you sure? Because I'm trying to understand what's going on, and you're beginning to piss me off. Why are you here?"

"I'm solving the immigration problem. That's all you need to know."

"What about checking with each other before doing anything? Damn it, if I did something like this you'd tear a strip off me."

Of course, I had done something *exactly* like this by contacting the federal government. I couldn't bring that up without completely undermining my position. My high horse had just thrown a shoe.

I took a big breath and let it out. "All right, what's your plan?"

"All you need to know is that it will make me rich, solves the immigration issue, and helps this country."

"What do you mean, 'make me rich'? Since when do you need money? You have something like 200 million dollars in the bank!"

"I don't answer to you."

"Kali, we're sisters. Please, let me help you."

"My sister was killed by terrorists. You have nothing to offer me. This conversation is over. Go home."

"Like hell it is! I'm not going..."

* * *

My words stumbled their way to silence. I was standing in my living room. Somehow, Kali had sent me home.

I tried jumping back to Majuro, but it didn't work. I got a sensation of the universe moving but I went nowhere.

I had no idea what was happening, so I sat down where I was on the carpet. Yoko Geri came over to see me.

"What's wrong?"

I didn't want to talk about it and hoped he understood.

Something was terribly wrong. My best friend and sister seemed to hate me, and she was determined to destroy everything that was good in her life.

I couldn't tell Mum, Dad, or George what was going on without knowing the whole story, and what I did know would hurt them terribly.

I've never felt more alone or helpless.

Yoko curled up in my lap, laid his chin on my hand, and purred.

GLOSSARY

Kalijiriki	Kalijiriki	The main language of the Otherlands. Pronounced Kahlee-yee-REE-kee.
Ov alishibishie wasi ko akao.	Kalijiriki	Your hovercraft is full of eels.
Banco de Finanzas	Spanish	Bank of Finance
Bienvenido al infierno, hermanita	Spanish	Welcome to hell, little sister.
Buenos días. Llévame al Holiday Inn Express.	Spanish	Good day. Take me to the Holiday Inn Express.
Chiquita	Spanish	Little girl
Aka wate	Kalijiriki	Oh crap.
delegación	Spanish	Police detachment
Federales	Spanish	Mexican federal police
Gringa	Spanish	White woman
Ich kann Deutsch sprechen als wäre es meine Muttersprache. Möchtest du, dass ich dir ein Wiener Schnitzel mache?	German	I can speak German like it's my native tongue. Would you like some Wiener Schnitzel?
Il Pizzaiolo del Presidente.	Italian	The pizzeria of the President. Named after a visit from Bill Clinton during his presidency.
La Rana Dorada	Spanish	The golden frog
la señorita hermosa	Spanish	The beautiful woman
Madre de dios	Spanish	Mother of God
Mi hermanita	Spanish	My little sister
Mogesalmebit' Kakhelebi restorani	Georgian	Welcome to the Kakhelebi Restaurant
¿Que hora es?	Spanish	What time is it?

¿Que pasa, hermana?	Spanish	What's happening, sister?
ron	Spanish	Distilled cane liquor
Kukofiki ingu uli?	Kalijiriki	Do you understand me?

ABOUT THE AUTHOR

G. W. Renshaw is a writer, martial artist, Linux druid, and actor who lives in Calgary, Alberta, with his lovely wife. He has a wide range of interests, from flint knapping to quantum cosmology. He will happily watch just about any film with monsters in it.

You can connect with G.W. at:

Facebook:
www.facebook.com/GWRenshaw/

Website:
www.gwrenshaw.ca/